THE
CRYMOST

DEAN H. WILD

ISBN: 978-1-940250-32-8

Artwork by Andrej Bartulovic

Interior Layout by Lori Michelle
    www.theauthorsalley.com

Printed in the United States of America

First Edition

Visit us on the web at:
www.bloodboundbooks.net

ALSO FROM BLOOD BOUND BOOKS:

*For Doris and Arlene—greatest joys, deepest sorrows.
And for Julie. Always for you.*

PART ONE:

A LONG DAY

CHAPTER ONE

LUCK IS A THING *that comes in many forms.*

The phrase popped into Mick Logan's head as he climbed the retractable steps into the attic. Hemingway, right here under the shapeless veils of insulation drooping from the underside of his roof and for no good reason other than it might have something to do, vaguely, with the task set before him. Of course, that would make it *luck comes in the form of a box.* And boxes there were in this narrow third floor area. Stacks of them on the dusty plank floor, each one marked in Judy's neat handwriting.

He gazed at them, hands on hips. It seemed like such a simple task: to go home, empty the clutter from a few cartons, and take the empties back to the village hall to use in the cleanup. Looking at them, however, invoked a prediction, a poor man's premonition of sorts, in which Judy pointed out displaced picture albums and stray fondue pots and asked what in the world he had been thinking. He listened to the unseasonably strong May wind whoop around the eaves outside, and he thought about going back into the morning light empty handed. Maybe come up with another solution to the box problem, one that didn't involve the controlled and sensibly charged wrath of his dear wife. He still had a few days to get the village hall cleaned out before the big vote. And maybe if he checked with Copeland's gas station again he'd come up with some boxes, because he was pretty sure Roger Copeland was holding out.

But things didn't get done by waiting. It wasn't how the city-dwelling Mick Logan ran his classroom all those years ago, and it wasn't how the small-town Mick Logan ran his village maintenance job, either. He bit down on his lower lip, harder than usual because it brought a dull flash of pain, and he gave the attic another, more intense onceover. A box caught his eye; a reddish-colored carton with only a corner showing behind the greater bulk, like a shy child shuffled to the back of the crowd. For some reason it seemed like a good place to start.

He dragged it into the open and felt ambushed by recognition as he brushed ten years' worth of attic dust from the counter-folded flaps on the top.

Written there in his own hand: CLASSROOM.

No revelation, no excitement. Just the last box he'd picked up from the school in those numb and hazy days surrounding the move from Royal Center to Knoll. His hands seemed to slow down as they undid the flaps and folded them back. He considered the jumbled contents with dull reluctance, drawing a mental breath, and then began to pick through the artifacts of his previous working life.

Textbooks and lesson plans were the bulk of it: *Intermediate Grammar, Introduction to Great American Literature*. A desk plaque reading MR. LOGAN was slipped in next to a rolled-up poster of twentieth century authors and poets. He ran his fingers through an assortment of desk pens and paperclips. Touching them was like tapping selected seconds of the past, bits of his time at Lincoln Middle School trapped inside flint-strikes of memory.

Pushed down next to a faded desktop calendar was a small bag made of sleek gray velvet, and he pulled it out before he could reason his way through whether this was a good idea or a bad one. He let it rest in his palm and considered its drawstring top. He was into it this far, might as well finish it. He opened it and dumped the contents into his waiting palm, his heart thudding with a slow, deliberate cadence.

The items clicked together in his hand; two chess pieces—a horse head knight as gray as the bag it came from and a darker king, each carved from a veined mineral, highly polished. The wind keened across the eaves as he thumbed each piece with slow, thoughtful strokes.

"Robbie Vaughn," he said at last.

His voice was barely above a whisper.

The house settled around him. Outside, something crashed over in the wind and rattled with a tin bucket sound. His flesh rippled beneath his Village of Knoll uniform shirt. His fist closed over the chess pieces.

The voice awakened in his memory belonged to one of the brightest, funniest kids he'd ever known. *That's a checkmate, Mr. Logan.*

He made an evaluative, almost congratulatory smile. Despite the remembered voice, his mental barriers put up long ago against all Robbie Vaughn matters were holding, and he could not let these psychological levees be breached by this discovery. No images came—not the upstairs school hallway drenched in merciless March sunshine, not the funeral home and its own unsympathetic harshness. All contained, properly cinched and calibrated.

Good.

One of the carton's corner seams split with a dry popping sound. It made him jump. Books spilled onto the floor. The remainder of the chess pieces, stacked in a loose jumble for the last decade, rolled out and clattered like gumballs. The wind slammed against the house again. If he were the type to believe in omens, he might have found a reason to be uncomfortable under his own roof just then. Instead he dealt the carton a hopeless swat. No longer of use to him. But stacked in the shadows behind it were more boxes. And they were empty. Luck, in one of its many forms.

Before taking the empties downstairs, he repacked the classroom stuff into a new, stronger carton. All but the velvet bag containing the knight and king, which he put in his pocket next to his car keys. There was some type of comfort in the act.

CHAPTER TWO

When Mick walked into the village garage, Harley Kroener's voice wheeled into the high-ceilinged space with an inflection of lament. "Goddamn it, why today?"

Mick looked at his friend who, parked at the ancient wooden desk in the corner, executed two quick movements at once. One was to give Mick a glance of acknowledgement, the other was to slam the phone receiver into its cradle. *Town bullshit*, Harley's expression told him.

"What we got?" Mick said and put down his armload of boxes. The village garage was aglow with morning light from the glass block windows. It smelled of grease and the ghosts of exhaust and grass clippings. "People sticking posters to the streetlight poles again, sneaky rascals?"

Harley made a humorless laugh. "I think we've got them cured of that, at least until this Mellar's nonsense is done. Once the rummage sales kick in, we'll have to start all over. No, this is something I can take care of before I leave town, I guess."

Mick gave him a head shake. "You're not even supposed to be here today. What is it? I'll fit it in."

Harley got out of his chair and it was like watching a juggernaut rise from the surf. To say Harley Kroener was tall was an understatement. And he was broad. Not fat but wide set, perhaps a little slouched under the weight of fifty years, but still formidable to behold. "I got out of the house because my pacing around was driving Beth Ann nuts, so whether or not I'm supposed to be here, this is where I'm staying. For another few minutes, anyway. God, I hate this medical consultation bullshit. And they'll probably tell me it's nothing, anyway."

Mick made no reply because they both knew doctors don't set up consultations just to tell a person there was nothing wrong, especially when they ask the spouse to be in attendance. He would expect a similar silence from Harley, if the shoe were on the other foot. "No, really, I'll do it, whatever it is. All I have on my plate today is cleaning up next door."

"And that state inspector is due. What's his name? Fyvie?"

"Nothing to it. I take him out to the old landfill, show him where the vent pipe is, and come back to town. Five minutes. Four if I take the truck out of first gear."

Harley slouched a little more. "Yeah, okay. Somebody has been messing with the manhole covers. They're offset all over town for some reason."

"Wow." Mick flashed him a smile. Knoll was not much more than a wide spot on County Highway L, seven streets that formed an unremarkable rectangular grid. The village was annexed into the sewer system of the nearby city of Drury, which gave it a distinction a step above other neighboring small towns. The manhole covers in Knoll numbered exactly three. "I don't know if I can find an extra minute and a half."

Harley's gaze swept over the paperwork on the desk and across the nail-studded board propped against the window. The board was a gleaming collection of village-relevant keys of varying age and size. "Point taken."

"Manhole covers, huh? Does it have something to do with the sewer backup at the firehouse, do you think?"

"Don't see how. All I know is if the town's shit hadn't bubbled up out of that firehouse floor drain we'd have a place to vote next week and we wouldn't have to worry about cleaning up that damned village hall as an alternate polling place. If I'm back early enough this afternoon I plan to be right next door with you to help box up some of those old town records."

"What part of 'day off' don't you understand? It's all going to be here tomorrow, still waiting, still a pain in the backside."

Harley went quiet, and a pulse beat at his grayed temples. Mick placed the expression after a moment and felt something wither inside. He was being what Harley considered to be cavalier. Mick could afford to be cursory and dismissive because he could easily move on to something better than hauling brush and running the village snowplow. Judy passed him the same look in quiet moments; a baffled wonderment, nearly an accusation, but not quite.

"Just as well," Harley said at last. "Beth Ann is due to pick me up. She hates this nonsense, too."

"You know Judy and I are rooting for you," he said and nudged the big guy's shoulder.

"Yeah."

A car horn sounded outside. Harley flinched and started walking toward the service door. When he opened it up, a gust of May wind shuffled the papers on the desk and made the tools hanging on the pegboard across the room sway and clang together. The board full of town keys caught the draft in a bad way and crashed over. Keys of passage to all the major doors, cabinets and ignitions crucial to the Village of Knoll scattered across the desk and jangled on the floor.

Harley glanced back through the door. "Jesus."

"I got it," Mick said and waved him on. "You get going before Beth Ann heads over to that consultation without you. Call me when you know something."

Harley nodded, seeming daunted and dazed before he closed the door.

Mick looked after his friend, bemused and heartsick. By tonight, Harley Kroener would have confirmation of the obvious and their quaint little town would have something new to gossip about. Knoll was a thirsty place when it came to gossip and there was always room for more.

Mick's gaze settled on the southeast corner of the garage, maybe because the landfill was in that general direction, and the new state inspector, a Mr. Fyvie, was due shortly to check the methane vent. Yes, that was on his plate, too, getting the new guy acquainted because the old-fart who used to come out, intent and familiar and barely noticed, decided to step through the door marked RETIREMENT. Then his thoughts circled around to luck again and at last returned to the town, and how it, as a collective, believed in omens and superstitions. It was why Cheryl Abitz kissed the lottery machine at Copeland's every time she bought a Powerball ticket. It was why there was a horseshoe nailed up above the door at the volunteer firehouse, and why the penny on the front step of the decommissioned post office just kitty-corner across the street from this very building stayed there year after year, disturbed by neither child nor chairperson. And it was why that other place, near the landfill, existed at all. Easy enough to find, *that place*, if you went up Pitch Road, veered away from the old dump and followed the arrow on the rough wooden sign lettered with a single word: CRYMOST. Omens, luck, phenomenon. For these, Knoll kept the door of acceptance wide open.

CHAPTER THREE

Mick began sorting through the spilled and scattered key collection but then abandoned the effort. Other duties were calling. Manhole covers needed to be righted before someone on the way to The Chapel Bar on Backbank Street or the F&F Feed Mill on the main drag dropped a tire in and ruined their suspension (God forbid it should be Cyril Vandergalien, mill proprietor, volunteer fire chief and acting village president; nobody needed to open *that* gate to administrative hell). One bad part: the key for the village hall, which he would need if he was to begin any type of cleanup next door, seemed to be AWOL. That meant he needed to fit in a stop at the Borth house so he could pick up a spare, provided Chastity Mellar Borth was home and was willing to part with one of her village-appointed keepsakes. And the landfill inspector was due around ten. Let's not forget about him. Jesus, whatever happened to quiet life in a small rural town?

Most of the days *were* quiet. Idyllic peace was Judy's plan when she suggested they not stray from Wisconsin after he quit teaching but rather find a sleepy, low-key town like the one where she grew up. Knoll turned out to be close enough to her new job in Drury and low-key enough to fit the bill. The day they toured the house on Garden Street and fell in love with it was the same day he spotted the HELP WANTED sign taped to the door of the village garage. The rest, as they say, was history.

Ten years later, they were part of the town, as accepted and immovable as the local landmarks or the village sidewalks. True, he and Judy were just sallying forth into their early forties, and one more big move was not out of the question, but he often felt—with a wistful sort of bitterness—there was a better chance of the Wistweaw River on the town's southeast edge changing course than there was of the Logans packing up and leaving Knoll. The same went for the Kroeners. Or the Prellwitzes. Of course, people *did* pack up and move away on occasion, but such endeavors were always accepted by the town populace with a resigned disappointment. Knoll liked to keep its own and it demanded, quietly, a brand of commitment. Even idyllic peace bore a cost.

He picked up Harley's desk phone and dialed the number pinned to the bulletin board above it. The Borth house phone rang only once, as usual, before the answering machine kicked in. He worked his teeth slowly across his lower lip. The receiver felt heavy and slick in his hand.

"Ms. Mellar Borth," he said at the tone. Never just "Ms. Borth", which discounted her historical attachment to the town and therefore was not tolerated. And certainly not "Chastity". The use of her first name would be a social—nay, a *moral*—faux pas. Chastity Mellar Borth was five years his senior but the difference between them was defined by something other than time. Mick, Harley, and so many others were part of the town, but Chastity *was* the town, by lineage and by the reverence granted to her by the town's inhabitants.

Formality out of the way, he finished his message. "Mick Logan from the town garage. I want to start clearing out the village hall today but I've misplaced my key. I'll be over within the hour if you want to leave one in your porch mailbox for me. Much obliged."

Quite a day, and it was barely past nine. As he went to the door, his hand bumped the pocket where the velvet bag rested and the knight and king slept in close comfort. *Slept?* Odd observation, but somehow appropriate. The wind gusted outside and rumbled across the roof of the garage and the town hall next door. The town hall, where neglected invoices, forms and documents stood in precarious stacks like a leaning city covered in dust. Should the wind get in there, the whirling cyclone of loose papers would seem endless. *Some things slept*, he mused, *while others raged around them, and should the two meet, unsheltered and laid bare, there was chaos to be had.* Not Hemingway, that. It was pure Mick Logan, and he thought it wasn't half bad.

He walked over to the truck, wind snapping at his collar, and he started the engine.

CHAPTER FOUR

Orlin Casper remembered his birthday celebration, already two days past, as a real whiz-banger. By ninety-five-year-old standards, anyway. He held memories of the party out before him as he staggered toward his easy chair by the picture window. He hoped he'd make it. The strength was running out of his legs with the ease of warm bath water. His ticker beat heavy and slow, pumping out its last as he tried to impose reminiscence over dread. Such a lovely birthday, not spent in this house on Meadow Lane, his residence of sixty years, but at the nursing home in Drury where the nurses had put balloons in his wife's room and somebody brought a cake. His dear Irma sat politely in her bed, the removed smile she wore throughout her five-year decline fixed on her face. A photo album was passed around and the nurses made an appropriate fuss over shots of proudly-owned cars, favored pets, and beloved relatives, including the two boys who both would beat their parents in the laborious race to the grave.

At one point during the party, Irma laughed and told him she'd found two dimes in the washer. "Double barrel luck," she called it, and then winked at him. Just lucid enough to make it cruel. It sent a shiver down his spine and tossed another grain into the remorse that ran and ran like an hourglass in the heart.

Yessir, a whiz-banger birthday, he thought and flopped into his chair. His nerve endings buzzed; his little pains, which grew in number too fast to count over the last few years, were absent. Fled. If this was the way out of this world, it wasn't so bad on certain levels. He evaluated his picture window view of Knoll, how she seemed to have her collar turned against the blustery day, and he thought of double barrels. Then he shivered. The air thinned.

He hoped someone would find the note on his kitchen table because Knoll—Mellar's Knoll when he was a boy and now just Knoll—was in for a whiz-banger of its own. His last moments lent it all the certainty in the world. "Somebody better figure her out," he said out loud.

The strange buzz in his nerves rushed in and ate everything up. The room darkened. He settled back, drawing his breath in gulps, then gasps, then sips. And at last he breathed not at all.

Knoll hunched against the wind.

CHAPTER FIVE

Chastity Mellar Borth switched off the answering machine's playback and made furtive glances around her dining room. There was no need for unease. The Logan man dropped by on many occasions, on village business of course, and he was always mindful to step onto the porch softly, and by no means ever try the bell next to the wide-set oak door or peer through her heavy lace curtains. Logan followed the regimen better than some of the people who'd been born in the town. And yet, dread seemed to linger, just out of reach.

She brushed past the broad mahogany table with its complement of twelve chairs, her movements easy and fluid. Her pain was dull today by regular standards, a mere complaint in her back and legs, and hardly noticeable at all in her scalp which was crowned by dark hair pulled tight, slick and severe and braided in back day after day. In fact, she barely sampled the selection of pills by her kitchen sink today. In her parlor she opened the dark wood secretary, took out the key to the village hall and folded it in her hand.

She bore no doubt Mick Logan would have the village hall ready. Aside from his respect for protocol, he was a reliable worker. The hall was a last-minute choice but sufficient in light of the odorous disaster befalling the firehouse, but truth be told the venue mattered to her very little. Where the town vote—the *initiative* was the proper term, she guessed—took place was outweighed in her mind by the very reason there was a vote (initiative) at all. Disgraceful how the fate of the old family store, Mellar's Mercantile, became a matter of gauche, almost whimsical preference. Green posters tacked up around the town rallied would-be voters to choose the *Mellar's In* option so the historic building might remain and be gradually, and expensively, renovated. Her own front window sported one. Opposing posters in red, for the *Mellar's Out* camp, demanded the razing of the old general store and fuel depot and the extrusion of its leaking underground tanks. At her last estimation, red posters far outnumbered the green.

She never dreamt that by her forty-fifth year she would see the old building, an icon of the Mellar family presence and a Knoll landmark, at the risk of being stripped from the town entirely. It seemed almost like betrayal.

A hot vibration shot up her arm and the key flew from her hand. She stopped and looked down at where it gleamed on the dull Persian patterns of the carpet near her plain, flat shoe. *This was a different pain,* she thought, and rubbed her arm through the checkered cloth of her sleeve. Almost a *dare not* pain which seemed brought on by pinching fingers instead of the usual, dastardly flares of fibromyalgia.

She stooped to retrieve the key, trying, not too successfully, to lock out thoughts of her father clamping her tender child's flesh between his rough fingers and pinching, telling her she *dare not* behave like the other girls, *dare not* listen to their wretched ideas or covet their trampy clothes. She was a Mellar, unique and above such lowbrow practices. Over time his pinches were replaced by scathing challenges to her usefulness and intelligence, and eventually by brutal silence. So many cruelties. And yet, the tears she shed at his funeral five years ago were genuine. Sparse, but genuine. It spoke to her character, she believed.

She opened the door, key in hand, and stepped onto the broad, shady porch. The house was the only structure on Tier Street. In fact, the street seemed more of a private drive off of County Highway L, also known as Knoll's main street called Plank Street, or locally, just The Plank. There was nothing inviting or friendly about her family home, no pretty garden flags or flowering shrubs, and the doormat certainly did not say WELCOME. The only splash of color was the poster in her front window. Green, of course. *Mellar's In*, of course.

From the house location there was once a clear view of the edge of town, where Mellar's Mercantile stood sentinel and The Plank took a sharp uphill turn toward Pitch Road and all that lay beyond it. A stand of oak and ash now blocked the view. She gazed off in that direction anyway as she stepped up to the railing mailbox, dropped the key in, and closed it again.

"There you go, Mick Logan," she said under her breath and squinted into the warm, gusty air.

Then she backed inside and shut the door, once again surrounded with the scents of faded velvet and oil soap. Pain awakened and thumped anew in her back and legs, shimmied down her spine. And was that a second painful pulling—dare we call it a pinch—on the flesh of her arm? She turned toward the kitchen. Perhaps it was time for a pill or two after all.

Oh, for the happy days when she was a married woman and Gregor Borth would come home to her. The pills and the pain were so few back then, until Gregor lost control of his car in a March ice storm. He slid through a turn onto Backbank Street and deposited the Cadillac in the icy Wistweaw River. The impact snapped his neck. She mourned long and often for her dear Gregor, and yet it was Daddy Mellar who often nudged into her thoughts. As he did now. Still giving those *dare not* pinches, should she try to forget him.

A pill was in order, all right. Many of them, if for no other reason than to quell her dear father's refusal to stay dormant in her thoughts. Ungrateful behavior on his part, considering all she'd done for him. Enduring his speechless grunting and combative nature at the end. Even going out after his burial to The Crymost place off Pitch Road, where the mourners of this crude, ungracious town went to toss away trinkets associated with their grief, as if sorrows could be so easily cast away.

She stopped in a shaft of sun just before the kitchen sink and scowled. A strand of uniform glassy beads was coiled around the bottles on her pill shelf. She reached toward it, coldness invading her with the same intimate ease as the pain often did. The beads winked at her. It was a rosary, black stones hazed with dried mud, the attached ebony cross swollen from years under the water. She picked it up and stretched it between trembling fingers, a puzzled groan like a high thin note working out of her throat.

Daddy Mellar's rosary.

The one she'd cast away into The Crymost five years ago.

CHAPTER SIX

The first two manhole lids were only slightly unseated. Easy work for Mick. He was making good time as he pulled up to the final lid at the right angle junction of Tier Street and Backbank. But as he stood over the last cover, pry bar in hand, he hesitated.

Look closer, part of him demanded. He worked the tip of the pry bar into the narrow gap between manhole lid and rim. The wind died down. He could hear the gurgle of the Wistweaw not far off of Backbank. The rest of the town was silent. In his teaching days, when his students fell unusually silent, it indicated something was about to happen. *In the wind*, his father used to say. He was convinced such sensations were a thing of the past, buried along with his other life, but here it was, standing with him ribcage to backbone, an old specter for whom a decade was a blink.

He pried up the edge of the cover, then, in an instant of pure impulse, he squatted to lift the lid as if it were an overly heavy hatch. Gobbets of wet mud were stuck to the underside as if flung up against the lid, and not long ago, considering the freshness and looseness of the muck. Not exactly an *in the wind* kind of strange, but it still struck him as odd. He'd ask Harley if this was common. If ever in the history of—

"Is waste water your business now?"

He jumped and looked around at the man standing over him.

Cyril Vandergalien wasn't a small man—too many beers and buffet dinners—but he was able to move with considerable stealth. Mick never heard him approach. He must have come from the firehouse across the street. Apparently, the village fire chief, performing his chiefly duties, found the need to switch into his village president mode.

"Not at all," Mick said. "But somebody's got to tend to the lids when they come loose, now don't they, Cy?"

"Loose." A light of suspicion flickered in Cy's eyes and his charcoal colored brows drew down.

"Every manhole cover in town," Mick said and seated the lid, then tapped it with his pry bar. With luck, this would be a case of close the manhole, close the conversation. "Some kind of prank, probably. I've got it handled. No problem. Just a quick—"

"Always digging right in and getting it done, aren't you, Logan? It's what folks around here like about you."

"I do what's necessary," Mick said, his hands tightening on the pry bar. "You know that."

"I know what's necessary and what makes sense can be two different things around here, and folks go with what makes sense in the end. Isn't that right?"

Cy shot a glance toward the firehouse. A red *Mellar's Out* poster was taped to the inside of the front window. All the properties under Vandergalien's watch sported one: his home on Forest Street, the feed mill, and, of course, the firehouse. He wanted to put one up at the village garage as well, but Harley told him where he could stick it.

"Thanks for the tip, Cy," Mick said at last and turned toward the truck. "I've got work to do."

"You got that village hall cleared out yet?"

"I'll get to it," he said into the wind. "When it makes sense."

A dark colored SUV pulled up close to where they stood. The driver leaned out of the open window, his face freckled and inquisitive, his hair a flash of red in the sun. "Either of you gents Mick Logan?"

Cy aimed a crooked finger. "That's him."

Mick stepped closer.

The man jutted his hand from the window. "Peter Fyvie. I'm here to take a methane reading at your landfill. I waited at the garage for a few minutes, thought about calling your cell, then decided to try to track you down. Nice day for a tour around your little town."

Mick took the hand. It was like shaking a cool green branch covered in thin bark. "Pleased to meet you. Welcome to Knoll."

Cy swept up and held out his own tough-as-leather hand for the man to shake. "Cy Vandergalien, village president. Sorry there was nobody at the garage to greet you. We get so busy. Priorities go right out the window some days, I guess."

"Actually, I'm half an hour early," Fyvie said. "I can't expect anyone to know when I'm ahead of schedule. Doesn't make sense."

A laugh built up in Mick and he hoped it wouldn't come spilling out. "No, it doesn't. If you want to follow me in your truck, I can set you to work right away, Mr. Fyvie."

"Very good. Thank you, Mr. Logan."

"Mick, please."

Fyvie glanced at the other man whose expression turned sour as he stood by the car. "Nice to meet you, Mr. Van Grinten."

"Vandergal—" Cy began.

He was cut off by the upward slip of Fyvie's window.

Mick climbed into his truck, laughing.

CHAPTER SEVEN

Just before the land assumed its steep upward pitch, a stretch of wild fields on the north side of The Plank accommodated Mellar's Mercantile: a two-story brick and wood hulk seeming to watch the world through a front-facing hole where a show window once resided. Leaning pines surrounded it. They reminded Mick of dark and swaying mourners attending a body in state. The property was village land, sold off to fatten the Mellar Borth bank accounts, which granted each Knoll citizen an equal say in the fate of the building by way of the upcoming vote. Even the village president got to put in his two cents, no more, no less. Right, Mr. Van Grinten?

He laughed again, but kept his eyes sharp. With the leaves budded out for the season, the Pitch Road turnoff was difficult to see, even if it was nearly at the crest of the hill. Something else drew his attention, however. A figure walked the roadside ahead, traveling downhill into town. Not so unusual; Knoll had its share of cyclists and joggers and habitual stroll-takers. Still, the lean male shape piqued his attention, perhaps because the man was covered neck to shoelaces in black. It seemed to be a suit. Formal, and the wind picked at some sort of draping on his back, sending it aflutter like a single dark wing. *A cloak?*

Broke down in his car perhaps. The figure was close enough now for Mick to discern a pallid face and a stout, black derby hat. Long hair fell around the man's shoulders in a sheaf of silvery gray—

Pitch Road yawned open to the right, bringing him back to the matter at hand. He cranked the wheel, his teeth gritted, and he wondered if the truck's back tires might drop into the ditch due to the sharpness of his turn, but they remained true. In his mirror he saw Fyvie's vehicle make a sudden drastic attempt at the turn and succeed as well. He slowed down and stuck out his arm to give Fyvie a wave—part apology and part congratulations for catching the abrupt change in course. Fyvie waved back, which was all right.

The road ended atop the first of two gentle rises, and it was there he stopped his truck. To his right was the landfill gate: two metal swing-outs barring the way like robotic arms. To the left stood a tilted sign made of weathered planks like a crude burial cross. Letters hacked into the crosspiece possessed a moldering starkness.

CRY MOST

Beyond the sign, a pair of wheel ruts trailed up the second rise and took an evasive, somewhat secretive turn through an opening in the attending tall brush. It was there he was looking as he climbed out of the truck and dug for his key to the gate.

Fyvie got out as well and made a relieved stretching sound as Mick undid the gate lock.

"Almost scenic sometimes, these landfill areas."

"If you say so," Mick said as he pushed the gate open. The former dumping ground for three surrounding townships was high land. Its coat of tender spring grass shimmered in the passing winds. "As long as you don't think too hard about what's underneath."

Fyvie laughed, heartily. "I do and I don't. Now if you'll sign off as admitting official, I will begin my appointed duties."

He offered Mick an open leather binder. Mick signed the form inside and then checked behind him at the not-too-distant spot where Pitch Road opened up to County L. By his estimate, the figure in black was due to pass by any minute, and he wanted to—suddenly *needed* to—see it happen.

There was no figure, however. Only Roger Copeland's tow truck rolling uphill, out of town.

"No security issues or anything," Mick said, pulling his gaze from the road. "Nobody has any business up here anymore. Just close the gates before you leave. Easy as that."

"I'll go along with easy," Fyvie said on the way back to his vehicle. The wind seemed to snatch at his shirt. "It's a short day for me. After this it's home to cut the grass and then pack up for a week at the lake, just me, my fishing gear and a twelve pack of Coors. Real Garrison Keillor stuff, right?"

"A little Americana is good for the soul," Mick said.

Fyvie laughed again. "It is. Thank you, Mick. Have a pleasant day."

"You, as well."

Mick climbed behind the wheel and sat a moment, his hands held out as if with indecision. It had been years since his one and only visit to The Crymost. Part of him demanded he ascend the path right now, all the way to the limestone ledge beyond the shrubs, and gaze out from the stark and dizzying height at the marshland stretching on for miles and the Wistweaw threading away from Knoll like a ribbon of silver. He might even get out of the truck and inch his way to the edge of the dropoff and peer uneasily down at the spring fed pool ninety feet below. And he would consider, as he did on his first day here, why the people of Knoll came to this place, sorrows in hand, and dropped their offerings over the edge.

Instead he waved to Fyvie, put the truck in gear, and got himself back onto the main road.

CHAPTER EIGHT

The landfill vent stack was six feet high with a crook top. It jutted from the landfill slope like the head of a contemplative water bird. Peter Fyvie parked the SUV close to it, hopped out and went around back to gather his equipment with considerable haste. A short day was, after all, a short day, and there was no sense in squandering even a minute. A good ten paces away from the pipe he pulled the telemetry box out and set it up: a suitcase on a tripod, to go with the bird-head vent pipe. *Yes*, Fyvie thought, *we're working a regular Wonderland today.*

The system came up, and while he waited for the first readings to appear he took out the handheld combustible gas indicator, no more than an oversized stopwatch in appearance, to get some preliminary numbers. The LCD window read XXX. He scowled. Low numbers were common. Negative numbers weren't unheard of if the ambient air pressure was great enough to affect emissions, but he'd never seen the handheld reading resemble the label on a cartoon jug of moonshine. He moved closer to the vent pipe.

No change.

"Come on, I checked you before I left the goddamn office."

He crouched next to the pipe to press the indicator as close to the source as possible, prepared for the rich odor of anaerobic decomposition to rush over him, but there was none. What he saw made him disregard all other thought. The vent pipe was riddled with rusty pinholes at ground level. Spring weeds poked from the gaps. Weeds and rust, for Christ's sake.

He went to the truck, his short day forgotten, and brought back his cell phone. The EPA was going to have some words with the Village of Knoll, yes indeed. He bumped the stack experimentally with the heel of his hand. It waggled, not a regulation vent at all but a decoy stuck into the ground, probably attached to nothing down below. He took photos, his hands trembling. Knoll was about to be served a pretty healthy helping of whoop-ass.

"Is there trouble?" The voice made him whirl around.

The man who stood a few paces away watched him with an evaluative sort of patience. *Pale,* was Fyvie's first thought. The second had to do with what the man wore: heavy black clothing and some type of cloak like a town official or church layman from an old movie. And there was something else peculiar about the man, but he couldn't quite place it.

"This stack," he finally said, because it was all right to talk to this strange man with the politely folded hands. "It's not...what it should be."

"Are you sure there is no mistake on your part?"

The man's long silver hair danced in the breeze. His face was wise but mostly free of lines. The face of a fifty-year-old but no older. And his eyes. Intense. More than that, they were fascinating. Green faraway pools you could dive toward but never reach, just fall forever.

Fyvie concluded he should walk away from this place, but his arms and legs were no longer his own. "No. No mistake, and there's going

to be problems. This will bring down some big trouble after I file my
... uh ... "

The final word was gone, replaced by a sense the man somehow
peered into his head.

The man's brow creased with worry, or perhaps effort. "How many
others will come because of this discovery of yours?"

The word was "report". Didn't matter now, anyway. "There will be
an investigation. Knoll's going to get really busy, really fast. This is a
clear violation, after all. And if you break the rules, you bring the
pain."

His mother used to say it while she dealt blows with the yardstick
or the leather strap or sometimes her wooden kitchen spoon, a
cigarette cramped in the corner of her mouth. *If you break the rules
you bring the pain, Petie. Don't you know that by now?* The memory
was savage, nearly blotting out everything else. Nearly.

"It concerns me," the stranger said. "Small towns frown upon
disruption. They prefer things to remain as they are, as they always
have been. But I see you are a man of convictions. Your family must
be very proud. You are a family man, are you not?"

"A girl. Two boys. And Linda." He felt a humorless smile crawl
across his lips. "They can be a handful."

"I can well imagine. Demanding, whining, taxing you with their
bad behavior. Why is it people can't simply toe the line?"

"Yeah, why is that?"

"I believe it's a lack of reverence," the man said, his gray mane
blowing. "At any rate, you need to move on now. Your day is done."

"Yes. Move on," Fyvie said as his feet shuffled forward. *I'm
sleepwalking*, he thought with distant amusement.

He collected up his equipment and stowed it in the back of the
SUV. Then he climbed behind the wheel and started the engine, his
face fixed with blank purpose, his hands twisting at the wheel. "I don't
want to do this, mister."

The stranger ducked close to the open window, his face creased
with strain, his eyes filled with shadow so they looked like holes. "Oh,
but you must."

And Peter Fyvie was sure of it, as sure as breaking the rules
brought the pain. He turned the vehicle around and tore up clots of
young grass on his way through the landfill gate, then turned toward

the uphill path and the barrier of shrubs. He bounced into the wheel ruts, raced past The Crymost sign, and maneuvered through a gap in the shrubbery wall.

The view opened up. A limestone outcrop of perhaps 100 feet in depth—not a lot of ground if you're piloting an eight-cylinder 4x4 with the pedal to the floor—overlooked a vista so grand it was startling. High. So very high. *Damn.*

He punched the brakes and fishtailed, slowed, but not enough. The SUV nosed over the edge of the drop off and plummeted toward the sprawling pond of murky green below. All the while, the stranger's smile remained caught in his brain like a crescent of cold metal. The vehicle struck the water with a jarring impact. He realized the singular electrifying agony of his own neck breaking. He was able to draw one last terrified breath before he sank, equipment and all, as if enfolded by waiting arms.

Damn.

CHAPTER NINE

Mick was filling up the village truck at Copeland's when the wind changed direction. It sailed down The Plank like a deluge in a rain gutter. A handful of grit blew in his face and yet he felt the need to look right into it.

It was a southeast wind, a Crymost wind. He'd heard the old codgers in town refer to it in such a way, when it roared high and heavy in the late winter, and they always said it with a knowing glance at one another over their spectacles. Men such as Orlin Casper or Kippy Evert, who lived on Field Street and sold not-bad-but-not-exactly-top-notch wood carvings of deer and wild birds at local festivals and craft shows.

With a hint of irony he noticed Kippy Evert's rusted-out Huffy three-speed leaned up near Copeland's front entrance. Maybe he'd mention The Crymost wind to the old geezer and see what developed. Another thought took over when he spotted Copeland's tow truck parked around the side of the building, however. It had to do with the stranger in unfashionable dark clothing.

Roger was stocking Pall Malls into slots above the cash register.

He glanced at Mick but did not stop his work. "Sorry Mick, no boxes today."

"This is how a man gets greeted at the Gas 'N Go?"

Kippy Evert was hunched over the register counter and scrubbing at a scratch-off lottery ticket with a quarter. He glanced up, his old eyes bright beneath shaggy white brows, and made an appreciable cackling laugh.

Roger shrugged and brought up some more cigarette packs. "Just telling you what I know."

Mick reached behind the counter for the town credit sheet so he could sign off on the gas. "I know you're just holding out on the boxes to bust my balls for some reason. But I need to ask you about something else. You took the tow truck out this morning?"

"Yup," Roger said. He'd switched from Pall Malls to Camels. "Did a battery jump just this side of Baylor."

"Then you saw the man walking the side of The Plank just past Pitch Road? Somebody all dressed in black, kind of like an old-time dignitary." He put the paperwork back in its place, another tankful on the village's credit account squared away.

"Nope. I didn't see nobody."

Kippy passed another bright-eyed glimpse. He was between tickets. "That inspector that's due for the landfill check-up, maybe?"

Mick shook his head. "No, I met him just before I saw the other guy. The walker was coming into town pretty determined. On a mission."

Kippy gave this some thoughtful consideration, then shrugged and went back to scratching. It was his last ticket.

"What's the big deal anyway?" Roger said and stuck a pack of Camels in his shirt pocket.

"No big deal, just got my curiosity up is all. Done with that box?" Mick said and pointed to the empty carton behind the counter at Roger Copeland's feet. "Sure could use it."

"I can't do that, Mick. And I can't say why, so quit asking."

Kippy shot a glance between them, as meaningful and wise as any comment about Crymost wind. "Maybe Cy Vandergalien knows why."

Roger leaned on the counter with both hands. "Look, old man. If you're done with your Tic-Tac-Dough you can get your ass out—"

A passing siren drew all their attentions outside.

Knoll's fire department also supported a spartan complement of medically trained first responders. It was the responder's vehicle that roared past Copeland's at the corner of Garden and The Plank, shot north toward Mick's home (a tingle of dread overcame him), and then made the hard right down Meadow.

"A sound I don't much care for, sirens," Kippy said, shuffling over to join them.

They all stared as if the incident had left some sort of contrail of calamity. On the counter, Roger's cell phone chirped. Roger picked up, spoke briefly and then put it down again.

"Orlin Casper," he said. "The Janzer boy was delivering his papers and saw him through the picture window, dead as dog shit."

Kippy drew in a ragged breath and clutched Mick's shirtsleeve. "Damn it to hell."

"Guess you just graduated to the oldest person in Knoll, old timer," Roger said and took up his phone again. There was, after all, news to spread.

Kippy blinked and wrung his spotted, heavily-lined hands. "Hell of a way to get a promotion. Can you do something for me, Mick?"

"You all right?"

"After a certain age, us old men turn into old ladies when it comes to getting bad news. I hate to ask, but I don't trust m' bearings right now. Could you give me a ride over to Orlin's place?"

"Not much you can do over there, from the sound of it."

"I know, I know. But I got to be sure of things. It ain't real lest I see the fuss, you know? You don't have to stick around, just drop me off, if it's not out of your way."

Kippy's Adam's apple bobbed in his wattled throat. He smelled of sawdust and coffee with cream. The oldest person in Knoll.

Mick nodded. "Let's put your bike in the back of the truck."

CHAPTER TEN

Their route took them past Mick's house and he gave it a passing glance: a narrow three-story with cement steps leading up to the front door. Nothing remarkable. Judy had already put her flower boxes under the windows. They'd be crowned with brightly colored blooms once she made a trip to the floral place in Drury.

"Wonder who will tell his wife," Kippy said as they neared the right angle turn where Garden Street ended and Meadow Street began. "Irma Casper's in a home with the Alzheimer's, you know. Damn shame. Pull over here. Don't want Cy Vandergalien getting all bent out of shape thinking we're penny-ante gawkers."

Mick complied. The Town of Knoll EMT van, its emergency lights dark and still, was backed up to the front door of Orlin's one-bedroom house. The drapes were drawn across the front picture window. Mick got out, took Kippy's bike from the back of the truck, and rolled it over to its owner. A moment later Cy Vandergalien and Nancy Berns came out of the house, two wide-set forms hunched over with grave discussion.

Kippy clucked his tongue. "Damn double barrel is almost lost," he said. "Except for me. And who am I going to pass it to?"

A harsh clatter drew their attention. Nancy Berns, with a case full of equipment in each hand, lost her footing and tumbled into the grass near the front of the van. Before he could think about it, Mick hurried toward her.

"Are you okay?"

She rolled onto her back and made a light, laughing sound. "I'm good. People my size bounce before we break, you know. I hope I can say the same for the equipment."

Mick stuck out a hand and helped her up. The hard EMT cases were on their sides but they seemed no worse for wear. He picked one up and handed it to her. "Everything seems intact. Any fragile stuff inside?"

"Not particularly. It's fully stocked so there's not a lot of jiggle room for something to break, anyway. We didn't bother to open them up for this one. You know?"

"I heard."

She brushed at grass stains on her knees and made a hopeless chuckle. "I hate it when I get all rattled. My head stays straight but my feet lose all sense of direction. Be the death of me one day."

He tipped a nod toward the front door. "Bad?"

"I've been to much worse, actually. Orlin is in his chair, just as peaceful as you'd like. No unpleasantness, no mess. But I've never had one leave a note before."

"Note?" He handed her the other case.

She motioned for him to move in closer. He could plainly see the smudges of makeup on her round cheeks and the intense glimmer of shared gossip in her eye. "Not a suicide note or anything, because this wasn't a suicide. But it was strange. And he wrote it shortly before he died because the pen he used left blobby ink on the paper, and the same ink was smudged on his hand. Left the note right on the kitchen table, in plain sight. The kind of thing you want someone to find. There was just something *drastic* about it. That's my gut feeling."

"What did he write?"

"Well, I'd like to think it meant something to him, poor Orlin, some last wish or request. Sad if his last thoughts were some kind of nonsense. 'Don't forget the double barrels,' it said."

Mick looked around for Kippy, but the old man was no longer next to the village truck. He was pedaling his bike south on Meadow, toward his own humble home. "Double barrels," Mick said under his breath. "Wow."

Correlation. It was a word he'd taught all of his English students because literature was full of correlative instances. *So was life,* he thought as he climbed into the truck and drove around to the Mellar Borth house.

The key to the village hall was in the wooden mailbox bolted to the porch railing. You ask for something, you get it. Correlation.

For no good reason, he shivered.

CHAPTER ELEVEN

The cluttered and cramped front office of the village hall was nothing new to Mick. He'd passed through it plenty of times. The flags for the street lamp poles were kept in the back storage room, the only other room aside from a closet-sized restroom. In fact, flags would be in vogue soon, with Memorial Day coming up.

Stacks of yellowed paperwork and unlovely cartons of clerical bric-a-brac stood everywhere. The place had not seen a town function or housed an election since long before the Logans moved to town. The town clerk's office duties were executed from Cy Vandergalien's living room by his wife, Alice, and all voting events took place at the firehouse until yesterday's sewer mishap changed the plan.

As he glanced around, Mick thought there were things in here Orlin Casper handled during his tenure as village president, back when Cy was in diapers. Landfill records in some of those rotting boxes were filled out during the days Kippy Evert ran the dumping ground and saw to its maintenance. Cleaning the place out was a big job, set down by Chastity Mellar Borth herself, and he was glad to accept the challenge alone. It kept the pressure off Harley.

Harley. As he stepped into the musty-smelling interior he wondered how things were progressing for his friend. He bumped a stack of old invoices and it toppled. Loose papers flooded the narrow walkway between dilapidated crates and piles of antiquated state and county forms and booklets.

"Dammit," he said, and blinked at what was exposed by the fallen stack.

A wooden box, cube-like, twelve inches on a side. Unremarkable enough, except for leather side handles and the padlock holding its flat lid securely closed. Near the lock, hand-written letters in red paint: LINR.

A chill found him. For a moment he might have been back in the attic at home, rummaging through the Lincoln Middle carton once again. He leaned closer and shades of Robbie Vaughn and the other boy, Justin Wick, leaned with him briefly before shuddering away. Correlation, or a slight case of the screaming meemies?

At last he picked up the wooden box by way of its handles and set it on the room's only piece of furniture, a desk just inside the door, where light from the single window washed over it. Definitely some hefty contents in there. Full of old town ledgers or handwritten tax rolls, no doubt. *Of course, it would be impossible to know*, he reasoned as he slipped his fingers under the padlock. Maybe he would go next door to the garage and get a bolt cutter just for laughs and—

The lock opened with a *snick* sound and then hung there. It seemed to beam at him like a crooked smile.

That's a checkmate, Mr. Logan.

He made a what-do-you-know-about-that laugh and slipped the lock free, then flipped the lid open. Folded yellowed sheets sat askance inside, but a black leather-bound book, thick and textbook sized, was what caught his attention. Two swatches of old fabric tape were stuck to the cover. On each swatch was a line of handwriting. *Deaths*, read one. On the other, *Mellar's Knoll now Knoll.* For a reason he could not name, his heart thumped heavily as he slid the book out and cracked the cover. Names in nearly faded fountain ink filled a ledger-like grid. Beside each name was a date. Knoll's dead, circa 1939.

His cell phone rang and he made a slight jump. He shoved the book back into the LINR box before answering. Harley was on the other end.

"What are you and Judy doing tonight?" his friend asked, his tone slow and even, not the regular Harley but a *yeah-it's-as-bad-as-we-thought* Harley.

He swallowed hard. "We're up for whatever you need us to do."

"Come over after supper. You and I need to have a beer, or two. And maybe a shot to go with it."

The tremble in Harley's voice was agonizing. Mick realized he'd closed the LINR box and set it aside without thought. "We'll be there. Tonight."

After he hung up he allowed a distracted brand of determination to take over. He dug into the piles of loose invoices methodically, boxed them and labeled them with a black marker.

The LINR box remained by the door, disregarded. He suddenly felt he had enough to deal with.

CHAPTER TWELVE

By twenty after five Axel Vandergalien wanted a joint, bad. He meant to light up hours ago, on his lunch hour, but his one and only jay was in the glove compartment of his goddamn Passat and he wasn't in the mood to walk around to the back of the feed mill to get it in the middle of the day. Besides, his uncle Cy would come down hard on his ass if he was caught toking up on the job again. There was enough ass-busting from The Uncle Cy camp on other matters. The old *Jesus, you're twenty-three frigging years old, boy, can you wear some clothes that don't have holes in them?* and *when you gonna get a frigging haircut?* stuff was getting pretty old, but who gave a fuck? Cy just liked to hear himself talk, mostly. Otherwise dear old Unky wouldn't allow him to run the mill for the better part of the day, seeing to the needs of the area's shitkickers and plow jockeys, would he?

But now, at last, it was jay-time. He closed up the F&F ten minutes early. *Shitkickers deferred until tomorrow*, he thought as he trotted down the outside stairs and rolled the big bay door facing The Plank to a closed position. The late afternoon sun threw longish shadows that were like a memory of summers past, or a promise of the season to come. During the warm months, the shadow thrown by the huge corn bin next to the mill building resembled, to him at least, a brontosaurus, like straight out of that Durasstic Park movie. Or Jurratic, or whatever. He'd thought it for years, some kind of childhood bullshit.

"Stupid," he said and then turned on his heel to walk around back.

His car was parked on a gravel plot at the back of the property, which left plenty of room for the shitkickers' big trucks to swing around and fill up from the long neck feeder attached to the side of the corn bin. A person was always making room, because the world revolved around the shitkickers and the cop lovers and the rule-making dickheads of the planet. *Too bad*, he thought as he slumped in behind the wheel, his hair masking his face like a black and oily curtain. He took the pre-rolled jay out of the glove box and lit up, thinking the afternoon shadows might indeed indicate spring, but sweet Mary Jane at quitting time tasted like high July summer, golden and warm and heady.

He tipped his head back as he exhaled, and closed his eyes. When he opened them, he saw the man standing next to the corn bin. He acknowledged the heavy, buttoned-up black clothes with a blurt of laughter. As if drawn by the sound, the man began to walk over, his hands folded.

"Shit," Axel said and thought about smashing out the joint or maybe tossing it out the window.

He was still on mill property and if this was one of Unky Cy's fuckstick cronies, he might end up with his ass in a jam after all. But his hand stopped partway to the ashtray as if his wrist has been snatched by an intervening hand.

If there was one thing Axel Vandergalien was good at, besides shooting pool and giving the bar girls in Drury and Baylor multiple orgasms, it was being able to spot a judgmental prick from ten paces. More to his credit, he could spot an all-out authoritative asshole from a mile. This guy was neither of those things, despite his long but conservatively straight gray hair (*thinks he's fucking Ichabod Crane or something*). This guy was searching, but for what?

Before he could stop himself, he got out of the car, the joint smoldering into the cup of his hand and he leaned against the door. "Mill's closed, Mister."

"Very good." The man's near-smile made him seem imperative and fascinated. He stopped a few paces away. "Then you have time to speak with me."

"Look man, I barely have the patience to talk to the townies around here. And you ain't no townie, so I really don't have time for you. You looking for directions or something, go to the gas station and ask 'cause I'm not a fucking GPS."

"Directions, no. But I may need a confidant while I'm visiting. Someone I can call upon in the next few days. Someone of a less than authoritative position, shall we say?"

"Good luck with that." Axel took a pull from his jay. He felt in his bones the stranger would make no judgments about it, and he was right. "Some days there's enough authority in this town to make me want to puke. Between that Borth bitch calling the shots like a goddamned queen mother and Unky—uh—my uncle who thinks every time he takes a shit God eats it, and a bunch of tight asses who think they're so much better than certain people, yeah, there's authority here all right. Knoll's crawling with it."

"But you're not on that same level."

He grunted. The sun was westering and bright, but a residual coldness seemed to be leaking out of the shadows. "They look at me like something the dog pissed on most of the time. Unless they need me to lug out their goddamn feed bags or work the truck scale when they're cashing out for the day. Then they go home and talk about my jail record and my tattoos and how I keep this job only because my uncle is letting me skate."

"So wrapped up in judgement," the man said with a dip of his shoulder. It was a gesture of confidence. "As if none of them have ever crept under the law."

Axel blew a plume of smoke skyward and put out his fist because he wanted a knuckle bump from this man. "You know it, Ichabod."

The man smiled, placed a cool finger on Axel's extended fist and coaxed it down. "The name is Thekan."

He said this with excessive care, as if not to have it confused with *deacon*, or *beacon*. Axel's hand seemed to descend down and down, as if his arm was loose elastic. The sunset world and the cool shadows leaned in to eavesdrop on him and this man who was so glad—

"I'm so glad we understand one another," the man said, and blinked his suddenly startling green eyes.

Axel wanted to look away. Couldn't. More than startling, they were frightening eyes, their centers white-green points of light. But for all the fear coiled inside of him, he also felt a desire to vent a while longer about the people of Knoll. Even old Unky Cy with his big mouth and his *Mellar's Out* posters and his gigantic *mother-trucking fuck*.

He laughed at this, a high giddy sound, and staggered uncertainly on his thick-lugged boots. He squinted at the man as he spoke. "Are you putting stuff in my head?"

"I am more of a sculptor just lately." The light was gone from his eyes. The shadows were back to normal, too. The brontosaurus stretched out in grand form thirty yards away.

"Right," Axel said.

"And I have a task for you. Do you understand it, should I need you to perform?"

He *did* understand. Without the exchange of a single word on the matter. *Weird as fuck, this Thekan. This Ichabod.* "I do," he said. "But when? How?"

His joint fell into the gravel. He didn't care.

"I will leave the fine details up to you, my friend." Thekan said. "Free will. Understand?"

He did, although he was pretty sure they hadn't discussed it. But then again maybe they had. His head was all fucked up. "Sure, I'll do it."

CHAPTER THIRTEEN

With the workday shaved and showered away, Mick went downstairs to find Judy in the kitchen packing up cookies for their visit. The evening held a sort of *big event* feel, but the big event promised to be a grim one. A starting point, where the Logans and the Kroeners began a journey with a potentially morose end.

"Why don't you wear the tan pants?" Judy said, stacking pecan sandies with capable ease. "Those black ones cut you at the waist, if I remember right."

He rolled his shoulders a little. As usual she was exactly right. "The tan ones are missing a button. I forgot to tell you."

She shot him a bright look over her shoulder and indicated the kitchen chair where her iced tea and her laptop sat, both glowing in their own way under the kitchen lights. There was also a spool of thread and a needle. Draped over the back of the chair were his tan pants, button intact and ready to go.

"You're too good to me," he said and emptied his pockets onto the table.

"And don't you forget it. What do you think you're doing?"

He grinned at her, his hands in the middle of undoing his belt buckle. "Just a quick change of clothes in the privacy of my own home. Besides, it's not the first time I've had my pants around my ankles in this room, am I right? Care to join me, lady?"

"If we had the time, maybe. Or if I had the energy. We took on three new clients today, and none of them are light accounting. All big stuff. What's that?"

He immediately knew what she meant. The velvet bag containing the chess pieces was on the table amid his other pocket cargo. Carrying them was automatic now, a response more than an effort. As he tucked and zipped, she took out the king and the knight and turned them over in the light.

"I came across them in the attic," he said. "They're from the school."

"I know they are. Some pretty deep memories here. You okay?"

He kissed her cheek. "As calm as can be."

Calm is not okay, it fired off in the depths of her gaze. *Was* he okay with it? The only counselor he'd gone to see—not after Robbie Vaughn's death but after his funeral (it took a miserable brand of delusion for him to appreciate the internal wreckage he was carrying around)—had warned him of false serenity. But this didn't feel forced or hastily constructed or false in any way. It felt *right*. Even necessary.

"It was a bad time," she said as she popped the pieces back into the bag and held it out for him, watchful.

"It was a long time ago" He dropped it into the nearest kitchen drawer filled with orphaned tools, pens and pencils, and matchbooks. "And I have moved on."

Judy touched his shoulder. He understood every meaning in it, appreciated every nuance. His Judy, diligent at his side. When something fell off, she was there to put it back, maybe not as good as new but still competently done.

"Now let's go see our friends," he said.

CHAPTER FOURTEEN

Harley Kroener's house, which sat on Backbank just a few doors down from The Chapel Bar, showed no signs its owner of thirty years might soon be a lingering supplicant instead of a master and caretaker. Its roofline remained as straight and stalwart as an unimpressed brow, caring nothing about needle biopsies and radiation therapy. Its long porch was a place where cedar scented memories lingered. Its front steps creaked in all the familiar places when Mick and Judy approached the door. *Such was the indifference of the world*, Mick thought.

"It has spread to his lungs," Judy said at the last minute, tucking a length of brunette hair behind her ear. "Tumors. Just so you know."

He was thankful she'd offered the information, because it seemed like a detail Harley might or might not share. A hopeless feeling of *ah shit* flared up in light of it, the same type of feeling that visited him weeks ago when Harley told him there might be cancer, and it might be bad. It made him ache in a way you ache only for those closest to you.

As he rang the bell, Judy slipped her hand into his and gave it a squeeze. A wooden sign dangled by lengths of chain from the porch ceiling. It was something Beth Ann picked up at one of the craft shows in Drury last autumn, a name plaque with *The Kroeners* burned into knotty pine in broad script. In the lower corner was a painting of a trout, mid-leap surrounded by drops of lake water, line and hook streaking from its mouth. The sign caught a breeze and the squeak of its rusted chain took on an almost conversational lilt—*here we go, here we go, here we go*. When Beth Ann opened up, Mick put on a soft and understanding smile. He had to stop biting his lower lip to do it.

Another element unchanged by the *big event* was the Kroener's hospitality. Beth Ann had lit scented candles around the undersized, randomly furnished rooms and she took Judy's light jacket with a smile. Harley stuck his head out of the kitchen doorway and sent a quick head dip of acknowledgement Mick's way, along with a wink. "There he is."

The women hugged. The men shook hands. It all felt natural yet odd and backward. No one needed to say it. When it was just him and Harley in the living room with a couple of beers and a plate of Judy's cookies, Harley lowered himself into the worn chintz recliner in the corner to get down to business. It was a long trip down.

"I feel like a total shit about this, Mick. The whole thing."

"What do you mean?"

"You know what I mean. You holding the bag at the garage while I come up sick."

Mick swigged his Coors like it didn't matter. "Take it easy on yourself. Things will get done."

"I've got Beth Ann to mollycoddle me, so you shut the hell up. We both know you're going to be running your ass off and it's not fair. I've got chemo scheduled for tomorrow, and they want to radiate my lung right off the bat, too. A real one-two punch. When I asked if I could come in to work right after, they laughed as if they were humoring an old man with old-timer's disease or something. Jesus."

Mick noticed how his friend appeared diminished for all of his size and height, and he realized he hated this *big event* even more than he'd first thought. "I've heard the treatments can take a lot out of you."

"Yessir. So, I'm going to wait."

"Wait? Is that smart?"

"Only for few days. Once this village voting nonsense is off our plates I'll start the whole ride. But listen, don't say anything to Beth Ann. I haven't told her yet. I'll do that tonight, before bed. Then I'll make my excuses with that dopey-faced Dr. Lambert in the morning."

"Fine, then here's the plan. You take most of the regular village work over the next few days while I get the hall ready for the big vote. By most I mean only as much as you can handle. And you have to promise to get yourself in for treatment ASAP right after we learn whether we have a *Mellar's In* or a *Mellar's Out*. Deal?"

He leaned forward and extended the Coors bottle. Harley clinked it with his own. "Deal. What a bunch of garbage we put up with, right?"

"Right."

"Speaking of garbage, did that gas sniffer from the state office collect what he needed at the landfill?"

"He didn't get back to me," Mick said. "I suppose if there was a real problem he would have tracked me down."

Harley's eyes grew hard as he eased back into his chair, as if to say *yeah, they'll track you down from now on, Mick Logan, because I'm no longer up to snuff. Never will be again, I suspect. You go on to the head of the class, and don't feel bad. Not your fault I faltered and fell.* Then he said, "I'm not going to let it lick me."

Mick tipped his bottle in a toast. His smile felt wide and somehow painful at the same time. "I didn't think you would."

Judy's voice came from the doorway. "Are girls allowed in this clubhouse?"

Beth Ann stood behind her with an air of composure despite her puffy red eyes. She held out freshly opened bottles of beer, enough for everyone. "I'm afraid we don't have the secret password, if there is one."

"Get on in here, honey pie," Harley said, switching on a bright voice and pressing some of the slouch out of his shoulders. "All the password you need is right there in your hands."

They all laughed, with hardly any strain at all.

They spoke as friends do, with seriousness and concern tempered with bouts of light laughter, never quite forgetful of the *big event* and the purpose of their company. Only once did the room become quiet, when Beth Ann professed how glad she was they could start Harley's treatments right away. Mick and Harley traded a quick *oh shit* expression and Judy picked up on it. Then Harley made some joke about the hospital being more on the ball than the local mail delivery and everyone laughed again.

They parted with more hugs and handshakes. Harley's grip on Mick was overlong, his countenance wide and heartfelt, and Mick supposed every parting would be on a similar order from now on. He wrapped it up by slapping his arm around Harley's broad back and he whispered, "Hey. You're still the boss. Always will be."

Harley responded with a rubber-lipped nod. His eyes shone in the air so sweetly scented by apple cinnamon candles. "Talk to you tomorrow, Mick."

Once he and Judy were outside he took her hand.

"Beth Ann is a mess," Judy said as they walked to the car.

"It's going to get worse once she finds out he's not going in for treatments right away."

She nodded, her suspicions confirmed. Clever Judy.

"Why in the world would he wait?"

"Because he's married to this town just as consummately as he's married to his wife."

"Careful, Mr. Logan," she said and stepped to her side of the car, "your poet's soul is showing."

"Just a little." He climbed behind the wheel, stroked by a light breeze which was still out of the southeast, still a Crymost wind.

On the drive home, Judy looked at him with part concern and part cool sensibility. "Is it just me, or does it feel like we've turned some type of corner overnight?"

"Yes, and the turn wasn't onto Easy Street, either. I hope you're okay with late suppers for a while because I think I'll be burning some midnight oil. Harley's tough but I can see this is already wearing him down. I might be taking over a lot of the town's work on my own."

"I thought about that. You know, Britta Kemmel says there's not a lot going on at the F&F right now. She ought to know since she lives across the street. Maybe Axel Vandergalien can help you out. I know Cy likes to keep him busy so he stays out of trouble."

"One Vandergalien with his nose in our business is enough, thank you."

"Just a thought." She yawned as the car eased into the driveway.

He put his arm around her as they walked to the house and she spoke with a sleepy tone while he unlocked the door. "I still like it here. We picked a good place."

"We did, didn't we?"

He could not say what made him turn around to face into the southeast breeze, but when he did, what he saw made him freeze with the house key still poked out in front of him as if to unlock the very air. A greenish glow spread skyward behind the treetop barrier of Garden Street like a paintbrush swipe of alien dawn. He stepped off of the porch to get a better view but the light diminished, burned low, and then went out.

Judy's voice leaked toward him, heavy with wariness as she stepped close to him. "Mick."

"I saw it," he said.

"What was that?" Judy asked, transfixed on the now dark and starry sky. "It seemed like it was close by."

"It did," he said. His lips felt cold.

Close by, in the southeast. The direction of the wind, and The Crymost.

PART TWO:

DARK
HANDSHAKES

CHAPTER ONE

TWO THINGS CROSSED Mick Logan's mind as he went through his morning routine. One of them was a lingering concern over Harley. The other was more pertinent and therefore more demanding: Judy's suggestion about getting some help with the village work. Like most of her ideas, it was logical and solid, and it definitely bore further consideration. When he left the house, the goodbye kiss he gave her was long and came with a deep hug, which brought on one of her baffled yet amused smiles. He loved those smiles.

He arrived at the garage feeling energized and a bit challenged, but in a good way. Judy said it best: they'd turned some sort of corner. What waited around the bend was still unknown, but he felt equipped to handle it. His mood changed when he walked into the garage.

Light streamed through the glass block window in a soft shaft. In that shaft, Harley was at his desk, his face in his hands. Mick stepped inside and cleared his throat. "Did we keep you up too late last night?"

Harley jerked to attention, a massive totem rocking on the bearings of the old wooden chair. "Hey, Mick. No, I stayed up only a little while after you left. Just long enough. You know."

"You told Beth Ann?"

"She didn't take it well, but I made it clear my mind is set on this. That was that. But for some reason I'm so damned tired today."

"Should have slept in. Can I trouble you for some coffee?"

Harley reached over and poured a cup. "I'm trying to keep it normal. I talked to Cy and he said if I need some half-days I can take as many as I want. Without pay, of course."

"He's a real prince. You knock off whenever you're ready today," Mick said and walked around to snag some garbage bags from the storage locker. "I'm going to get started next door. Rap on the door when you go so I know you're leaving."

"If I knock on the door over there, it will be to tell you it's time to break for lunch. Shit." Harley's face compressed, and his hands grasped at his right side. Mick set his bags down and rushed over, uncertain, but Harley was already coming out of it, relaxing.

"I'm good," Harley said at last. There were dark hollows under his eyes. Lack of sleep, maybe. Or the rolling machinery of hurt and worry doing its dark work. "Pain just grabbed me for a second. It's done it before."

Mick gave Harley's shoulder one of those age-old nudges and once again his friend's eyes passed a message of heartbreak.

"I mean it. Leave whenever you're ready today," he said and gathered up his bags and his coffee cup for the road. "Things will get done around here."

He hurried to the truck, his decision to make a side trip now firm. The F&F Feed Mill opened early, and he wanted to find Cy in residence.

CHAPTER TWO

There was no one in the front loading bays of the F&F so Mick went around to the back and climbed the metal stairs to the upper office. Axel was kicked back in the padded desk chair with a bag of chips in his lap and a cigarette smoldering between his fingers. Or something akin to a cigarette, judging from the smell.

When Axel saw him, he jumped to his feet and stubbed the smoke out in a nearby open drawer. "Fuck, man."

"I didn't mean to sneak up on you," he said, reminded of the days when he'd catch a student up to their tricks. The feeling was one part authority and about four parts amusement. "Sorry."

Axel indignantly slammed the drawer. Corn chips were scattered around his feet like flakes of yellow paint. "Nobody comes up here but Unky—uh, my uncle."

"That's who I came to see. Both of you, actually. Is he here?"

"Over at Copeland's, settling up the gas bill, and then wherever else he goes most days. Cat napping, maybe. What do you want?"

"I have a job for you, if Cy gives the okay."

"I already got a job."

Mick's expression changed a little, to an even more teacher-like *is that so?* look. He couldn't help it. "This would be just a few hours. Village work. Easy stuff."

Axel's eyes flashed with acrimony in return. "Uncle Cy tells me about you lazy-ass caretakers. Fucking janitors is about it. Scooping up elephant shit after a parade is all you do around here, and you can't even get that done right. If you want somebody to work their nuts off while you and that dumb shit Kroener sneak around and blow each other all day, look someplace else."

"For your information, Harley Kroener is sick and it's going to be just me doing village work as of next week. I thought, with your family's interest in the town, you'd be happy to help out. Keep the town clean and tidy, because there's a thousand different kinds of elephant shit in a place like this, Axel. And it all needs shoveling."

Heavy feet sounded on the outside stairs accompanied by a jangle of keys, lots of keys. A Cy Vandergalien amount of keys if ever there was one. Mick smiled, and felt more like a teacher than he had in years. "You might want to start by cleaning up the mess under your chair."

Cy stopped just inside the door. "Logan. What the hell are you doing here?"

"Just having a chat with your nephew about working for the village while Harley deals with his health issues." He pointed. "It seems Axel has a drawer full of reasons not to help out, however."

Cy stalked over to the drawer and yanked it open, then glared up at Axel whose face was a few shades paler, his lips pressed thin. "Toking up on the job again. Goddamn it. You, boy, have just bought yourself some extra duties. Some big ones."

"I do enough for this shit hole."

"You going to do a little more or you'll be wearing my size ten-and-a-half in your ass. The in-floor corn grinder down by the loading bays needs to be cleaned up, and I think you're just the man for the job."

Axel's eyes went wide. "That thing's out-of-date, illegal, and dangerous. You need a certified technician or some such shit to clean it. I know you do. Jesus."

"Let's just say your certification came in written on Zig-Zag papers." He plucked out the partial joint and shook it under Axel's nose. "And if you want to keep this job and the shit hole in my basement you call an apartment, you'll jump right on it. Get me?"

Axel's eyes lowered down to slits.

Cy dealt Mick a brief acknowledgement before going on. "And I think it's good if you do some village work, too. Something we can measure, make sure you're getting the job done. Like cutting grass, maybe. Appropriate, since grass is your favorite pastime anyway. Don't you think?"

"You gonna let that jerk have his way?"

"This is *my* way, boy. Nobody else's."

He shot Mick a conspiratorial look. Mick returned it with a nod. "It would be a big help if you could trim up the roadsides and ditches, the strip in front of the old mercantile, and the lawn at the Borth house. You can use the Swisher. It's a rider with a 60-inch deck. It's old but it gets the job done. Starting tomorrow. Mornings are best."

Axel put up his hands as if showing off the black stars tattooed on his knuckles. "No go. I've got to work here tomorrow morning."

"Not no more. Not after this horseshit," Cy said with another peek inside the drawer. "You put your goddamned doobie out on my copy of the quarterly report, you numbnuts. You're a village employee, mornings, as of tomorrow. And you can spend your afternoons downstairs in that grinder pit figuring out how to scrape ten years' worth of corn dust out of the blades. Clear?"

Axel collapsed a little all over. "Fucking ridiculous."

"Clear? Or do you go to my place right now and start packing your miserable possessions for easy transport to points unknown, pot papers and all?"

"Yeah. Clear," Axel said. "I need some air. Jesus."

He dealt both of them a glower on the way out. After he was gone, Mick made his way to the door. "Thanks, Cy. I didn't mean to cause a family dispute or anything."

Cy grimaced and took out his quarterly report, brushed fussily at the burned hole in the center of the top page. "To deal with an asshole, you gotta be an asshole sometimes. And don't think I did any of it to help you out, Logan. I made a promise to straighten that boy out and I mean to keep it, that's all. Now get back to work. Jesus, what's with all the damn corn chips on the floor?"

Mick turned away and slipped out of the door.

Axel pushed the Passat up to seventy just outside the town limits, only half aware of the needle on his gas gauge ticking over the E mark like an admonishing finger. Best if he went back into town for some gas at Copeland's, but he'd have to go easy at the pump. His entire claim to financial liquidity at the moment consisted of three crumpled dollars. Rip-assing away from the F&F was a dumbass move, childish, like a tantrum. But he thought his Unky Cy expected it, in a way. Hell, even that Logan dickhead didn't seem all too surprised by his exit.

Oh, but they'd all get something they didn't expect real soon. All he needed to figure out was where to get enough gasoline to do the job—three dollars wasn't going to cut it. But like Ichabod/Thekan had said, the details were up to him. He'd find a way. There was always a way.

At last he turned the car around, leaving heavy black streaks in the middle of County L.

CHAPTER THREE

Chastity Mellar Borth trudged from the car to the house, her arms loaded with groceries. The pain was like an anvil and hammer today; it clanged away inside her bones and brought with it something new, a mordant thump in the back of her head. The only promise of relief was the company of her cool, dark rooms and her pills. But soon, the changes would rain down.

She stopped just before mounting the porch steps. *Changes?* A silly thought, a random particle covered with its own nasty jags, probably related to her headache which was bad enough to affect her vision on the way home. Affect it to the point of hallucination. Perhaps a call to Dr. Zugge was in order, as long as she was ready for a confrontation on the matter. He would tell her in his drawling, long-suffering tone how blurry patches and blind spots were common with severe headaches. That part she'd heard before. But what does it mean, dear doctor, when road signs changed before your eyes? Yes, during her drive not five minutes ago the green sign board at the north end of The Plank changed, clearly, and in a rather entertaining way. One second it read KNOLL above the tiny designation of UNINCORPORATED, just as regular as clouds at dawn. Then, with a sort of flicker/switch, it read MELLAR'S KNOLL in stark bright white letters.

As she drove up on it, hands locked on the wheel of the Lincoln, the only words she was able to find were *Whose idea . . . ?*

Then the letters shifted again. Her dear old family name turned dark, each character withering and dropping away, like leaves from a long-dead tree.

Hallucination, she could hear Dr. Zugge's drawl as she struggled now to take out her keys without spilling groceries into the dirt, *is a common result from overt mixtures of pain medication, you know.*

Well, an overt mixture waited for her inside and she could barely wait to administer it.

She poked the key toward the door lock and thought something was not right. Her noisome *Mellar's In* poster was not visible in the window immediately to her left. That was because someone was standing in front—

"Allow me," the man said and stepped out.

She made a stifled cry, unable to move.

"Who . . . ?" She assessed the man's intense but neutral face. There was something soothing about it, unlined and framed out by a mane of gray hair the way it was. *Such heavy clothes*, she thought on a deeper level, *and not a drop of sweat despite the warm day.* "Who . . . ?" she asked again.

"My name is Roderick Thekan," he said with a slight smile as he reached for the grocery bags. She surrendered them without thought. "I am a judge by trade, with some very old connections to this town. And I've come for a visit."

"I don't know you," she said and the truth of it allowed her to come back to herself a bit. She jabbed the key into the lock. "And this is private property, which means you're trespassing."

"But I hope to change that, since I would very much like us to spend the next days together."

"Together?"

It came out much less harsh than she'd intended. The lock tripped, but she made no effort to open the door.

"It was once your family's duty to play host to the politicians and businessmen and clergy who visited Mellar's Knoll—forgive me, *Knoll.*"

In her mind, the word *Mellar's* fell away again, corroded scraps carried by the breeze. "Why would you call the town by such an old name?"

"As I said, my connections here are old ones. I am a bit of a historian, you will find. And I am called to be, in the case of your town, a witness to change."

"Is this about the mercantile?"

He smiled over the top of her groceries. "All things have a cycle. Beginnings, endings, recurrences. It's the guts and glory of history. Continuation despite grim and sometimes terminal outcomes. But your doorstep is not the place for such conversations. We shall have plenty of time for discussions at your dining table or in your lovely parlor over the next few nights. If you will have me as your guest, that is."

His long fingers tightened on the bags. A Styrofoam carton complained inside. So helpful, this man. And he had come so very far. She was uncertain how she knew, but in her mind, it was undeniable.

"None of the rooms are prepared for guests."

His smile broadened, thin and sharp above her bread and celery. "Tonight, I have much business which will keep me out late anyway. But tomorrow evening I hope to lay my head here. I think we will make complimentary companions."

One of his pale hands swept out and brushed her wrist. His eyes captured pinpoints of light from the morning sun. Green-white light. It startled her, and yet surprise was washed away by another sensation—or rather lack of sensation. The arm he touched was devoid of pain, leaving only a blank, healthy, *liberated* sensation from shoulder to fingertips. He pulled away and the sweet relief faded. Aches leaked back in, instantly, heavily.

She'd heard of such things: Reiki, touch therapy, other such outlandish practices, but perhaps there was something to it. And perhaps this judge, who was sworn and bound to serve people in the fairest of ways, was sent by divine guidance to relieve some of her agony. Sent as mysteriously as Daddy's rosary. Perhaps not all the Mellar family's good fortune had been exhausted as she once believed. Changes may, indeed, be raining down.

She pushed the door open and nodded for him to go in.

"Tomorrow," he said and handed the groceries off. "We will spend more time. If I'm welcome, of course."

He waved his hand as he stepped off her porch, his lovely, healing hand.

"As you say," she called after him, "it's my family duty."

CHAPTER FOUR

The village truck was nearly loaded to capacity and Mick was glad for it. The gloom of the village hall's back room was unpleasant, and the musty smells of old record books, invoices and newspapers—something he'd hoped to get used to as the hours wore on but did not—were cloying. One thing was for sure, the fresh air during the drive to the Baylor Disposal Facility would be a blessing.

He entered the back room for one last armload, his sights set on a shoulder-high stack of newspapers in a far corner. They were ancient copies of the *Drury Daily Courier*, yellowed with age. He fed them into a trash bag a few at a time, barely glancing until an extra bold headline caught his eye.

TUBERCULOSIS IN MELLAR'S KNOLL?

The accompanying photo was of The Plank and Forest Street intersection. The village hall and village garage were in plain view along with a familiar brick building, the signage of which declared it a parlor of optometry and watch repair, which would one day house a branch of the Bank of Dunnsport. The facing corner building, most recently a failed and shuttered attempt at an ice cream parlor called Ice Dreams, was plainly some type of hat and dress shop for ladies. Like its modern day counterpart, it was out of business judging from the soaped windows and unreadable but somehow mournful banner across the door. A dray horse pulled a wagon away from the camera on the way to the F&F. No cars traveled the streets, but if there were they would have been of the Coupe or Packard variety. No pedestrians wandered the sidewalks.

He glanced at the first few sentences of the article, momentarily fascinated.

May 16, 1939—Mellar's Knoll, WI
County Desk

The recently voted decision to pull up the remaining wood underlayment on rural areas of County Highway L should have little impact on traffic in and out of Mellar's Knoll, even though the road serves as the town's main street. There is virtually no travel here. The fair town, which is nestled on the northern bank of the Wistweaw River, has taken numerous visits from Doctors P. Jessup and M. Sherman of Drury and Dr. C. Clairville of Baylor in attempts to treat various illnesses spreading throughout the town and laying low its citizens. Little activity can be seen as one rides down the main street, passing shuttered windows, barred doors and shops left still and empty. According to physicians Jessup and Sherman, lethargy and melancholy are the primary symptoms which, in most cases, result in forfeiture of fortitude, and death. A strain or collective strains of tuberculosis and consumption are suspected. Visits to the neighborly town should be done with high caution . . .

"Hey." Harley's voice gave him a start. "Ready for lunch?"

There was pain near Mick's mouth. He was biting his lip. Hard. "I am." He dropped the paper into the trash bag and fumbled it closed. "I'm right behind you."

CHAPTER FIVE

"Listen," he said after they unpacked their lunches at the garage desk. The open bay door let in a sweet-smelling spring breeze. "I talked to Cy this morning. Axel Vandergalien is going to help us with the lawn cutting. He starts tomorrow."

Harley shook his head as if the whole thing was inevitable. "Isn't that a little like pissing over the dam?"

"I'm sorry. I should have asked you first because I meant what I said last night. You're still the boss."

Harley bit off a chunk of his chicken salad sandwich, ruminated a little, then said, "He's a goldbricker, and he'll be a pain in the backside. But maybe Cy will cut us some slack if we have his nephew on the crew, so there's an upside. Now, let's talk about something else. Cleanup going okay?"

"Lots of paper waste, newspapers galore, but it's a secondhand education for me in a way. Did you know there was a suspected TB outbreak in this town in the thirties?"

"Heard of it. Whatever swept through town nearly emptied her out, the way I remember my granddad telling it. And right after is when the name of the town changed and we were known as just plain old Knoll."

"A dark handshake." The words fell out, a lurking thought made manifest.

"A what now?"

"Something somebody said to me once."

"From your days at the school?"

Days at the school, indeed. The Robbie Vaughn days, with Robbie's words—*dark handshakes*. It was Robbie's assessment of Shelley's *Frankenstein*, and how the doctor and the monster come to accept one another and reach their individual resignations with mournful loathing. A brilliant analogy, in Mick's opinion, energized by discovery and a bit of self- congratulations as the rest of the class looked on, reverently silent as one of their own took a valid, scholarly leap before their eyes.

"Yeah." He snatched up his paper lunch sack. "Old stuff."

"Can't discount the old stuff," Harley said, his eyes suddenly sharp. He wadded up his lunch wrappers and a majority of his sandwich and tossed it in the trash barrel. "It's there whether you want it or not."

"Well, I've got a truckload of Knoll's old stuff I need to put someplace else. But let me ask you something first. Did you see anything odd right after Judy and I left last night? A flash of light, kind of green in color?"

"Nope. Not sure what it would have been, either. Transformer blowing out would be my first guess." Harley gripped his side again, his face set with painful concentration. "Damn, that's a bad one."

"Two in one day is too many," Mick said. "Go home and rest."

Harley flashed him a defeated expression. "It's passing. Besides,

I need to get the Swisher tuned up for the friend you're bringing on board tomorrow. I gotta be good for something around here."

"Always will be and you know it. But I'll feel a lot better if you're out of here when I get back from Baylor."

As Mick stepped outside, he thought about dark handshakes.

CHAPTER SIX

The Crymost was no more than a glimmer far back in his thoughts. That changed when Mick drove by Pitch Road and saw Kippy Evert up there, tooling his bicycle past the dump gates.

He turned in, and slowed to a crawl, feeling every bit the stalker. Once Kippy slipped through the barrier of tall shrubbery at the top of The Crymost path, Mick shut the truck down, climbed out and strode up the path with slow cautious steps. *Rude and ridiculous*, he thought, *spying on an old man during what was likely a very private moment*, but a sense of fascination kept him going.

He stopped where the parted shrubs stood like sentinels and he crouched down to watch. Kippy's bike lay on its side, its back wheel twirling lazily in the sun while its owner trod the hundred foot expanse of limestone toward its termination point. Mick remembered how the sheerness of the drop off captivated him the first time he'd seen it; such a clean and angular end as if the shelf of rock was trimmed by an enormous blade swung from the heavens. And then he'd felt what The Crymost exuded like a rolling, enveloping wave. He'd felt it then, and he felt it now.

Some places inspired awe with their beauty, or granted serenity by means of their visual and perhaps aromatic offerings. What The Crymost offered its visitors was a sense of melancholy. The localized heaviness in the air was what no doubt inspired the town's founder, Josiah Mellar, to declare it an official place of weeping. The quote Mick heard one of the town's geezers recite went something like: "We shan't build upon or otherwise deface the land herein, but reserve for weeping this most lachrymose of places."

The ledge area was known as The Lachrymose for many years, and even though its name was simplified and reformed through the decades into Crymost, its designation remained sacred. Widows in black gowns and high button shoes wept there as they dropped loved one's possessions into the spring-fed cauldron far below. Parents parted with medals from two world wars, Korea, that dastardly surrogate mother and eater of young Vietnam, and more recently Afghanistan and Iraq. Grandchildren flung hair ribbons and baseball cards. The jewelry of the sick, the toiletries of the dead—the pond floor was surely lined with strata of those things, scoring the decades. And the people of Knoll still came whenever their hearts wore a wrapping of sorrow. And so, here was Kippy.

He watched Kippy inch close to the drop off and fling out his bunched hands. A smallish wooden box sailed outward from those hands, yawned open on tiny hinges as if releasing a silent scream, then flipped end over end, out of sight beyond the ledge.

"There you go, old boy," Kippy said. "You sleep now. I'll try to do right."

And that was it.

Mick hurried to his truck feeling suddenly obvious and guilty. To drive away would seem ill-timed and rude, so while Kippy emerged with his bicycle at his side, Mick fussed with the tailgate in a nothing-to-see-here-just-minding-my-own-business sort of way. He tipped the old man a casual wave.

Kippy waved back. "G'day, Mick. Say, you're not dumping trash here are you?"

"Not here," he said and dusted off his hands. "I'm on my way to Baylor."

Kippy's gaze was cutting and yet comforting. "Last I heard, you got to Baylor by staying on The Plank for about twelve miles or so. Less'n there was some business you had up at The Crymost first."

"Yeah, I'm sorry, Kippy. I'm not sure what was going through my head," Mick said. "I saw you and I got a little curious. I've seen some odd stuff in this direction lately."

Kippy grunted. "You saw last night's flash, too, huh?"

In that instant Mick realized he was more than comfortable around the old man. The easiest way to put it: they were on the same wavelength. "Have you ever seen the dump light up in your years here? Or the marsh? Anything up here?"

Kippy considered the handlebars of his bike for a moment. "My suspicion is it wasn't the landfill or the marsh, t' be honest."

"Does it have to do with double barrels?"

Kippy made a near-smile. "I guess my lips got a little loose yest'idy. I do appreciate the ride, by the way. You're a good man. Probably why I feel so open with you. And why, since there's some old stories I need to share with somebody, I'm figuring you're a good, solid person who will keep them well."

Wavelengths. Yes indeed.

"Tell me, then." He rapped the side of the truck. "This stuff can wait."

"Not here. Not now. I've got a dear friend to bury tomorrow. My thoughts will be quieter once Orlin's in the ground."

Mick thought of the wooden box sailing through the bright air. The burial process had, in a way, already begun. "Understood. You know where to find me when you're ready."

"I do."

"And, I'm sorry." Mick had a cruel vision of Orlin Casper's funeral, attended by only two mourners: an addled wife who endured the ceremony with all the emotion of a potted plant, and Kippy with a dark suit jacket thrown over his faded flannel shirt.

"Me, too," Kippy said, then mounted up and pedaled away.

After a few seconds, more distantly: "Hey Mick."

"Yes?" Mick shouted after the old man.

Kippy pedaled on, unheeding. He was soon a small dot navigating Pitch Road to its end.

The voice came again, behind him. Louder. "You. Mick Logan."

He whirled around. The green slopes of the landfill met him. No one stood in the broad expanse. The vent pipe with its shepherd's crook top held court to an empty plane. Still, an expectant heaviness radiated toward him.

"Logan." The voice again. Almost goading as if to dispel the underlying thought a trick of sound might be at play.

He ducked under the landfill gate with part disbelief and part fascination, his gazed fixed on the vent pipe and its twisty strand of midday shadow. Part of him understood he'd pinpointed the source of the voice even as a more rational side attempted to wrestle it down.

"That's it," the voice rang in the air, hollow, sounding locked up but very loud. "You're just about here. Come on."

Sweat broke out on Mick's forehead and trickled down his back as he stood in front of the vent pipe. He crouched and then craned his head up to look into the downward facing outlet, to validate the impossible. The interior of the pipe was a lightless, empty throat. He pushed up close. Closer.

The voice burst from the pipe's interior. "Just. About. Right!"

A bloodless hand pushed out of the pipe's dark maw and stretched open like a ghastly blooming flower. It snatched at him. Cold fingers skittered along his cheek. Mick flinched and stumbled back. The pipe rocked to and fro, taking on the appearance of an oversized metronome. Old metal flaked and broke loose at ground level. A bony crunch followed, and the pipe toppled to the ground with the sweeping grace of a felled tree.

"What the hell is going on?" He directed the question at the fallen pipe, more precisely at the open outlet end which was only a lightless (and handless) hole once again.

"You'll get it," the voice from inside was patient, and perhaps a little bit familiar. "You're a bright guy. And I don't want to see you hurt by what's coming, so you better listen. There's not a lot of time."

"I don't—"

The pipe shuddered once as if from a passing blow, and he sensed the change in it. Coldness. Vacancy. He gazed at it as if dumbfounded by its sudden stillness, confusion joining his other emotions. *Hallucination.* A quiet suggestion drifted toward him as he backed away.

Mick got into the truck and leaned his head back, his teeth planted firmly on his lower lip. If what he'd just witnessed was indeed a hallucination, it was a very real one, which made it bad, as bad as the one he'd experienced at Robbie Vaughn's funeral. The time since Robbie's burial, a ten-year barrier of acquired confidence that was as much cocoon as it was armor, threatened to drop away with hopeless ease. What made the mind so cruel unto itself? Why mock the senses and conjure such phantoms? The voice from the passenger seat made him jump.

"Better get moving."

Peter Fyvie sat next to him, gas bloated and dripping, blind-white eyes agleam. Greenish water blurted from his mouth and splashed on his chest. "It's close, Mick. And it's hungry. It took me. And it will take you, too."

He goggled at the shape next to him, unable to follow the urge to leap from the truck and equally helpless to act upon the baser instinct to strike out. Instead, he squeezed his eyes shut. *Hallucination.* His inner voice was no longer a suggestion but now a demand. Better to accept that which presently sat at his side as hallucination than accept it as real. It was an old affectation, a Robbie's funeral affectation. *Hallucination is better than real. Better than real.*

When he opened his eyes, he was alone in the truck, drawing deep whistling gulps of air. *Hallucination,* came the demand again, but the word's meaning and impact crumbled into nothing when he looked to his right. The seat next to him was soaking wet.

CHAPTER SEVEN

The drive to Baylor and back gave him the opportunity to work through what he'd seen and attempt to find some reason in it . . . to no avail. Back in Knoll he rushed into the village garage, located the number of the state inspector's office next to the desk phone and dialed it. He was told Peter Fyvie was unavailable, which he interpreted as government-speak for "on vacation". Real Garrison Keillor stuff, remember? He hung up a little too heavily and Harley looked up from his work on the Swisher engine.

"Something going on?"

"Trouble at the landfill. The methane vent pipe isn't . . . what it should be."

Harley straightened up with some effort. "Cy is going to shit his pants when he hears about it. Do you think that Fyvie fellow has called him yet?"

Mick gulped. "I don't think so. I don't know. But I, uh . . . " He ran a hand through his hair. It shook.

"Mick, are you all right?"

"Yeah," he said, finding some of the rational Mick coming back at last in the safe and familiar surroundings. Rational enough to know he wasn't ready to talk to Harley, or anyone else, about hallucinations or suspicions that said hallucinations might be something more. Something real. "Just a long day. Let's close her up."

Harley nodded and squatted by the Swisher to finish up. He gripped his side when he did it and made an exasperated sound deep in his throat. "I can call Cy, if you want. Tell him about the pipe."

"No," Mick said on his way back to the truck. "Let's wait until I can . . . uh . . . let's wait."

When he got home, the smells of dinner filled the house, wonderful and rich. Judy met him in the front hallway.

"Hi," she said, and her expression immediately tightened. "What happened?"

Even for his dear Judy, who could read him well, he was not ready. "Nothing much. Just anxious. Axel Vandergalien starts work for the village tomorrow."

"Wow, give you guys a tip and you jump right on it."

"It's how things get done, lady." He grinned and reached around playfully for her backside.

"Hey, go wash up. I've got to check the meatloaf."

He felt better with fresh clothes and a clean face. When he came into the kitchen, Judy was transferring green beans from a pot into a ceramic serving dish. "Too bad about Orlin Casper," she said.

"Kippy says funeral's tomorrow."

"Yes." She paused. Funerals were a delicate subject. Always would be. "I placed an order with the florist in Drury so there will be something there from us."

"Okay."

"Something else is wrong, isn't it?"

He sighed.

"I thought I saw something at the landfill today. Something weird." It felt good to get it out, but mentioning it put the dripping horror of Peter Fyvie in front of him again and he hoped she wouldn't ask for details. "But I've got it handled."

"Do you?"

Her expression was like a cloudy stone flashing with multiple facets. *You thought you had things handled once before, and you were wrong,* one of those flashes said. *You're being foolish and stubborn,* said another. Yet another asked, *don't you remember how awful it was back in Royal Center? Are you willing to put us through that again? Ignoring it won't make it go away, you stupid, pigheaded man.*

A mean flame began to burn in his brain and in his gut like a double-ended fuse. He stalked to the junk drawer, took out the chess pieces in their velvet bag and gave them a vehement shake. "It always comes back to this, doesn't it? That one miserable, terrible incident is like some secret, festering sore in our lives, always there in the back of everything we say and do, and I'm sick to death of it. Yes, finding these things brought me a little closer to the old days, but it's not a reason to haul out the Valium and call the shrink brigade. I had a bad day, Judy. Confusing as all hell. And coming home should be my shelter from it. Instead, I get the stink-eye and the third degree." The moment seemed to balance on a pinnacle. The next words were out before he could stop them. "It's goddamned humiliating and it's the last thing I need from you."

The wounded look on her face filled him with self-loathing. He stomped into the living room and flopped on the couch, searching for a perfect, healing next step. The answer, in his experience, was to wait. *Let it settle* was their unspoken motto in these matters. Maybe not the clearest path to resolution, but it kept them from having anything close to an all-out fight for eighteen years.

After a short while, Judy came into the living room and sat next to him on the couch. She rested a hand on his arm. "I'm sorry. I worry too much sometimes. Still friends, right?"

He took her hand, looked into her eyes. "Yeah. Always. God help us both. Things are okay with me, really."

She got to her feet. "And I believe you. Do you want to pour us some iced tea while I finish setting the table?"

He smiled. *Let it settle.* "I'll be right in."

She glanced back before she left him. Her worry was still there, like a fine crack in her capable demeanor. She was turning his words over in her head. He sensed it as surely as he smelled the meatloaf in the other room or felt the copper-warm ray of sun streaking in the living room window. *I thought I saw something weird, but I'm okay.* His one relief: she didn't seem to notice he'd put the bag with the chess pieces in the front pocket of his jeans. There was a strange soothing quality in knowing they were near.

At last he got up to pour the tea.

CHAPTER EIGHT

Mick had the dream for the first time in years. It was always more memory than dream, and that made it cruel.

"Do you have time?" Robbie Vaughn stood in his classroom doorway and drew Mick's attention away from the stack of ungraded assignments on his desk.

He said he did, thankful to disparage the endless essays proclaiming Robert Frost as the most influential American poet of the twentieth century. After an hour, he'd had enough of apples tumbling down and roads not taken. The chessboard was already set up near the window, a focal point in the glow of late March sunset. So they played.

They talked of things significant only to the moment and yet pertinent for the ages as the black numbered wall clock swept time away.

"Track and field this year?" Mick asked at one point, the nominative left off because such casual speech seemed to fit easily into the moment.

Robbie's deep and innocent eyes studied the game with eager intensity, yet he managed a half-smile. "You kidding?"

"Just thought you might like to join in with some kind of activity."

"You mean not be the nerdy kid who hangs around with the teacher after school?"

"Not what I meant. There's opportunity, that's all. Meet some people, work as a team."

"Nope. Who would I meet chasing a ball or jumping hurdles anyway? The same people I see in the halls here every day. People I'm not interested in teaming up with, mostly. There are *by-yourself* people in the world, Mr. Logan, and I guess I'm one of them."

Robbie slid his bishop forward. His slender limbs, aglow where the sun touched the downy hairs of youth, moved with a grace that made up in confidence what they lacked in strength.

"You can't do everything in the world by yourself, you know."

"No, but I think I'm smart enough to know the difference." Another half-smile graced his face. "I've had years of practice already."

Mick offered an appreciable nod and focused on the game more closely. His king, already cornered, had become smothered by his own pawn and was highly at risk. In this particular "by-yourself" game,

Robbie definitely took the upper hand. Mick moved his knight, hesitant. Robbie leaned forward, his intensity now burning bright as he studied and re-studied the configuration of pieces in the upper corner of the board. At last the boy reached across the board, beaming. "That's a checkmate, Mr. Logan."

Robbie took up his knight and claimed Mick's blocked-in king in an exaggerated capture.

They laughed and Mick congratulated the boy with a hearty and somewhat wistful handshake. Students like Robbie were rare, and their stays all too brief.

"Thanks for the break," Mick told him and got out of his chair, "but I've got seventeen more Frost essays to grade before I go home."

"Gotta go home and study anyway," Robbie said. The last rays of March sun streaked through the window and gilded his face. His eyes glinted. "I hear some guy is planning a pop quiz on poets other than Robert Frost for tomorrow."

"The guy's brutal from what I hear." Mick smiled. "A real tyrant. Especially after he receives a whipping on the chess board."

They both laughed. Robbie left him, the doorway shaded by fading daylight.

The painful choking noise came from the hall less than a minute later, and he stuck his head out of the door with a sudden unexpected skim of sweat on his palms. An instant *in-the-wind* sensation put him on high alert.

The building's central stairwell gave access to four floors of classrooms. Its turns and landings formed an open shaft of veined marble and mahogany. Gazing into it always assaulted Mick with rolling swells of vertigo. Two boys grappled at the central railing which, on this topmost floor, formed a sort of pen around the dizzying space. Justin Wick, a burly and notoriously discontented student from a family of money was one of the boys. Mick had him in third period American Lit and found him to be a brooding, uncooperative sort. The other boy was Robbie. He was on the wrong side of the railing, kicking out to gain purchase over the open expanse of the shaft. His hands gripped the other boy's forearms desperately and Justin Wick, feet firmly planted on the hall floor, shrugged in an attempt to shake him off.

Mick meant to rush out and break up the scuffle, but the precariousness of their off-kilter positions locked up his muscles. A hasty or brutish attempt to break it up might result in success on Wick's behalf and grant Robbie a three-story fall.

Dark handshake sprang into Mick's thoughts. Robbie's *Frankenstein* assessment. Except this was another type of dark handshake playing out before him.

The will of the dream took license then, because Mick shouted. "*Hey!*"

It filled his head with the resonance of a cathedral bell and echoed down the hall, but in reality he'd only been able to manufacture a dry squeaking sound. Justin Wick's voice rang out instead.

"You gonna get an A now, brownnose faggot? A for asshole?" Justin then sensed Mick, turned from his business with a snap of his head and a fluff of dirty blonde hair, and glared directly at him. "Is he, huh? Is he gonna get an A?"

"What are you doing, Wick?" Mick managed to say. "Pull him in right now."

There was no stunned regret in Justin's hard face over a prank gone too far. There was only heartlessness and lack of reason. It hit Mick like a kick to the stomach. Still, he rushed forward.

"Fly, little fairy," Justin said forming a wide set but ultimately cold smile. "You just fly on to the Land of Nod. Sounds like a fairy place, someplace hungry for fairies like you, so that's where you gonna go."

"No, Wick. Stop it."

Justin Wick's eyes narrowed to slits. "The Land. Of. Nod."

He disengaged Robbie's desperate hands with a pinwheeling of his arms. Robbie fell without a sound.

Mick froze. He heard a heavy clunking sound against the third floor railing below followed by a breath of silence, then another looser, batting sound, more distant against the second floor mahogany. The final soundless gap was longer and the awful smacking sound on the marble lobby floor stole his breath like a gut punch.

Justin Wick laughed and motioned to the stairwell shaft with a goofy did-you-see-that expression. Mick's dream essence intruded— or was it a memory of a different kind? Doors slammed all around him, around the entire building. Classrooms once filled with meaningful ideas and passions shut up as if by a mighty wind. Rooms of warm light, sealed.

And then something new. Justin Wick stopped his infernal laughter, his face pale and grave. He turned and spoke directly to Mick.

"Hey Logan. Welcome to Wonderland—"

Mick sat up with a cry caught in his throat. Judy was next to him, her hands folded between her pillow and her cheek, her breathing slow and easy. Undisturbed. Good.

He rolled over in the moonlit dark, his heart pounding, his teeth working over his lower lip. *Wonderland, The Land of Nod. Wonderland. The Land of Nod.*

He slept, not at all.

CHAPTER NINE

Cy Vandergalien was glad to see the windows dark when he pulled up to the house. Alice wasn't a problem; she hauled a book and a bag of cheese puffs off to bed most nights and was conked out by eleven at the latest. His nephew was the one usually knocking around in the basement playing his crazy-ass music too loud, puffing his joints, and pounding the piss out of his broken down laptop. But tonight, all was quiet. At the ripe old hour of straight-up midnight, Cy could finish unwinding from the trials of the day in peace.

Not that he wasn't pretty loose already. The boys from Elmore Excavation spent it hard and fast tonight at The Chapel Bar. Cy wasn't much for sucking beer on a weeknight, but he wanted to be sure the gentleman's agreement he put together with Johnny Elmore was going to stick. *Mellar's Out* needed to win the initiative, first thing, and judging from the number of red posters popping up around town, he was confident the desired outcome was in the bag. Then old Johnny could move in and raze that shithole of a mercantile building. Once cleared—at the village's expense, of course—the land could be had for a song if a person had the right "ins" . . . and nobody possessed more of the right "ins" than yours truly, village president and all around nice guy. Then it was a matter of Elmore Excavating buying it from him for a ridiculous and extravagant amount, Elmore claiming a sizable but much-needed business expense—all major tax breaks invited—and one Cyril A. Vandergalien walking away with a tidy bundle of profit free and clear by this time next year. *Nothing helped a man unwind better than money in the pipeline,* he thought as he climbed out from behind the wheel, gave his car a pat as if it were an old chum, and stepped into the moonlit driveway.

"Good evening." A voice came to him from some distance away. "Cyril Vandergalien?"

A man walked toward him, streetlamps throwing his shadow out long and narrow and reaching.

"Evening, and you got him," Cy said back since he was not foreign to after-hours meetings or clandestine encounters. Sometimes, they were the best kind. "Up kind of late, aren't you, stranger?"

"Late it is," the man said. All decked out in a dark suit he was, with a tightly-knotted black bowtie. He removed his hat and took a stance at the end of the driveway. His gray hair fell around his shoulders. "And we both have obligations to keep, so I'll make this quick. I'm wondering if you might direct me in one small matter."

"I'm off the clock and I'm bushed, but if you make it quick I'll try to oblige. Shoot."

"I have some interest in the old Knoll town records, but I am unsure where to find them. My usual . . . intuitions aren't guiding me. They're blocked, almost."

"Everything you want is at the old village hall. Mick Logan's been working there these past few days straightening her out, so he can probably dig up whatever you need. You got family here, doing one of those genealogy things or something?"

"I am somewhat of an historian of late." The man's eyes searched the night. "Logan. Logan. That name seems to be blocked as well. How curious."

"Blocked? What the hell does that mean, Mister . . . ?"

"Thekan." His hand came forward. "I'm the Honorable Judge Thekan. And my mission in your town will be brief but quite critical. Pleased to meet you, Mr. Vandergalien."

Cy's hand became enveloped in the other man's grip. Cool flesh, unpleasant almost. The whole exchange took on the qualities of a dream, right down to the low, buzzing sensation that traveled from Thekan's palm to his own and the almost perceptible points of light trapped in the man's eyes. When Cy spoke, the words slipped around in his mouth. "Seems there was something else I wanted to ask you, but for the life of me—"

"Ah well. Forgotten is foregone."

"Right." Cy narrowed his eyes. "So, you plan to stay in town for a while?"

"A few days. If I'm welcome, of course."

Cy's thoughts hitched as if through a mental pothole. Damn, what did they put in the beer down at Chapel's anyway?

"Welcome as any," he said at last.

He dug for his keys with the sudden urge to rush inside and curl up next to his snoring Alice. In the same instant a green glow lit up the sky to the southeast, beyond the cozy houses crouched along Knoll's streets. Northern Lights was his first assumption, but the glow lacked the familiar restless shimmer of the aurora, and it was not in the north at all.

"What the hell?" he said.

"Lovely," Thekan said with a casual flick of his hand. "Like an awakening."

Cy felt the words take shape in his mouth like a mass of dark and feeding fish. "The Crymost."

Thekan's stare hardened. "Your state inspector told you all about it, remember? Called you on your telly-phone."

"He did?" Cy asked even as the memory pushed in. "Oh yeah. He did call me. I think. Didn't he—?"

"Just this afternoon. And he told you to expect such an oddity for a while. A natural phenomenon."

"Yeah, phenomenon. Completely—"

"Completely harmless. Completely natural, yes. But we digress, and you were on your way to sleep. Gentlemen's agreements can be exhausting, after all. And you forgot to mention to your excavator how you want him ready to begin the razing of that dreadful building immediately after the voting results condone it. The very next day, in fact. It would be for the best."

"Right. The best. Guess I'll give old Johnny a call in the morning. Not sure why I forgot it. Been a hell of a day."

"You'll do all those things tomorrow with no trouble. But now it's time to rest. Gentlemen's agreements, after all."

"Rest. Yeah."

Cy trudged into the house and undressed as he crossed the bedroom. He climbed into bed wearing just his undershorts. The greenish glow over The Crymost was plainly visible when he glanced out the window. Completely natural, but people were going to notice.

Best to spread the word about it first thing in the morning. No sense in letting speculation run wild.

On another, uneasy level, he thought about deals in the dark.

A few of Knoll's citizens drove up to Pitch Road to investigate the green glow as the night wore on. Most, however, stayed in town, gleaned information from those who came away from The Crymost with firsthand accounts and passed it on, spinning a web work of information, phone to phone, house to house, street to street as the hours wore on.

In the way of stars and formless dreams, the glow was swept away by the sunrise. Talk of it over breakfast was brief for the most part, sometimes even disregarded. It was Knoll business, Crymost business, and there were many who concluded in the reasoning daylight it was best not to challenge the ways of the town's lachrymose place.

Cy Vandergalien's phone was on the kitchen counter, muted. When he stumbled down for coffee and switched it on, it lit up immediately.

PART THREE:

WONDERLAND

CHAPTER ONE

AT A LITTLE PAST eight, Mick had already fielded three calls on the garage landline regarding last night's light show. He placated each caller with his lack of excitement on the matter—he'd been in Knoll long enough to know how to assuage the public at large. While he dealt with them, Harley gave Axel, who showed up on time and actually appeared eager, a rundown on how to operate the Swisher.

The fourth call came in while he was getting ready to resume his cleanup of the village hall. It was a reporter from the Drury Courier who wanted to know if Cy Vandergalien might want to provide a statement about the glow in time for the afternoon edition. Mick considered the aggravation Cy was sure to find in such a request and said "Sure, here's his home number," before hanging up.

Harley came over and hitched his pants with a grimace. "Well, for better or worse, I got our boy over there ready to roll."

Axel blinked at Mick slowly from aboard the Swisher, then fired it up and guided the mower out of the bay door. His first morning would be easy: the roadsides of The Plank at the town's outskirts and then the patch of lawn around the old mercantile.

"I think he got it," Harley said while he hung up some stray tools. "Seemed alert enough, but I got nothing back from the boy, really. Like I was talking into an empty room."

Mick stared through the open bay door and listened to the diminishing growl of the Swisher. He was reminded of another person who spent much time in a state of aware blankness. Justin Wick, scourge of Lincoln Middle School, slasher of teachers' tires by way of a butterfly knife, which was confiscated after he held it to the throat of a terrified seventh grader who thrashed just enough to cause an inadvertent but very deep slice just below the jawline.

The kitten Wick supposedly mounted in splayed-out fashion to the back wall of the family garage with a pneumatic nail gun was a legend of the darkest proportion, a tall tale with no proof to back it up, and yet Mick was sure he was not the only one who could too easily picture Justin's enamored fascination over the small creature screeching and writhing toward slow death. Doubt over the accuracy of the tale was cloudy at best among the Lincoln faculty. Most of them had grown weary of Justin's endless string of student lunchroom shoves and chokeholds, of his brooding classroom presence and volatile hallway assaults to the point of frustration. The rumors of him toting pockets full of street drugs through the halls of Lincoln dwelled likewise in the foggy land of maybe-maybe not. The notion that Justin was trouble with a capital T was upheld by most of the school, and the idea that he would one day come to no good on a devastating level went without question. None of them, whether upholding these thoughts as pitying or prophetic, realized how soon the devastation would come.

Mick shook himself. Too much, too soon after last night's dream. He needed to shut it down hard and fast and get his day started in earnest.

But a trailing thought stuck with him as he went back to work. It slid in uneasily, summoned by the past but clinging to the moment, pitying and prophetic in its own way in regard to the blank and brooding Axel Vandergalien. *Trouble*, it said, *with a capital T.*

Midday clouds rolled in and gave the day a harsh, steely glare. Mick came out of the village hall at noon, ready for lunch. Today the workload was easy: pertinent old receipts and invoices required boxing and transport to the firehouse for safekeeping. Harley sat outside of the bay door in his creaky high-back chair, his hands folded across his stomach, his bagged lunch untouched at his feet. The hollows under his eyes seemed very deep.

"Cy says he's got it on good authority the glow up to The Crymost is a natural occurrence." Harley said. "Nothing to worry about. He's going to put something in the Drury paper to that effect tomorrow."

Mick dusted his hands off and thought, *be ready, our so-fair town makes the papers yet again.*

They both looked up at the familiar sound of the Swisher's engine. Axel guided the mower expertly up to the bay door and killed the engine. There were flecks of grass caught in his hair. His jeans were shaggy with clippings from cuff to knee.

"Roadsides are done," he said, almost righteously as if they were expecting them not to be. "And the mercantile, too. Christ, what a shithole."

"Yard's all frost heaved," Harley consorted. "Riding over it kicks at the kidneys a little. Did you gas up when you were done?"

"Forgot." Axel hopped down. "Copeland's is at the other end of town, old man."

"There's a couple full cans in the back of the garage," Harley said watching him closely. "They should tide you over."

"Ten gallons each," Mick threw in. "They're heavy."

Axel gave it a moment's thought and then shifted inside his clothes. "I'll handle it, but can I do it in the morning? I'm supposed to be at the mill about now."

Mick and Harley exchanged glances and Mick nodded. "Go on then," Mick said. "I'll put the Swisher away. Thanks."

Axel stalked off, swiping the green shag off his jeans.

Harley stared after him for a moment, then stood and turned to Mick. "Do you mind if I punch out too? I'm bushed."

Mick took in the laborious way he lumbered toward the trash barrel and dropped his uneaten lunch inside. "Do what you've got to do."

"Whatever it takes to get past the rough patches," Harley countered and raised a massive mitt in a parting wave.

Mick waved back. Harley Kroener, unwell and possibly (probably) fading. Axel Vandergalien, unreadable at best. Rough patches sounded about right.

Axel strutted all the way from the village garage to the back corner of the F&F lot where he'd left the Passat. Once there he toked up, drew in the smoke and allowed it to leak out in slow, luxurious coils. The corners of his mouth turned up slightly, accommodatingly, at thoughts of the project.

Full gas cans. In the village garage. Perfect.

CHAPTER TWO

Roger Copeland strode into the back room of the Gas 'N Go, taking the first few steps in the dark as usual because the motion sensor light was on the fritz and God didn't he hate the dark. In such a windowless pit it was just this side of unholy.

He barked his shin on a stack of cardboard just as the switch did its duty. Goddamned Cy Vandergalien and his cockamamie ideas. So what if Cy wanted to give Mick Logan a little good natured challenge and have every cardboard box in the town broken down and stashed out of sight? Fun was fun, but why the lot of them required stashing in the back room of his store, he didn't know.

He winced at the fire spot of pain on his shin and limped over to the countertop in the back where he kept a number of toolboxes at the ready. He opened one up to pull out a screwdriver. That damned cash register drawer was stuck again, and—

His hand went to the object on top of the box's contents with a dreamlike slowness. He picked up on the thin gold chain so the pocket watch dangled just inches before his eyes. There was no mistaking the relief image on the lid: a locomotive belching smoke, its front catcher like a wedge of perdition. His granddad's pocket watch. The cover opened with a *snick* sound, exposing the yellowed watch face ringed in Roman numerals. A crescent of greenish water bubbled under the crystal's bottom. The engraving on the underside of the lid caused his breath to catch in his lungs.

JERROLD COPELAND
25 YEARS OF SERVICE
SOO LINE RAILROADS

He snapped the lid closed and cradled the watch in his palm, transfixed. By all standards the timepiece should be a dream, a phantom of the mind, but here it was, undeniable. As real and true as his memory of taking it to The Crymost a decade and a half ago and flinging it over the edge.

Sheila Wiedmeyer bought her grandmother's house on Meadow Lane just after she was married. She loved the place for its memories more than its charm, and Patrick didn't seem to care one way or the other. There was so much of Grandma in the house, and in the town, it seemed a shame to deny herself of either. She was sentimental and nostalgic at heart. Yet, the nostalgia of Grandma's three hat pins, the fancy old-world ones with the long shafts and shiny stones set into the tops, was suddenly lost on her, mostly because they sat—of all places—atop the stack of clean towels in the laundry room basket, and they were coated in mud. She picked them up using a washcloth, afraid to make direct contact because this was one of those weird things you saw on the ghost hunting TV shows or that old *Unsolved Mysteries* program with Robert what's-his-name from when she was a kid. *A once in a lifetime occurrence*, she decided, because she was neither clairvoyant nor psychic, even if she sometimes wished she was. This was a gift, eerie and unexplainable, and she knew right away she would tell no one else about it. Not for a while. Maybe never.

Jim Schraufnagel (Old Jim to his friends because his hair had gone prematurely white at an early age but now, decades later, his mane was thick and lush while most of his friends were down to a fringe and a wisp) studied the war medal on the coffee table with concern. His father-in-law had been the only honors-bearing serviceman in the family, and as far as he knew, this wasn't his, not covered in grime the way it was. A couple of the guys and their essentially hairless scalps were over for a game of sheep's head yesterday. Maybe one of them left it. He'd ask around next week when they played cards again. He scooped up the medal and stashed it in the kitchen cupboard next to his coffee filters and his Metamucil, then put it out of his mind.

There was no way he could know how his wife, in the ground at Willow Valley these last three years, had flung the object into The Crymost pool the night after her father's funeral. She had done it without telling him.

Cy Vandergalien sat at his kitchen table, his late lunch untouched. The object he turned over in his fingers, a brooch with a blue center stone of cut glass and an oval frame of sterling silver, was tarnished and mud encrusted. It was his mother's, and he was pretty sure it had been pinned to her breast when they buried her a couple of decades back. And yet, when he hung up the phone after talking with Johnny Elmore, who promised to mobilize his demolition equipment the minute the *Mellar's Out* vote was final, there it was, next to the message pad on the counter. He scrubbed at it with his thumb until the stone gleamed and glittered, and he thought, *forgotten is foregone.*

"Cy." The voice, like the brooch, was his mother's, ragged with sorrow and cigarettes, just as he always remembered it. Only it was no memory. It rang stark and real and as loud as a handclap in his sunny yellow kitchen. He jumped in his chair. "This ain't a good place anymore. Not for you nor for anyone else."

In an instant the source of the voice, be it memory or other less welcome possibilities, was gone from him. He felt it blink out, sensed its absence. He looked around, heart thumping, a fine layer of sweat drying on his forehead. The brooch was like an aching clot in his over-tight fingers. He relaxed his hand and watched it glitter in the sunlight. Somehow the sight of it helped to focus his thoughts.

"Jesus, Ma," he muttered.

Alice wandered into the kitchen, eyed his uncompromised sandwich and lumbered over. "What you got there?"

He slid the brooch into his front pocket. "You got the second-quarter newsletters ready, yet?"

She grabbed his sandwich and took a luxurious bite, then brushed at the corners of her mouth with a plump pinky. "Working on it. They should go out the day of the vote. You look peaked. Is your heartburn bad today? Do you want some Rolaids?"

He blinked slow, contemplative. "Just listening to my gut all of a sudden. I don't think I want anybody up at The Crymost for a while."

She blinked, her cheek packed with partially chewed lunchmeat. "You worried about last night's glowy stuff? I thought your state inspector said it was okay."

"Not worried," he said as his fingers worked over his mother's brooch through the fabric of his pants. "Just careful."

CHAPTER THREE

"You are Logan."

Mick turned around and squinted at the man just outside of the village hall's open door. His first suspicion was state inspector, checking up on an absent Peter Fyvie (and that would confirm the unthinkable: that yesterday's Fyvie hallucination was no hallucination at all and Fyvie's words—*it took me*—were not only real words, but true words), but then he noticed the man's cloak and dark hat. His thoughts harkened back to the man walking the roadside the other day, and he feared he might have done a comedic type of doubletake. If he'd reacted at all, the stranger's face did not indicate it, however.

He put down his work. "I am. What can I do for you?"

"No favors," the man said with a concessionary tip of his head. He made no attempt to enter the hall. "I make it a point to be familiar with the key citizenry when I visit a so-fair town such as this."

Mick went to the door and stretched out his hand. "Who told you I was a key citizen? My wife?" His mild curiosity was replaced by an unsettled feeling as they shook. "What brings you to Knoll, sir?"

"The name is Thekan. I'm a court judge by profession. I'm also a bit of an historian. Town records are of particular interest to me."

The man's eyes grew hard. Mick blinked. Was there a sense of intrusion, like a mental pressure as if one of the man's cold thumbs pressed on his brain? Certainly not.

"Plenty of old records here," he finally said. "But if you want to browse through them, you'll need permission from the village president."

"I have seen him already, thank you." Thekan's courtliness took on an edge. "It appears you are reorganizing the room. Are the records to be moved?"

"Invoices and accounting stuff will be moved to the firehouse for a few days while we hold a town vote. Everything else stays right here."

"I'm so pleased to know it." Thekan rested a hand on the doorjamb as if testing its sturdiness. His smile was accommodating with a certain level of perplexity. "And so pleased to make your acquaintance, Mick Logan. But I have many more stops to make, and must make wise use of my time here. I'm sure we'll meet again. Until then, have a pleasant day."

Mick nodded in reply as the judge strode away. *So-fair town,* Thekan had said. Old-world language, he supposed, for an old-world duck.

He went back to work, frowning.

CHAPTER FOUR

Mick was just finishing the after-supper dishes when Kippy Evert called.

"Funeral's done and I've had a nap. There's time for some old stories now, if you want. I'll be down to Chapel's," the old man said.

A single car sat in the parking lot of The Chapel Bar when Mick pulled in. Twilight shadows were swallowing the finer details of the world, but he was able to pick out evidence of one more patron— Kippy's bike was leaned up next to the front entrance. The building was long and narrow, and if not for the Bud Light sign ablaze in one of the tiny front windows, the place would have appeared closed.

Mick approached the huge double doors where a Presbyterian preacher once greeted his Sunday congregation. Long ago, Sunday buckboards circulated from the mercantile to this building, then known as the Mellar's Knoll River Church, so the family might hear this week's sermon and go into the world better people. Now folks came for a different type of communion, and they went into the world merely *feeling* like better people. Mick smiled as he grasped one of the door handles and opened up.

The interior was large and open, yet dim. Behind the bar at the far end of the room, Will Adelmeyer, owner and sole proprietor, rested on the heels of his hands in classic bartender fashion. His checkered shirt was cuffed at the elbows, his smooth jaw set in a dutiful almost-smile. Kippy sat on a barstool just to Will's left, a full pilsner in his hand. The two of them seemed nostalgically perfect just then, like an image struck on photographic tinplate.

"Get that man a shot and a beer," Kippy said as Mick strolled over.

Will tipped Mick a quick nod and went to work. He was a young man, at least ten years Mick's junior, but he had the bartender swagger down to an art. Mick stuck out his hand for Kippy. "You get Orlin put to rest?"

Kippy shook with him. He was still in his black funeral suit, his tie pulled down, his collar unbuttoned to show a spill of neck wattles. "He's in the ground," the old man said. "I hope to God he can rest. Thanks for coming."

Mick settled into the stool next to Kippy. "Glad to do it. But if it's private stuff you want to talk about, I'm not sure I'm the one who should hear about it."

"Not private," Kippy said and took a long pull from his beer glass. "If anything, it's a very public matter, especially when things are rising to the top th' way they are. You better start on that beer, you're going to need it."

A nicely-headed glass had appeared as if by magic at his elbow. He took it up, nodded at Will Adelmeyer who stood nearby as dutiful as ever, then raised a toast toward Kippy.

"To old things shared by new friends."

The other voice came from a corner table near the electronic dart boards. "Goddamn fools made a failsafe. Thass what they thought."

Roger Copeland brooded over a row of empty shot glasses as he spoke, gazing at a pocket watch cradled in his palm. "Something pissed off is what they got. What *we* got."

Will leaned over the bar. "Hey, Roger. You promised if I poured you that last hit of Wild Turkey you'd keep from going all mouthy, so pipe down or I'll lock you in your car and leave you for dead in the parking lot."

Roger slouched back in his chair with a pout. "Bushit. Thass what your Wile Turk is. Buncha bushit."

Mick exchanged a look with Will, part amusement, part concern. Will leaned in and lowered his voice. In his eyes was the sad turmoil any longtime barkeep must harbor, ghosts of a hundred confrontations high and low. Or a thousand. "He's been here since five. Who's running the Gas 'N Go, I don't know. Probably Stu Rueplinger since he's laid off from the machine shop in Winter Lake."

"Who does he have an issue with?" Mick asked.

Will's response was a dismissive head shake. Kippy expectantly watched the two of them.

"I'm sorry," Will backed away. "You guys have business to discuss and I don't mean to get in the way of it. I'll camp out in back for a while if you want to talk freely."

Kippy marked him with a crooked finger. "You stay right where you are. What I'm going to say has more than a little to do with this place of yours too, Will Adelmeyer."

Will blinked, intrigued. Over his shoulder, an electronic strip sign's scrolling LED lights proclaimed Chapel's Summer Pool Leagues were forming now. "How am I part of the subject of the day?"

Mick decided to take a chance. "Does the term 'double barrels' mean anything to you?"

"Double barrels. Whiskey barrels? Shotguns? What?"

Kippy set down his glass, hard. "Let's not unhitch the horse and drag the wagon home. If I'm going to tell this, I'll do it in a sens'ble order lest I leave something out."

Will said, "Easy, Kippy," and promptly filled the old man's glass. "We'll do this your way. No reason not to. Here's one on the house. Now, we're all ears, right Mick?"

Mick was reminded of the one thing he'd always admired about Will Adelmeyer; his deft ease with handling people. He passed an appreciable nod Will's way. Then he toasted Kippy with the shot glass this time. "We're listening. Really."

Kippy folded his hands and bowed his head. When he spoke it was with slow determination. "Let me start back when people died here all of a sudden. A couple years before Japan's antics converted this country into a card-carrying member of the WWII club, this was." It was pronounced *dub-ya dub-ya two*.

Mick nodded. "You mean 1939. The TB outbreak."

Kippy cackled. It sounded bitter. "T'was a sickness, all right, but t'wasn't TB."

"My great grandfather once mentioned diphtheria," Will said. "He was three sheets to the wind at the time, talking about how the family came to buy this place right after the town emptied out back then."

"I 'spect if you'd go back in time, you'd find a lot of folks had their own tidy explanation for what cleaned out the town in '39. But if you put 'em all together, none of 'em would jibe. Because none of 'em was true. I was a young pup when I learned the die-off in '39 wasn't the first of its kind for the area around Knoll. And it was the idea of another die-off that got a particular group of men of this town a little scared somewhere around the year 1960. They put together a plan and they recruited us younger men for the grunt work to make it happen, and by recruited I mean put us to service with a father's command. All in secret, because Knoll doesn't talk about its ways, or its ravagements. Me and Orlin was young bucks in '60, a bit younger than you are right now, Will."

"Grunt work doing what?" Mick asked.

"Digging, mostly," Kippy examined his hands as if picturing the shovel in them now. "Endless digging. Some of us with flashlights, some of us with old gas and oil lamps. Like a regular gold rush team, we was. Only there wasn't any gold. We assumed it was part of the sewer project 'cause this was when they laid in the city sewer lines from Drury, but there was heavy digging equipment all over town, so we was puzzled over why they needed us to move any earth at all. And we were never told the purpose. We had ideas, though. We heard things. And we weren't dumb, either."

"What was the purpose, Kippy?" Mick asked. "Some type of bunker? Fallout shelter?"

"I'll admit, bombs were on the top of a lot of minds back then. Wasn't a few years further into the decade and we'd all sweat it out while Russia threw its weight around by way of Cuba. But this was something else. This was Knoll business, and Knoll business alone. What we figured out, and there was three of us working this end of town, was the group of our fathers and grandfathers thought they could stop the next culling in Knoll, or at least put in a way to stop it should signs of it start to rise up. And I'm not talking TB or measles or explosive damn diarrhea. I'm talking something hungry like a big fish in a deep pond coming up to gulp as many little bugs as it can before going under again, only the swim takes decades to finish. And instead of bugs, it wants people. Knoll people."

Words jangled in Mick's head and twanged off his nerves: *It's close, and it's hungry. And it will take you, too.*

Will's voice was full of controlled patience. "You're not saying something ate up the people of Mellar's Knoll in 1939, are you? With all due respect, I hear a lot of crazy talk at this bar, but I haven't heard anything like what you're saying since Charlene Plotts came in high on cheap cut crack and told me a troop of Donald Trump clones was stalking her. It's sad to think someone's brain can cook up stuff like that. It's sadder to think the person actually believes it."

Kippy gulped at his beer. "You Adelmeyers are all a bunch of hardheads. Something in your genes, I 'spect. But I ain't on crack—for cripes sake my blood pressure meds make me woozy some days—and I ain't demented, either. I saw demented today at the funeral. Poor Irma Casper is hardly the bubbly bride that Orlin took home after the war. And see? I'm already off m' rails. Let me get back on 'em or we'll be here 'til sunrise.

"Us younger men started asking around about the die-off, asking anybody who might know something, and when we pooled our findings, we were able to piece together an account that scared the shit out of us.

"Did something swallow up Knoll citizens back in '39? In a way, I'd say yes. But it was smart in going about it. It took each person a little at a time over a period of days, hollowing them out until they fell. Looked like a sickness, but that was just the ongoing effect. This thing, whatever it was, wanted life. Just life. And it knew how to draw it off. We got wind of older accounts, like a die-off when Mellar's Knoll was just a trader's post along the Wistweaw, and one before that wiping out a village of Ho-Chunk just across the river, and it's like there's a pattern to it. Four generations give or take. If it comes back again, you can bet it's going to want more lives. Just drink 'em up. I have no doubt the same idea is what got our daddies rolling out some bleak ideas in the 60s about what could be done. The government had the commies to worry about back then. Knoll had something else. So our dads and grandads cooked up something they called the double barrel."

Mick drained his glass. After the last few days, a story such as this left him teetering on another fulcrum of belief. It was becoming unbearable.

"Okay," Will finally said. "This is Knoll, home of The Crymost. I can see where some folks might believe in some kind of once-a-century boogeyman. But breaking their backs and the backs of their sons digging up the town to put up some secret defense against it? Nobody's going to go to those lengths."

Kippy lowered his brow. "Young man, I spent better than three months under this town digging 'til my hands bled and my shoulders felt like sprung rubber bands."

Will filled the old man's beer again. "Hard to buy the reasoning. That's all I'm saying."

"Granddad wasn't good enough." Roger Copeland's voice rang out once again. "Did'ja know that, Kippy? Yer old man and his 'lil group wouldn't let him in on the big plan, juss gave him grunt work. Twenny-five years with the Soo Line and all they gave him to do was chuck dirt from under the old mercantile, sum bitches. Rotten, rotten sum bitches."

Roger stood and his chair tipped over. He stumbled but caught himself, dipping at the knees like a tightrope walker in slow motion. Mick was on him before he could fall and bark his head on something.

"Easy there, Roger. Easy."

Will was at Mick's side in an instant. "It's all right. I got him."

"Sum bitches!" Roger cried out.

"Yes." Will took him from Mick with the aplomb of a parent transferring an exceptionally large baby and lowered him into a new chair. "We're all just sons of bitches, right? The whole darn world."

Kippy went on. "Us grunt diggers did the secondary work where the machines couldn't get. The backhoe men, paid on the side from working the sewer lines, did the main digging at night. They also laid in the slab concrete. There was the mechanics. Orlin ended up there after a while. He was a smart one, that boy. And there was the record keepers. Must have been twenty of us working the project, all told. All dead now, 'cept me."

"Mechanics?" Mick asked and went back to his beer.

"The double barrel boys," Kippy said with importance. "The engineers."

"And what was their deal, Kippy? What were they building?"

"Don't know, exactly. I took a job in Royal Center and moved out of Knoll before it was done. But the old town, she beckons like a forlorn lover. By the time I moved back, Ed Sullivan was showing the Beatles and this country's young Catholic president was cold in his grave. And all the work was done, the double barrel, whatever it was, the sewer and the secret tunnel too, complete and covered up, and not spoken of."

Will clapped his hands together as if dusting off the chore of planting Roger, agape and unconscious, back into his chair. "Okay, Roger here corroborates there was some digging, but a tunnel? What would be the point of tunneling under Mellar's Mercantile?"

"Don't know that, either. My digging was done somewhere else. Right under our feet, in fact. My end of the tunnel, which I expect comes out at the mercantile, runs out of the basement of this bar."

"Sorry old man." Will's face contorted like he'd bitten into something sour. *Yes*, Mick thought, *perhaps the Adelmeyers were a bit hardheaded.* "There is no tunnel in my basement."

Kippy climbed off his stool, weary but determined. "Come on. This won't take but a few minutes. Downstairs. Now."

The basement was damp and as openly huge as the upstairs. It was also very clean. Orderly stacks of liquor cartons and beer kegs were placed around with plenty of room to walk between.

Kippy shuffled around, his head swiveling like the needle of some anatomical compass. Then he pointed at a spot near the stairs where the stone wall was lighter in color, the mortar smoother in texture. "Sealed up now," he said.

"That?" Will said. "I see it so often I forget it's there. But if you're talking about a passageway across town to the mercantile, I'm afraid you guys screwed up your directions. This is the wrong side of the basement."

"There's a tunnel behind that seal, but not *my* tunnel. That's the moonshine tunnel. Goes straight out to the Wistweaw. In prohibition days, 'shiners would bring their goods down the river at night and drop it off at the church. Some folks came here to pray. Some had needs other than spiritual, but nearly everybody stopped at the old river church in those days. So my daddy said."

Will gaped, dumbfounded. "Nobody ever told me—"

"Funny thing about hist'ry. If it dies off with its keepers, it dies altogether."

Mick spoke up. "Where is your tunnel, Kippy?"

The old man ambled over to where a massive wooden shelving unit stood lined with boxes of receipts and invoices. It was reminiscent of the filing system at the village hall.

"The mouth should be just behind here."

"This, I've got to see." Will tapped Mick's arm on his way by. "Do you mind?"

"To adventures with new friends," he said.

The two of them moved the boxes to the floor in no time. With a little grappling they dragged the shelving structure away from the wall, arms straining, teeth gritted.

Kippy motioned toward what they revealed: a crude wooden door set in the wall. "And there you are."

It was adorned with veils of dusty webs. Looking at it sent a shiver down Mick's spine. Not a playful haunted house shiver, but something visceral like the sounding of a deep, elemental chime.

"And it goes all the way to the mercantile?" Will worked the rusted latch.

It opened freely. Air rushed out, musty and damp, with a slight mineral essence. Not the dry moldering smell Mick expected. The light leaked in only far enough to reveal the first few feet of smooth concrete flooring and walls.

Mick spoke almost involuntarily. "Complete and covered up."

Will grinned at them. "Is it crazy that I want to grab a flashlight and take a stroll down there right now?"

"Be a good walk," Kippy said peering into the blackness. "Maybe dangerous too, depending on how the frost and spring thaws have had their way, throwing things around like a bratty kid. And I 'spect somewhere along the way we'll find the double barrel, whatever it is. But it's late and this old geezer's been to a burial today. Thoughts of underground places don't sit well with m' peace of mind just now. It happens when you get to the age where you know your name's on the Reaper's calendar, most likely on the top page, circled in red."

"I'm pretty curious, too," Mick said. "But Kippy's got a point. Let's pick a day soon when the three of us can go at it fresh."

Will conceded and closed the door. The sound of it echoed in the tunnel behind. "I should get back upstairs, anyway. If Roger comes around, I hate to think of the mess he'd make helping himself to my back bar." He took the lead and they ascended the steps. "I will admit I'm wild to see what they concocted to hold back whatever kind of scourge they thought was coming, whether it was germs or soul-suckers from the deep."

"You can make light," Kippy said, grunting with each upward step, "but the facts remain."

"Are they facts?" Will asked as they gained the main floor. "Yes, people died here. But aside from that we've got a bunch of suspicions and hearsay. Stories."

Kippy shuffled back to the bar. "Damned, hardheaded Adelmeyers."

Will ignored the remark and patted a sleeping Roger Copeland on the shoulder. "Like a rock. I suppose I can do the right thing and take him home, if you gents don't mind watching the shop until I get back."

Mick moved on a surfacing idea. "How long will you be?"

"Ten minutes to run him home, plunk him on his living room couch and come back here. Is there a problem?"

"No, but I might duck out for a short trip, too. I came across something at the village hall that might be related to tonight's disclosures, now that I think about it. It's an old journal that tracks the deaths in this town at about the same time the town name was changed. It won't take long for me to get it, that is, if you gents are up for a gander at some old town records before we call it a night."

Kippy nodded. "That I can do."

"I say what the hell." Will slung Roger's arm around his neck and hoisted him to his feet.

Mick walked over. "I'll help you out with him before I go."

"And I," Kippy Evert said and shuffled behind the bar to fill his own beer glass, "will be right here waiting."

CHAPTER FIVE

The knock on Chastity Mellar Borth's front door came late. She put aside her reading, went to the front window and nudged the heavy lace curtains aside. Her heart pounded. The man on her porch was standing close up to the door which made only a hint of his shoulders and the curve of his back visible from her viewpoint. Deep inside of her, anticipation entwined with excitement.

"I've come for my room." The voice smote her with its directness and its familiarity. "If you'll still have me."

Her hands trembled as she unlocked the door and opened up for him. "Of course, Judge. You're welcome." Light from inside washed over him. She blinked hard because she was staring at his hands— those thin-boned wonders able to draw pain as easily as an autumn reed draws pond water—the way a famished woman might fixate on an imminent meal. "Please come in."

Thekan stepped in, his cloak draped over one arm, and swept the derby from his head. The breeze of his passing made her shiver.

"I hope you didn't go to too much trouble." He said and turned around in the middle of the room. It was a grand move, almost theatrical. "My needs are simple. Just a soft bed."

"No trouble," she said. In truth, her efforts took up most of the morning, refreshing the room at the top of the stairs while her muscles and bones cried out with each move.

Thekan eyed her with chiding calm. "I won't have you exerting yourself," he said and inched closer to her. "At least, not unnecessarily."

He laughed, and she followed it with her own. The girlish sound of it revolted her on some deep level, but on the surface, it was pure release. As a counterpoint, her pain paced in its den and pawed disdainfully at the walls. *Might you touch me*, she nearly blurted, *just a tap*?

His brows raised. "Upstairs?"

"I beg your pardon?"

"My room. I assume it is on the upper floor?"

"Yes. Of course. Yes."

"And have you told anyone I will be staying here?"

"No." She hadn't seen anyone to tell.

He closed in, a breath-stealing type of nearness.

"You should." He tapped a white index finger in the air as if dotting an *I*. "The town might receive me better if I have the endorsement of someone significant. Someone who cares about Mel—about Knoll so deeply. It is, after all, a wary place."

Oh, how she wished the inches between them were even fewer, so his miraculous flesh might dimple her skin. She shivered from her shoulders to her shoes. The imagined touch of his flesh flared to a heated memory of husbandly contact, of her Gregor's dark-haired bulk writhing against her, pressing, prodding. She looked at Thekan with a sense of guilt and yet wondered what other miracles his hands might deliver. "The town has needs."

"Towns, like people, are miraculous things. Each one with a place and a purpose." He leaned further toward her. His eyes were lighted eldritch lamps, eerie to behold, but acceptable, too. Miraculous. His hand cupped her cheek, and his fingers crawled to where her hair tensed into the braid at the back of her neck. "When their calling comes, it is only proper to resign to it."

Breath left her in a massive shudder that delivered strange, pleasurable constrictions to her breast, her loins. "The town has a calling." She agreed, the certainty of it secondary to the waves of insinuating warmth radiating through her, tingling at her extremities. Discreet sensations slipped into play, as astounding as old music squeezed note by note from a sheltered organ, pleasant yet nerve-tightening. "It always has."

His hand clenched at the back of her neck, rough but forgiving. A vise in velvet. His other hand settled on her hip, as if to initiate a dance. "And together we will lead this town to its ultimate destiny."

He massaged her hip, sent small electrical impulses through her skin to a deeper awakening part that caught fire like a long-damped fuse. A cool draft touched her back. The door was still open to the night. Someone on Tier Street might see them in this uncouth embrace, but the concern dulled, faded, died. Another wave of warmth rolled deep in her belly, drew her toward Thekan and the faint underlying foulness wafting from his mouth.

"Yes, I want that," she said and it was more breath than voice. "I want everything you said. Everything."

"Good." Thekan took a series of graceful backward steps up the staircase, pulling her along. With each footfall she felt a fragment of her pain drop away until, at the top of the stairs, she was a weightless and brightly washed vessel. Her nerve endings burned with only one true and clear heat now. A ravenous heat.

Thekan flung open the door to his room and swept her inside. "All I need is a soft bed, after all. It's been so long."

She climbed onto the freshly laundered spread and lay back for him.

His hands tensed into greedy claws as he lowered himself over her. Drops of dark red flooded the corners of his eyes and dripped down. Within seconds his cheeks were striped with crimson. A droplet pattered onto her chin and she flinched at it, certain of its make up by its weight and the light sanguine odor, but disregarded it the same way she disregarded his cold hands tearing open her blouse and plucking away her bra with a gentle mastery of finesse.

"We get what we want then, both of us."

He ground his hips against her thighs. The hot rigidity thrust against her caused her to gulp at the air. She meant to draw it all inward like a mighty storm to consecrate the moment. Pull in the room, the house, the whole town with her wanting breaths. "Yes. Oh yes. Yes."

"Onto our purpose, then."

She clamped her trembling hands on the sides of his face. Where his eyes once gleamed there were now only dark pits. Streams of red flowed from them. Another miracle from his well of dark secrets. She kissed his scarlet cheeks furiously, tongued the ragged rims of his eye holes, lapped the slick depths of his leaking sockets.

His breath washed over her in a dark wave. It blended with the rustle of cloth and the tearing of her skirt. A groan welled out of her, long and ripe with fulfillment.

One floor below, the front door wavered on its hinges and closed quietly against the night.

CHAPTER SIX

"There was something about this the minute I saw it," Mick said and set the LINR box on the bar.

Will and Kippy perched on neighboring stools with enough space for Mick to stand between them. They glanced from him to the box with a quiet type of curiosity.

"In my day we used to keep all the town records in those kinds of lockups," Kippy said. "At some point, some smarty decided to get rid of them and use regular file cab'nets."

"Well, this one stayed behind," Mick said.

Will squinted at the box lid. "L-I-N-R. What does it mean?"

They both deferred to Kippy who replied with a shrug. Then Mick tipped back the box lid.

An idea blew by him: *Harley should be in on this.* Not many others, aside from Cy Vandergalien, possessed the same deep commitment to the perpetual clockwork of this town. But the hour was late, the clock next to Will's LED strip sign—which now declared *$1 shooters Fridays 6-8* with scrolling dot-to-dot importance—read a quarter of ten. Harley would no doubt be fast asleep.

83

"This was filed away at the village hall?" Kippy hooked his finger into the open box and dragged it closer.

"Buried is more like it. And this is why I thought we'd all find it so interesting."

He pulled the book out right under Kippy's nose and set it on the bar. He tapped the tape label that read "Deaths".

"Mortician's records?" Will asked and lifted the cover fussily between two fingers.

"Mortality Log," Kippy commented and took charge, flipping the cover open to reveal a ledger-style grid filled with handwritten entries. "Buddy of mine kept one in the field during dub-ya dub-ya two, and he fussed over it like a mother hen. At least, at first. Name, rank, serial number, and he made a list of wounds and injuries, indicating what was most likely the death-dealer if there was a mess of them. I think his pen got a might heavy after a while because he cut back to just name, rank and serial. Then one day he put the book down and did nothing but stare out at the horizon. Did it long enough to get himself sent home. Was a janitor at the canning fact'ry over to Drury until 1980 when he put his mouth around the business end of a Remington shotgun." His finger slid down the page. It made a dry scraping sound. "Olivia Rebedew, May 17, emphysema. John Pesch, May 17, heart failure. Emily Wozniak, May 18, consumption. William Zehren, May 18, diphtheria. All 1939. What'd you call it a short while ago, Will? A once-a-century boogeyman?"

Will ducked in closer to study the page, his eyes sharp and hard. "TB. Infirm lung. Melancholy? So many different things, all within a few days."

"Like I said . . . " Kippy tipped another scholarly finger in the air. "Doesn't jibe, does it?"

Mick looked directly at Kippy. "Jibe or not, what did those double barrel boys have in mind with the tunnel? You must have some idea."

"Told you, I left town before they was done, long before they laid in the concrete walls. Dads were supposed to fill in their sons on the matter, generation to generation so we would always be ready, but my dad never did lemme back in on it. What little I know came from Orlin, and he only spilt a little bit on a few drunk nights shortly after I came back."

Kippy hooked a finger in the box again and picked at the papers resting inside.

"I just don't know." Will paced to the back of the bar. "This is Knoll, for God's sake. The down-low is about Jimmy Conger's wife running off with that cowboy wannabe from Fond du Lac or how the Prellwitzes haven't paid property taxes for three years."

"But sometimes there are darker handshakes," Mick said, mostly to himself. "Almost always, in fact."

The question twisted around in his brain with restless aplomb, bumping against the walls of reason, heady with disdain—did something roll toward Knoll with its lips parted in preparation to eventually yawn and gulp? He'd been warned long before Kippy's story, after all. Peter Fyvie's presence (ghost? memory? Or was it an hallucinatory manifestation?) offered words that fit the bill almost too perfectly. *It's close, Mick. And it's hungry.* The affirmative was so damned hard to accept. Common sense rejected it out of hand. Still, the bar gloom seemed to tighten around him.

"You have something else here, Mick," Kippy said. He slid a paper from the box, a large document folded into a tight packet. His old man's fingers struggled to undo it a layer at a time. "Darned if it doesn't have Orlin's writing on it. And it's dated '60 to '61."

"About the tunnel?"

"Even better," Kippy said, assessing what was in front of him: a drawing rendered so long ago the ink appeared purple-brown. Dashed lines, notations of measurements, very technical. And a large legend at the top, still undisclosed because the last fold had yet to be turned back.

"Maybe we should stop." Will's face was pale. "Something's happening. Can you feel it?"

Mick nodded. The constricting gloom seemed to lower, to steal his breath.

Kippy said, "Schematic—"

The rest was cut-off by a bone-rattling boom. The lights went out. Beer glasses chattered like crystal teeth. Bottles shattered. Will's strip sign blazed in the sudden blackness, red and green beads of light spelling out L-I-N-R before it coughed sparks and dropped from its hanger. The silence that followed seemed deafening in its own right.

"Jesus," Mick called out, gripping the bar like a man caught at a ship's rail during a sudden swell. "Everybody all right?"

"Fell off the damn stool." Kippy's voice was thin and breathless in the dark. "Can I get a hand?"

"If I could see your hand." Mick groped for him. "Will, got a flashlight? Anything?"

"Breaker box is in the basement. Give me a minute. I'll try to get to it without breaking my neck. Worst case, I've got a brand new generator in the storage room down there."

Mick caught the sleeve of Kippy's suit and felt the old man rise easily, which was a good sign. Tough old Kippy. A moment later the lights came up. Neon stuttered. A chorus of electric motors started up around them, an under-the-breath buzz not noticed until it was subtracted from the air and then put back.

"I think we've got some trouble," Kippy said as he climbed back onto his stool and pointed at the ruined LED sign nestled amid broken glasses on the backbar. "L-I-N-R."

"I saw it," Mick said. "This is going beyond weird, Kippy."

"Far beyond."

"What the hell just happened?" Will walked over from the basement door. He seemed pale and utterly lost. "Every last one of my breakers was tripped. And this mess up here. Jesus!"

"We brought it on." Kippy tapped a bunched hand on the paper he'd unfolded just before the building shook. "Because we're close to something here."

"I'll ask again," Will said and thrust a plaintive hand at the blackened sign with its fried electrical cord. "L-I-N-R, same as on the box. What does it mean? What the Christ does it have to do with—"

"Will."

Mick pointed to the legend printed on the paper in front of Kippy. They all read it over.

LET IT NOT RETURN. L-I-N-R.

"What the hell?" Will said and it sounded like a plea.

"Answers without conclusions," Mick said as he held up the unfolded sheet. It was, as Kippy had assessed, a schematic drawing of some sort, for a large rectangular apparatus. The words *double barrel* were written at an angle near the LINR legend. At the bottom, the signature of the chief engineer was printed in neat block letters: *Orlin Casper*.

"We need to take our time with this. Think it through and compare notes. And like the tunnel, we need to approach it with clearer heads in the light of day. In the meantime, don't share this with anyone. Hell, nobody would believe us if we tried to describe it, anyway." They nodded and Mick glanced at Will. "Do you want help with cleaning up back there?"

Will toed some broken glass and shrugged. "No worse than when the cut-ups from the Baylor Picnic storm in here every August. I can handle it. Damn, that sign cost me a hundred bucks."

They were all picturing it, Mick knew, because it was branded in their memories. The sign. The double barrel schematic. LINR, Let It Not Return. "Let's get you home, Kippy. I'll give you a ride."

"'Preciate it," Kippy said and brushed at his suit as he stood. "I'm so rattled right now I might drive m' bike into the weeds. I wish there was somebody else we could call in on this, but no names'll pop into my head."

There was Harley, if he felt up to the task. Mick resigned himself to asking his friend privately first thing in the morning. Then he slipped the mortality log and the schematic into the box. Before closing the lid, he froze with a mixed sense of hope and reluctance. "There might be someone else. Is this who I think it is?"

Will was sweeping up, but he stopped to look at them. Mick turned the box and allowed them to read the tape label stuck on the underside of the lid.

LINR—Property of Francis P. Vandergalien—LINR

"Yep," Kippy said. "That was Cy's daddy."

CHAPTER SEVEN

"I'm scared, Mick," Kippy said in the parking lot while Mick loaded his bike into the open trunk. "I know I'm the last one. I can feel the truth of it beating inside of me, harder than my old ticker. Out of all the diggers and engineers and runners, I'm it. I'm also sure another die-off is on our doorstep, turning the knob one tick at a time and grinning wide because it can almost taste what's on the other side. That's beating hard inside me, too."

Mick glanced into the back seat, where the LINR box sat, a source and instrument of dismay. He screwed down the defenses around his thoughts the way he'd been taught after the funeral, the way he practiced frequently over the years.

"We all need to settle down," he said at last.

Kippy turned his head and he once again reminded Mick of an anatomical compass, only this time he pointed squarely with his finger. "In fact it's better than at our door. I 'spect it's shining a lantern through the keyhole."

Mick followed his finger to the southeast.

The Crymost was glowing again.

CHAPTER EIGHT

When Mick arrived at work, Harley was at the garage desk turning a greasy hunk of metal over in his hands. The morning sun showed flashes of an open metal port with a metallic flap closure in those huge fingers, and it made Mick think of schematic drawings . . . and of the box locked up in his car. With a pang of nervousness he considered how to best approach the details of the previous night with Harley. This was hardly on a par with casual conversation like *did you catch the game last night?*

He gave the desktop a jovial knock, just to get the ball rolling. "What's with the carburetor?"

"Out of the Swisher," Harley said. The hollows under his eyes seemed nearly black. "Axel couldn't get her started up this morning. Neither could I, so I sent him packing for the day. The choke pull-off on the damn thing is all twisted up."

"I can drive into town and pick up a replacement if you want. Today's my day to paint the village hall interior and I'll have some time while the first coat dries."

"I'll manage the drive if I need it. Pour me a coffee, would you? My hands are black with grease." So was the desk top. And there was a smudge on his cheek like an inky exclamation mark.

"Listen, Harley, last night I was talking with Kippy Evert and the subject of the Knoll die-off came up. So did some other stuff."

"Well, Kippy's got to have some mournful things on his mind of late, what with Orlin's funeral and all."

Mick set a cup of coffee down where Harley could reach it. "But there's more. Did you know there's a tunnel under this town?"

"Sewer access. Sure."

"Something more. Something Kippy and a bunch of other men from Knoll helped dig out in the early sixties."

"Gotta wonder about Kippy sometimes. He seems with it for somebody just over the eighty hashmark, but there's a way a man's mind works after a point, if you know what I mean."

Mick leaned on the edge of the desk. "I saw it, Harley. The mouth of it, anyway. It's in the basement of The Chapel Bar. Will Adelmeyer didn't even know it was there until Kippy showed him. And there's supposedly a machine of some sort in there, something called the double barrel."

Harley set the carburetor down as if it were exceedingly fragile, his face fixed on the desk. "Oh."

"He says it was designed as some kind of precaution against another die-off. He said Mellar's Knoll emptying out in the '30s wasn't a natural fluke or an accident, but something that cycled through on some sort of agenda, and that it's coming due again. It sounds nutty, I know, but at the bar last night Kippy, Will and I—"

Harley pivoted in his chair. His fists jutted out and shook like those of a child throwing a tantrum. He was staring at a point in distant space. "You'll have to catch me later, I think."

"Harley?"

The big man's face lost all color and crumpled with pain. The grease mark on his cheek was like a black hole in parchment. Mick thought later he was fortunate to be standing because it allowed him to ease Harley to the floor before he toppled out of the chair.

"Goddamn," Harley said through gritted teeth. "Can't breathe."

"Hang in there," Mick said, wrung up in polarizing bands of concern and panic.

He got out his phone and forced a layer of calm over his thoughts. Then he clasped his friend's shoulder while he dialed and waited for the 911 operator to pick up.

CHAPTER NINE

Everything seemed to happen with the loose cohesion of dreams. The village EMTs bustled in with record speed—Nancy Berns and Stu Rueplinger were on duty today—and Mick tried to stay out of the way. Harley was out cold and it scared Mick. *Unresponsive*, he heard Nancy call it. The ambulance came screeching in and men in crisp blue shirts and soft-soled shoes deployed with a sort of steely efficiency, cinching Harley to a stretcher and hoisting him up like some collective machine. They spoke in factual bursts as they worked, and one of them informed Mick they were taking Harley to Hillside Hospital in Drury. Mick was on the phone with Beth Ann at the time, alerting her, and he told the ambulance tech that was fine.

He called Judy on the way to Drury, and it wasn't until he was in the hospital admitting area that he realized he'd left the village garage wide open. Knoll would just have to be on its honor for a while. It seemed only a few minutes later when Judy came down the hall, her face set and grim.

"What do we know?" Her eyes betrayed a parallel to his own deep running thought: *It's too soon for Harley. Too soon.* "Where is Beth Ann?"

"No news yet. And Beth Ann should be here any minute. She was working at the branch in Baylor today."

"God, I hope she drives carefully. She gets so rattled. What happened? Were you there?"

"Right next to him. You know how people say so-and-so just keeled over? Well, one minute we were talking and I . . . what's the matter?"

Her eyes were very intense in the diffused hospital light. Penetrating. "There's more going on with you. All the time. Don't think I can't see it."

Damned eighteen years of marriage.

"Number one, I'm worried about Harley but I'm coping. But there are things from a few days ago I need to come clean about, and something happened at the bar last night. Here is not the place to go into it, though. We need someplace private and quiet."

Her hands sought his out and gripped them tight. "Bad?"

"Confusing to say the lea—"

"Oh God," the voice from down the hall made them crane around. Beth Ann ran toward them, her Bank of Dunnsport blazer slipping off one shoulder. A swatch of hair blew across her face like a mousey-brown shadow. "Oh, Judy. Have you heard anything? Where is he?"

Judy caught her by the shoulders and began speaking to her, direct but gentle. At that instant, Mick's cell phone rang and their portion of the corridor seemed like a pocket of contained chaos. The call was from Cy.

"Where the hell is everybody? I'm looking at a wide open but empty village garage right now. Gordy Prellwitz tells me there was an ambulance."

"It's Harley. He's suffered a—I don't know, an episode. We're at Hillside."

"His wife there?"

"She just got here."

"Then you don't need to be handholding him. I got a job for you. Meet me at Pitch Road. We're going to shut her off."

"The Crymost?"

"Damn right. I don't want anybody poking around up there for a while. Reporters, people who believe they're in an episode of the goddamn *X-Files* or think they're Ansel freaking-Adams. Just makes sense to keep everybody away."

"Right now, Cy? Really? Can't it wait until we've got some word on Harley, for Christ's sake?"

"Kroener is going to pull through or poop off whether you're sitting vigil over there or not. There's town business that needs doing, and I say it needs doing now. Don't give me a reason to paste the help wanted sign in the village garage window on my way home from Pitch Road."

"That's dirty pool, even for you."

"It's what makes sense, Logan. Meet me over there or you're out."

"Goddamn it." Mick shook himself as if it might calm his trembling insides. For all of its shitty use of an upper hand, he saw the thinnest sliver of agreement with Cy's insistence they shut down the road to The Crymost. For a while at least. "I'll be there in half an hour."

Judy convinced Beth Ann to sit in a nearby chair and then stepped away to inform the admission desk of her arrival. Mick caught her on the way back. "I've got to go."

"Go where? You can't leave."

"Cy has declared The Crymost off limits and he wants the road blocked right away. He was very insistent. Brutally." He made sure his expression was very direct. "I'm not wild about leaving right now, but it seems I don't have a choice. And I have to admit, given the circumstances, I think Cy's idea is a good one."

"What's going on, Mick?"

He left her with a look that promised someplace private and quiet soon, very soon.

CHAPTER TEN

Axel drove down The Plank toward the village hall for the third time, his gut full of steely tightness. The time for Ichabod's project was here. The certainty of it arrived with the same fingers-in-the-brain sensation that accompanied the details of the task.

A funny and weird son-of-a-bitch, that Thekan/Ichabod. Equally funny and weird was how everything came together. Sure, he intentionally messed up the village mower's carburetor with a few jabs from a screwdriver, and hopefully that overgrown bag of shit Kroener wouldn't notice it was intentional. Then he drove by the garage an hour ago, just for the hell of it, and fuck if there wasn't an ambulance parked out front and a bunch of commotion to go with it. When he rolled past the garage a second time, there was Mick Logan climbing in his car and heading for who knew where, and not another soul around even though the garage was still open. *Perfect.*

A third pass for good measure showed not a soul, just the morning sun shining into the open garage door. He pulled around back and went right for the ten-gallon gas cans. Full. Heavy.

He dragged one around to the village hall next door, and a tiny bud of thought bloomed. The opportunity for a little retribution was open to him, something personal to top off Ichabod's project. Logan was one of the big-idea dick wipes in this town, which made him a pain in the ass. Plus, he squealed to Unky about the roach in the drawer the other day. So, maybe it was time to fuck with him. *Flame-fuck him, in fact.*

The back door of the village hall was a flimsy hollow-core, warped and peeling after years of conversation with the elements. It was locked, but three good tugs broke the jamb and the door swung out at him with a shudder and a creak. He slipped into the back room that was full of boxed papers and began to slop gasoline around. Then he went to the front office, a space tidier than such a shithole deserved. There was a ladder and some buckets sitting around, as if Logan was getting ready to paint the place up. *Oh, there'd be a splash of color, all right. Real soon.*

He parked the gas can, still half full, under the kneehole desk next to the front door and covered it with loose sheets of newspaper. Then, in a move he felt showed exemplary prowess, he unlocked the front door ahead of time, so Logan could boogie right on in. He left through the back again, and with a second flash of genius (*man, your brain is a fucking machine today*), he pulled some lengths of weathered two-by-fours from a pile behind the building and tilted them against the door in a series of diagonals, bracing the door closed.

Then he pulled around behind the old Ice Dreams shop across The Plank where he could watch and wait. It might be an hour before that fuckwit Logan showed up, or it might be half the day, depending on what the ambulance business was all about. But he was sure Logan would be back. Everything was lined up too perfectly today for him not to show. He fired up a joint, put on his best under-the-weather voice and called his Unky at the F&F. The grilles were off the in-floor grinder, but they would have to stay that way until he felt better and could resume the cleanup. Unky Cy said it wasn't a problem. The mill was closed for the day anyway because Cy was a little under the weather himself.

Everything was falling into place today. Everything.

CHAPTER ELEVEN

Mick found Cy about a hundred yards down Pitch Road erecting a six-foot steel pole on the shoulder. When Mick got out of the car, Cy scowled and armed sweat off his forehead.

"About time. This is a two-man job if ever there was one."

It wasn't, but Mick nodded anyway. "A lot of things in this town are. You hold it while I sink it in."

He took up a pole driver and had the pole standing tall and firm in less than a minute. The second one went just as quickly. "Ground's pretty soft, yet," Cy said, distracted, and glanced toward the rise at the end of Pitch Road. "Good thing."

"Anything you want to get off your chest?" Mick asked as they strode to where a heavy tow chain rested in the grass. They dragged it over to hang it between the poles. Mick imagined they must look like men holding a tug-o-war with grade 80 alloy steel instead of rope.

"If there was, what makes you think I'd share it with you?'

"I can handle you dragging me away while my friend is in the hospital. If you want to be the boss man and pull rank like that, I guess that's your prerogative. But at least talk to me. I'm not the enemy, Cy. I'm just trying to figure out a few things about this town of late. If we can add what you have and what I have together, maybe we can come up with some answers when people start asking questions. Because once you start chaining off roads, you can bet the questions will come. And the speculation."

"This here is just me listening to my gut, Logan." He secured his end of the chain and stepped back. His hand worked over his shirt pocket where an oval-shaped object made a noticeable bulge. "My gut has made more decisions for this town than the damn village board can ever count. And Knoll hasn't suffered yet."

Mick stepped back, too, chain mounted and swaying. "And what does your gut tell you to do next? After this?"

The man's mouth pressed down into a hard line. "When I think of it, I'll let you know. Now get back to town and get to work, 'cause you ain't off the hook yet. You got a cell phone so you can get a call if something about Koerner comes up. In the meantime, my boss man prerogative, as you put it, sets me up in a place where I still call the shots and that village hall isn't going to paint itself. Your place is in the village doing what we pay you to do."

"We'll see about that."

"Damn right we will. Get to the hall, Logan, and get to work."

Cy marched to his car and executed a squealing U-turn onto The Plank.

Judy called with news just as Mick climbed into his truck. Harley's blackout was brought on by a calcium imbalance in his blood, she said, and they were going to keep him for a few days. He was sleeping and would remain sedated until at least dinner time, so there was really no point visiting until later that evening.

"Okay," he told her, "then I guess Cy gets his way on this one. I'll get a little work done around here and go back to Drury after supper."

Mick's next order of business was to check the messages on the garage answering machine. There was one. It was Kippy Evert, sounding excited and a little breathless.

"Mick, don't know if this means anything, but I remember you asking about a sort of man-in-black fella the other day at Copeland's. Don't know why, but it got me to thinkin' about some old books I keep in the cellar. Something else t' throw on the pile when we talk, I guess. Sorry t' hear about Harley. Hope that all works out."

At last, Mick went over to the village hall, a gallon of paint in each hand, and walked right in.

The air in the hall was rank, but any further consideration he might have given it slipped behind other thoughts racing through his head, the primary one concerning the private, informative time he promised his wife. The phrase *forces at work* crept in, quiet and logical. So much he needed to share with Judy. And Harley, too. The evening, still hours away, promised to be rough.

He put the paint cans down and went in the back room to find some brushes. The back room storage shelves, so neatly arranged, made him think of Judge Thekan asking about town records. In turn, his thoughts swung inexplicably around to the tang in the air. Familiar. In fact, it was—

The first sound was like a metal washtub hitting the floor in the next room. A second later the building seemed to expel a mighty breath around him, a sound-stealing *whummm* noise followed by the slam of the front door. The pieces came together in his head with alarming clarity. A wave of heat blasted in from the front office and knocked him off his feet. Flames, like the spill of a yellow and blue tide, roared toward him.

And then, the voice from the dark back corner.

"You better get over here, Mick. And you better hit it high."

Axel ran across Forest Street and ducked behind the bank building. The fire took off kickass style the minute his match hit the gasoline, so there was no need to worry whether or not he'd fucked it up. But he wanted to watch. Why he didn't run back to the Passat, he didn't know. Maybe it was fortuitous—

"Fortuitous of you to come this way."

The voice startled a slight cry out of him. He whirled around. "What the fuck, Ichabod?"

The Judge wasn't wearing Ichabod clothes anymore. He was in regular stuff, a sport shirt and slacks, like a shoe salesman or the guys in the used car lot in Drury. "Walk with me to your vehicle. Once there, you should make a call, as any good citizen would."

Axel blinked and kept pace shoulder to shoulder with Thekan. The front window of the village hall was a frenzy of contained flames. Smoke leaked out around the door and through a seam in the roof. "If I call they'll know I was here. Not cool."

"It's a guarantee someone has already noticed your car behind the hat shop—or rather, the confectioner's parlor. It's a small town, my friend. Places to hide are an illusion. But affectations are practically a matter of record."

"What's that mean?"

A gray finger swept around and nicked Axel's throat just above the Adam's apple. He opened his mouth to balk but in the next instant his brain seemed to go buoyant, like a large foggy balloon. The village became a Technicolor panorama, the street jostled on hinges and rollers. "Whoa, fucking mega-hit. And I wasn't even smoking."

"Oh, but you were, should someone ask," Thekan said, his voice a buzz in a box. "Just now, in your car. There will even be a few fine citizens who will attest to seeing you. When you happened to notice the village hall catch ablaze, you called on your telly-phone as fast as your fingers would allow."

When they reached the Passat, Thekan opened the door and a billow of sweet smoke boiled out. A pair of doobies were stamped out on the shift console. Totally fucking hilarious.

"I am primo-grade stoned, man. How'd you do that?" Axel slumped in behind the wheel, his eye immediately drawn to the plump wallet-sized bag on the passenger seat, clear plastic stuffed with telltale shreds of green. "Is this my payoff for your dirty deed done dirt cheap?"

This was uproariously funny, but he cut his laughter short when his thoughts turned toward Mick Logan, how the poor shithead was probably frying to death at this very moment. The reality of what he'd done was suddenly a weighty thing. He felt sick.

"No deed goes unrewarded." Thekan studied the village hall with narrow eyes. "And it is a relief to know certain concerns can be so easily swept away. A change that rivals alchemy. Similar to how past remorse becomes motivating fire when the inspiration is right." He twitched as if coming out of a daydream. Dreamy old Ichabod. "You should start dialing now. Slowly, of course."

"Slow dial for a quick burn."

The phrase immediately struck Axel as gut-wrenchingly funny. He managed to poke out the numbers on the dial pad through his laughter. His eyes were filled with tears.

Mick scrambled to his feet and whirled toward the voice in the back corner. The sight of the speaker froze his heart. Peter Fyvie, wet and bloated, gestured to the back door like a nightmarish game show host fawning over a prize. Mick's thoughts swung back to the last time he'd seen Fyvie in such a condition, in the passenger seat of his truck. That time he tried with all his might to push the image away as hallucination, despite evidence to the contrary. This time such an estimation was harder to justify. The man shed droplets which pattered on the hall floor, staining the wood with very real, very dark starburst splatters. Firelight threw Fyvie's shadow deep and wavering and undeniable on the wall behind him. And the smell of him, a chalky mineral scent blended with the gassy notes of new rot, crept under the rank gas-and-smoke vapor filling the room. *Dead*, Mick thought, *so very dead*. Fyvie gave him a wide let's-do-this smile and greenish water trickled from his lips.

At last, Mick rushed forward (*I'll do this, that door is the only way out, but dear God don't you touch me*). He shoulder-rammed the door and met unreasonable resistance. He staggered back. Ribbons of flame unspooled along the perimeter of the room behind him, festooned the walls in fluttering streaks, rushed and spread in ravenous rivers. He prepared for another pass at the door, his skin prickling in the mounting heat.

"I'm almost out of Knoll so listen to me before I'm spent, Mick," Fyvie gurgled above the roar of flames. His cloudy eyes bulged, mottled with points of refracted firelight. "The door is blocked on the other side, but the braces are all pretty low. Hit it lots higher."

Mick didn't question it, simply rushed the door shoulder first, leaping at the last second to strike it higher up. The upper half of the door jumped away from the frame, offering a glimpse of clear, sunny air before it clapped shut again. The wood surrendered in a diagonal crack from doorknob to top hinge.

"What the hell is this, Fyvie?"

Sharp smoke filled the room, clouds of it churned overhead. Flames danced around his ankles, seared his skin like the touch of summer steel.

"This is fear of discovery." Fyvie slipped around behind him, his skin steaming, and humped up against Mick's back in a sodden embrace. "Now move it. I'm not much of a fire barrier."

Mick rushed the door again, with an even greater leap. The upper portion of the door let out a splintering crack and dropped away. He dove through the opening and came to rest face down in the dust and gravel parking lot, the clammy weight of Fyvie still on his back.

"The Crymost is giving everything back," Fyvie's voice bubbled in his ear. "It always does just before it feeds. But this time is different. This is the first time it's worried about being stopped. So it brought that judge back, too. As a paver of the way."

"What?" He wanted to move out from under Fyvie's miserable, sodden weight. The smell of him was wretched. But he also was loath to interrupt what this well-meaning, life-saving, very dead non-hallucination had to say.

"The opening Thekan used is still in play. Some of us have managed to spill through. Some want to help, some don't give a shit. But the kicker is we're all weaker than Thekan by a mile. And we're briefer."

"We?"

"The dead, those who've crossed over but remain connected to Knoll in some way. Beyond the pale. Whatever you want to call it. The time for all of us is limited, and sooner or later we'll all be pulled out of Knoll and drawn back to where we belong. Then it will be just the townspeople, Thekan, and The Crymost. Sooner or later Mick . . . all of us . . . gone . . . "

Mick rolled over at the precise moment Fyvie's weight evaporated from him. *Gone again, just like in the truck. Gone, perhaps, for good this time. Out of Knoll.*

"Fyvie?" he said anyway. "Why would it use Thekan? What's his connection?"

There was no response.

He got to his feet and shambled toward the garage, dialing his phone as he walked. He coughed. The fire roared inside the village hall. Thoughts roared just as loudly in his head. On the other side of the building, the front window of the village hall blew out.

Welcome to Wonderland.

CHAPTER TWELVE

For the second time that day, events moved with the cohesion of a fevered dream. The garage interior was filled with smoke but seemed exempt from any radiant heat for the moment, so Mick transported garage property a piece at a time, just in case the fire leapt over. He took the items to the curb facing The Plank. People began to gather and gawk and voice concerns. Some of them pitched in, helping him move items, but he couldn't say who they were. Just dream faces. His thoughts brushed alternately across the undeniable presence of Peter Fyvie (his shirt still clung to him in back with the unpleasant dampness of Fyvie's juices), and the men of the 1960s Knoll—the diggers, the planners, the double barrel boys—hustling in dutiful silence under a contained but growing panic.

To accompany the rest, a word flashed through his mind, with resistance because it slung inflammatory mud at the intellect. *Supernatural.* It seemed too foreign, too easily applied even after what happened at the bar, even after not one but *two* encounters with an undeniably dead Peter Fyvie. He attempted to push the word aside but it refused to comply. Like a funhouse character on a spring, it kept popping into his line of sight.

Fire trucks arrived. People in fire suits toted hoses, began to beat back the flames of the village hall and to saturate the garage to protect it. At some point, Nancy Berns sat him down on the curb, draped him with a blanket and handed him an oxygen mask with a portable tank. She demanded he sit still for a few minutes so she could check him over.

"Somebody blocked the back door," he said, knowing it sounded senseless and out of context, but he needed to get it out.

"We'll check it out, Mick," she said, her round cheeks plumping with a smile. Calm, official, soothing. God love Nancy Berns. "You should call your wife. Get yourself home."

He wanted nothing more than to hear Judy's voice. But the garage needed to be squared away. "I need to help out first," he said to her, and the logic of it was a living thing. It stirred the air between the two of them. "You know how it is."

"I do," she said and plumped her cheeks again. "There's a spare fire jacket in the back of the pumper, if you're sure."

He nodded his thanks and got to his feet. When he regarded the blazing village hall, he shivered.

CHAPTER THIRTEEN

Chastity Mellar Borth pulled her car into the broken remnant of parking lot next to the mercantile. It was still a regal building in her eyes, spoiled by disrepair and neglect but no less grand at its core. What would Daddy say if he knew she was willing to let it go now? Thekan wanted it gone, after all, and was willing to go out among the people of Knoll to secure the *Mellar's Out* vote. He told her so while he slipped into the shirt, one of Gregor's, which she brought to his dawn-lit bed with almost ceremonial pride. The mercantile stood in the way of his dark miracles, or perhaps threatened them. She knew it without him saying it, and for that reason alone it must go.

But enough of this maudlin farewell. Change was upon her. Upon Knoll. The tightness of the low-heeled pumps on her feet and the naked sensation of her legs below the knee-length hemline of her new skirt seemed like alien sensations, proof of how long it had been since she attempted to dial into the mainstream. But the town's destiny was on the horizon. Thekan drove the point home many times throughout the night. *Many times*, she thought with a controlled but enthusiastic smile.

"I am a paver of the way," he said while she lay next to him, breathless and slick and delightfully sore, the after-sex sheets bunched between them. The pits of his eye sockets glimmered and throbbed deep and red. "A time for feasting is coming to this place. As it has come many times before. When the land was young and wild the feast claimed only herd animals and flocks of birds that squawked in confusion over what drew them to the ground even as their lungs burst and their guts constricted. Later came the natives who conformed with reverent, dutiful surrender, and at last the farmers with their harsh German and Norwegian and French insinuations brought their sensible suspicions. Now that the land is crowded with houses and barns, taverns and shops full of souls, there is a risk of defiance. There is a need for liaison before the feast can make another claim." A clear teardrop slipped out of his pulsing eye socket and coursed down to his trembling chin. "So, I am here, unsure of how but certain of my purpose."

Poor Roderick Thekan, tormented, indentured and admittedly unpleasant to behold during certain intimate moments. But brimming with feats of wonder. *Like the mercantile itself*, she thought with a sigh brimming in its own right, *spoiled to the eye and yet grand at his core.*

Dark miracles, she thought as she glanced at the mercantile once more, then into the backseat at the box she'd picked up from the printer's. In it were posters. Red. They said *Mellar's Out* in large black letters.

"You better go, Cy."

It was his mother's voice again, this time sounding a bit like the days she'd warn him out of the house before the old man came home to dole out a reprimand with the strap or the yardstick, and it stopped him in his tracks on his way to the table.

"I can't," he said under his breath, his eyes darting. "For Christ's sake, I run this town, Ma."

"Time to run *from* it. Mind me, now."

"This ain't right, you talking to me."

He clutched at the shirt pocket made bulgy by the blue brooch inside. He supposed, pressed up to the table with his fist at his chest, he resembled a man having a heart attack. That was no good. Alice was in the front room, the TV blaring while she worked on the village newsletter. God forbid she should see him in such a state.

His phone rang and he snatched it up, almost grateful for a distraction. Mick Logan was on the line with three matters at hand: the fire at the village hall, the fact he was closing up the garage for the day, and what option was left for the upcoming vote since the hall, like the firehouse, was now out of service.

"Button up the garage," Cy said and walked out to the back porch. "We'll talk about the rest tomorrow."

His backyard was sun drenched, a meticulously mowed and clipped source of pride, but it offered no solace to him at the moment. *A fire*. Another peculiarity in their fine village. That scoreboard seemed to tick up at an alarming rate.

"What's happening?" he asked and aimed it deliberately at his ma, in her grave for twenty years.

There was no answer.

CHAPTER FOURTEEN

During the short drive home, true fatigue settled over Mick. His arms and legs ached and his throat was raw with the aftereffects of smoke. When he walked into the house, Judy was there despite his insistence she stay with Beth Ann. She met him with a huge embrace. "Are you all right? Really? You look exhausted."

"I think I'll live, but a shower would be nice."

Afterward, they sat in the kitchen with the back door open. She poured glasses of iced tea and he gulped his down. It felt blessed on his parched throat.

"I know you've had a big day," she said, "so I'm sure you won't mind if I take a raincheck on everything we need to talk about. I know it's important and I really want to hear it—I *need* to hear it—but Beth Ann asked me to help her with something right after supper. Can we talk later tonight, when I get back?"

He drained his glass and refilled it from the frosty pitcher near Judy's elbow. "My head's going in nine directions at once right now, anyway. Things need to settle. And I want to drive to Hillside and sit with Harley, bounce a few things off him. Later will be fine."

"Good," she said. "Now why don't you take a quick nap before you fall over? I'll put a pizza in the oven."

He smiled at her, his best most reassuring smile. Under the table, his free hand worked at the chess pieces in his pocket.

CHAPTER FIFTEEN

Two dreams repeatedly haunted Mick Logan in the six months after the tragedy at Lincoln Middle School. Both of them dwindled in frequency after a while, but like tenacious relatives, they sometimes put in an appearance for old time's sake. There was the memory-dream of Robbie Vaughn's fall into the stairwell, and there was the funeral dream, also a memory-dream but possessed of a throbbing, grim undertone all its own. This dream visited him as he slept on the living room couch.

It is a short dream, in two quick scenes, with him and Judy wearing business-like black. They enter the funeral parlor assessing islands of darkly dressed strangers who are engaged in low-voiced discussions. Judy's face is set and worried; she doesn't want to be here but doesn't want Mick doing this alone. And frankly, for all of his insistence on coming, he's ready to make a hundred-yard dash for the huge double doors behind them and burst out into the light misty rain.

But he holds it together, following Judy's lead—bless her for cutting the path through the heavily resistant air—up to the coffin where there are more islands, not of people but of flowers. Multitudes. More of a logjam, really. Two people a bit older than Mick stand vigil there wearing identical wrung-out expressions. Mick stammers through a weak introduction, and he refuses to look at the body in the pleated white compartment. Then, just as he takes the moist hand of Mrs. Vaughn and gives it a light squeeze, he does look. His words die on his lips.

For one moment it is Robbie in repose, powdered and dapper in a navy blue suit and tie. A bit too pink in the cheeks. And there is a strange, miniscule bead of something cloudy in the lashes of his right eye. A grim and logical part of him identifies it as adhesive to keep the eyes shut, one of many feints to lock Robbie in the illusion of sleep.

Then the suit grows short at the cuffs, strains at its buttons and it is now Justin Wick in the coffin, his dirty blonde hair splayed like an insult on Robbie's fine white pillow, his larger frame violating Robbie's space. Mick goggles at Mr. and Mrs. Vaughn, his mouth working, fish-like. *Surely they must notice, must see the change in the body before them.* Their weary red eyes fill with alarm, aimed at him, not at the coffin.

"Mick." Judy catches his sleeve. Her voice is tight and urgent. "What is it?"

Justin jacks himself up on his elbows and twists his head around. His face cramps and stretches until the gum on his lashes lets loose, left then right, and the strand of silk keeping his lips closed breaks and flutters like sprung piano wire.

Mick reaches out as if to embrace the dreadful figure in the coffin, entwine it and crush away the image, make it gone. His hands tremble. His throat works, unable to create anything more than a high, keening sound, but in his mind the words are huge and blaring. *Where's Robbie? What have you done with Robbie?*

Justin laughs while the great Mr. Logan is being pulled toward the door by his wife, who appears sick and pale over the whole thing.

"Nod," Justin says and laughs again. "Dontcha remember? The Land of Nod. It's a hungry place. There's always room for more."

"Please, Mick," Judy is saying. There is a terrible, strained sound to her voice. She is dragging him now, her feet wide set for leverage, her black purse swinging like a pendulum, bopping between them with each step. "We're going to the car now. Jesus. Come on."

The Vaughns are in each other's arms, confused and wounded by the display. People rush to the couple with comforting hands and extra tissues, blocking out the coffin, but not before Mick can see it one last time, the logjam of flowers, the satin pillow, the soft lining brilliant yet barren. The coffin has changed once more. It is now empty . . .

Mick jerked awake and swiped a trembling hand across his sweaty forehead. The sun was low and brooding.

"You awake?" Judy called from the kitchen.

"Sure," he said and got up on wobbly legs.

Outside, someone started up a lawnmower and began the round and round maintenance of their yard.

CHAPTER SIXTEEN

When Mick walked into the hospital room, Harley was on the phone with someone, his huge gesturing hands at risk of swiping a nearly-cleaned dinner tray off the bedside table. Mick was glad to see it. He brought the LINR box around and set it on the nightstand next to some gift shop flowers. With an appreciative warmth he saw the card stuck amid the blossoms read *From Mick and Judy* in Judy's fine script.

Harley hung up the phone and considered him with a speculative banality. "That was Kippy Evert, of all people."

Mick lowered himself into a chair near the foot of the bed. "And what did Kippy have to say?"

"He told me about the fire at the village hall. Otherwise it was the usual namby-pamby horse crap when you call somebody's hospital room."

Mick set his hand on the box. The wood felt cool and unpleasantly damp all of a sudden. "No horse crap here. I want to tell you what I know. What I've seen, heard, and felt for the last few days. It's all truth, even if it might sound off the wall. Do you feel up for it?"

Harley gave a slow nod. His eyes gained some of their dark hollows back and his mouth was a thin line, tense with concentration. "Let me get the nurse in here first. I've got to take a leak something fierce. This goddamned I.V. Then we can get to work."

"All right," Mick said and found he was grateful for the last minute opportunity to organize his thoughts.

Judy Logan went to the door and gazed out at the last rays of daylight—molten strokes laid over the streets and sidewalks of Knoll—and a nagging voice rose within her. *What would Mick say?*

The answer was a simple one. He'd say she had no business at The Crymost, no matter what her friend wanted to do. Based on the peculiar lights up there, of course, and the trivial if somewhat mysterious matter of the road to said Crymost being chained off by decree of village authority. And let's not forget the insights her husband wished to share with her in a few hours, which no doubt orbited around The Crymost as well. It was a perfect storm of reasons to stay away.

"It's not just for when somebody dies, you know," Beth Ann had said earlier, her eyes wide and wet in the afternoon light of the hospital lounge. "It's for any heartache, and this is a big one. I'm going tonight, after dark. Please, come with me?"

It amazed her now how firmly she decided to keep any word of it from Mick. Part of it stemmed from a sense of justification. If Mick was able to take on certain rogue behaviors—leaving the hospital when poor Harley has just been admitted for example, not to mention his secretive moodiness of late—then she was entitled to her own asides. A wild curiosity about The Crymost stirred within her that begged to be sated after all, and this was a rare chance to witness a very private Knoll practice firsthand. And on a more heartfelt level, the act (dare she call it a ritual?) might bring her friend some relief, if only of the emotional variety.

The sun slipped below the horizon just as she pulled up to the Kroeners' door. Beth Ann came out with a light jacket over her shoulders and a large cylindrical object clutched to her breast.

"Thank you for taking me," Beth Ann said as she climbed in.

The object she held was an ornate ceramic beer stein with a fancy hinged lid. Overly large, but with a sense of generosity rather than gluttony, rather like Harley himself. It seemed a fitting token, given its purpose.

"Of course," Judy said.

She glanced toward the southeast. Her stomach tightened.

CHAPTER SEVENTEEN

The nurse put Harley back into bed, checked his IV and glared at Mick, intimating it was time for patients to pursue much needed rest. Then she strode out on foamy soles, away from their waiting silence.

106

"I promised to tell you what I know," Mick began. "So here it is. I believe that state inspector, Peter Fyvie, never left town. And I believe there are forces at work in Knoll."

He spoke easily about Fyvie's sudden appearance in his truck and about his later encounter with Fyvie inside the burning village hall, keeping his voice even and logical, managing to put a frame around his thoughts to deflect any self-doubt. Not screwing down, but fortifying.

"So, you think that Fyvie guy is dead?" Harley asked after a point. "Of course, he'd have to be if he looked the way you described him."

"I would love for it to all be some kind of daydream, but he touched me, damn it. Rode my back, heavy and wet and real enough to keep the flames off. So, do you want to hear more? Because if you think I'm nuts already, I can stop."

Harley's gaze became fixed on a point in the corner of the hospital room. The fluorescent glow from his over-bed light accentuated the seams in his face. "My dad always feared the family car running out of gas. As a kid I'd watch how he puffed away at his pipe and checked the gas gauge over and over when we were on a drive, worried, as if the needle might drop from full to empty in a heartbeat. One of those tics that makes one person different from the next. And he was that way until the day he died.

"In 1985, Beth Ann and I drove home in a blizzard. We'd been married all of three years by then, and I was damn fool enough to believe we could make it to Madison and back despite the weather. Like a bigger damn fool, I left with a near empty tank. We ran out of gas just the other side of Baylor. Total white-out where mid-afternoon was like being wrapped in a sheet, so you couldn't tell east from west from Shit Can Alley. Would have been a person's last mistake to try to walk back to town. Good way to get found in the spring, just bones wrapped in a rotted winter coat and a gas can in one hand.

"The county plow went by while we sat worrying over what to do, and this was back when Verne Prellwitz—Gordy's dad—was driving for the county. He was a half-blind maniac and he damned near shoved us right off the road. Buried one side of the car clear to the top, and never slowed down. Beth Ann's scream pretty much capped my feeling like a jackass, and in those few seconds I was just about out of my mind with worry and self-disgust, thinking about the wisdom of my old man, four years in his grave by then. 'You had it right, Dad,' I even said.

"And just like that somebody patted my hand, a *there-there* kind of thing. Wasn't Beth Ann either; she was still curled up on her side of the car from reacting to the plow's near miss. I realized I was being egged on. Not *there-there*, but *let's go*. Without thinking about it I cranked the ignition, and the engine caught right away. Stayed running, too, and we drove the twelve miles home, the gas needle on E the whole way, and the air blowing out of the heater vents smelling of pipe smoke. My dad's brand. I have no doubt about it.

"You don't have to plead much of a case if you want me to believe those who've passed on can grab the reins on this side when it matters. The only ones who are lacking something upstairs are the ones who can't make room for the idea. Or *won't*. What puzzles me is why a complete stranger like Fyvie is jumping in on your behalf."

"Maybe because whatever put him where he is now is what's at work in Knoll. Maybe because I was the last one to talk to him. His final connection to the earthly plane."

Harley accepted this with a quiet nod. "So what else is there? One death doesn't make for a revived die-off, after all."

Mick summed up the incident at The Chapel Bar next: the tunnel, the blackout, the exploding LED sign. Then he drew the folded paper from the LINR box and handed it over. "Do me a favor and use your mechanical good sense to tell me about this drawing."

Harley took the sheet two-handed like a man reading a daily paper. After a moment he said, "Part schematic, part assembly plan."

"But to assemble what?"

"A pump of some kind. And a big one, too. A six-footer is my guess. There are impellers here . . . " He indicated with a thick finger. His eyes played over the image with growing interest, like a plunderer surveying a treasure map. "And there's another outlet down here with a fan of some kind."

"A pump," Mick said and examined the drawing from behind Harley's shoulder. Tension built in him, a sense they were closer to answers the men of 1960s Knoll took to their graves. It was like a weight on his heart. "For water?"

"This one's for liquid." Harley pointed at one part of the drawing, then dragged his finger to another. "But something else goes here. Air, maybe. And these are intake pipes, one next to the other. Whatever this thing is, it's meant to pump out two things at once."

"That explains the name." Mick pointed to the legend at the top of the drawing. "Double Barrel."

Anything else he might have said caught in his throat.

Tension whorled around them like a living thing. Tension and *intrusion*. Harley's sudden, hectic expression confirmed it was more than Mick's imagination. The overhead lights flickered.

"Time to put that away." Mick motioned to the paper. "Last time we took it out like this there was an incident, if you recall my story."

"Ignition and primary vent," Harley said despite the warning. "Look at it come."

"Put it away, I said."

"Just now."

"What?"

"Mick, I'm telling you, some of the notations on this paper weren't there a second ago."

Fixtures vibrated in the room. Mick felt the small hairs on his body bristle out in waves. The LINR box toppled over. The mortality log skated out ceremoniously to the middle of the floor and flopped open. They both stared at it.

At last Mick snatched up the LINR box and thrust it toward Harley. "The drawing. Put it away. Now."

"Wait." Harley extended a white, trembling finger. "Look at that, Mick."

From the nightstand a pen lifted off a book of crosswords and sailed across the room like a slow-motion torpedo to hover just inches above the mortality log. The television screen in the corner became awash with a frenzy of white static. The telephone at the bedside rang, and they both jumped. A wall speaker, presumably for emergency announcements only, issued a series of crackles, but neither of them acknowledged it. They were transfixed by the pen, which jabbed—tip down—onto the open page in the book and moved with harsh strokes. Mick took a step closer. Harley patted his arm with concession. "Take it slow. This is something we don't want to get in the way of."

The phone rang again. Harley knocked the handset from its cradle. It landed on the nightstand, mouthpiece up, and a reedy, distorted voice buzzed from the plastic. "Out of Knoll."

Harley glared at it. "What the hell?" And then he shouted. "*Jesus, Mick, watch out!*"

Mick felt a whoosh as the mortality log, suddenly airborne, sailed just inches from his head. Harley, despite his size and weariness, managed to leap out of the bed and duck out of its path. The book crashed into the wall above the bed and then flopped onto the mattress like a mortally wounded bird.

The wall speaker blared into the crackling air. "*Out of Knoll!*"

Seconds later, the charge in the room diminished, dissipated, vanished.

"You okay?" Mick asked.

"Yeah, sure, for a guy in a dress." Harley tugged the back of his hospital johnnie together. There was a bloody patch on the back of his hand where his I.V. line tore free during his book dodge. In kind, his I.V. unit began to emit a three-note alarm over and over. "What was that all about?"

Mick gave the book a cautionary poke. "Somebody trying to tell us something."

"I'm not sure I get the message. *Out of Knoll.* What the hell does that mean?"

"Fyvie said it to me during the fire, too," Mick said and flipped through the book until he found the page bearing the freshest entry.

At the same time, Harley picked up the schematic drawing, which had fluttered away when he leapt out of bed, and spread it open on the sheets. They stood side by side, each studying what was laid out in front of them. The room seemed very still despite the electronic chirp of the I.V. alarm and the more distant, off-the-hook alarm of the phone receiver.

Mick read the new entry in the mortality log. "The Honorable Judge Roderick Thekan."

It was penned with a shaky infirmity, but then again a pen infused with life for brief seconds could not be held to good penmanship. Not in Wonderland. The newest date, which was aligned with other dates of passing on the page, was May 21, 1939. The cause of death: blank.

"I was visited yesterday by that stranger I saw walking into town. He asked me about the records at the village hall." Mick's lips felt very cold. "As it turns out he is a judge named Thekan. One hell of a coincidence, if you know what I mean."

"Crazy thoughts aren't always wrong thoughts," Harley said and took up the schematic. "Not after what we just saw happen in here. And this is what I've got to contribute, now that the room is a little calmer."

He tapped the paper again, and this time Mick saw the word right away, how it was attributed to a part of the drawing by way of a dotted line. "Igniter," he said, "like a furnace. To heat something?"

Harley's eyes turned hard. "Nope. To cause some type of combustion. Or explosion."

Those eyes also swam with the signs of fatigue now. It was easy to forget, given their little distraction, why Harley was here. "Why don't you get back into bed," Mick insisted.

He pressed the nurse call button and told the responding voice that Harley's I.V. had come out. A moment later the nurse with the foamy soles came in and straightened up, admonished Harley for being too rough and gave Mick, who put everything back into the LINR box, a smoldering glance on her way out.

Once the room was theirs again, the air seemed gravid, this time with possibilities.

"Will and Kippy should come up here with me tomorrow so we can all hash this out."

"Good idea." Harley wrung his hands in his lap. His eyes bore more than weariness now. "But make it late morning. They've got me down for tests at the goddamned crack of dawn."

"You're the boss," Mick said, and stepped to the door. Then, with a flash of correlation: "*Out of Knoll.* You asked what it means. I think it means we're running out of help. 'Listen to me before I'm spent' is how Fyvie put it. And he said once the help is gone, it will be just the townspeople, Thekan, and The Crymost."

"Our help is leaving." Harley's eyes drifted closed, his voice turned thick with the grayness of onrushing sleep. "Which means those of us who know something better move on it. Hell of a thing."

"It is," Mick said and backed out of the room, suddenly made afraid for Harley again by the way the big man was tipped back against his pillows, mouth open, hands curled loose at his sides like old wood shavings.

He spoke in a soft tone from the doorway. "I'll see you tomorrow, big guy."

Before he left, he turned out the light.

CHAPTER EIGHTEEN

Judy parked at Pitch Road's new chain barrier, got out and ducked under with Beth Ann right behind. She brought a flashlight but didn't bother to turn it on. A watercolor streak of last-light on the horizon accented their way for the time being. Besides, it seemed rather natural to initiate this lowly ceremony in the dark.

"Will Harley notice his beer stein is missing?" she asked.

"There are five more like it gathering dust in the back of the dining room curio cabinet, so I doubt it."

Judy merely nodded. They were nearing The Crymost fork and the air gained density, as if the darkness moved around them in mounting waves. She switched on the flashlight, lowly ceremonies be damned.

"Do we need to say anything?" she asked. "When we get up there, I mean."

"No. The Crymost will know."

They stopped just inside the barrier of bushes. An elvish, green glow blushed up from below The Crymost ledge and it gave Judy the sense of being in the presence of a huge, slowly-waking animal.

"Okay," Beth Ann said.

She inched up to the edge of the outcrop. For an instant Judy's feet nearly took over and sent her across to pull Beth Ann back before she was snatched away by whatever hungry thing might cling to the unseen side of the ledge. She fought it down. Beth Ann tossed the stein over with a two-handed lob. The offering twirled end over end, limned in green light and dropped out of sight. Peaceful.

"There. I've done my part." Beth Ann turned back with a light sigh. As she looked past Judy, her expression changed to puzzlement. "Who are they?"

Judy whirled around.

Four people occupied the way out, spaced randomly in the gloom. Three men and one woman, each facing The Crymost drop off. Judy swept her light across them and found no solace in the details lent by the flashlight's glow. The woman's clothes were old fashioned, a long woolen dress buttoned up to the throat. By contrast, a miserable looking young man closest to the barrier of shrubs wore a Kurt Cobain

T-shirt. His hands, lashed together with coil upon coil of narrow twine, dangled near his crotch. The other two gentlemen were older, one wearing what appeared to be a century-old banker's suit and mutton chop sideburns, the other a farmer dressed for the field. None of them truly stood, she saw with real shock. They were suspended, their feet dangling inches above the ground.

Beth Ann came up behind her and dug fingers into her shoulder. "What do we do?"

Judy found no words. Her thoughts came up again and again against the improbability of those dangling feet like a trapped thing.

At last she took an infirm step forward, her light held out before her. "Stay right behind me."

"They're part of this place. They must be."

The man closest to them, the banker man, ignored them as they passed him. His mouth remained a harsh line beneath a wild mustache as bushy as his sideburns. The pockets of his long coat bulged, Judy noticed. To each wrist and ankle a brick was tied with frayed twine. He was wet. Soaked, in fact. The redolence of wet cloth came off of him in waves. Droplets from his shoes pattered in the grass. She forced herself another step forward before she realized Beth Ann was no longer behind her.

"Help him," her friend said. She was not addressing Judy. "Please, tell me The Crymost will help my Harley."

"Hey." Judy swung her light until it fixed on Beth Ann, who knelt before the woman in the dark dress.

The woman considered her supplicant with yellow-skimmed eyes which were hardened by a type of growing alarm.

"The results of this place are of another stripe now," the woman said. It sounded as if the throat under that heavy collar might be riddled with holes. "Energies are bolder. I do not know why I tell you this. Only that something moves me to do so."

"You're like angels," Beth Ann stood, her hands clasped and trembling at her breast. "Angels with a message."

Judy took another step. The twisted brand of hope on her friend's face frightened her, and the air took on a sudden foreboding, as if she, Beth Ann, and the strangers were being observed with calculating malice. She glanced behind at the drop off, where the glow increased in intensity, before striding up to her friend. "We need to go."

"Shit's on the move," said the farmer man. His white hair was plastered in wet ringlets to his scalp. "Even the Lachrymose don't understand all of it. Don't like it none, neither."

A thick hunk of metal resembling the harrow from a plow sat on the ground just below the man's dangling boots. A length of rope tethered it to his waist. Words shook through Judy like a tolling bell. *Drowned. Suicides.* It jarred her and somehow freed up her mental channels. She reached out and snagged her friend's wrist.

"The aperture closes ever tighter," the man with the mutton chops spoke into the glow, "and those who mean to help will soon find their chances ended. In moments, we will fade. At last, an ended goodbye."

"No!" Beth Ann broke away from Judy and clutched at the woman in the dress, twisting the fabric of sodden sleeves in her fists. "Not before you help my Harley. Just one blessing. Just one. Please."

The woman reached out and nearly but not quite cupped Beth Ann's chin in her pallid hands, her expression soft, her yellowed eyes on the verge of being filled with hurt. Her words were made slurry by dribbles of greenish water leaking through her teeth. "The Crymost is at work in exceptional ways just now. By its nature, it will succor regardless of its own desires, because you have made your plea in the proper way. I believe your man will once again hold you in strong hands."

"Thank you," Beth Ann sobbed. "Oh, thank you, good God, thank you."

"Enough," Judy said and took her friend by the shoulders.

Beth Ann succumbed and allowed herself to be led away. Judy brought their pace up to a stumbling run, the rapturous look on her friend's face bringing to light one more truth she had no business knowing. Prayer, possessions, and sometimes the body as a whole might be flung out in offering, just so relief from the unbearable might be known. Some convictions were naïve and yet inherently valid, the viable currency of the soul.

The last stranger in their path was the young man in the Cobain shirt. Beads of water in his immature beard caught The Crymost glow like gems. He held out his bound hands. His shoulders jerked and popped. His dangling bare feet waggled. The front of his shirt bumped outward as his ribs muttered and cracked. Judy gave Beth Ann an extra push. The last thing she wanted was for those cold, twine-bound hands to give her shoulder a chummy rap.

"Hey," he called after them. "It's spontaneous, baby. That's the beauty of it. We're just trying to help."

She continued her stumbling run and did not let go of Beth Ann until they reached the car. They drove back to Knoll, their breaths fogging the windows while The Crymost glow stole deeper onto the horizon.

CHAPTER NINETEEN

Mick had powered down his cell phone before he went to see Harley and did not switch it on again until he was on his way back to the car. It rang immediately, flashing a message regarding six missed calls.

"Thank God," Judy said when he picked up. "Come home, Mick. Come home right now. Beth Ann's here and it's . . . oh God, just come right away."

The drive home from Drury was an agonizing eternity, and when he got there Judy met him at the door. Her pale expression alarmed him further. "What's wrong? Are you and Beth Ann okay?"

"She's in the guest bedroom, sleeping," Judy said and wrapped him in a deep and desperate embrace. Her words became muffled against his chest. "It's a good thing she carries her Valium wherever she goes. What's happening in this town, Mick? With The Crymost?"

A sick dread flared up in him. "What about The Crymost? What happened?"

"Not here."

She led him through the kitchen and onto the back porch. He'd waited too long, his sick dread told him, and now something had happened to Judy, and this was going to lead to him telling her everything. It must. They sat across from one another and held hands like people preparing to embark on an unknown, perhaps treacherous endeavor.

An hour later it was all done. Judy told her story straight through, and he did his best not to interrupt. Then he told his part, which took considerably longer because he started with the supposed TB outbreak in the '30s. When he was done they stared at one another, their binding acceptance leaving it all indisputable.

"So what do we do?" she finally asked. "And why does it have to be us? I'm relieved as hell you're not having your old issues from the Robbie Vaughn days because for a while it seemed like a real possibility, but this seems irrational in its own way, to try and build a defense against something so . . . *unnatural*."

"Why me? Think about what we've got . . . " He raised a finger to mark each of his points. "Harley is sick, Orlin Casper is dead, Kippy is pretty spry but his age alone makes him a concern as much as a help. That leaves me and Will Adelmeyer. I'd take some help. Hell, I'd welcome it with open arms, but this isn't exactly a town vote where you can recruit supporters with red and green posters."

"*Us*, Mick. I said us."

His jaw tightened. "Not in a million years. I don't want you involved any further in this." He got up and rested his hands on the porch railing. The night moved by as quiet and complacent as the Wistweaw on the other side of town.

"I'm already involved." She stepped up behind him and placed her hands on his shoulders. "Four very dead-yet-talking people clinched it for me. And I'm going to hold my ground like any self-respecting Knoll resident. "

He turned around. "Emotionally nailed to the town?"

She shook her head. "To the man trying to protect it."

CHAPTER TWENTY

Kippy Evert lost track of how long he stared at the small wooden box with its crude attempts at embellishment. One of his first forays into woodworking. It was swollen from its time in the water.

Orlin took to the box right away on a long ago day down in the basement workshop. Offered him twenty dollars for it, but Kippy said he should just take it. Orlin did, and used it for years, maybe for matchbooks or cufflinks or some such. Then one day when Orlin's wife was being shipped off to the rest home in Drury, he returned it. Downsizing, Orlin said, a term for squeezing an ocean of life's memoires and possessions down to a regrettable trickle. Kippy accepted the box and put it in a prominent place on the end table next to his reading lamp. Until he took it to The Crymost on Orlin's behalf, not two short days ago.

"And, here y' are, back again," he said to it, softly. "Damnedest thing."

He assessed the books recently placed on his end table and weighed their meaning and how they fit in with Orlin's box. This joined with the weighty sense of something coming—not the something brewing at The Crymost exactly, but an offshoot of it, a bit of business directed solely at him, due any time now, and he shivered.

The knock on his door was gentle, and he got up almost immediately as if an old friend might be calling at this late hour. "The Judge, no doubt. Let's get this show on the road, then."

Kirkpatrick Evert, you are too reckless, his mother used to say. But carelessness wasn't usually stitched up the back with suspicion like this. *Or fear*, he decided as he shuffled across the living room, box in hand.

The man on his porch stood rigid, gray hair blowing in the night breeze, eyes alight with anticipation. There were green-white points where his pupils should be. *Aw, hell.*

"Thekan, ain't it?" he said and stepped aside to admit the man.

"Evert. The digger," Thekan replied, his dark shoes whispering on the carpet, his sport shirt crackling.

Kippy executed a quick movement he hoped Thekan would not notice, a lean out of his door as if to snatch one last breath of clear air before this buggerfest got ramped up. His hands performed a quick, efficient task, setting a singular object on the porch floor, then he turned back to face his guest.

"I assure you, I'm alone," Thekan said.

"So I see." He closed the door, swallowed hard. "Alone and calling late. Why is that, d' you suppose?"

Thekan smiled, slow and conciliatory. The door lock, untouched, engaged with a metallic snap. The window in the kitchen, which was open just a crack, closed with an efficient thump. "Circumstances call for it."

"I 'magine they do," Kippy said, a tremble stirring within him more fiery than he'd known in years. He strode to the end table where a stack of old books rested in the lamplight. "I've been doing some checking up on you. See, not everything gets stuck away at the village hall. Sometimes when a man works for Knoll for a while, his basement gets used as an overflow for certain things. Things a man might forget he kept, until he takes a look."

"I'm aware. But now it's time for this town to forget, one piece and one person at a time, so there can be no resistance to that which stirs in the stones outside of this town. I am prepared to wipe you clean, Evert the Digger, in any way necessary."

"Can't wipe this."

Kippy pulled the top book from the stack on his end table. The significance he'd hope it might hold became apparent. In Thekan's presence it hummed like something electric. The Judge gawped at it.

"Got your number, don't I?" Kippy said. "This here is a detailed account of how, with a single decree, you took the God out of this town in '39. Don't take a genius to figure out you're back somehow, a godless thing come to make more godless work. Ain't it? Just look at you."

Kippy advanced and Thekan stepped back in kind. He had the son of a bitch's number. Damned if he didn't. The book was Irma Casper's, and he found it in a carton of items from the old river church he'd kept for years. When he came across it, it stuck out because it was wet. Like Orlin's box, it was a recent arrival.

"See, there's always gonna be folks who remember." His heart hammered, his breath felt sharp and clean in his lungs. "Once we get it all figured out, there's folks in this town gonna put a stop to a few things. Maybe as soon as tomorrow. His'try lives, shithead."

Thekan jerked his shoulders as if wrenching out his next words. "I will not be deprived."

Invisible force struck the book in Kippy's hands. The sensation brought home boyhood memories of a hardball defying the protection of the oiled mitt and jarring every bone and tendon from fingertips to shoulder. The book was sundered as if by a shotgun blast, loose pages fluttering ceilingward from the hardboard spine. They withered and darkened as they skirled about the room, twisting into meaningless curls of ash.

Kippy staggered backward. What a foolish old man he was. What stood in his house was a pernicious thing, and Mick Logan would have told him so. Will Adelmeyer, too, because even an Adelmeyer wasn't too hardheaded to see it. Kippy spat out the word topmost in his mind.

"*Foo!*"

It was a ridiculous word, old, something from childhood funny papers, but it helped him break away and run to the nearest door. The cellar. He felt too slow and yet fumbled all the way down the stairs and into his workshop.

He rushed toward his workbench and carving table. Thekan sprang down the stairs behind him, wolf-like. The pegboard across the room, full of dangling chisels and wood rasps, glared in the fluorescent lights like an arsenal. Kippy dove on it, snatched a three-quarter inch chisel and rushed back, confronted Thekan at the bottom of the stairs. Thekan regarded him, evaluative, like a patron assessing some incompetently done museum exhibit.

"Evert the Digger, the Carver, the Rememberer," Thekan said. A drop of blood bobbled in the corner of each eye. "I didn't ask for this obligation, you know. My awakening and the realization of everything bestowed upon me were rather alarming at first. But I hope to do well. It's a promise older than the both of us. Do well and know your reward. Too bad your contrariness has left me only one choice."

Kippy felt cold energy swirl through the room. The clatter from the pegboard behind him was like an icy chuckle as blades and chisel tips turned erect. He formed a quick and grave assessment: at least twenty chisels back there, maybe more, all tensed like quarrels waiting to be fired, all aimed at his back. "This doesn't end with me, you know."

"I'm aware. But I have more time. Unlike you. Goodbye, old man."

Kippy felt an explosive rush of air as his chisels, lovingly worn smooth by his own hands, streaked toward him. He tensed, and then knew a second explosive rush, this one of unbearable mortal pain assaulting his shoulders, his back, his spine.

Aw, hell.

CHAPTER TWENTY ONE

Morning. Mick crept past the guest room door and eased down the stairs. He found Judy in the kitchen drinking coffee.

She poured him a cup and handed it over. "We should get this hammered out before Beth Ann comes down. What's the plan?"

"I still want to round up Will and Kippy and see if we can't all have a sit-down with Harley sometime today. After town business, of course. I'm guessing Cy will want to talk about the town vote this morning because we only have two days and nowhere to hold it."

"What about that old Ice Dreams shop?"

He shook his head. "It's a dump. And there's really no time to get it ready. I'm not sure what the answer is."

"I'm available for today's meeting too, you know." She finished her cup, set it aside. "I took the day off. After last night I just . . . there's so much to process—"

"Wonderful." Beth Ann's voice made them look around. She bustled into the kitchen, her phone to her ear. "I can do that. Yes, I will." She was pulling on her jacket with errant tugs. Her face was lined with sleep and her hair was a pillow-tousled mess. She flashed them what was either a beaming smile or a frantic grimace. "I'm leaving now. Thank you."

Hysterical was Mick's assessment as he got up, ready to stop her from bolting deliriously through the back door and into the dewy morning. At the last minute he held his position.

"They're releasing Harley," she said, bypassed Mick and gave Judy's arms a celebratory shake. "Better than that, they're giving him a clean bill of health. His tumors are gone. Gone! The Crymost and the angels have smiled."

"Are you sure?" Judy's eyes turned toward Mick, clouded with concern.

"I'm sure that they're sure. His white cell count is normal. Everything's normal. They say his recovery is miraculous. Miraculous. Oh, thank you, God." Her car keys jangled in her hand like a string of charms. "Thank you, angels!"

Mick reached for his own keys. They were in his pocket, next to the chess pieces. "One of us should drive you."

"You two have done enough," she said, her eyes brimming. "Thank God for you. My dear friends. Harley will be back home in an hour. Healthy. What a beautiful, beautiful blessing."

She swept out of the back door, her joy so glaring it seemed reasonless.

Mick moved up behind Judy and slipped his arms around her waist.

"I want to be happy for them," Judy said, rubbing her hands over his.

Outside, a cloud passed over Knoll, turning the bright outdoors into a shadowed mockery of the warm day on tap.

CHAPTER TWENTY TWO

Mick stepped onto the front porch, his day mapped out in his head, an excitement over Harley's recovery batting back and forth from light to dark. How oddly the pieces flowed in tandem, the mundane and the unnatural. What happened in Harley's room, for example. And what Judy saw at The Crymost. They coursed through the everyday now, twisting and sluicing and impossible to ignore or discount, subterranean tributaries of a brighter surface stream.

He trotted down the front steps and nearly ran into the woman coming up his front walk. He blinked at her unexpected mode of dress—a loose colorful blouse and a pair of light slacks—unexpected because this was Chastity Mellar Borth, and he'd never seen her in anything but ankle-length denim skirts and drab tops.

"Good morning, Ms. Mellar Borth. To what do I owe this honor?"

She smiled at him, something she obviously had yet to perfect. "Good morning to you too, Mick Logan. I'm on a mission of servitude today, delivering Knoll some news and some posters."

She tapped at a stack of oversized paper rectangles tucked under her arm. Red *Mellar's Out* posters.

"You've had a change of heart, I see," he said.

"About a great many things. The town vote will be held on my property in light of the disaster at the village hall." She held up a poster and indicated where the new location was plainly printed. "The Mellar legacy needs to change with the times. Be part of the town's progress, not its past. There will be an open house, punch and cookies while the voting takes place. It's time to strip some of the mystery off the Mellar name, don't you think?"

She held out a poster and he took it. He caught himself scowling. "I must say, you know how to ensure a turnout. There are a lot of curious people in Knoll. If they don't come to your house to vote, they'll come just to be nosey."

She laughed and her eyes sparkled just a little. "I've been closed off to the town for too long." She walked away from him with a friendly wave. "Say hello to your wife. Make sure she comes to vote."

"We will, but just so you know, I think we're leaning toward the *Mellar's In* camp."

She picked her way down the sidewalk as if her feet were woefully unfamiliar with her new sandals. "You just come and make your mark. We'll be glad to see you."

"What about Cy?" He raised his voice because she was nearly to the next door down Garden Street. The Merks. There were plastic toys strewn in the yard. "Is he on board with this?"

"He will be once we tell him," she called back and then let herself into the Merk's enclosed porch to knock on the door.

We?

He tried to call Cy on the way to the garage but got no answer. Then he called Axel. No answer. Moments later he got his first good look at the interior of the village garage and how a scrim of soot covered everything. His thoughts took a new, pedestrian turn toward how he might begin to clean the place up.

CHAPTER TWENTY THREE

Axel stopped packing long enough to see who called him, then tossed the phone down on his bed.

"Shit."

Logan. The not-dead testament to how screwed up things turned out. What the hell was he thinking, pulling such a dumb stunt? Just a matter of time before someone fingered him for the fire, no matter what that judge said.

He crammed more stuff into his duffel bag and his hand came across the plastic pouch old Ichabod left him with, still pretty full. The shit was high test. Maybe something cut into it. Looking at it drove home the source of his latest troubles. Thekan. Even if he packed some damn fine weed, a freak was a freak. He stuffed the bag down deep and pushed some socks—not clean but still going along for the ride—on top, then he slid his rolling papers in next to it.

His immediate plan was a simple one: hole up in Royal Center for a few days if he could get some old drinking buddies to take him in. If not, he'd go all the way to Madison. Lots of childhood friends in Mad City who might let him crash—

His hands stopped their work. Across the room, a doorway was opened into a long hallway and Auntie Alice's laundry room. The stairs were at the far end. It was there a nearly non-existent light was splayed, like a blush. A man stood there, just a shadow, and the posture reminded him of a vulture perched on a branch. A sliver of brighter light lay across the face, picking out the features of Thekan the Judge.

"What are you doing here?" Axel asked and stepped in front of his work. "I don't want anything else to do with you, man. You're bad news."

Thekan strolled forward, into the room. "This is how you treat the one who would put you in a place of importance in the destiny of this town?"

Thekan's eyes did not yet burn with their familiar eerie light, but they were about to. Axel could somehow tell.

"What the hell do you mean?"

"I require hands to carry out more work in these last crucial days, to guide the fate of this town in a particular direction."

"I ain't no politician." He picked up a wadded T-shirt for his duffel, tossed it down again.

"But you are useful," Thekan said, and the light *was* in his eyes now, faint but alive with electric heat. "I specifically chose you. With me you are welcome, and you are wanted."

Axel scowled at the odd flutter in his chest. A man was speaking, not in the room but in the past, in his head, telling him he was useless and nobody wanted him because he was such a fuck up. The words stung more than anything he'd heard in his then fifteen years of life, but not because of what they said. He had shivered and sweated when he'd said, "Please, Dad," just before rough hands took him away. He blundered into a bright stench filled with harsh noise, hard beds and harder eyes staring out from behind iron bars.

"That's bullshit." His voice sounded small and far away now. "Nobody ever chooses me."

"Exoneration takes time." Thekan was next to him, his hands spread in demonstration. "And proper circumstances. I find you to be a joy, my dear Axel. And I reward joy with joy, do I not?"

Two of Thekan's fingers plucked the air. Axel felt his lungs fill up with sweet, lulling smoke. It was like an embrace. He reveled in it for a moment, then blew out a breath. "I fuck everything up. I tried to kill Logan, you know. Fixed it so he'd burn in the fire I set for you. But he got out somehow."

"Still, it would have been a favor to me had you succeeded. Mick Logan troubles me in ways I can't explain."

"You're not pissed at me?" He was close enough to touch Thekan now, to know the heat of contact what might come from someone who didn't degrade, didn't despise. Instead he drew another deep breath, which was sweeter and headier than the one before it. The room took a lazy spin. "You don't think I'm a shit?"

"One doesn't think such things of those they have faith in," Thekan said, his stare blazing now. "I have faith in you, dear Axel. Much faith. Stay."

There was a sliding sound behind them as items slipped from the duffel and onto the bed as if plucked by dutiful hands.

"What are you?" The question seemed to come from many places in Axel's brain, some of them he didn't understand.

"The one who lifts you up instead of treading over you. The one who gives instead of takes and trusts instead of suspects. I offer much, so much more than the entity which brought me. Where I am willful, its reactions are automatic. Automatic and perfunctory. I am here, and I mean to stay."

"Stay," he heard himself say.

Thekan's arms spread wide. Axel fell into them and wrapped his arms tightly around the man. He pressed his cheek to the man's breast. The cold squirming presence under the shirt did not repulse him, not really. Nor did the pervasive scent of rot, a singular puff, which whorled at him and then was gone. The man's fingers traced over his scalp in long contemplative strokes.

"Will you serve me a while longer? Leave what you know of me unsaid, leave my reputation here solid and untarnished, at least until this town sees its inevitable end?"

"I . . . " Axel squeezed his eyes tight. There were tears in them. Bitter tears. "Yes."

CHAPTER TWENTY FOUR

When he was ready to take a break, Mick called Will Adelmeyer. "I think today's the day we check out that tunnel of yours. Harley's on the way home and I'm hoping he'll be up for tagging along."

124

DEAN H. WILD

"Fine by me. But you caught me on the road. My liquor and my beer get trucked in, but when it comes to the pickled eggs and Slim Jims, I'm on my own. Can we do it after lunch?"

"I'll be there with my flashlight in hand."

"And maybe some holy water."

He meant it lightly, Mick could tell, but any levity immediately evaporated.

"I've got more to tell you when I see you. A lot more."

"Yeah, I had a feeling."

Mick hung up and reached into his pocket, touched the chess pieces resting there. He barely noticed the couple who stepped in through the open door. Not until Harley Kroener said, "Soot did a number on this place. Holy Christ."

Harley and Beth Ann smiled at him from just inside the bay door. Beth Ann was latched to her husband's arm as if they were strolling to a church picnic. Mick walked over and gave his friend an energetic and well-practiced shove to the shoulder. "I heard they kicked you out. And I see you didn't know any better than to come to work."

Harley was in a Village of Knoll work shirt, cleaned and pressed. The expression he wore was steady and knowing. "I told my honey, here, the same thing I'm going to tell you. I'm feeling too good not to work."

"But only for a few hours," Beth Ann said. "You might be feeling spry but there's no reason to abuse the angels' gift. You should be going to church right this minute to show your gratitude."

Harley patted her hand. "You can thank God enough for the both of us."

"By the way, Beth Ann," Mick said, "keep this afternoon open. I want to call some people together and talk a few things out."

Harley planted a kiss on her forehead. "You really need to hear what's going to be said, honey pie."

Beth Ann stepped away, her eyes shining. "Call me. I'll meet you."

"I will." Harley waved as she disappeared through the bay doors.

"How are you really?" Mick asked after a moment. "Is it a miracle?"

"Damn close to one. I woke up feeling like a kid again, and those pains in my side: gone. Do you think it has something to do with last night? With all that weird horseshit going on in my room?"

125

Mick considered him carefully. "Did Beth Ann tell you anything about what she did last night? She and Judy?"

"She said she asked some angels for help. In fact, she's been babbling about God and angels all morning, as I'm sure you noticed. I've never seen her like that before. You know how we are. Church is a formal thing, like doilies you put out just for company. Once the tea party is done you put 'em away until next time."

"Then we've got more to talk about."

"Better hold that thought a minute." Harley pointed toward the door.

Cy Vandergalien stalked in, a black backpack slung over one shoulder. He listed to one side when he walked as if the weight of the pack was throwing him off.

"There's not much time," Cy said and his scowl lent him the appearance of a trout stunned to find itself at the bottom of a creel. An unshaven trout at that. "Get yourselves to work on setting up."

"You mean for the vote?" Mick said. "It's out of our hands, from what I hear. Chastity Mellar Borth is taking on the particulars."

"Yes." Cy stood before them, his sleepless eyes twitching. "She asked for those portable voting booths we got down at the firehouse. Your number one job is to get them set up in her front yard. Weather's supposed to hold, so they can stay up overnight. All but the wiring for the in-booth lights. You'll have to do those tomorrow morning."

A decorative brooch glittered on Cy's shirt front. A woman's brooch with a large blue stone. Mick considered it with a quiet worry. He gave equal consideration to the posters Cy clutched tight against his side. Green posters. *Mellar's In.*

"Is everything all right, Cy?"

He'd heard Cyril Vandergalien laugh a few times in his life, a deep and uneven sound. What came from the man's mouth now was more like a frantic cackle. "*Everything* is never all right, Logan. There's always something going to hell somewhere. When most things are off the beam is when you've got to worry. Put these up. Everywhere."

Mick glanced at the posters Cy practically shoved into his hands. "I thought you were a *Mellar's Out* kind of guy. What has changed? Do you know something new?"

"What I know is I got an insurance adjuster coming out in a couple days to snuffle through what's left of the village hall," Cy said and stepped toward the bay doors, "and a fire marshal from Royal Center who's itching to study the burnt remains on account of you said you suspect somebody lit her up. I don't know why, but I've been putting them both off as best I can. Some of this other stuff is my way of pushing back, following my gut, Logan." He suddenly seemed more weary than ever. "In the next few days, I suggest you do the same."

PART FOUR:

THE LAND OF NOD

CHAPTER ONE

BY THE TIME MICK and Harley transported the voting booth sections and assembled them in the front yard of the Mellar Borth house it was nearly midday. They arranged the booths into a pod of three, facing inward with a vinyl privacy flap at the entrance to each carrel. *Carrel*, a word from his school days. Not quite accurate, but Mick still liked it.

He noticed two newly constructed stages on the property, a tiny one bearing a podium and PA system, and another larger structure near the carriage house/garage where a pair of workmen were arranging power cables.

"She having a band?" Harley said as they put the final touches on the carrels. "Looks more like the Baylor Picnic than a town vote."

"Trying to sway tomorrow's crowd in her favor, maybe?" Mick said and indicated the *Mellar's Out* posters which covered each window at the front of the house. Patriotic bunting covered the porch. He was sure by tomorrow, when the voting opened, there would be balloons as well, and perhaps streamers trailing in the wind.

A sudden breeze swept across the yard and snatched away one of the canvas coverlets meant for the booths. Harley responded by sprinting after it and grasping it before it escaped into the open fields behind the house. He walked back with a pleased smile. He was barely winded as he handed the canvas back to Mick. "What? You suddenly look like you got a mouthful of crap from somewhere."

"This is as good a time as any," Mick said. "Our wives went to The Crymost last night, and Beth Ann asked for help. For you. And now you can bounce around like a kid. Thought you might like to know."

Harley dropped the coverlet inside one of the carrels and gave it a punch for good measure. "The Crymost?"

"There's more. I'll squeeze it into the rest of the plans I have for our day if you're on board with it. I say we round up Kippy and our ladies and get ourselves over to The Chapel Bar. Maybe do some tunnel exploration. Hunt down a certain double barrel."

"Sure," Harley said with a stunned blink. "Why not?"

CHAPTER TWO

The memory was caught up in Cy Vandergalien's head, sudden and relentless. Amber light was a big part of it because it was close to bedtime (little Cy was in his pajamas, which were blue and had rocket ships on them) and his daddy used an old-fashioned square lantern with cloudy orange-brown windows to light up the garage workbench.

"Jes' doing my duty here, son," Daddy whispered, and executed a little stumble-hop as if the ground tried to skate out from under him. His breath smelled sharp and maybe a little bit fruity; it overpowered the grease and gasoline perfume in the back of the garage. "You looka this, and look good. If you don't 'member it and draw it back for me, I'll knock it into your head but good. Got it?"

Daddy's eyes gleamed with a familiar meanness in the amber light. If Momma knew Daddy's eyes were gleaming that way she'd beg them to come in the house. He almost wished she would.

Daddy showed him a piece of paper, and Cy thought it must be a treasure map, only this one didn't have a big X to show you where to dig for gold like the ones on cartoons.

"This's our place." Daddy's finger tapped the paper. "And this's the bar. That there is the dump."

A map of Knoll, then. A map of home. Daddy saw it was sinking in, puffed out his lips and then traced his finger along a singular pencil line that intersected the streets of the map in a funny way. "This is what I gotta show you. See it? This here? See that bitch, the way she goes?"

Cy nodded. It was important for this to sink in, he could tell, not by what Daddy said but by the way he trembled despite his fruity-breath looseness. This was not sharing like giving him a drag off of his cigarette for laughs but sharing like teaching. Sharing something of heavy significance.

"Now you," Daddy said and flipped the sheet over. He made quick slashed marks with a pencil he took from his pocket—the pencil said F&F FEEDS on it—to make a rough rendering of the town and then he handed the pencil over. "Draw the line I just showed you. Garden Street is at the top, down there is Pisch Road . . . *Pitch* Road, goddamn it. Draw."

He drew slowly and not very straight, but he connected the areas of town just the way Daddy showed him. He even put dots at each end because he knew maps did that sometimes.

"Holy Christ, you got it," Daddy said. In the amber light he seemed unreal, like a hunched shadow you could pass right through. "Okay, I showed you what I was s'posed to. Now remember it. For the rest of your goddamned life."

Cy evaluated the line with a seven-year-old's fascination. "What is it?"

"Some dipshit's idea of good air. Supposed to be a shaft, but it works more like a passage to the double barrel. And don't think you can go farting around in there. Only one 'scuse to go down there, ever."

"What?" he asked and his eyes felt very wide.

"Bad fucking news, is what." Daddy made another stumble-hop. He grabbed the edge of the workbench just in time to keep from falling over. "Your gut'll tell you. Now get out of my sight . . . "

The memory walked with Cy until he got to the place where the southern end of Garden Street hooked around and became Backbank and he was standing before the sign for The Chapel Bar. The Wistweaw chuckled behind its barrier of trees just to his right. He could see glints of it through the branches. There was no other sound in Knoll just then. No indication that the town was fucked. But he knew it was, because his gut told him. Hell, his own ma told him. It was time to share what he knew for all of Knoll to see. It was time to draw. He took a can of black spray paint out of his backpack and began to make his mark.

CHAPTER THREE

"Your judge is making the rounds today, did I tell you?" Harley asked him as they drove over to Field Street in Mick's car. "Beth Ann and I saw him when we got back to town. Like a door-to-door salesman, he was."

Mick managed an acknowledging grunt.

He felt anxious. Kippy didn't answer his phone. It could be that the old boy was tooling around town on his bike somewhere, but a deeper undercurrent of dread ran strong and steady in his head. He choked up on the steering wheel and parked in front of Kippy's house.

"Bike's here," Harley observed.

Both of them noticed the small wooden box near the front door as they approached, and an extra, nearly silent alarm went off in Mick's mind. He knocked, hoping Kippy would answer with sleepy seeds still in his eyes. When no answer came, he turned the doorknob. The door opened easily.

"Kippy?" he called inside.

When they were answered by silence, Harley said, "Maybe he's out back."

They stopped in the living room where the cover of a book, its pages strangely absent, was tossed next to Kippy's tatty sofa. Mick held it up so Harley could read the hand notation on the ancient cover.

"River Church notes. I.C."

"He said he had some ideas. Maybe he found a connection between the die-off and the church." He raised his voice. "Kippy?"

Harley tapped his shoulder. "The cellar door is open. Look."

Mick's feet turned heavy with dread. Old men fell down sometimes. Old men got sick. Old men were perhaps more vulnerable to forces preferring to be left unchallenged.

He went first, switched on the stairway light and went down the first step before the smell of blood hit him.

Kippy Evert was a motionless sprawl midway up the stairs, arms outstretched, one hand clinging stiff and gray to the lip of the next riser. His back bristled with jutting metal objects and his face was turned toward the upstairs door, toward an escape that never came. Mick glanced at his filmy blue eyes as if to confirm what the blood and the rigid posture already told him. His knees buckled with cruel acknowledgement.

"Ho, Jesus," Harley said and snatched the back of Mick's shirt. It was the only thing that kept him from pitching headlong down the stairs. "Come on. We don't need to get any closer."

"He's dead," Mick said, only because the words needed to come out. They were blocking everything else. "And somebody . . . do you see?"

"Yeah," Harley said, and took a moment to stare and to process.

Two of the long objects in Kippy's back were pressed in deeper than the others. On the step above Kippy's head and then another step two risers higher, which put it near Mick's current position, were spade-shaped prints rendered in blood. Shoe prints. Going up.

"They stepped on him," Mick said. It was another blockage that required clearing. "Whoever did this stepped on his back on the way out."

Harley tugged his shirt again. "Let's go make some calls. On the porch, in the fresh air. Damn."

They took a moment to lean on the porch railing and collect their thoughts. A car sailed by and Geralyn Medford waved from behind the wheel. They did not wave back. At last, Harley nudged him. "You want to get out your phone, or should I use the one in Kippy's living room?"

"Let me check one thing before the whole place is locked down as investigative evidence."

His gaze switched to the box near Kippy's door, knowing with impossible certainty it was the one he'd seen Kippy toss into The Crymost only a few days ago. He picked it up, turned it over, opened it.

"Not the kind of thing you leave outside, usually, is it?" Harley asked.

"Not unless you want somebody to notice it," Mick said and took a single slip of paper from the interior of the box. He read it and turned it over for Harley to see.

An equation of sorts was written in a halting hand.

THEKAN = CLOSED DOWN RIVER CHURCH = IRMA CASPER

"Kippy's research."

"Orlin's widow?" Harley took the note, eyed it. "What's she got to do with this?"

"I.C. is Irma Casper. That book inside, or what was left of it, was hers. Probably full of information about the church, and anyone involved in its closing, judges included."

Another car rolled by, this time with a friendly toot of the horn.

"Jesus, we better call before half the town sees us standing out here," Harley said.

Mick put the box and the note in his car before making the necessary call, waves of sick rage pulsing through him.

Soon Field Street was lined with official vehicles including a Twin Lakes County Sheriff's car and a coroner's van. Neighbors gathered in clutches, and Mick and Harley were separately questioned on the scene. When the detective questioning Mick told him not to leave town, Mick asked if he was a suspect.

"We'll be in touch," the detective said and snapped his notebook closed, ending the exchange.

Harley was still talking with a second detective, so Mick took the time to call Judy.

"I heard," she said with a hundred questions stirring behind her words. "Connie Gassner told me you were there, and not to call you because the police were talking to you. What happened?"

"I'll give you details when I see you, but the Cliff's Notes version is this: I think Kippy was on to something about the die-off and it got him killed."

"God, Mick. Where is this headed?"

"You should call Beth Ann."

"Already did. I'm on my way to see her right now."

"Good. You two stay at Kroener's. We'll come as soon as we can."

Behind him a van sporting the logo for Channel Seven News pulled up and Jim Scanlon himself, star of the local evening news, climbed out, brushed at his silver hair and set his square jaw.

Harley walked over a minute later. "God, I hate this shit. Been through it before, when George Bintzler keeled over on a job just the other side of Pitch Road. I was mucking out culverts for the spring runoff when I found him. And the cops' first protocol is to think you're not a finder at all, but some kind of killer."

Mick put on his best gruff detective face. "We'll be in touch."

His phone rang and he was met by Will Adelmeyer's voice. "I think you better come over to the bar. There's been a development."

He dealt Harley a *what now* expression. "We've got problems right now."

"I heard. Just come as soon as possible, okay?"

CHAPTER FOUR

Will Adelmeyer came out to meet them when they got to The Chapel Bar.

"This wasn't here when I left." Will indicated a spray-painted line traced across his parking lot. It continued between the houses on the other side of Backbank in an easterly attitude. "But I get the feeling it adds to our worries. This and poor Kippy. Was it murder?"

"We know it was," Harley said.

Will nodded slow and thoughtful. "Here's the other thing," Will said at last and swept his hand close to the painted line. "Look at the way it starts at the edge of my building and goes off this way. It almost seems like somebody is—"

"Tracing out the tunnel." Mick finished it for him because he saw it too. "That means somebody else knows about it."

Will furrowed his brow. "But who?"

The voice from the sidewalk made them all turn to look. "Why don't you ask Cy Vandergalien?"

Nancy Berns stood on the sidewalk behind them. She held the leash of a tiny, breed-ambiguous dog who was currently doing his business in the terrace grass. When none of them spoke, she went on. "Cy is painting a line all the way through town, across people's yards, over the sidewalks, the streets, leaving empty spray cans as he goes. I thought maybe it had something to do with tomorrow's vote, but that can't be right."

Mick watched her. "How did he seem to you, Nancy?"

"Nervous." She stooped to collect her dog's deposit in a plastic bag. "But after poor Kippy, I suppose we're all going to be a little twitchy. Who would want to murder a nice old man like him? And right here in Knoll."

Mick approached her. "Listen, Nancy. We're trying to keep close tabs on what's been happening in town. Sort of watchdogging. Do you think you can do something for us?"

An intrigued smile blossomed on her face. "Name it."

"If you hear anything out of the ordinary, whether you're walking your dog or out on one of your emergency calls, could you let us know? Me or Harley, or Will? Anything at all."

She laughed as if he'd just made a gross understatement. "In this town, I can almost guarantee there'll be something. Sure, I'll keep you posted. By the way, last time I saw Cy he was crossing Tier Street. Maybe twenty minutes ago. It looked like he was painting his way right out of town, in case you're interested."

"Thank you, dear," Harley said and waved her on.

Mick dialed Cy and got no answer. He glanced plaintively at Harley and Will. "Are you thinking what I'm thinking?"

Harley began walking to the car. "You bet your ass. Let's go."

"Guess I'll be opening the bar late today," Will said and followed them.

Mick drove with Harley riding shotgun and Will in the back. There was no sign of Cy on Tier Street, just the diagonal line of black paint across the pavement.

"Let's go right to the mercantile," Mick said and made the turn onto The Plank.

"Somebody's out there, all right," Will said as they pulled off the road near the mercantile's weedy driveway. "But it's not Cy. Why are they in the middle of the parking lot like that?"

Chastity Mellar Borth's gleaming black car was parked thirty feet or so from the side of the building. Two people stood near it, examining the ground. One was Chastity Mellar Borth wearing a colorful, very new blouse and skirt combination. The other was Thekan in a white shirt with cufflinks and charcoal slacks. His hair was pulled back into a ponytail. They looked up at the sound of the car.

"Let's go make nice," Mick said. "Test the water."

"Left my diplomat's hat at home," Harley said.

They got out and walked to the shoulder where the drive-around at the front of the mercantile fed into the remnants of the parking lot. This left an expanse of twenty feet between them and the place where Chastity and the Judge stood. The paint line lay stark and neat on the shattered shell of pavement between them.

Mick said the first thing to come into his mind. "Something historical about that line, Your Honor?"

Chastity took a step forward and placed her sandaled foot on the paint. "Nothing historical about petty vandalism, Mr. Logan. Nothing in the least."

"Not much of a vandal, making a single stripe."

The line, he saw now, ended just behind Thekan's heels, even though Cy's last abandoned spray can rested another thirty feet away next to the building.

"An uncreative attempt," Thekan said and held out his hands over the sorry state of Knoll's miscreants. He glanced backward at the mercantile, but only fleeting. "If there is a message here, I'm afraid it is lost on me."

"And yet, somebody went to the trouble," Mick said.

His eyes remained fixed on Thekan's black dress shoes with their unfashionably pointed toes for two reasons. First, he was unable to stop replaying the image of the bloody spade-like shoe prints on Kippy's stairs. And second, the paint line near Thekan's feet was fading inch by inch, as if evaporating off the earth as he stared. A few days ago he might have gawped at such an occurrence with amazement, but not now. Not after Peter Fyvie, and the bar, and Harley's hospital room. Now his regard was one of dour acceptance.

He heard Harley mutter behind him. "What the hell? Do you see that?"

"I do."

"People with flawed agendas sometimes go to great lengths," Thekan said, his shoulders rigid, his eyes hard. "Too arrogant to see the futility of their actions. Sometimes they need a sign to direct them, to shoo them away from their needless acts like summer flies. Do you believe in signs, Mr. Logan?"

"I believe in a lot of things, Thekan. Signs from the past. Signs from the dead, even."

From behind him, Will said, "I want to go, now."

"Yeah," Harley said and put a hand on Mick's shoulder. His voice sounded strained. "Me, too."

Mick's first reaction was to challenge the two men behind him, but it was quelled by the sensation of an idea being dashed against the back of his head, like an outside thought searching for entry. Its message leaked in with the sketchiness of a storm-ravaged radio signal. *You want to leave this place,* it said, *you want to leave this place now.*

It was all the explanation he needed. Thekan was getting inside Will's thoughts, and Harley's. His own well-formed mental doors of resistance, on the other hand, were holding. He wondered for how long. "I think your vandal is on to something, Thekan. Does it trouble you that people are figuring you out?"

"Presumption has always troubled me." Thekan's hands swept out before him as if making a presentation. "Especially when it inspires the uneducated. Stay away from this, Mick Logan. Listen to your friends. Go away from here."

"How long do you think it will be before this town realizes what you are? Some know it already, am I right?"

Mick directed his gaze at Chastity Mellar Borth. She turned away from him, her face hard and neutral. Then he inched closer, his heart hammering, an accusatory finger aimed at the Judge.

"You might be trying to clear the way for whatever is descending on this town, but certain things can't be erased or eradicated from the world, Thekan. And there are those of us who have a pretty good idea of what's coming. And we mean to fight it."

"You challenge that which you know little about." Thekan raised his hands like a pastor commanding his congregation to rise. "That, Mr. Logan, is folly."

"We won't be intimidated."

Thekan's eyes narrowed to slits. His mouth trembled. "Folly," he said again.

A hot spot of pain bloomed on Mick's right shoulder. It was followed by the sound of a stone tumbling away. He clutched at the pain, his gaze caught by hints of motion around Thekan's feet. Broken pavement vibrated there, restless, as if trying to tear free of the ground. Before Mick could react, a softball sized hunk of tar and concrete tore free from the ground and rocketed forward, catching him on the thigh.

"What the hell?" Harley asked again, just before an acorn-sized fragment clopped him on the forehead and drew blood. Half a dozen more scraps of pavement lifted in the air, suspended in the sunny May afternoon.

"Let's go," Mick said. "To the car. Now."

They all turned in retreat. A chunk the size of an apple caught Mick's elbow and sent pins and needles up to his shoulder and down to his fingertips. Another struck him on the shoulder blade. Another bounced off the fender of his car with an efficient clunk. Will let go with a throaty "Holy crap," as a particularly large portion slammed into his lower back and nearly sent him sprawling.

They got into the car and Mick pulled away quickly, but not before one last look in the rear-view mirror. Chastity gazed after them with dazed astonishment. Thekan stood in the shade of the mercantile trees, his hands on his knees, either panting with exhaustion . . . or laughing.

CHAPTER FIVE

"That was some kind of freakshow," Will said from the backseat. A trickle of blood trailed down his cheek to his chin. His hair was mussed in a way that would have been comical had the circumstances been different. "The rocks was one thing. But it was like he was in my head, too, telling me I should leave."

"What was it you said about this?" Harley asked. "Forces at work? That's what we've got here, all right. Thekan included, the murdering bastard."

"You noticed his shoes, too," Mick said.

"Sure as hell did."

Will sat forward. "What about his shoes?"

Mick's hands twisted at the wheel. "Kippy Evert's killer stepped on him like he was some kind of garbage, and left shoe prints in the process. I bet you ten to one the prints will match those outdated shoes of Thekan's."

"Then we've got him," Will said. "If the cops are told about it—"

"They'll question him." Mick made a suggestion at the futility of it with his hand. "And that might be nothing more than a waste of time. You saw what he's capable of doing to people's thoughts. More than saw it, you were subjected to it. What's to say he won't fill up their heads with a bunch of dismissive reasoning? Put them pretty much in his pocket? It seems he's already hooked Chastity Mellar Borth by the gills, and who knows how many others in town since he's been making the rounds like a regular circuit preacher."

"Only it's not the good word he's spreading around, that's for damned sure." Harley touched the bloody knot above his eyebrow and winced. "He's dangerous. And he's got us singled out as troublemakers now."

Mick parked in front of his house and looked directly at both of them. "Are we up for a car trip? After we let the wives know we haven't been trucked off in county jail jumpsuits, of course."

Will blinked. "I thought we were going to tour the tunnel this afternoon."

"Since we're clearly in Thekan's crosshairs, I think there's something else we need to do first," Mick said.

Harley was already nodding. "Irma Casper."

CHAPTER SIX

Mick would think later about the phrase *best laid plans*. But initially, when Judy met them at the Kroener's door, what registered was the scattered clumps of earth and broken crockery in the front entrance and his wife's harried expression. "I was just about to call you."

A moan from the living room punctuated it.

Harley, who was just behind Mick, pushed past the both of them and rushed in. "Beth Ann. Oh Christ, not now. Stay still." Then over his shoulder he said, "Could I get some water and a cold rag?"

Judy responded and Mick let her go. The air felt heavy and electrified with urgency. The calm sway of the trees outside was like a contrary gesture from another world. He ducked into the living room.

"Migraine," Harley said. "One of her bad ones." He was on his knees next to the couch where his wife was stretched out, pale and panting.

Judy returned, cloth in hand. "We were talking and she just went down. Like a dead faint. She took a bunch of houseplants down with her."

Harley took the cloth and began daubing his wife's cheeks. "How bad is it, honey pie?"

Beth Ann's hair fell across her face in stray tangles. A rim of blood seeped into the outer edge of her left eye. "My miracle," she said with a cracked type of discovery. Her arms creaked upward to receive him with underwater slowness. "Oh, praises be. Oh, angels."

Will stood in the doorway, seeming lost. Mick shrugged. "I never knew she was prone to migraines."

"She mentioned it once, but—what happened to you? Your lip is bleeding." She glanced at Will, noted his injuries and turned back, more wide-eyed.

"I'll explain in a minute," he said. "How is she, Harley? Do you need anything else?"

"Just to get her up to bed is all," Harley said and eased Beth Ann to her feet.

"I'm not seeing so well," she said, her searching left eye halfway flooded over with crimson. "Oh, Harley, it's a bad one." And then to Judy, "I'm sorry to be such a disappointing bother."

Judy intervened, slipped an arm around Beth Ann and led her to the hall, speaking in the low confident tones of friendship. She glanced back at Mick before mounting the stairs and the meaning in her expression was clear. *Go to it, Mister. Whatever it is, just go.* Mick's heart swelled. His brilliant Judy.

He stepped up to Harley. "You need to stay here. Be with your wife."

"I hate like hell to leave you boys."

"You'll hate leaving Beth Ann even more. Don't sweat it. Will and I can handle this."

"Sure." Will stepped up, his hands working against one another. "We've got this nursing home thing."

"Bring back something. Anything. Jesus, I hope Irma's lucid."

Mick nodded. "Me, too."

CHAPTER SEVEN

The Drury Meadows Long Term Care Facility used a lot of white in their decorating: receiving desk, walls, side tables, ceilings, and floors. If it was an attempt to project sterility or bright cheer, it failed. The place merely seemed uncertain and blurred as if viewed through a cataract eye. Will fidgeted next to Mick, taking it all in with a sort of controlled alarm as they waited. Finally, he said, "It's as if everyone here is waiting for something."

The profoundness of it left Mick without a reply. It reminded him of Robbie Vaughn's dark handshake.

A nurse in powder blue scrubs came up and took them to a day room large enough to hold a dozen people but was, at the moment, empty. They sat in worn and faintly stained armchairs near a bank of windows overlooking a stream lined with old willow trees. The sun threw rectangles of light at their feet.

The nurse slipped away for only a moment and returned pushing Irma Casper in a wheelchair. Irma was petite, as Mick expected. She wore a flowered blouse a mile too big for her, stretch slacks and slippers patterned after ballet shoes. What he didn't expect was the conspiratorial expression on her tiny, lined face. It shone beneath her sheaf of thin, white hair and added a brightness to her nearly colorless eyes.

"Hello, Irma," he said and got out of his chair to crouch next to her.

"Hi," Will added with a wave.

The nurse seemed satisfied with the exchange and stepped away.

"Irma, we're from Knoll," Mick said. "Do you remember Knoll?"

There was a slight twitch in her jaw, but there was no change in her expression of unshared secrets.

Will sat forward and looked directly at her, almost into her. His hand covered one of the thick-veined claws on the wheelchair armrest. "We want to know about the old church. And a man who we think helped shut the place down. A man named Roderick Thekan."

Sighing violin music, so low it was nearly nonexistent, was drifting down from an overhead speaker. It cut out. Came back with a crackle. It made Mick think of Harley's hospital room. Then thin notes of sound escaped Irma Casper's throat, so light they seemed to sail like dandelion fluff. "Thekan. The judge from Royal Center."

"Yes." Mick leaned closer. "That's the one."

Irma's voice startled them. "Thekan did more than shut down the church with a casual bang of his gavel. He took the last breath."

"His last breath, Irma?" Will added his other hand to his grip on her. "Did he die there?"

Her brow furrowed as she stared into a well of memories. Outside, the sun slipped behind a cloud. Wind stirred the willows. The music cut out again, and this time it stayed out. "No. He *took* the breath *from* the church. Forced all the good air out. Knocked the sanctity right out of the place with one thoughtless decree. All in a day's work for him. Even though the town needed that little bit of godliness in light of what was coming, as it turned out. Took it and regretted it, I'd say. He died all right, in his Royal Center home, a week after he made his foolish decree, right while other folks started passing away in Mellar's Knoll."

A shiver, part chill and part obsession, fell over Mick. "How did he die, Irma?"

Her slippered feet began to bounce on the footrests of her chair. "Who knows why men of power make the decisions they do. But they make 'em, just like that." Her free hand rose into the air, her wizened fingers pinched, and she made a twisting motion. "I believe he was warned not to shut up the church, warned by those who knew better, but he went ahead. And when Knoll folk started dying not two sunrises later, he felt the weight of what he done. Unbearable weight. He locked himself up in his home, agonizing over how to make it right, and realized he couldn't because the dead were piling up in Mellar's Knoll like cordwood. Ending it all for himself was his final decision. And that he did. With two nails and a board."

Every telephone in Drury Meadows rang in unison, creating a single sustained note. The overhead lights blinked. The air seethed with energy. Mick felt the small hairs on his body bristle. Will looked around, pale but determined. "This is unbelievable."

Mick nodded and then, with revelation, he said to Irma, "What do you mean by nails and a board?"

She raised her gnarled fingers in the air near her eyes in a forked fashion. "Done it himself. Board was laid out on his kitchen table with two big old spikey nails, points up. Slammed his head down, hands behind his back as if he was at some kind of pie eat. Them nails went clear through his peepers and into his brain meat. He should have brought some of the good air back first, if he was so sorry. It coulda been done. Still can be done for all I know, if you got the right fire of devotion in you."

The lights went out and the gloom was nearly suffocating. Alarms ramped up from rooms where critical equipment sensed the loss of power. Nurses scattered.

A voice cracked from the overhead speakers, a yawning and distorted declaration. *"Out of Knoll."*

Toilets flushed in every room. The seething air turned heavy. The halls filled with shouting nurses. "Shit," Mick said.

Irma's eyes fixed on Will, burning with imperative need. Her free hand clamped down on his. "My Orlin wants you to know you need the good air at your backs, boys."

"And the tributes." Will raised his voice, his face twisted with bafflement over the words coming out of his mouth. He jerked like a man being electrocuted. "We sent as many as we could. Sent them while The Crymost began its stirring." He attempted to free his hands from the grip entwining them, but was unable. With panic, but more control, he said, "Mick, what's happening to me?"

"Enough, goddamn it."

Mick reached over and pried the old woman's hands away from Will's. A heavy blow shook the building. The window behind them cracked in a huge silver X shape. Mick staggered back into one of the armchairs. Residents' voices rose up from the halls and the nearby rooms in a chorus, some of them sprung from dusty vocal chords unused for months, or years. What they exclaimed was clear for all of its feeble ululations. "*Out of Knoll.*"

The character of the air changed with the abruptness of a summer dust devil's collapse. It took on the stale, vacant attributes one not only accepted in such a place but came to expect. The music and the lights blinked on. Drury Meadows returned to its proper cataract state.

Will backed away from Irma on unsteady feet. "Wow. My heart's going ninety miles an hour and my balls feel wrapped up somewhere around my kidneys. Was I really talking about The Crymost just now?"

"You were. Should you sit down?"

Will shook his head and set his gaze on Irma. "Is she going to be all right? If she got the same vibes I did, I'm surprised she's not stroking out right now."

Mick crouched next to Irma's chair once again. "Irma, what is good air? How do we get it? And these tributes that were sent, who has them?"

Irma slumped, her eyes dull windows, devoid of any brightness or conspiracy. He thought of a vessel with its contents poured out.

"We're done," he said to Will and stood up again. "Goddamn it."

CHAPTER EIGHT

"So, there's good air, which I kind of understand," Will said when they were on the road, "and tributes, which are trinkets pushed over here by some kind of creepy intervention but probably look like they're barfed up by The Crymost. And spooks shouting 'out of Knoll' at us."

Peter Fyvie flickered through Mick's thoughts. "Ghosts. It's a simple term, but you can use it."

"Great. So we got Boo-Berry and Christmas Yet To Come tossing knickknacks around town. Unbelievable."

"You're not as hard headed as Kippy might have thought. Good for you. And I think our 'out of Knoll' crowd is more like Hamlet's father, laying it on the line for us, planting ideas, using any mouthpiece they can find, hopeful we'll do something about it." Mick was starting to relax. They turned onto Highway 130, which meant home was only a half hour away. "Something sure brought the chaos to Drury Meadows back there."

Will made a humorless laugh. "Chaos again, you mean. Like at my bar, or what you told me about Harley's hospital room."

"It makes me believe we're on the right track about certain things."

"And certain people. Our friend the Honorable Judge Suicide, to be exact."

Mick slowly nodded. His heart was thumping in an agonized way he hadn't known since he looked into Robbie Vaughn's coffin and found it empty. "But Thekan is no ghost. Hell, I don't know exactly *what* he is. Everything is so balls up. My head is a mess."

"You found a dead body today for crying out loud, and then faced off with His-Honor-Dead-Head—we've both got the bruises to prove it—and talked with an old lady who was serving as a ham radio for the great beyond with me as the speaker system. I think you put in a full day, my friend."

When summarized in such a way, it seemed stymying. His old therapists would have had a field day with it. "But we have so much we need to find out," he said and scowled into the late afternoon light. "And I feel like we're running out of time. Don't you?"

Will said nothing, just struck a thoughtful pose, hand to mouth. At last he said, "One thing we can do is show up for the vote tomorrow and do our damnedest to make sure Mellar's Mercantile is voted to stay, because for whatever reason, it's part of the whole 'Let It Not Return' plan which makes it something we need. Am I right?"

"The mercantile," Mick said, nodding, "and good air."

CHAPTER NINE

Mick found Judy in the living room. The TV was on and there was a half-finished beer on the coffee table. Uncharacteristic of her, especially before dinner. She got up when he walked in.

"Harley wants you to call him," she said. "How severe is this, Mick? How deep does it go?"

"Deep," he said and took her in his arms." How is Beth Ann?"

She relayed Harley's information. A dose of medication—the heavy stuff, as he worded it—put Beth Ann in a restful state. "I've never seen a migraine affect someone in such a way," she explained with controlled anguish, a Judy-type of anguish if ever there was one. "And her breathing was so labored, like she couldn't get enough air."

He took some of her beer. It was cool and rewarding. Almost gracious, but he said nothing. Judy's words, part of them or perhaps all, set off a deep-running correlation he was unable to pin down. It slipped by him and was gone in a blink.

"Are you zoning out on me?" Judy finally said.

"Sorry. Bells going off for no reason."

"I've told you what I know. It's your turn." She tapped his hurt lip which was now an angry scab. "Tell me everything."

Before he was done they moved to the kitchen. There was a casserole in the oven and the sun painted the wall with the color of polished brass. He took his shirt off as he talked. A good sized knot had formed on the elbow struck by Thekan's pavement hail and he held an ice pack to it. After an officious inspection of his back, Judy informed him his shoulder blade was badly bruised. He felt no pain there, only a dull ache when she pressed on it.

"We should turn him in, press charges," Judy said.

He walked around and began to set the table. "Turn him in to whom? Last time I checked, Knoll was fresh out of exorcists."

Another alarm bell went off in his head. *Source: unclear.*

Judy leaned back, arms crossed, lips pressed together. "I can't believe we're alone in this, the few of us."

"Others have got to be noticing. I think if we try, we can get some neighbors on board. They should be people we trust, however."

"Those with an open mind, you mean. That's going to be a tough one."

His phone rang. It was Cy Vandergalien. His voice was defeated, somewhat ghostly. "Did you see it?"

"The line you painted in honor of Knoll's secret tunnel? Yes, we saw it."

"The line that *was* painted, you mean. It's been rubbed out like it never happened. And it's not really a tunnel. It's a shaft."

Mick felt a new coldness drift over him. "A shaft for good air?"

"Where did you hear that?"

"We've got to talk, Cy. I mean it."

"If you want to talk anytime other than now, you'll have to do it long distance because tomorrow I will be across the Illinois border. I've got family in Itasca, you know."

"Please, don't abandon Knoll now. You know too much. At least give us some guidance before you go."

"We can meet up, but not for you or Knoll or anybody else's sake. I want to see that shaft, I guess," Cy said with a hint of his old determination. "For real, not just a line on an old map."

Mick gripped the phone tight enough to make his knuckles ache. "We can go down there right now if you want. Will Adelmeyer will let us in through the bar basement, and I know Harley will want to come."

"Not now," Cy said as if such impromptu planning was unheard of in these matters. "I'll put my trip off a few hours more. I'll go with you and whatever band of monkeys you want to bring. Tomorrow, after the vote. Then I'm in my Ram and down the road."

"We'll be glad to have you. Until then, be careful. Got it? Cy?"

He'd hung up.

They ate in silence and afterward Judy brought beer onto the back porch for the both of them. "How did we end up in the middle of this? Why us?"

He wanted to say it was inevitable, they were marked as beings who were not allowed enduring rest. There were stretches of peace, like long lulling railroad rides, but harsh places waited down the line. Dark stations. You stepped off when your stop came up, clutched what little baggage you owned and hoped to find your way through the fog and the night.

One of those stops for them was at a station called Robbie Vaughn, labeled in neat, tombstone lettering. It harbored shocking death, mental anguish and the grim yet satisfying news of another youth— Justin Wick—meeting his end at the Cedar Ridge Boys' Detention Center via an overdose of smuggled-in narcotics the night of Robbie's funeral. This new station stop was designated by a placard twice as large as any others, and painted in spider-thin letters that seemed to squirm if you stared too long. And its name was Crymost.

He wanted to say it out loud, but Judy would just tell him his poet's soul was showing, so instead he said, "Because we're in-the-thick-of-it types of people."

She nodded, as if it were the perfect answer, and squeezed his hand.

CHAPTER TEN

"God, I love pussy," Axel said and immediately found it uproariously funny.

He laughed out loud, despite the young woman splayed beneath him in the back seat, panting as he slid into her with a ravenous thrust. Funny despite, or perhaps on account of, the two primo joints he'd rolled from the Judge's bag. The effect burned bright and hard inside of him. *Hard.* He laughed again, and it slipped along deliciously with the sensation engulfing his cock.

The girl, whose name was Charlotte, or Charlene, or something, gave him a puzzled upward glance that melted away beneath a soft moan. Bar sounds traveled across the parking lot like the music of dreams. Rusty's Roadhouse, the place was called, and it was on the outskirts of Baylor. One of his favorite hangouts. The women always seemed to be hot and ready. Whatever Rusty was serving them, Axel wanted a bottle to take home.

He drove himself deep with the press of his hips and Charlotte or Charlene made an equally immersed moan. Headlights flared past. Not a problem; the regulars at Rusty's knew what the back row of the parking lot was reserved for and steered clear. *Respect among pussy-lovers,* he thought and snorted more laughter in the back of his throat.

When the car door opened at his back and the cabin became flooded with interior light, he did not immediately grasp what was happening. A hand bunched his shirt collar and dragged him out, and things began to gel. This was Charlotte or Charlene's boyfriend, and he was about to be at the receiving end of some roadhouse wrath. Goddamn it. He planted his feet and turned around. His pants were around his ankles. His dick bobbed in the air and it made him feel somehow idiotic, but it also fueled his need to defend himself. His fists clenched.

But there was no boyfriend. Thekan stood in front of him, his face hard. "We have work. It has to be now."

"What the fuck, man?"

Thekan glanced into the back seat and his pupils flared. "You're done here, understand?"

Charlotte/Charlene slipped into her panties and denim skirt as casually as tamping out a cigarette and let herself out of the opposite door. She walked toward the roadhouse with dreamy indifference and did not look back.

"What kind of work?" Axel groped at the clothing wreathed around his shoes and attempted to pull them up, but came away empty handed because he was standing on a majority of his jeans and underwear.

"Heavy work," Thekan said to him. "Necessary work."

Thekan's hand latched onto his cock, heavy and hot. It made him jump. "What the hell?"

The hand on his organ squeezed hard, a single flex. The climax that flared through Axel's body seemed to draw every muscle and tendon toward a central molten core and then release in a thousand flashpoints. His breath left him in a shuddering gust. His cum shot out in a blurt across Rusty's Roadhouse pavement. And as he was poured out, so was he filled up. The heavy work became clear in his head. It was at once loathsome.

"Now pull yourself together," Thekan said. He scrubbed his hand on the leg of his trousers as he spoke. "We'll meet at the mill."

Axel pulled up his pants, with greater success this time. His primo weed buzz was fading, soaking away as quickly as the jizz on the blacktop. "Does it have to be?" he asked.

Thekan backed toward his ride, the Mellar Borth bitch's car. He dangled the keys playfully in the air and the engine turned over. "I'm afraid it does."

CHAPTER ELEVEN

Chastity Mellar Borth stood up from her bedroom vanity and took a tentative step toward the door. The heels were the highest she'd worn in a long time but the pain in her feet was a mere mumble compared to the roaring agony that lived in her bones and muscles only a few short days ago. Such comparisons made it hard to think about Roderick (not the Judge anymore, not after, well, not after certain repeated intimacies) with any type of suspicion. She owed him for her well-being, and for the imminent return of the town to her hands. Even if the mercantile was (will be) voted away, the setup in her front lawn, so much like a sleeping carnival, was a final wooing to bring the village of Knoll back into the arms of a Mellar, as it should be.

But what he'd done today, to Mick Logan and those others, sullied her appreciation. Roderick's gifts went far beyond a touch-and-heal marvel. They crossed into the territory of volatile and worrisome. Even frightening.

She stared across the hall to the room where Roderick sometimes slept. Sometimes, when he wasn't in her bed pursuing needs which grew rougher, more ravenous with each encounter like a restless wheel picking up power and momentum at every turn. Was it madness to question him? Wasn't there always a fine line between suspicion and curiosity, as fine as new silk?

She opened the door to Roderick's room. Sparse and tidy. He'd brought few possessions with him, and a majority of the clothes she brought for him to wear (Gregor's) were neatly folded and stacked on the dresser. Unremarkable. But there had to be something of interest here. Something to satisfy her curiosity.

Suspicion.

She went to the closet. The dreadful wool suit he'd worn the day they met was draped on a hanger. Almost automatically she slipped her hand into the front pocket of the jacket. *Let me find, let me know.*

She found something. Many somethings. Cool and loose like tiny soft seeds. Some of them seemed to stick. She pulled out her hand.

Maggots covered her palm, her fingers, her knuckles. It was like wearing an undulating glove that broke into a thousand specks and slithered over her wrist, up her arm. Her thoughts clashed with new revilement and dark fear. The mirror above the dresser goggled at her like a surprised and betrayed eye. The windows yawned like blaming mouths: *he knows you're here, knows you suspect.*

A tiny white shape wriggled into the neckline of her blouse. It explored her breast with a feather-light nuzzle. She screamed and shook her swarming hand wildly as she ran back to her own bedroom.

Daddy's rosary, draped over her mirror, clacked against the glass as she swept by. She grabbed a handkerchief from her dresser, scrubbed at her arm over and over, even though the wriggling whiteness was already gone. Perhaps never there at all. A sob escaped her. Across the hall, the door to Roderick's room swung shut with a thump.

He knows I suspect. Oh, God, he knows.

CHAPTER TWELVE

Mick decided it would be better to sit down with Harley and fill him in. Judy followed him to the car. "Not without me, you're not."

Harley let them in. His eyes were red and fretful. "Let's sit in the living room," he said, keeping his voice low. "Beth Ann is sleeping and the sound travels less from there."

Mick went through everything quickly. Harley's first question was directed at Judy.

"And how is all of this agreeing with you?"

"It isn't. But I can't deny it. Not after what I've seen, and not when the people I love dearly are in it up to their eyeballs. I just wish we knew what the hell we're supposed to do."

A thump on the stairs made them all look around. Beth Ann stuck her head around the corner, her expression shrouded in the slack remnants of drugged sleep. Her left eye glinted, an unpleasant crimson jewel.

"Oh, company," she said.

One hand skimmed over her unruly sheaf of hair. A small gold cross glittered at her throat.

Harley glanced at his watch. "Time for another pill, isn't it, honey pie?"

"I hate taking them," she said with a shrug of near embarrassment.

"Do you want to sit with us?" Judy moved over to make room between her and Mick on the sofa. "What we're talking about involves you, too."

"Thanks, but no," she said and fingered her cross. "I can barely see straight for the pain."

"All right." Judy got up to give her a gentle hug. "We'll talk tomorrow."

Beth Ann nodded and stepped away, toward the kitchen.

Mick watched it all with intensity. Far back in his head another quick slip of correlation. "Good air," he said.

The doorbell chimed. Harley went to answer it, said only a few words, then returned to the living room with Nancy Berns at his side. She seemed a little daunted, but her eyes were as bright as ever.

"Hi Judy, nice to see you." Then to Mick, "Funny how I went to your house first and when I didn't get an answer I came here, and here you all are."

She made a nervous laugh and shifted a manila envelope from one hand to the other.

"Take a load off." Harley motioned to a chair next to his own. There was a basket of knitting on the arm. Beth Ann's chair.

"I can't stay. I just came over because, you know, what we talked about this afternoon."

Mick sat forward. "You found something?"

"Sort of stole it, actually." She handed the envelope to Harley. "It's Cy's."

Harley slipped his cheaters on and dug into the packet of papers with interest.

Nancy went on. "Cy hasn't been himself lately. Forgetting things, daydreaming a lot. And with the spray painting business this afternoon, I'm worried about his state of mind. Anyway, that—" she aimed a stout finger at the pages in Harley's hands "—was in his locker at the firehouse. He's usually pretty protective over that locker. Me and Stu Rueplinger joke about how he keeps the family fortune in there. But today, it was hanging open and the only thing inside was that. I don't know if it's the kind of odd you're looking for, but it raised my eyebrows, I'll tell you."

"What have we got?" Mick asked.

"It appears Cy was planning on buying up the mercantile property and then selling it off for a nice profit. Got a bunch of paperwork drawn up already, including a village order to begin tearing the mercantile down immediately after the vote passes. It explains his big push on the *Mellar's Out* campaign. Let the village foot the bill to raze the place and pull those leaky tanks out of the ground, then buy it all up as open land."

"But he's for *Mellar's In* now," Judy said.

Nancy nodded. "He made us switch all the posters at the firehouse, red to green, just like that." She held out her hand as if to receive a handshake, and then flip-flopped it in the air. "It's a state of mind thing, I tell you."

"Or his realization," Harley said, "that we need the mercantile to stand because it's a major part of our concern."

"What concern?" Nancy eyed them, still bright but penetrating too. "If you mean the funny feeling in the air, or the run of local catastrophes, or the glow at The Crymost, you don't have to twist my arm to convince me it's all connected."

"We're trying to piece it together ourselves," Mick said. "And we'd appreciate any other help or information we can get. From anywhere."

"I'm with you. And I think a lot of other people in town will be too. I can work the crowd at tomorrow's vote and see what else I can drum up."

"That's our plan, too," Judy said. "More or less."

"Thank you for your help," Mick said.

"And one other thing about Cy." Nancy held up a finger in a lest-I-forget gesture. "Not only was his locker nearly empty, but he cleared out his desk at the firehouse. And the mill is closed down tight as a drum. None of it looks good."

"We plan to meet with him right after the vote," Mick said to her, but not before passing a wary glance to the rest. "He wants in on our findings too."

"I hope something can be done," she said. Her eyes still twinkled with a lively Nancy Berns twinkle. "Knoll is a dangerous place these days."

"Be careful out there," Mick said.

"You know it," she said and made another nervous laugh on her way out.

Mick bit his lip, unaware of it until the split-open portion began to bleed. Harley came back from seeing Nancy out and let out an anxious breath. "Tomorrow," he said.

They acknowledged it with a grim nod.

CHAPTER THIRTEEN

Will Adelmeyer walked from the bar to the front door and sipped a scotch. *All praise the righteous and the good.* The thought surfaced in the back of his mind. It was not a memory but something he found banging about in the clutter of his head one day while reflecting on the history of his bar. It evoked images of a congregation standing from their crude pews lined up where his table seating now shared space with the dart machines and a booth housing almost-legal video spin and win games in deference to an occupied altar, which was now his back bar, the shrine of piety and salvation replaced by the glitter of temptation. The phrase visited him from time to time, like the chime of an old clock, neither an annoyance nor a comfort.

The occurrences of the last few days seemed heavier when he was alone, and he thought about calling Mick Logan, just to touch base. Instead he drained his glass—normally he didn't touch the wares of his back bar when he was alone, but tonight he made an exception—and stepped up to his narrow front windows.

The view was not much, just a segment of Backbank Street and a pool of light from the streetlamp. But as he watched, two cars drove by: Chastity Mellar Borth's Lincoln and Axel Vandergalien's Passat. Axel's car followed the other so closely its grille was nearly planted on the other vehicle's bumper. It reminded him of a dog running nose to tail with a companion. The Lincoln swerved as it passed the bar and took out the Carmichaels's mailbox across the street. The streetlight gleam offered a glimpse of the driver: broad shoulders and the fall of a silver ponytail.

He backed away, contemplating, and poured another scotch.

CHAPTER FOURTEEN

Cy Vandergalien paced around the upstairs mill office, the desk lamp throwing wild shadows across the walls. His mother's brooch was in his palm, nested in a pocket of painful divots. He checked his watch. It was only a matter of hours now before he'd be on the road to Itasca with his dear Alice at his side and this town long gone in the rearview mirror. Just as well to wait until after the vote. Alice would never leave until the ballots were counted and the matter decided anyway. Goddamn contrary, frustrating, loveable Knoll. Leaving was hard, but necessary. His gut told him as much. So did murder and weird lights and disappearing paint. So did his dead ma. How the hell do you argue with something like that?

The back service door of the mill was downstairs near the larger rollup entrance to the loading bay. He knew every creak and groan of the mill like the caresses of an old dusty lover, and the squeaking hinges of that service door came to him, faraway yet familiar.

His nerves sang like violin strings. No one had business here after dark. No one. He slipped his hand into the top drawer of his desk and pulled out an old revolver. It was his daddy's. Heavy. Loaded. He crept to the office door and waited at the top of the stairs, listening.

Down below, the back door of the mill slammed loud and clear. *Shit.*

He jogged down the stairs and let himself in the main bay, then flipped on the lights, his eyes darting over the bulging, dusty feed sacks, the support beams shaggy with webs and chaff. The depths of the main floor seemed too shadowy despite the rows of 100-watt fixtures dangling overhead.

He kept the gun low at his thigh and stood in the middle of the bay floor where trucks dropped their loads into the floor grinder pit and then drove right on through. Or would drop their loads if Axel had not removed the grate segments over the pit and propped them against the wall like abandoned cattle gates during his cleaning efforts.

"Come on out now and I won't turn you in for trespassing," Cy shouted.

A form separated from the shadows at the back of the bay and stepped into the light. It was that judge fellow.

"You're not allowed in here. It's after hours." Cy meant it, but it felt like loose rags in his mouth.

Agitated pigeons fluttered in the rafters. He glanced up, and when he looked back, Thekan was closer even though he'd heard no rustle of clothes, no tap of a shoe.

"I go where I must. To clear the way."

"There's nothing that needs clearing in my mill, Mister." Another shape caught his eye, this one mostly hidden behind the vacuum line designed to pull the ground feed out of the belly of the grinder once the augers had their way. His stomach drew down with trepidation. He nudged the gun forward. "You and your friend better get packing."

Thekan smiled with resigned acceptance. "If only you had let old memories lie. Forgotten and foregone."

Peripherally, he noticed the other shape lean in. Was that Axel? He wasn't able to check, his eyes were locked on Thekan, his ears abuzz with Thekan's words.

"But you are a willful man, Cy Vandergalien. Demonstrative to a fault. In need, perhaps, of a reprimand."

A third shape staggered into the light from the other side of the bay. Cy's limbs went numb. What appeared at first to be a walking silhouette revealed itself as a repulsive imitation of life. It wore a black suit with narrow lapels and frayed buttonholes that looked much better in the black and white wedding photos that once sat on the family piano next to his grade school pictures. The hairless head, a strangulated purple so dark it was like a scoop of late twilight, tilted with pleased discovery. "Ahhhh," it said.

Cy swallowed with a throat made of stone as the shape hurried over and its hand, riddled by rot, reached for him.

"You drew that line real good," his father's voice bubbled out of the rotted grin, wet, as if he'd gargled with the rich gasoline once perfuming their family garage. "Just the way I showed you. But still, looks like you screwed the poochie in the end, boy." Amused delight swirled through eyes deep set and slick. Fingers reached out, stroking the air. "Screwed the poochie."

"Don't touch me," Cy whimpered.

Feet, bony and shaggy with some sort of black growth, clicked on the bay floor. "Come here, son. I gotta lay one up side your head."

Cy took a long step back. The gun wobbled with hopelessness in his hand. "I'm leaving, Daddy," he heard himself say. "It won't matter anymore. Just go back to wherever the hell you came from."

"Nope. Got a duty, boy."

His father leaned forward. Without thought, Cy fired the gun. The bullet twanged off of something metallic across the room. What followed was a yowl of pain from behind the vacuum pipe in the corner, and an indignant, "What the fuck?"

The other shadow. *Axel*.

Daddy cozied up, wrapped in the essence of mold. Under it was a sharp, fruity odor. Cy pulled back. When he spoke, it was a plea. "I'm stayin' in town, aren't I?"

"Yes," Daddy said. "You are. Staying for good. Just like me."

Cold hands clamped over his head the way a clergyman might grip a penitent to shake the wickedness out. Then they pushed.

Cy staggered backward. His landing foot dropped into the open air over the grinder pit and his weight pulled him backward. The fall was a short one. He marveled as he landed on the cruel spiral edge of the grinding auger how sharp it was after all these years.

Axel limped over to the wall-mounted grinder controls. Pain blasted outward from the bullet hole just above his knee; it felt as if his whole damn leg was on fire. The green start button pulsed like a bleary reptilian eye. It seemed to ask him, patiently, what he was waiting for.

"Finish it," Thekan told him from across the bay. He stood alone. The other guy, the *thing* in the moldy black suit was gone.

Axel let his palm hover over the button. "Why don't *you* do it? Same way you start up cars and open doors like some fucking Gary Houdini?"

"Harry. That was Harry Houdini. And to all things there is a purpose, my boy."

Axel glanced at the edge of the open grinder pit where his uncle's shoes had scuffed it. He wanted a joint. He wanted to run.

"I do this, and then I can go?"

"You can run as fast as you are able," Thekan said with a smile.

Axel's leg throbbed in time with the button. A groan rose from the floor pit, accompanied by subtle stirring sounds. Next on the agenda: cries of pain and calls for help, ramping up to threats and accusations. Goddamned Unky Cy.

He swatted the button, hard. He shouted to drown out the winding roar of the motor but he still heard the laboring of the auger. The lights dimmed as mauling blades did their work. He punched the stop button only ten seconds later with a sob. A red button. As red as the scent that churned the air. He shouted again, this time into ensuing silence.

Thekan stood before him and gently cupped his chin. "Done."

Run, fucking run. Axel slipped away, his wounded leg screaming. The segments of floor grinder grates were on his left, heavy steel, tough enough to withstand the weight of large farm trucks. When one of them swung outward from its resting place and blocked Axel's path like a section of fence, he fell back hard on his ass with a startled cry. The grate leaned over him as if with evaluation and then it dropped. He scrambled backward, too slow, and heavy steel slammed down on his already wounded leg. He heard the bone snap.

Axel screamed again. Thekan stood over him. "You're going to be the answer to many questions in this town," he said and nudged the sole of Axel's free foot. "Welcomed and wanted. Oh so wanted."

A nostalgic tightness came across Axel's toes. New shoes. Just like in grade school. A wallet swelled in his back pocket, and the name Kirkpatrick Evert ignited in his brain with its coming. New shoes, new wallet and his fresh sweaty hand prints on the grinder controls. The equation came together quickly in his head.

"*You fuck,*" he shouted through gritted teeth. "*You set me up, you stinking rotten fuck.*"

"Rest now." Thekan's tone was soothing. He rubbed his fingers together as if sifting herbs into a pot. "Still and quiet and done."

A lulling primo-weed tranquility crashed over Axel. He barely noticed the pair of spent doobies and how they dropped near him like insects perishing around a porch light. He wanted to pull the wallet out and fling it away, and work out of the stiff pointy shoes, but it suddenly didn't matter. Nothing mattered because every last particle of him was being swallowed by long, luxurious ribbons of descending sleep. Deep sleep. Still and quiet.

PART FIVE:

DANGEROUS
WATERS

CHAPTER ONE

Harley PICKED UP MICK at seven am. The morning was bright despite gray clouds stacked on the horizon like battleground sandbags. They traded looks of anticipation as they drove across town.

"Do you trust this?" Harley asked. "Doing the final setup like this? We'll be in Thekan's territory. Alone."

"It's too close to the actual event to cause a stir," Mick said. "The most we'll get out of him today is a speech to the people of Knoll during the proceedings. A nice as pie schmooze."

"And I wonder what it is he's going to say. 'Hey, the scourge is just around the corner. Here's a gun. Avoid the rush.'"

Harley pulled onto the shoulder of Tier Street. Ahead of them, the Mellar Borth house crouched like a huge beast humiliated by the patriotic bunting pinned to its hide. "Let's wire us up some lights."

As they unloaded the truck, a curtain twitched in an upstairs window of the house and Mick did all he could to ignore it, focused on toting the interior lamps and the cables meant to run through the heavy metal backs of the voting booths. When he reached the carrels he stopped, his muscles tightening, his heart picking up in pace.

Harley came up behind him. "What we need is to put big old stickers on these three voting stations telling folks to Vote *Mellar's In*. What do you think?"

"I have a better idea," he said as he set his cargo in the grass. "Do you see what I see?"

Harley's face grew quiet and calculating. Five plastic wrapped packets of ballots were stacked in the carrel in front of them. Next to the packets were slotted wooden ballot boxes, one for each carrel.

Mick rapped his knuckles on the closest box. "Remind you of anything?"

"If we cut a slot in the LINR box we have it'd be a dead ringer," Harley said. "But a fourth ballot box won't do us any good."

Mick shifted some cables around for effect, in case they were being watched. "It will if we stuff it with *Mellar's In* votes and then swap it for one of the others. What do you think our voter turnout will be like today?"

"Three hundred," Harley said and tinkered with one of the light fixtures. "Give or take."

"And we've got five hundred blank ballots. Thank God for minimum orders at the print shop, is all I can say." Mick slipped one of the packs of paper off the stack and pressed it tight to his stomach. "I'm going to go back to the truck and call Will. And Nancy Berns, too. I think she'll want to help us pull this off."

"Take all the time you need. I got this. I'll place a box at each station and open up the stacks of ballots. Harder to notice what's missing if they're unwrapped."

"That's why you're still the boss," Mick said and headed toward the truck.

CHAPTER TWO

An hour later Mick hurried across the bar parking lot with Judy right behind. It was going on nine o'clock, which meant the vote would commence in two hours.

"There's Will," Judy said and pointed to the front door of the bar.

Will held the entrance like a hotel doorman and followed them inside. "Gang's all here," he said.

Nancy Berns stood just inside the door and greeted them with a cautious nod. Harley got up from one of the side tables. Beth Ann remained seated, her eyes downcast, her migraine's grip as deep as ever. Harley gave Judy an earnest look. "She's not very comfortable with this ballot-stuffing idea," he said. "Thinks it's some kind of sin. Which I suppose it is. But she wanted to come, headache and all, bless her."

"I'll sit with her. Nancy, let's get started on marking up those ballots."

"Just steer me toward the pencils," Nancy said.

Harley brought out their ersatz ballot box. The LINR was neatly sanded away and the lid sported a freshly cut slit. "There she is. And I got to tell you, working on this thing felt weird, like I was sending Thekan a signal somehow. We don't need him barging in here about now, doing whatever weird shit he's got up his sleeves."

Will spoke up. "I don't think he's able to barge in. Not here, anyway." He worked at something he kept palmed in his right hand, and it made a faint clicking sound. "You remember how yesterday, at the mercantile, Thekan was in the parking lot, but pretty far away from the building? Weirdly far?" They nodded. "Last night I saw him drive by here, and he swerved as if he needed to put as much distance as he could between himself and my bar. Like he didn't dare come closer. Or couldn't."

"Makes sense, in a way," Mick said. "Otherwise, if there's something at the mercantile that he doesn't like, or feels threatened by, why not take care of it himself?"

"Or get somebody else to do the job," Harley said. "I know he had me close to walking away against my will yesterday."

Will raised his eyebrows. "Something about certain places jams his frequencies."

"Good air, maybe," Mick said and glanced across to where the women were grimly marking ballots the way they might write out tallies of some dreaded disease. His gaze lingered on Beth Ann, just for a second, and then skipped away. "Or what's left of it."

"What we should do is go down to that tunnel right now," Harley said. "Make sure the double barrel is there in the first place. The way we're doing it seems ass-backwards, don't you think?"

"We wait for Cy," Mick said firmly. "We need him."

"You should stay out of there," Beth Ann spoke up. Her crimson eye twitched behind its drooping lid. "Harley told me about it. I think it's dangerous. Bereft and dangerous."

An idea circling in Mick's head finally found correlation. "You may be right," he said and stepped over to take her hands. "And I want you to think about something. When this church was deconsecrated, a big part of the tunnel's importance was taken away. Up until then it supplied an essence to the double barrel pump or whatever else is waiting for us in there. Good air. We learned about it yesterday. I think the essence is weak now, nearly gone, and it needs to be strengthened."

Beth Ann's face was a mix of trust and terror. "What does that have to do with me?"

"We don't have a minister of our own, and I doubt we could pull one in to help. But your fervency lately, your passion, makes you the next best thing. You could bless the tunnel for us. Not go in, just do it from the entrance downstairs."

"Oh, Mick, I don't know," she said with a helpless smile.

"We need this, Beth Ann. Think about it. Please. But not for too long."

"I will," she said and clutched her cross necklace. "A few minutes. Just give me a few minutes."

Mick took his place next to Harley. "I hope you don't mind."

Harley shrugged. "It makes sense, but I don't see her going for it."

"Maybe Cy can officiate if we need him to," Will threw in. "He's a sort of authority figure, right?" He gave the object in his hand another click.

"What is that thing?" Mick asked him.

Will showed him a metal disc about the size of a stopwatch. Its face was a row of tiny windows, each with a single digit number inside. A plastic tab poked out of the side. "It's a tally keeper. Push the button and the number goes up by one." He clicked it to show them. "I use it to track drink tabs when somebody has a party at the bar. I call it my clicker. I thought it would come in handy today."

"It will." Mick patted his shoulder. "If you stand watch over a single ballot box, and can tell us when a hundred votes have dropped in, we can make our swap."

"That's what I thought."

Harley made a half-smile. "Damned if we don't make a fine team of cheaters, the three of us."

"These are done," Nancy said from behind them. She held out the stack of ballots, all marked in favor of *Mellar's In*. "You boys can fold them and stuff them in."

Judy piped up from where she sat next to Beth Ann. "And fold them in odd ways so they're all different from one another."

"In fact," Beth Ann added, "don't fold some at all. We want this to look good."

"The six of us," Harley corrected as he parceled out the ballots. "The whole cheating team of six. Now let's go, a couple at a time, and make this happen."

CHAPTER THREE

When they arrived at the Mellar Borth property, other people were already milling about, chatting in small groups. In the bright mid-morning sun, the grounds were inviting with their orderly placement of tables bearing punchbowls and cups, an easel supporting an ancient photograph of the mercantile in its heyday, and two stage platforms, on one of which a musical band of local repute called Shifting Sands was tuning up.

Mick took Judy's hand as they stepped onto the grounds. He wondered if any of this was valid, this festival atmosphere on private property, if fruit punch and a cover band were on the books as acceptable trappings for a town vote, if maybe the whole event could be scrapped on some sort of compliance issue. But it was too late to change the schedule now; everything was in full swing.

The six of them met up casually, hailing one another as if it had been days instead of minutes since they'd spoken.

"You're prepared, I see," Mick said with a gesture toward the wheeled apparatus at Nancy Berns's side. It looked like a white beverage cooler with a large red cross sticker on the top.

Harley followed up with a sly smile and a wink. "Somebody put you on duty at the last minute?"

"You never know when you might need some first aid."

She patted the side of the container. The LINR box was inside for now, but they would need to find some way to make the exchange when the time came.

"Look at them come," Judy said, shielding her eyes.

Cars were pulling onto Tier Street one after another. People walked up with the measured flow of a migrating herd. "Floodgates are open," Will commented under his breath.

"Typical Knoll," Nancy said with a nervous laugh. "If you're not early, you're late. I'm going to start working the crowd."

With that, she wheeled her first-aid cooler away, nudging elbows and greeting people with her broad smile.

"We should all do the same," Mick said. "At this rate anybody who is going to vote will be here in the next ten minutes."

"Look sharp," Will said with a nod toward the elevated stage near the voting carrels.

Chastity Mellar Borth mounted the platform, gazing out at the activity in her yard as if surveying a wonder of nature. Mick thought she appeared almost radiant; only a slight crease of worry around her mouth spoiled it. Behind her, Thekan stepped up, his face set in a hard imitation of pleasantness. Thekan the abomination, the levitator of stones and the killer of Kippy Evert. Looking at him chilled Mick's blood.

"Split up and mingle," Mick said. "He can't watch all of us at once. At least I hope not."

"Come on, darlin'," Harley said and put his hand at Beth Ann's waist, "let's blend in and do some campaigning."

Shifting Sands ran a few practice riffs and batted a sample drumbeat or two. The chatter on the grounds was becoming a buzz peppered with friendly laughter.

Will held up his clicker. "Once this deal starts, I'll casually make my way to the right-hand side, the voting station farthest from the house. When I reach about ninety-five, I'll walk away, toward the band. Is that good enough for a signal?"

"Perfect," Mick said. "All I need to do is figure out how we can switch boxes under Thekan's watchful eye. He's too smart to think we won't try something today. And he's intuitive."

"More than intuitive, in my experience."

Mick slapped him on the shoulder and sent him on his way. When he turned around, Roger Copeland was standing there. His eyes were red, as if from a night's worth of drinking, but he seemed eager about something. His smile was tentative. "H'lo, Mick," he said.

"Roger. Voting *Mellar's In*, I hope."

Copeland's smile widened. "I knew it. Your wife and Harley Kroener already asked me the same thing. You guys got a thing going, don't you?"

"What do you mean, a thing?"

"Pushing the vote to one side. I'm all for letting the old building stand, too, just so you know." He fingered a pocket watch chained to his hip. "I sorta feel like Knoll needs it. Isn't that crazy?"

"Not crazy at all. We think so, too."

"This town doesn't need any more changes or shakeups. Not after Kippy. And The Crymost lighting up at night . . . I'd make sure the votes went right, too. I'd put in a fix if nothing else."

"Yeah, well . . . "

"Mick." The voice from behind him was Nancy Berns's. Her eyes were bright with determination. "I got our man. Gordy Prellwitz."

She pointed out the slouched, potbellied and very familiar form standing at the edge of the crowd. He was talking with the people from Elmore Excavating, his balding head bobbing appreciatively. One of his hands gripped the handles of a yellow Rock-a-roo mounded full of baby blankets.

"He'll do it?" Mick asked.

"In a heartbeat," Nancy said. "He and the wife have got their grandbaby for the week but Gloria is carting the little bundle around showing it off, so Gordy's just toting an empty Rock-a-roo. The box will fit, no trouble, and he can walk right up to the voting booth with it, and raise zero suspicion."

"Goddamn," Roger Copeland said, "You already got a fix going, I see."

Mick passed a glance of resignation to Nancy. "Keep it to yourself, would you Roger? I can't go into details, but this thing has got to go our way. It's important."

"No sweat, Mick. Hell, I'll stump for the *Mellar's In* vote, too, if you want. Don't know how many folks will listen since I'm no Cy Vandergalien, but I'll give it a shot."

"Thanks, Roger."

"Have we seen Cy, yet?" Nancy asked and surveyed the crowd.

"He'd be a big help about now," Mick said.

Roger pointed. "Alice is working the registration table, talking to your missus."

Judy and Alice were indeed involved in conversation. Behind them, the band was warming up with an up-tempo version of "On Wisconsin". Nearby, Harley and Beth Ann chatted with Stu Rueplinger, and Will stood near the carrels with the Bellamys who lived on Meadow Lane just a door down from Orlin Casper's place. Gordy Prellwitz caught Mick's eye and tipped him a confiding but discreet wave.

Mick's teeth scrubbed across his lower lip. All was in place, with a tense but otherworldly feel like *Lord of the Rings* by way of John Clancy. Things were going to fall into true soon, and without mercy.

The band stopped. Chastity Mellar Borth stepped up to the microphone and put up her hands. The crowd noise fell to a hush.

"Welcome, Knoll, to this important occasion. Today, we make a historic decision on behalf of our town, and I hope I have made the experience a pleasant one for you. No matter what the outcome—"

A voice from the crowd rose up. "Whatever, lady. Where's Cy Vandergalien?"

Soft chuckles traveled across the grounds.

Chastity seemed reserved and amused, very diplomatic. "Whatever the outcome, we must remember this is the day a significant part of Knoll moves toward long awaited change. A rightful destiny."

Harley caught Mick's arm as he passed by. "Everything ready?"

"As ready as it's going to get."

Mick moved on, cut between the Carmichaels and the Joneleys and met up with Judy. "Alice is upset," she said before he had the chance to ask. "She hasn't seen Cy since last night."

"Damn it."

Chastity raised her hands up again because the crowd was stirring, anxious to get on with it. "Before we open the registration table for you to collect your voting ballots, one per customer, and our friends in the band play some music to entertain you, I thought we might have these proceedings condoned by a man many of you have come to know over the last few days."

"Cy Vandergalien," someone shouted.

Laughter popped up in small islands and sank away.

"The Honorable Judge Roderick Thekan," Chastity said and stepped back, her hands pattering against one another, her mouth still etched with barely-there worry lines.

Applause spattered like sparse droplets. The crowd's interest deepened, however. There was a collective sensation as if everyone was leaning in as Thekan took the microphone.

"Good morning, Knoll. As I have introduced myself around town, I have met many fine people and I am compelled to give you counsel. The face of your town is on the verge of change, and today's proceedings will determine what that change will be. This venue is casual, light-hearted, and for that you must thank your so-fine matron. But keep our purpose in mind. Keep your decision at the top of your thoughts as you cast your vote. Raise it to the heavens. Speak it plainly to your souls."

Judy tugged Mick's sleeve and turned away from the stage with a sound of distress. "He's getting to me. I don't know how, but I can see myself marking up one of those ballots for *Mellar's Out*. I can practically feel the pencil in my hand."

Thekan seemed unnaturally taller somehow. Almost heroic, Mick thought. His voice was an up-winding engine, gaining fervor, generating power. "The mark you make today shapes a part of the future for Knoll. Your vote seals a fate, and I'm sure there are some of you who came here with uncertainty over which way your decision will fall. Let me assure you the inner voice is the just voice. It is your sensibility and your deepest known truth. Therefore, for any who are unsure, I advise you to listen to your innermost, unscathed thought on the matter. Acknowledge it before doubt can cloud it. Listen to it and follow it through. Listen to it wholly. Listen. Listen . . . "

Mick caught Harley's attention from across the crowd. The look Harley returned was on the edge of dread. Will shook his head as if coming up from a dip in cold water. Nancy worked her way back to Gordy Prellwitz and spoke to him low and imperative. Many others in the crowd stared at Thekan with thunderstruck silence.

"So prepare and vote confidently," Thekan said with an appreciative nod. "Today you help to confirm a destiny. Today you will initiate change in your town. You have all become pavers of the way. Thank you, Knoll, for allowing me to participate in this so-important event."

Applause rose up, more emphatic this time.

Judy turned to him, pale and shaken. "Is it some sort of group hypnosis?"

"He's stuffing ballots in his own way. Come on, let's get in line and drum up some last-minute sympathy for *Mellar's In*. Just to be sure."

"It's going to be hard," she said, her eyes wide with concern.

Chastity grinned and took over the microphone. "I declare the polls officially open."

The crowd moved with a fluid synchronicity, first to the registration table and then into groups around each carrel. Shifting Sands, who was breaking in a new drummer, fired up an old Carl Perkins song about Kansas City.

Mick took a quick account. Judy was working the crowd near the carrel across from Will. Harley and Beth Ann were in the back, making their point with a couple of women in nurse scrubs, one of which he recognized as Emma Balog from Forest Street. Will was hawking like a funhouse barker to funnel voters to his carrel, one hand uncharacteristically buried in his pocket where he kept the clicker going. They were doing their best, Nancy included.

Mick made his appeal to Mrs. Merk and the Goldapskes and the Fergusons from Garden Street. Thekan and Chastity likewise worked the crowd, and more than once he caught Thekan's hard glare aimed directly at him, suspicious and uncertain and with more than a little warning in the mix. He kept going until he saw Will stroll toward the band and flash his palmed clicker as an all-clear.

Go time. The air turned to lead in his lungs. He glanced across the crowd at Nancy who also took note of Will's cue and tapped Gordy Prellwitz on the arm. The box had apparently been transferred to the baby carrier because Prellwitz immediately got in line at Will's carrel. Judy was just stepping away from casting her vote, her smile wide but fixed because she too had noticed Will's signal. The time seemed right for Mick to cast his own vote, perhaps in the carrel across from where their cheater's box was about to be planted. He turned and ran bodily into Roderick Thekan.

Thekan stepped back and caused the man behind him to stumble.

"Hey, watch it mister," the man said. It was Roger Copeland. "Oh, sorry, Judge."

Thekan paid him no mind but stared at Mick with evaluative calm. "Are you pleased with the turnout, Mr. Logan?"

"Are you?"

"My appreciation holds no bearing I'm afraid."

"Besides," Roger popped up," the good guys are going to win this, hands down. No way they're going to lose, right Mick?"

Thekan whirled around and Copeland shrunk beneath his gaze. Mick's first reaction was to shout *don't look at him*, but it was too late. Mick could almost feel information pass unspoken between the two men.

"Pardon me," was all Thekan said before he stalked off to the stage nearest the carrels.

Mick looked around for the others. Gordy Prellwitz slipped into the carrel, the baby carrier on his arm. Nancy was chatting with a group of women. Harley was shaking hands with a man Mick couldn't identify. Judy was walking toward him but making helloes on the way, stepping in time to Shifting Sands's version of "Taking Care of Business", which whirled high and twangy in the sunny air.

It was Will who caught his frantic expression first. Will, who instinctively broke away and rushed toward Gordy Prellwitz. People were jammed around the carrels, voices high and excited. Mick pushed his way in. He wasn't sure what he meant to do but they'd thrown Gordy into dangerous waters and, like Will, he needed to jump in, to defend.

Thekan mounted the platform and gazed down at the carrels, an imposing silhouette. Chastity came up behind him, brushed his shoulder with concerned hands and he shrugged her off. With a pang of hopelessness, Mick saw Thekan's gaze settle on Gordy's booth. He was too far away to be heard, to intercept, to do anything. Will was closer, but not close enough. Thekan tensed. He was too far from the microphone to be heard and yet when he spoke Mick understood him plainly. "Not today."

A charge leapt into the air like a rush of spilled lightning. The lights inside the voting carrels exploded with harsh pops. Feedback screeched from the band's speakers, and the lead guitarist of Shifting Sands threw his guitar down with a shout, goggling at his smoking fingers. The carrels shook with seizure-like frenzy; Mick could see the press wood sides pulling away from the metal backs as if wrenched by unseen hands. The voters inside goggled around, stunned.

"Gordy!" Mick made an attempt, but his voice was lost in the surprised shouts from the crowd.

The triad of carrels exploded. Fragments of wood and metal whickered through the air. Slips of ballot paper sailed up like leaves stirred by a passing bus. The crowd scattered in a hail of shouts and wounded screams. Mick saw Gordy stagger backward, his face studded with mini stilettoes of wood. One of the metal booth backs flew outward and caught Jack Hamilton, who taught English at Drury High, full on in the throat. He fell backward, spouting a spume of blood from his mouth. Mick was nearly to Gordy, who still clutched the baby carrier.

"Thekan knows," Mick called to him. "For God's sake, drop that thing, Gordy!"

Dangerous waters, a part of Mick recited as Gordon Prellwitz addressed him with a dazed, splintered and blood-streaked face. Thekan glowered at them, and that same panicked part of Mick recited *he's not done yet*. Thekan writhed as if shedding an invisible overcoat of pure power. The Rock-a-roo exploded into flying pieces with a lick of green fire. The explosion flung Gordy back, a violent pirouette that ended in collapse, the arm which held the Rock-a-roo a second before now gone in a burst of bloody fragments. He rolled in the dirt and clutched at his gushing shoulder stump, producing deep, rasping screams. A crescent of mangled Rock-a-roo rocketed deep into the crowd and plunged into Melody Carmichael's abdomen as her husband tried to lead her away. He continued to pull on her even after she was down, her midsection pumping blurts of crimson into the grass.

Shouts and screams came from everywhere. Mick twisted around, trying to take it all in at once. He saw Judy helping a woman who kept a bloody hand clamped over her right eye. He thought it might be their neighbor, Mrs. Merk. He saw Harley and Beth Ann across the way, safe and hurrying toward the perimeter.

"Jesus." Someone rapped him on the shoulder. It was Roger Copeland. "I did this, didn't I? I told him what you were doing somehow, that judge. I didn't mean to but I told him without saying anything. Jesus."

"You didn't tell him," Mick said. "He took it from you."

Roger stumbled away goggling at the chaos, a lost traveler in a land where the common language was screams and the air reeked of ozone. Mick watched him for a moment, then crouched next to Gordy Prellwitz. "Come on, Gordy," he said and then stopped.

The man's mouth was a dark gash, frozen and silent, his splinter-ravaged face paper white, his wide eyes sightless.

"Goddamn it."

"This is null," Alice Vandergalien screeched and beseeched the sky with fists full of crumpled ballots. "It's all null. God, this is insanity."

Thekan whirled toward her on his platform and executed another of those writhing shrugs. Alice planted both pudgy hands against her chest as if applying a corsage of ruined ballots to her bosom, and then she dropped to the ground.

Mick caught a glimpse of Nancy Berns, who was yelling into her cell phone and tending to a woman with a gash in her scalp. "Nancy," he called out and motioned to where Alice Vandergalien lay. A siren whooped at the other side of town. Someone, Stu Rueplinger presumably, had high tailed it to the firehouse to put the emergency vehicle into play.

Mick realized he was standing once again, with his arms held out, doing his best to coax those around him back toward Tier Street. "Leave the premises," he shouted. "We don't know if those wires are still live or anything else. Vacate the premises now, come on."

People responded, blindly, some of them calmed as if in appreciation of being instructed.

"Hey, you better sit down, Mick." Will Adelmeyer came up and put a hand on each of Mick's shoulders, gazing at him with an odd directness. There was a jagged scratch on his cheek. It reminded Mick of wax paper violated by a dull knife.

"What do you mean?"

Even as he spoke he felt the first hot and heavy thuds from his left shoulder. As he followed Will's gaze he saw a shaft of raw wood, neat and slender for all of its brokenness which lent it the appearance of a 12-inch ruler jutting from just below the ball of his shoulder. Blood was oozing out, bright and glittering in the sunlight.

"Come on," Will said and started to lead him away. "Before you fall down."

And fall I might, he decided as a light, disconnected feel took him over. He glanced back at Thekan who stood at the podium, slumped and spent, and yet somehow satiated. His lips moved across teeth gone suddenly broken and yellow, and in spite of the din, Mick once again heard every word.

"How do you like the turnout now, Mr. Logan?"

A low, plaintive sound rose into the air, the protest of a disturbed beast or the groan of massive ancient machinery made to run after years of rusty slumber. The crowd hushed momentarily and looked around to place the source. The southeast.

The Crymost.

The sound faded as quickly as it came, and in congruity, the crowd returned to calling out and vacating the grounds, more restless than before.

Mick traded worried glances with Will. Judy ran up behind him, already in capable mode, and led him out to the car.

"We can't wait anymore," he said under his breath as the first real pain erupted in his shoulder. "We don't dare."

The Knoll First Responders vehicle pulled up in a cloud of spring dust. Gordy Prellwitz's wife, wrangling a squalling baby in her arms, found her husband, fell to her knees and began to weep.

CHAPTER FOUR

"Twelve goddamn stitches," Mick said as he got to his feet in the procedure room of the Baylor Clinic. He was still shirtless and he regarded the bandage on his shoulder with disdain. "Jesus."

Judy held out his shirt for him. He eased into it while they waited for the clinic nurse to come back with word of his dismissal.

"Is it even safe to go back home?" Judy asked him. She looked exhausted. "We both saw what Thekan did. What defense do we have against something like that?"

"But did you see how exhausted he was afterward? I'm hoping he ran his battery down with today's big blast. That will give us some time."

"But it's not just him. It's The Crymost too. You heard that sound. That groan. It's hungry, like you said. And hungry things are driven things, Mick."

"The alternative is what? Hide? Run away? Neither of us is set up that way and you know it. Let me find out about the tunnel, see if the double barrel even exists. If it's a bust, if those men from the '60s were hoping to hold back a flood with the equivalent of two sticks and a paper bag, I'll help you pack and have the moving van at our door in the morning. Deal?"

Her sigh was long and low. "Please don't go running off the minute we get home. Give the glue some time to dry."

He nodded, and as if on cue, the nurse came back wearing a quiet smile.

Once he was home, the kindling pain in his shoulder, banking like an old boiler furnace, joined forces with an encroaching sense of exhaustion. He stretched out on the couch, but a moment later a call came in from Harley. "You need some quiet time, so I'll make it fast," his friend said.

He listened, with Judy standing vigil in the doorway.

Gordy Prellwitz was, not surprising, pronounced dead at the scene. Jack Hamilton's larynx was crushed by the flying barrier, and there was other internal damage to his throat and upper chest. All of it was too much; he died in the ambulance on the way to the hospital. Mrs. Merk lost her right eye (when he heard this, he passed a miserable glance to the right, as if he could see through the wall to the Merk's house next door), and Alice Vandergalien was in critical condition following a massive heart attack. She was due to be airlifted to a Madison hospital where specialists were standing by. Melody Carmichael's abdominal wound was deep and damaging. She was in critical condition as well and might not make it through the night. Both of the Belamys took wood impalements similar to Mick's in severity: Mr. Belamy in the calf and Mrs. Belamy on the left side buttock. Shifting Sands's guitar player was out with second degree burns on his fingers. There were lots of minor cuts and bruises on lots of other folks.

"Thekan's nowhere in sight," Harley threw in at the end. "Coiled up resting, is my guess. And if he was willing to put on that kind of show, it means it's close, doesn't it? This thing that's going to happen?"

"My gut tells me it is," he said.

After they ended the call he gave Judy all the updates, which she received with stony acceptance. His lids grew heavy as he talked and when Judy asked if they were going to check the tunnel tonight, he was already on the verge of sleep. The last thing he said came out without any thought on his part.

"Have to," he said. "It's just us, Thekan, and The Crymost."

CHAPTER FIVE

Near sunset, Stu Rueplinger drove the First Responders van down The Plank, the fatigue of the day weighing on him like millstones. His dirty blonde hair, thick for a man of forty, stood out in tufts starched by dried sweat. The scene at the Borth house had been a wild one, but it kept him and Nancy and Jerry Sterr jumping for a while. So many folks; so much blood.

They'd nearly cleared out the trauma box in the van, which was a first. But they helped a good share of people before the Baylor and Drury EMTs started arriving as backup. The truth was, Stu liked the atmosphere of disaster—in small doses at least. He had tried to talk out some of his excitement while he gassed up at Copeland's earlier, but Roger seemed particularly glum on the subject, which was understandable. Some folks folded up in the face of calamity while others took up the reins of responsibility.

The man in the road seemed to come out of nowhere, the way an image flickered to life on an old antenna television set. It was that Judge Thekan fellow, and he was dangerously close to the front of the van.

Stu punched the brakes and swerved to the side of The Plank to keep from hitting the man. The sudden shock must have knocked his awareness out of kilter because when he looked around, the Judge wasn't in the road at all. He was standing near the F&F bay door where farm trucks made their drop-offs and pickups.

The Judge seemed a little drained in his own right. Hurt, maybe. *So many people*, he thought again, *so much blood*. He shut down the van and climbed out, his heart hammering.

"You okay?" he called out and began to walk over.

Thekan smiled at him. "Awake," he said and slipped around the corner of the building.

That couldn't be right. Made no sense. Stu wanted to follow him but a groggy voice from the other side of the bay door drew his attention.

"Help me. No more dicking with Ichabod," the voice said. It was a pronouncement and a lament rolled into one. "I just want out. Somebody fucking help me."

Stu pushed and the door trundled open on overhead suspension wheels. "Hello?" he called out.

"Fucking hello yourself, feast meat," the voice called back.

"Axel?" he said and stepped into the dark.

A moment later he ran back to the van and snatched his cell phone off the dash. Damned if they didn't have another mess in Knoll.

CHAPTER SIX

"You're looking better than last time I saw you," Will said as Mick stepped from the cool evening air into the bar. "How's the shoulder?"

"Stiff but functional. Although I promised the boss I wouldn't do any rock climbing tonight." Mick passed a smile to Judy who stepped in behind him.

"He thinks some ibuprofen and a long nap have made him all better."

"Things were bad here for a while after we left, I understand," Mick said.

"Chaos." Will touched the scratch on his cheek. It was not deep, but still described an angry red line from the crest of his cheekbone to nearly the corner of his mouth. "Cops. Reporters. The last of them left just before dark. I think I'll open up tomorrow night with some kind of two-for-one special. This town needs to drown a few sorrows."

"Maybe," Mick said and sat with Judy at one of the tables. "Are we the first?"

"Yeah." Will glanced through the front windows and jumped. "Uh-oh. Roger Copeland is coming. Can't he see I've got the closed sign up?"

"I asked him to come," Mick said. "He's got an interest in this and I think he'll be of some help. Nancy will be here, too."

"I keep thinking about how quiet the town is tonight," Judy said. "Usually a fender bender on The Plank is enough to keep the town talking for hours. But on the way over I saw nobody chatting on their porches or stopped on the sidewalk to gab. No one in the streets at all. It's eerie."

Mick took her hand.

Roger Copeland stepped inside. He wrung a greasy ballcap between his hands like a drifter invited in for a late supper. "H'lo."

"Roger." Mick ushered him in while Will continued to man the entrance. Through the open door, he could see the Kroeners just getting out of their car. "How are you?"

"Still shook, I guess. Can I get a shot of Turkey, Will?"

"I'll pour us all something once Harley and Beth Ann are inside."

Roger sat across from Judy but kept his eyes downcast. His hands shook. "Damned if I know what I'm doing here. I didn't understand half of what you told me on the phone, Mick. But I want to help."

"I'm hoping tonight will clear up a lot of things," Mick said and swung back around to address the Kroeners as they stepped inside, Beth Ann in particular. "I'm glad you came. Are you up for helping with this?"

There were dark pain circles under her eyes. The left one remained a glossy red blank. "I'm willing to give it a try."

Mick nodded. "Thank you." He strode to the bar, then turned to face them all. They waited, attentive. *It seems class is in session, Mr. Logan.* "Thekan made a big mistake this morning."

"Overreacted," Will said as he stepped behind the bar to fill shot glasses.

"And Knoll paid a terrible price for it. Terrible. But we've got to keep going. The price will be more dire if we can't figure out how to stop this die-off, this *culling*."

"Culling. Jesus," Copeland said. "I don't see what a tunnel has to do with keeping something like that from coming. It don't make no sense to me." He worked his hand over the pocket watch at his side. "Goddamn tight, lightless places like that."

The front door burst open and they all looked around. Nancy Berns hurried in, out of breath. Stu Rueplinger was right behind her. "It's Cy," she said in a trembling voice. "He's dead."

She waited for their shocked responses to die down and stepped over to one of the tables to lean on it. Stu followed her. Mick and Harley stood on either side of them like sentinels.

"I would have called one of you," she said, "but we were tied up with the authorities and the mess at the F&F."

Stu spoke like a man haunted. "He fell into his old ramshackle corn grinder in the mill floor. When those augers started up, they just—"

"Sit down, everybody," Mick told them.

Nancy continued, still breathless: "It seems Axel pushed him in and then turned it on. Some kind of fight, I guess, because Axel was shot. He broke his leg trying to get away, but—"

"Slipped in those ridiculous shoes, I thought," Stu broke in. "And it wasn't just me. The cops were interested in Axel's shoes, too."

"But *what*?" Mick said to Nancy. "Go on."

She took a deep breath. "Well, he was as high as a kite. He must have laid in there for hours, even smoked a couple of those marijuana cigarettes. There were spent butts on the floor next to him. And he wasn't just high, he was talking nonsense. I think he snapped, emotionally, over it all."

"Here," Will said and put a shot glass in front of her.

She downed the contents and handed it back without a flinch. "Thanks. What I find funny is there wasn't a spent match or lighter in sight, nor any ashes. I'm no hop head but you can't smoke cigarettes and not produce any ash. Am I right?"

Harley looked at Mick. "Thekan set him up."

Judy stepped over to join them. "What would be the point?"

"Axel wasn't no threat," Roger Copeland said. "Pain in the ass, maybe, but he don't have the ambition to make himself a concern to Thekan."

Beth Ann came forward as well. Her fingers rubbed absent circles at her temples. "But fingers will be pointed at him now."

"That's right." Mick turned to Stu. "What did you say about his shoes?"

"The cops were making notes about them," Stu said, his eyes bulging a little. "Otherwise I wouldn't have noticed. But they weren't like the shi—uh the stuff Axel usually wears. They were dressy-like."

"Pointed in the toe?" Mick asked and let out a conclusive breath when Stu nodded to the affirmative.

"The stairs," Harley said under his breath.

"Yes." Mick returned to his place in front of the bar. "If Axel is pinned in the murders of Cy and of Kippy Evert—and I'll bet a million dollars the shoes on his feet will match a bloody footprint found in Kippy's house—it knocks the investigative presence in this town way down, keeps the outside world, police, news media, the whole works, from speculating and snooping while the die-off moves in."

Will came around with full shot glasses for everyone. "It doesn't change what happened at the Mellar Borth place."

"No." Mick knocked back his drink. The motion put a hot stitching sensation in his shoulder. "But it still cuts interest in Knoll down by a good share. At any rate, we should talk to Axel. Tomorrow. First thing."

"No go," Stu said. "They're taking him to the health center in

Allycegate after his leg is set and casted. He's under 72-hour psychological evaluation. No visits, no phone calls. Not even from the cops."

"Damn, that might be too long," Harley said.

"We're it, then." Mick said and reached out for Beth Ann. "Are you ready?"

Her fingers laced cold and tight over his. "I am."

"One for good measure," Will said and passed out another round of shots.

They all took one, without hesitation.

CHAPTER SEVEN

They went down the stairs one at a time and gathered around a table Will had set with a row of flickering candles and several flashlights.

"I thought it seemed too dark down here," Will told them. Mick smiled, thinking the gesture was just right.

"There she is," Harley said and strode over to the tunnel door. He opened it with hesitation and stuck his face inside. He filled up most of the opening. "In all her glory."

"Going to be a tight fit for you," Mick said.

Roger made a distressed *gaaaa* sound. "Damned tight places."

"More room than the crawlspace under the kitchen at home," Harley said, plucking a flashlight from the table and shining it into the tunnel mouth. "Nice smooth concrete. Like a walk in the park."

Beth Ann stepped forward. "What do you want me to do, exactly?"

"Just say a few words," Mick said. "We need a blessing of some kind, I think, and you're the best candidate for the job."

"We'll help you," Judy chimed in. "Hold hands everybody. Make a chain."

It was a simple request, but it felt resoundingly right. They linked hands, wordlessly, forming a loose S shape in the flickering light. Beth Ann was at the end near the tunnel, with Harley by her side, and she closed her eyes, seeming soothed and ready. Mick felt the energy almost immediately, like a surging current.

"I want . . . " Beth Ann began, then shook off the attempt.

"Go on, honey pie," Harley said.

"The light and breath of goodness is invited into this place," Beth Ann said, the fingers of her free hand plucking at a gold cross around her neck. "May the angels bring them—"

A gust of air turned the candles' light to a raddled gasp.

"Jesus," Stu exclaimed.

"—and plunge them deep and revealing to part these dangerous waters. Amen."

They all traded uncertain glances in the silence. *Done*, Mick thought, *as easy as tying a shoe, as mundane as mailing a letter.* However, the energy in the air switched to a feeling of constraint, as if dark water was pushing against an unstable dam. His hand went to his pocket where the chess pieces rested in their velvet bag. It seemed ages since he sought their comfort. "Okay," he said. "We've accomplished something. Look."

A glow radiated from the tunnel, deep and slow but increasing, the way distant fog builds on the horizon. As it grew it took on color. Crymost green.

They all stared. "What in the world—?" Nancy Berns said, her eyes wide.

The wall behind Nancy and Stu, which was the stone and mortar plug at the opening to the old bootleggers' run, blew open with a deafening billiard ball crack and a disgorgement of stone and dust. Nancy leapt away with a harsh bird-like cry and collided with Will and Judy, nearly fell but kept her feet because Will caught her under the arms. Stu, however, stumbled over a batch of still-rolling stones and went down with a cry of pain.

At the same time, the tunnel door before Beth Ann swooped around, slammed with a thunderous boom, and shattered into bits of raw lumber and rusted nails. A shrieking rush of air pulled the fragments into the gloomy throat of the tunnel.

The tunnel glow winked out. Beth Ann stared after it, her mouth pulled into a rictus. "What have I done?"

They were no longer an S-shaped chain. Each of them stood independently and a little dazed. Nancy and Roger bent over Stu, who favored his left ankle as he struggled to get up. Will and Judy went to the newly opened bootlegger's run. Harley put his arm around his wife and muttered reassuringly to her. Mick stood by them and stared into the open tunnel.

"You did just what we needed you to do," he said. "Thank you."

"You can thank me when the angels swoop in here and carry you safely to whatever it is you need in that tunnel."

"Mick . . ." Will shined a flashlight into the bootlegger's run. "This run must have blown open at the riverbank, too. There's fresh air coming in."

"Good air," Judy added.

"Then we should get down to business," Harley said, "and go in."

"Do all of us need to go?" Roger Copeland asked with some concern. He was crouched down, watching Nancy tend to Stu's ankle, which was swelling by the second. "That space looks tighter than I think I can stand."

"Stu is out," Nancy said, apologetic. "He's going to barely make it upstairs on this sprain, so tunnel-tromping is not an option unless one of you wants to carry him."

"Damned if that ain't my luck," Stu said. "Sorry guys."

"I've got an idea," Mick said.

Once again, he was at the head of the group and once again the attention was turned toward him, almost supplicating. "We're pretty sure the tunnel comes out at the old mercantile, but we don't know what shape the underpinnings of that old place are in. It's not a bad idea to have a detachment above ground, in case we need help getting out. That would be Roger, Stu and Beth Ann. We can stay in touch by cell phone. Judy, I want you to go with them."

She stepped over to him, her face neutral. "I don't think—"

"You're not a fan of small dark places, either. And I think Beth Ann will do better if you're with her." He took both her hands and leaned in close to speak into her ear. "And I want somebody from Team Logan on both sides of this thing."

She met this with a look of concession. "Beth Ann will ride with me. Roger, if you drive Stu it will give us enough car space for everybody once we're back together at the mercantile."

Roger nodded.

Nancy stood up and nudged Judy's elbow. "They'll be okay. They're smart enough to take one woman along, so common sense will be up to a decent level." They exchanged smiles.

"Are we ready?" Mick said, an anxious flutter in his gut.

Will grinned. "Fresh batteries in our flashlights, good air at our backs and guardian angels treading the streets above us. Gotta be ready."

A cell phone chirped. Nancy pulled hers out and answered it. When she hung up she let her gaze sweep across all of them.

"Alice Vandergalien just died," she said.

CHAPTER EIGHT

Mick went in first, followed by Harley, Nancy, and at last Will. They shined their lights around, taking in the dimensions of the tunnel. Harley needed to stoop, but only a little. Mick could sense the closeness of the concrete ceiling like a looming presence. It made him stoop, too. There was not quite enough width for two people to walk abreast, so they walked in a scattered formation which allowed them all to see what was ahead.

"Fine job," Harley commented, running his fingers along the wall.

Their lights picked out only a miserly portion of space, and soon enough the passage in front and behind them was swallowed by the dark.

"Good air or not," Nancy said with one of her humorless laughs, "this is not a nice place."

Sheaves of webs, heavy with dust, clung to the walls or hung down from the ceiling and fluttered like desiccated trader's silk. She batted at a swatch of it with her flashlight and grimaced when it clung to the outer casing. She picked it off with a shudder.

"My aunt Delores lived in an old farmhouse in Lamartine," Will said. "There was a root cellar with a dirt floor in the basement. It smelled like this, only the air didn't feel the same. Her cellar felt empty, lonely almost. Something's alive here. Waiting."

Mick nodded. He couldn't have said it any better.

"And it feels like it's going to go on forever," Nancy said and shuddered again.

"It's a twenty-minute walk from my house to the south edge of town," Harley calculated, "Including corner turns and waiting for traffic on The Plank. We should be out to the mercantile in about the same amount of time."

Will inspected the ceiling, evaluating the joints between slabs sealed with trowelfuls of hydraulic cement. "We must be under Backbank Street by now."

"Farther," Mick said and glanced at Harley. "Past your house for sure. Under the Austin's yard, I'd say."

Harley said, "That's plenty far for me to start asking this. Where is the wreckage from the goddamned door? The pieces got sucked in here, we all saw it, but I don't see a single sign."

"You haven't been watching," Nancy said and aimed her light at the wall. She pointed out a scratch, shallow but fresh. "There's a bunch of these along the way."

"Good air hard at work," Will said and cast a dubious look ahead of them.

Mick was certain they were all considering what sort of powerful force might pull wood fragments this far and farther, and they were all pondering what they might do if it came again, or if The Crymost glow came back, bringing other unknown forces with it.

Then Mick's light fell on a rough basketball-sized opening in the wall ahead. "What caused *that*, do you suppose?"

"We're under Forest Street, is my guess," Harley said as they walked up, training their lights. He stuck his face close to the hole. "Right up next to the sewer line access. Something blew through here, strong enough to pop out a weak spot."

"Just now?" Nancy asked, her eyes wide. "When the door blew apart?"

"No, I think it blew through the other day," Mick said, "with pressure strong enough to loosen all the manhole covers around town. Am I right, Harley?"

"I'll be damned," Harley said.

Mick began walking again, shining his light from side to side. "Let's keep going. The door debris and that first blast of air had to be drawn toward something. It's got to be ahead of us somewhere."

"Yeah," Will said. "That's what I'm afraid of."

"Maybe the double barrel pump, whatever it is, uses sewer gas as an explosive agent," Harley said. "It was meant to ignite something, after all."

"Maybe," Mick said.

Gentle gusts still slipped around them from behind, sailing like tatters into the darkness ahead. Good air. Mick took out his phone and dialed Judy. He got no signal. "So much for Team Logan," he said.

Nancy's light flickered out, came back. She rapped it with her palm. "Oh Jesus, don't go out on me."

"Those are brand new," Will protested. As if in defiance, his light made a single off-and-on-again wink, then went dark. "Damn it."

Nancy shook her head. "The lights, your phone. We're getting in pretty deep here, boys."

"Let's keep moving," Mick said.

"Wait. Look." Harley aimed his light to where a small dark shape the size of a bunched food wrapper rested.

They moved up in a tight knot. The object was the torn-away head of a stuffed animal, a horse judging from the thick yarn meant to represent a mane. The fabric was matted, the neck stump leaking curds of nubby filling. Its plastic eye glowered at them.

"It's wet," Harley observed, almost casually.

"How did it get here?" Nancy said, leaning over it.

Will crouched and poked the head with his defunct flashlight. "Yeah, that air blast pushed or sucked everything else out. Why not Hi-ho Silver, here?"

"I'll say it again," Mick said. "Let's keep moving."

CHAPTER NINE

Judy called Mick from the road but got his voicemail. She concluded the tunnel was some type of signal blocker.

She slowed the car as they passed the F&F. The front bay door of the mill was open, the way barred by a strand of yellow police tape. A man in a dress shirt and wearing a shoulder holster crouched near the floor grates just inside, contemplative. In the glow of the mill overheads the scene was eerily timeless like an afterhours museum exhibit.

"Poor Cy," Beth Ann said with a sick rasp. "I prayed for him. Just now. Please don't think I'm weird because of it. I couldn't bear it if you thought less of me, Judy. I really couldn't."

"After today, we could all use a little more . . . well . . . something."

She reached over and patted Beth Ann's hand.

"I wonder what our boys will find under the streets of this town."

"Answers, I hope. Simple, safe, low-risk answers."

It was Beth Ann's turn to pat her hand. "If Harley were here he'd say we passed low-risk about half-a-day ago."

They smiled over everything hanging between them. Then Beth Ann snapped her attention to the road ahead, her face stretching with surprise. "Stop. Stop the car!"

"What?" Judy asked, but it was a secondary reaction. She was already standing on the brake. They were just out of town, the last streetlight at the corner of Tier Street and The Plank a hovering ball behind them.

Less than two hundred feet from their front bumper, a green radiance flowed across the road like a plasma river. A glow, but not a glow. Light managing to maintain a shape.

Beth Ann's eyes flashed in the illumination. "I've never seen anything like it."

"Me neither," Judy said. The thought trailing behind it was *what's coming for Knoll is close now, almost ready to make its move.*

"It's coming from—"

"I see that."

The glowing mass spilled from the show window space in the Mellar's Mercantile store front. It spread as they watched, nosing toward town, and toward the car.

Roger Copeland's headlights went out behind them followed by the thump of car doors. Roger strode up and Judy nearly smacked him with her own door when she opened it. "Is it safe, do you think?" she asked as she got out.

The glow halted and humped backward. It reminded her of an exposed grub retreating back into tilled earth.

Roger watched it, hands on hips. "Don't know. But something just grabbed its attention from behind. Looks like it's crawling back into its hole."

"Hang back," Stu Rueplinger said. He limped badly and helped himself along by hanging onto Beth Ann's car. "We don't know what that shi—uh, stuff is all about. Let it go. Just let it go."

As they watched, the glow slipped back into the mercantile window like the tail of some bloated beast. Judy's stomach turned in on itself. *Come out, Mick. Oh please, come out of there.*

A voice made her look behind them. "Told you it was closer than ever."

A pair of car doors slammed. The Schelvans from Backbank Street were parked just behind Roger's car. Another car crept to a halt behind them and a pair of youngsters tumbled out of the back, made to stop short when an imperative voice from the passenger side demanded they keep their asses next to the goddamned car. Judy was able to see silhouettes farther down The Plank as people walked from town with slow, curious steps.

"What do we do now?" Beth Ann asked.

At that moment, the green glow ignited over the crest of Pitch Road. *Back in its den, whatever it is*, Judy thought with some relief. Back at The Crymost.

More cars arrived. People got out, advanced. It felt like that morning's vote at the Mellar Borth house all over again.

"What the hell?" Roger said and pointed toward the street ahead.

A variety of items rested on the pavement where The Crymost glow languished moments before. They were odd shapes, disordered and seeming somewhat forgotten, like waste washed up on the shore.

Beth Ann opened her window and craned her neck to see. "Paved with good intentions," she said under her breath.

"Get out of the car," Judy said, unsure of what came next, but unable to fight the need to do something. She turned to Roger and Stu. "Keep an eye on things. Don't let this get crazy."

Stu blinked at her. "How?"

"I'm not sure, but we're in the front of the line, and we know more about what's going on than anybody else. That makes us the gatekeepers."

The crowd moved in a weary unison—men in pajama tops and shirts and ties loosened in after-work attitudes, women in aprons and bathrobes and business suits and fuzzy slippers. They were all faces Judy knew with varying degrees of familiarity, but their dull determination made them equally detestable and frightening.

"Judy, what's going on?" a man (she thought it might be Corey Schelvan, but she couldn't be sure) called out to her.

Roger took a stance at her side. "Everything's under control, folks. No need to get jumpy."

"But there's stuff in the street," a woman challenged. "It wasn't there ten minutes ago when I came home from work. It came from that glow, didn't it?"

A consorting buzz ran through the crowd. More cars pulled in farther back. They were lined up on both sides of The Plank now. There had to be at least thirty people on the scene. A child demanded, "Are those toys in the road, Mommy? Mommy? Are they?"

Beth Ann tugged her arm. "What can we do? We can't stop them from looking."

"I don't know," she said and leaned against the car, arms crossed.

"Hey," Stu shouted and waved his arms. Hopping on his good leg, he reminded Judy of the comedy relief at a county fair grandstand show. "Those things in the road are a real traffic hazard, you know? We should clean it up before somebody drives through and blows a tire, or has a bad accident or something. Am I right folks?"

Another undertone, this one laced with notes of approval. Judy smiled at him and he smiled back.

"It's like the angels told us the other night. It's throwing everything back," Beth Ann said with sick wonder. "And why do I feel it's almost done? That this is the last of it?"

Judy gazed at the clutter in the road but said nothing.

CHAPTER TEN

Chastity almost didn't go in, but at the last minute she turned so sharply the upstairs hall runner twisted under her heel. Roderick stood at her bedroom window, hunched and panting, gazing at the place where The Crymost glow stained the sky. She was unsure which was stronger, her fear of him or her loathing, but she held them in check as she stepped up behind him.

"What could put you in such a destructive rage, Roderick? What is coming to this town?"

His fists trembled at his sides.

"Death. A cycle that follows an ancient path. It sleeps long and feasts furiously. And it's aware of the changes aboveground. Fearful of the opposition it might meet. So it brought me, bestowed me with undreamt of gifts, and in my zeal I brought attention and angered the opposition. Now it's restless and anxious and angry. Tomorrow must be the day I bring it an offering of many souls to touch, to expedite the feasting. It will be my atonement."

She swallowed past a thick knot in her throat. "And after that, what becomes of you? Of me?"

He turned toward her. *Sunken*, she thought when she saw his face and his yellow eyes. The odor around him suggested old meat left in a hot tin box. The front of his trousers was tented. She looked away and caught the view of the town. Her thought of *poor Knoll, I'm sorry Knoll* was a sigh of regret.

"I ask one final willful task of you," he said. "To help me atone."

Knoll was devising a defense. Roderick had angered the opposition, thank God. She swept over and lowered herself onto the bed. "It's too late to say no, I suppose." She hoped he did not see the pulse of fear in her forehead veins. Knoll needed time to devise, to act. Needed every minute. "I'll do what you ask. But later. After."

She reached for the top button of her blouse, but his hands beat her to it and he fell on her, pressing her into the mattress, his mouth trembling and spurting dots of foam.

"I feel next to nothing," he said, his eyes greenish lamps dialed low, rivulets of red welling in the corners. The silk at her collar muttered when it tore. His other hand worked at a place much lower, pulling away fabric, freeing flesh. "It's a betrayal, to be given good flesh only to wreck it with this numbness. This failing. This *rot*."

Poor Knoll, the words gained in volume in her head, as if to block him out. Her flesh rippled in kind to block out the rasp of his rough hands as they tore her smart summer slacks and the silkier layer underneath.

"I know you are anxious to go," he said in a voice nearly devoid of air. "I disgust you now."

"As I said," she gasped and drew up her knees to open the way for him. "It's too late for me."

His breath fell icy on her throat and his tears traced slick crimson across her breasts.

Please do something, Knoll, before it's too late.

He pushed in. She screamed and latched onto him, her fingers splayed over the jutting knobs of his backbone. The flesh covering them was thin, soft. Unraveling meat. She wept.

CHAPTER ELEVEN

"I don't know," Harley said. He stopped and gazed ahead of himself, a weary explorer just now aware of the miles he'd put on. "We should be to the mercantile by now."

They all stopped and trained their lights on him; all but Will, who clutched his dark torch like a war club.

Nancy nodded. "We're in for a really long haul if this thing goes all the way to The Crymost."

"Which it might," Harley agreed. "That Crymost glow got in here somehow, after all."

"Or it could end just a few more paces ahead," Mick said and swung his light around, "it's hard to tell in the dark."

"You know we're in it for the duration either way." Nancy chuckled. It was punctuated by a lazy flicker of her flashlight. "But the sooner we get out of this awful cramped place, the better."

"Maybe sooner, then," Will said and folded his hand over hers to guide the beam of her flashlight. "Up there. Do you see?"

Mick led the way to where dark fragments were scattered on the tunnel floor. He nudged the closest pieces with his shoe. "Old wood. Rusty nails. I'd say these are the door pieces we've been waiting to find."

"All the way up here," Nancy said with dark wonder.

Harley shot his light forward. "Yeah, we're close to something all right."

They instantaneously aimed their lights, a collective conscious. Other objects lay ahead in a jumble: a ragged red stocking cap, a set of keys, a silver spoon gleaming like a dull beetle shell. Mick started as his gaze fell on what he thought was a chessboard propped against the tunnel wall. His hand jerked to his pocket in acknowledgement, and for a moment he felt the sudden cold weight of Robbie Vaughn humping onto his back, and Robbie hissing wetly in his ear, *Fyvie sent me, Mr. Logan. He says there's no way out, this time.*

Then he saw the playful lettering on the board, nearly lost under a coating of grime. CHECKERS. The simple cousin of the intellectual game. It helped him to shrug off the dreaded sensations. Near him was a doll buggy, wheels up and filthy, an ashtray in the shape of the state of Florida, a softball. And at the very edge of the reach of his light, an open door frame was set into what would otherwise be a dead end.

"This is it," he said.

The others' lights were already dancing across the opening. Just inside was a deadfall of broken rafters and loosened hunks of fieldstone foundation, a ruined portion of the mercantile basement, plugging the way through up to three-quarters of the height.

"How's your backs, everybody?" Harley asked as they shuffled closer.

"Damn it," Mick said and reached through to give a length of fallen rafter an indignant shove. His stitches sent out a shockwave of protest, but the rafter actually moved a little when he pushed. A few particles of plaster sifted down and rattled at his feet.

"Do that again," Will said and sidled up next to him. "I'll help."

Harley attempted to push his long arms between Mick and Will to help. "If it just happened when the door blew at our end, it can't have settled too bad. It will be pretty unstable."

"Oh," Nancy said and gave the tunnel ceiling a dubious glance. "How unstable, exactly? Because I don't feel like getting turned into mashed Nancy down here. I'd help, but you three already look like sardines in a can, the way you're standing."

"It's okay," Mick told her as he pushed in unison with the others. "I think it's giving way."

"Yeah," Will rasped and ducked low to give Mick more room. "Harley, can you give us a little more?"

"Trying," Harley said. "Why is it so goddamned wet? Can you feel how wet the wood is?"

Will's voice was bright and yet morose. "Crymost juice."

The barrier gave way with a loud crash. The broken rafter tumbled away with the ceremony of a falling idol and debris crashed inward, clearing the opening. Mick lit the way inside, his heart hammering against his ribs.

"Take it slow," Harley warned him.

But he was through the opening in the same instant. His words came out with no effort, as if he was a conduit for the announcement and not its originator. "Here it is. Here's the double barrel."

He saw only the machine, a gray metal box the size of an alley dumpster. It was fed by several lead pipes stretching away into a crumbling hole in the far wall. The rest of the room, twelve feet on a side—palatial compared to the area they just left—was lost on him. He was barely aware of the others following him in. He set his hand on one of the metal side panels of the machine as if testing it for heat or cold. The double barrel, so much resembling it's crudely sketched likeness.

Nancy's light flickered around the room disclosing broken machine parts and forgotten tools, the mangled shred-nests of mice along the bases of the walls. "That's quite a smell," she said. "Is that gas?"

"Fuel oil," Harley said.

"The reason so many people wanted this place torn down," Will added. "A forgotten fuel tank was leaking somewhere. Judging from the smell, I'd say it's close by."

"Maybe not so much forgotten as hidden," Mick said. "Our leaky tank might be part of the double barrel, left behind full and ready on purpose."

He ran his fingers along one of the pipes and then held them up for Harley to see the oiliness.

Will raised his brows. "You can't run an engine on that stuff, can you?"

"No," Harley stepped up to examine the double barrel and lay his hands on the pipes. To Mick his countenance was that of a wild eccentric realizing the validity of some madcap theory. "The oil is for burning. And there's a mixer here. An igniter is probably somewhere on the other side of this wall. Electric from the looks of it, which is how the whole shebang is operated, pump and all."

Will ran his gaze along the ceiling. "Electric? I don't see any power cables."

"A battery, maybe," Harley checked the floor around the double barrel.

"Here," Nancy said and dragged a canvas tarp off of rows of car batteries stacked in a far corner. Each one was ruptured and wore a beard of long-dried corrosion. "Not any good, though."

"Would my generator back at the bar work if I brought it down here?" Will asked.

"Like a charm," Harley smiled.

"Then things are looking up," Mick said.

"Yes, they are." Nancy stepped over to a door next to the defunct battery pile. She jiggled the knob, and when it opened she said, "Because here's our way out. Looks like the mercantile basement proper." She followed it with a humorless Nancy Berns laugh.

"If I'm right," Harley gazed at the wall with its infusion of pipes, "this deal mixes fuel oil spray—which is the only way you can easily ignite the shit—with another agent to run it past an igniter and make something go boom. Judging from the direction these lines are headed, that would be Pitch Road, provided the lines go straight all the way."

Will joined Nancy at the open door as she shined her light into the adjoining room, a broad expanse lined with rotting shelves and moldy sacks. The beam played along dusty wooden steps going up. Mercantile basement, indeed. "It mixes fuel oil with another agent such as what?" he asked.

"It's called a double barrel," Nancy turned and grinned at them. "Gunpowder, maybe?"

Mick tapped another one of the pipes with a sudden certainty. There was only one word for what he felt just then: correlation. Damned if it wasn't.

"Methane," he said. "If these lines run all the way to Pitch Road, that explains the fake vent pipe at the old dump. It was a decoy, making everything look nice and normal, when the methane is really bottled up underground waiting for this old contraption to work its magic."

Harley grunted. "Goddamn."

Will spun around. "Give it both barrels and the dump goes boom, takes The Crymost with it."

Mick nodded, unable to ignore the hot excitement in his belly. "All orchestrated from a safe distance, and protected by good air. Right here."

"Goddamn," Harley said again, squeezed in behind the double barrel and crouched as if this new revelation demanded closer examination. "Sounds crazy on the surface, but I've cobbled together enough projects in my day that had no business working but ended up filling the bill."

"Will it be enough?" Nancy stepped back to join them. "Blowing up The Crymost, I mean. I think our problems come from a little more than rocks and dirt and a pool of old green water."

"The men who put in the tunnel and the double barrel seemed to think so," Mick said and rapped a hand on the double barrel's sheet metal side.

"We're not safe, guys," Will said, his face suddenly blank as he stepped up to Nancy's side.

Harley shrugged. "If there's a clog in one of the lines, or if it's not vented properly, something might blow up in our face, but otherwise—"

"No. Not the machine," Will said and pointed. "I mean that."

Thin greenish light burned inside the pipe-accommodating hole in the wall just above Harley's head. As they looked, it intensified with onrushing speed.

"Get down," Mick said and instinctively dropped into a squat.

Harley ducked just as the glow spread above their heads, revealing itself as something more substantial than light. It seemed to be an amorphous bladder full of foxfire. Nancy made an attempt to turn away, but the glow descended on her like a rushing tide, washed over her, bathing her in green. It flowed over Will a second later. He stared out from it, his brow furrowed as if he was caught between several clashing thoughts. Shadows ran over objects in the room like the fingers of a sightless being and a muted sighing sound wafted into the air. *Its voice*, Mick thought, *the voice of The Crymost*. And there was more, a sense of animal intelligence, more instinct than reason.

"Will! Nancy!" he called out. "Get through the door to the mercantile basement if you can."

They both marked him with dull, confused stares, but then Will rallied. He broke free of the green glow and ran through the basement door, his arms and legs jackknifing, his clothes and hair wet with Crymost juice, his eyes wild. Nancy remained bathed in green radiance, gazing into space. Her flashlight dropped to the ground and shattered.

"I should have grabbed her," Will said from the doorway, his face stricken. "Shit, why didn't I grab her?"

"Don't worry, we'll get her on our way through. Come on, Harley."

"Yup," Harley said and stood up, as if unaware of the overhead stream of radiance feeding the mass around Nancy. His head and neck were instantly bathed in it.

Will shouted. "Oh, shit."

Mick reached for Harley's arm to drag him out but saw there was no need. The Crymost glow recoiled, repelled. In the next instant it vanished the way a spotlight stills to darkness when its power is cut. A ghostly afterimage of it slipped through the door to the mercantile basement and up the stairs. The room around them became a confusion of clanks and clatters as objects fell to the floor from a dropped height. Crymost objects.

The mercantile let out a low, settling groan above them. Plaster dust streaked across their flashlight beams.

"I don't know about the rest of you," Harley said, his gaze and his light trained on the ceiling. "But I think we should get a move on. I'm getting a bad vibe about this place coming down around our ears, people."

"After what I saw you just do," Will said, "your vibes are the law. Let's go."

"We'll never make it," Nancy said, dour and almost prophetic, and showing no intention of going anywhere.

Mick dashed around and pushed her ahead of him. She was soaked to the skin with Crymost water but she responded with loose, sleepwalker's steps. Miserable tearing sounds came from above as the mercantile shifted and shed hunks of stone and broken wood. The four of them rushed into the main basement, large pieces of foundation and plaster crashing to the floor as they gained the stairs. Mick was the last one up. Loud thuds like pursuing footsteps made him look around to where broken segments of the basement ceiling fell on the risers at his heels, smashing the wood. He gave Nancy one last mighty shove at the top, and as he burst through the upstairs door into Will's waiting arms, the stairs fell away behind him in ruins. He leapt up and landed hard on the wood of the main floor.

Will helped him up and said, "Mick, Nancy's not good." There was a tremble in his voice.

Nancy was hunched in Harley's arms as if drawn up against the cold. Her eyes looked out at them, wide and yet empty, so different from just moments before.

"We'll never make it," she said.

Mick winced at the hopeless sound of it, but it was Nancy's hair he stared at. It was completely white.

"Let's get her outside," he said.

CHAPTER TWELVE

Fuck you, Ichabod, Axel Vandergalien thought as he dropped the manual shift of the hospital transport van into cruising gear.

The world rushed by outside and the appearance of it was strange to him—long streaks of color turned to threads the way blood thins in the rain. The flimsy hospital gown drooped off one of his shoulders and the hem was bunched to the side. Anybody looking in would see his worldly goods, bag and all, hanging out. But fuck them, too.

A single, clear fact blazed in front of him like a dripping sun, so real he could touch it. It pushed aside the idea that his busted left leg, in a fresh cast, slug removed, debilitated him like a stone anchor. It overpowered the memory of his slipping away from the nurse who was doping him up. He barely remembered hobbling outside like an overwound broken toy and jumping into this van, which was left idling next to the storage garage marked HOSPITAL PERSONNEL.

Only one thing flamed on in his head. Thekan was some kind of double-crossing, uncle-killing freak with nothing but dangerous intentions toward Knoll, and for once in his life Axel Herman Vandergalien needed to do the right thing. He needed to pull Thekan down, or at least get the people of Knoll to pull him down. Somehow.

"No. Go back to the hospital, dumb shit," Unky Cy said from the row of seats behind him.

In the rearview Axel could see him, mostly pulled apart in bloody chunks and then restacked, half-assed, as if that Pablum Picasso artist had gotten ahold of him. Next to him was Auntie Alice grinning with that stupid patience of hers, her fat cheeks taut and purple and a little shiny, her lips as black as engorged leeches.

"It's too late. You need to turn this truck around, honey," she said, and her eyes, bulging and dotted with red snaps, tried to blink but failed. "Or it's going to get very bad for you. The Crymost is going to do what The Crymost is going to do. That Thekan creature is just a part of it. You can't change anything."

Axel focused on the road and shrugged his shoulders.

"Fuck it all," he said again and pressed the accelerator as hard as he could. "I gotta tell somebody."

CHAPTER THIRTEEN

Touching The Crymost items was unnerving at first, but as she continued to collect them and deposit them in a damp but serviceable wicker basket she'd found, Judy felt more at ease. Beth Ann helped her, wordless and grim. Many of the townspeople had gone home, but a few remained to pick through the curiosities like browsing sheep. This relieved her as well, but she was still worried for Mick and the others. It seemed they were below ground for longer than a reasonable amount of time.

She glanced over at Stu, who had borrowed a pickup truck from one of the curious passers-by—Dave Bortner, perhaps. He limped around, transferring Crymost items to the truck bed for transport. Good old Stu.

At last she turned to Beth Ann. "I think it's been long enough. I'm going over to the mercantile, just to assess the shape of things."

"Let me take those over to the truck," her friend said and took the basket from her, "and I'll be right behind you."

Judy nodded and stepped into the street. Roger Copeland stood across the way gabbing with one of the browsing villagers, and she was glad to see him. They would make an adequate rescue team, her, Roger and Beth Ann, should it be needed.

As she crossed the center line she heard a crash from inside the mercantile. Something large. *Huge.* Perhaps part of the old building itself.

She stopped, her eyes locked on the gaping window opening of the mercantile, her mind playing out a hundred scenarios, her heart jackhammering. At the same time, she saw headlights coming into town from the south, but it did not fully register. All she could think about was Mick and the others and what might have befallen them. A hateful, tingling fear found a foothold in her heart.

The roar of an engine sank in next. The street became ablaze with headlamp light. Her shadow stretched out as if trying to break away. A white van bore down. She whirled to face it. Tires shrieked. She felt oblivious, betrayed, hopeless.

Her feet lurched forward, her vision and awareness blurred, and then crashing sounds filled the world.

CHAPTER FOURTEEN

Mick raced through the dusty wooden compartments of the mercantile ground floor. The open socket of the show window, draped in young vines, appeared in his flashlight beam and he hurried toward it with the others right behind, the two men helping Nancy along.

The sound of a racing engine barely registered as he stepped through the window opening into the fresh air of night. Then the screech of tires rose like a strain of sickness. It was the metallic crashing noise and the tinkle of scattering glass that finally awoke the dread in him. *More awfulness*, a part of him announced, *more and more awfulness.*

The scene on The Plank was described in surreal brights and darks by crosshatched beams of headlights. People stood in the road, some of them making distressed cries. A shadow ran toward him, huffing.

"Mick. For crissakes, you better get over here."

It was Roger Copeland, he realized as he broke into a run. On the opposite side of the road sat a pickup truck and a white van, yards apart, equally mangled. Puddles of ejected liquid shone on the pavement. Silhouetted street people began to gravitate toward the vehicles, and he felt the needed to go too, but as his feet hit the road another shape captured his attention. A solitary shape, arms clutched together, feet on the center line of The Plank.

"Judy?"

She turned to him and her arms flew up almost wing-like as if now, with him here, they could fly above the scene together, evaluate and decide what to do. He wound his arms around her. She fiercely gripped him.

"He missed me by inches," she said against his neck. "Crazy, crazy idiot."

"Who?"

She pulled back to give him a reason-filled look. "Axel Vandergalien. He came down the hill in that van. So fast. He swerved away from me. And he hit . . . oh God."

More people gathered around the wreckage, several on their cell phones. *Like crows*, Mick decided, spreading the bad news via wireless signals instead of treetop caws.

"There's Beth Ann," he said with some relief and pointed at the form standing just paces from the crumpled pickup.

He shouted for Harley, but his friend was already on the way over to his wife, muttering under his breath with racehorse urgency. Then Roger Copeland was back. "Mick, come see what we can do. We got a man down."

"Axel," Mick said. "I heard."

"No, it's Stu. He was right next to that pickup when it got hit. Come on. It's pretty bad."

Judy looked behind him and said, "Here's Nancy and Will. Maybe Nancy can—oh."

Dawning understanding crossed his wife's face the moment she got a good look at Nancy Berns. Without hesitation she took Nancy's arm. The trembling, stunned Judy from moments ago was gone, put away with the offhanded consideration of an old unwanted overcoat. "I've got her," she told them.

"Come on, Will," he said. "Let's see what's going on."

Stu was flat on his back near the peeled and snarling grille of the pickup. A mangled front fender stuck out above him like a broken wing. A crowd stood nearby. Someone had spread a light jacket over Stu's stomach as if to keep him warm. A deliberately placed trail of sweatshirts, a bathrobe, a couple of paper grocery sacks described a path between Stu and the truck like a bizarre footpath.

Stu seemed pale and unaware in the wash of headlights from the nearby cars, but as Will and Mick crouched next to him, one at each shoulder, he turned his head and managed a tired smile.

"What happened?" Mick asked, and let his gaze pass over the jacket on Stu's stomach. A rosette of blood was seeping through it.

Stu raised a shaking hand far enough to aim a finger. "Damned van came out of nowhere. Piece of metal bit me pretty hard in my gut. Might be some internal bleeding."

Mick looked around. At least two bystanders were phoning for help, thank God, but this felt urgent. It felt dire. "Listen, Stu. You're the expert in these matters. What do I do?"

"I might need surgery to fix this. And I ain't got no goddamned insurance for that."

Will pulled at the jacket coverlet up from the bottom, creating a barrier that prevented Stu from seeing. The wisdom of this was something Mick would marvel at later. At the moment he was simply unable to look away from what other well-meaning souls in Knoll meant to cover up.

Just above Stu's belt buckle, a ragged hole spilled a coil of intestine that made Mick think crazily of clock springs. A ropey length of it trailed off under the collection of cloth and bags and ended where a crescent of truck metal was hooked neatly through it, as if the pickup's one purpose was to unspool Stu's insides like yarn pulled off the skein. Blood pumped out in freshets and spread into the gravel.

Will let the coverlet drop without a word.

"Cold," Stu said. "I must be bleeding bad, huh?"

Mick squeezed his shoulder. "The ambulance is coming. Be here any minute."

Stu nodded and then looked up at the two of them. His face was a white moon. "If I'm bleeding bad, can one of you put some pressure on the wound?"

They traded a wordless exchange. At last Will rested his hand on the bloodied jacket. Gentle. This response, too, was something Mick would marvel at later. "There," Will said.

Stu's hand was still elevated and Mick grasped it out of instinct. "That better?"

"Yeah, thanks guys."

Stu shivered and let out a long, ragged breath. His eyes searched the night and then settled on Mick, and that was it. Peaceful dullness took possession of his features. Emptiness.

Mick gripped Stu's hand even tighter for a moment, then let it go. Will slipped off his shirt and spread it over Stu's face and upper body.

Dropped. The word seemed to tumble through Mick's head. They were all becoming singled out, dangled and dropped by malicious hands, and there was nothing he could do about it. Was there ever? *Maybe not, Mr. Logan.*

"Axel's a mess." A voice from behind sent Mick to his feet. "How is Stu doing?" It was Roger Copeland, who stepped up and took in the scene with a defeated "oh".

Sirens wailed in the distance. Will stood up and wiped his hands on his undershirt creating maroon smudges. "Come on, Roger. Let's get people out of the street," he said. "We don't need any more takedowns tonight."

"Yeah," Roger said.

Another hand, this one on his shoulder. It was Judy.

"Oh no, poor Stu."

"Yeah. Where's Nancy?"

"I put her in the car. My God, her hair. What—"

"Come on."

"Where are we going?"

"To seize an opportunity," he said and led her around to where the van had apparently flipped after impact and rolled back up on its wheels.

Its cab faced away from the street, one weak headlight throwing amber light into the ditch. Onlookers stood near the driver's door, which hung open drunkenly, but none of them moved in to help. A mess, Roger had called Axel, and it put an unpleasant tug in Mick's gut as he pushed his way up to the mangled opening.

From the waist down Axel seemed pressed into the crumpled metal, a neatly-fitted puzzle piece wrapped in a hospital gown, meant to pop in and out of place with the flick of a finger. The steering wheel jammed against his chest promised to be a hindrance to such popping, however. Another hindrance: the jag of crumpled truck roof buried in his skull.

Mick's first thought was *somebody ought to put some pressure on that.*

The smells of hot engine oil and blood whorled out at him. "Axel. Why this? Why did you come back?"

Axel rolled his eyes, his hair in sanguine strings. A trickle of red leaked from the corner of his mouth. "Motivating fire, I guess. That's what I was told once. Past remorse becomes motivating fire. But everything I do ends up a clusterfuck, man." He winced and gave an accusatory grimace at his chest, where the steering wheel pressed in impossibly deep. "That's the part Ichabod didn't get."

Mick leaned a little closer. "Ichabod. You mean Thekan?"

"Killed my Uncle Cy, then set me up as the one who did it. He's got something on the line, you know. Something that's coming to Knoll real soon. A hungry thing. And its reactions are automatic. Like an animal I guess. Ow, aw fuck."

"Some of us have an idea about what's coming, too, and we mean to beat it," Mick said. "We mean to beat Thekan too. What do you know, Axel? What can you tell us?"

Axel grunted deep in his throat. "He thinks he's got the town in his pocket, but he's also worried some of the people, or maybe a lot of them, will get a whiff of the rot under his skin. One thing Knoll is good at, it's sniffing out the ripe stuff. Me included. I guess they were right. Look at the shit show I caused tonight." His eyes fluttered with approaching unconsciousness. "By the way, sorry about the village hall fire. It was a fucking stupid move. I'm glad you made it out."

"Mick, the ambulance is here," Judy said. "We better get out of the way."

Sirens whooped close by, deafening. Running feet approached. One hectic shout proclaimed something about the Jaws of Life as emergency vehicle lights swooped around the wreckage.

Mick let Judy lead him back to the opposite roadside where Harley and Beth Ann waited. They blended with the other bystanders for a while and watched while stretchers and medical kits were rolled out. And Mick thought of jaws, yawning open, waiting. Waiting.

CHAPTER FIFTEEN

From behind the bar, Will said, "Let's do it, right now. We can roll my generator down the tunnel, hook it up to that double barrel machine and blow The Crymost to kingdom come before midnight." He moved around in the half-light of the lamps over the bar in his blood-smeared undershirt. The rest of them sat on stools like a clutch of time-weary patrons: Mick, Judy, Harley, Beth Ann, and Nancy.

"I'd be right there with you," Harley said. "But there's one thing we need to check on first: breather pipe. The write up on the double barrel plan says there needs to be a breather, probably on The Crymost proper. Without venting, the whole damn shebang might blow up internally and take whoever is pushing the start button with it. No way to tell if those double barrel boys got it done or not unless we check."

Will stopped in the middle of pouring a beer. "The Crymost might have done something to make them forget. I can tell you firsthand how easy that green glow gets into your head and starts moving things around. In that basement, I could feel it in me. In my thoughts." His arms, Mick saw, were alive with goosebumps.

Nancy made a low moan in the back of her throat, as if in concurrence.

"Then get ready, gentlemen," Mick said as Will set out beers for all of them. "It seems we need to go on a breather pipe hunt."

"Not tonight," Judy said to him. "You're exhausted, we all are. And The Crymost, or whatever lives up there, is on high alert. This town has seen two disasters today. There's no need to walk into a third."

"Tromping around up there is a job for the daylight, anyway," Harley said.

"Daylight and faith," Beth Ann announced. Her clear eye seemed haunted; the bloody one drooped, afflicted. "I'll pray we have those things on our side tomorrow."

Harley gave her a squeeze. "You do that, honey pie."

Will stretched and let out a huge yawn. "I for one am all for hitting the hay."

"I don't care for the idea of some of us being home alone, however," Judy said and gave Nancy's arm a gentle squeeze.

"We'll take her," Beth Ann said, more brightly than seemed possible. "We've got the spare bedroom off the attic. And I want to do this. I need to, I think."

"All right then," Mick said and stepped away from the bar. Will came around to join the rest, and once again Mick found himself standing separate, facing them, all eyes looking back with acceptance. "Let's keep each other safe."

Class dismissed, Mr. Logan.

CHAPTER SIXTEEN

Chastity leaned against the bathroom sink to keep from falling down. Her legs were weak and the pain between them was a broad and twisted cord lacing her anus to her pubic bone. On her face, streaks of blood like war paint—not hers, but the stuff that leaked from Roderick's empty eye holes while he gyrated and rammed into her. She splashed water on her cheeks, thought about cupping some warm soap suds between her thighs but then didn't.

"We're nearly done for tonight," Roderick called out from the bedroom. "Then you can rest."

Nearly done. Part of her cried out against another rough penetration. Against the texture of the emissions he produced during his final, brutal thrust this last time. His semen possessed a disbanding property, like it scurried inside her. Images of the larvae she'd mined from his pockets only the day before flowered open in her brain. She shoved them away, but they only opened again.

Another part of her insisted she relax because the tone of his voice intimated business now instead of lust. What she needed to do was put herself to rights, stagger back to the bedroom to trade her tattered blouse for a fresh one, strip away the remaining ribbon of waistband and put on new panties—or perhaps just a skirt because the thought of fabric touching her crudely-rubbed flesh made her sweat—and stay the course a while longer.

Come on, Knoll. I've bought you all the time I can afford. Somebody do something.

It was a stealthy hope, as quietly creeping as the trickle of spunk working down her legs. She wiped it and rinsed her fingers without looking at what might go spinning down the drain.

Roderick stepped up behind her and she squeezed the last ounce of strong, unaffected posture out of her frame. He was wearing slacks and an open shirt. His empty eye holes, rimmed with starbursts of dried blood, housed the beginnings of eyeballs mushrooming back into place. He held out her bathrobe.

"Just this," he said and draped it over her shoulders. "We need to use the telly-phone. For one call."

His hands massaged her neck, hard and rough.

"In a minute," she said and turned on the water taps. "I want to wash my face."

"Of course. I'll be downstairs."

Downstairs. *By the telly-phone*, she thought, and what might have once amused her pushed her to the brink of screaming. She scrubbed her face and pressed a few handfuls of water against her inflamed lower regions after all, then blotted with a towel. She did not look down even once. Instead she thought about what she might do if Knoll did not show its rebellious head soon. *Daddy's rosary might be a help and a comfort*, she thought as she pulled on her robe and tied it closed. It presented itself to her under strange circumstances after all. As strange as Roderick's arrival. And hadn't she picked it up frequently throughout this day, as if subconsciously asking for its help? It was downstairs at the moment, resting on her kitchen pill shelf, and she suddenly wanted it in her possession. Wanted it more than anything.

She stepped across the bedroom, gave the mussed and crimson stained sheets barely a glimpse, and went down to the kitchen where she plucked the rosary from its place just as Roderick moved up on her in a dark swoop.

"Ready?"

She slipped the rosary into her robe pocket, quite adroitly she thought, and hoped he hadn't seen. "Yes," she said. "Whatever you want. Who do you need me to call?"

"Everyone."

She frowned at the wall phone hanging before her. "You know how this works, right?"

He lowered himself into a kitchen chair. Gaunt. His eyes, now restored, held a dull shine. "I know how it works for me."

She took up the receiver and stared at the dial in its curved underbelly. Words churned in the back of her head the way a dust storm looms on a desert horizon. Roderick's words, what he wanted her to say, being fed to her via the telegraph of dark miracles. Her other hand stirred the beads in her robe pocket, flicked at a gilt edge of crucifix.

"Three rings," he said, "and you can start talking."

There was no hanging up the phone, no capability of rebellion in her muscles. She pressed the receiver to her ear upon the first ring. *I called from this phone to tell them Daddy was dead.* She clung to the thought, a desperate scrap of thinking still her own. Ring two. *This same phone rang the day they told me Gregor was in a terrible accident and I'd better come to Hillside Hospital right away.*

The third ring, and then a chorus of voices in ragged unison, unraveled at each end. "Hel-hello-lo-o?" mixed with a garble of voicemail salutations.

Knoll. Everyone in Knoll, or close to it. Roderick's dark telegraph commanded her vocal cords, engulfed her awareness, except for that one small shred of thought, like a bit of bright cloth fluttering in a high branch.

"Fellow Knoll citizens, this is Chastity Mellar-Borth. I want you to know I am in a state of great remorse over the tragedies befalling our fair town today. It is easy to reflect in solitude upon our losses, but this is a time to find solace in fellowship in our community. It is time we unite to console one another, kindly and properly. And we are fortunate enough to have someone among us who is willing to offer us guidance in such matters. The Honorable Judge Thekan would like you to attend a gathering of guidance and fellowship."

Roderick sat forward, his grin triumphant, his yellow teeth nearly snapping at the phone cord dangling between her breasts. She held her stance, her pocket hand working rosary beads with sweaty strokes.

"Meet us tomorrow at The Crymost, won't you? It will be a time to face our sorrows as a community at the place which knows our sorrows best." She clenched all over and homed in on the ache and burn between her legs. It sent an arrow of clarity through the words, summoned mental pictures of those Knoll citizens already lying dead in the morgues and funeral parlors of Drury, Allycegate, and points in between.

"We'll gather at . . . " the word "noon" clacked deafeningly from the dark telegraph. She felt her mouth begin to form the word. But no. Knoll needed more time to rebel, to defy in a way she seemed unable. Someone was out there, planning, devising. She knew her town well enough to be confident there was at least one. The idea shook through her, followed by another. She gave words to them both. ". . . at *sunset*. Bring a special memento, significant and curious if you have one. I know I will. And let us hope we'll find easement of our agonies by the beautiful blush of twilight."

Roderick snatched the receiver from her hands and pressed it close to his mouth as if to devour it. "Come to The Crymost," he said, so close his hair tickled her cheek. His corrupted smell was overpowering. "At sunset, as she says."

His eyes flashed at her, a universe of a thousand camera bulbs and he cast the receiver down. It shattered on the floor, spraying components.

Chastity pressed herself against the wall. There was nowhere to run from him; her tiny telly-phone nook was a miniature prison.

"Sunset and mementos?" he said, his breath a cloud of swampy rot. "You wouldn't dare plot against me, would you?"

"Against you?" She put as much lilt into it as she was able. Probing sensations whirled around her head, trying to worm their way in, meeting a barrier formed by her thought-scrap and the still-fresh soreness between her legs. "What is it you think I could do? I just wanted that little speech to sound more like me than you. Really, Roderick."

"Some in this town conspire."

"You might think so, but who would be so foolish after what happened this afternoon?"

She tried to slip by and he stepped in closer. "Mick Logan is a main concern. A threat, really. And I will find a way to reach him, reach *into* him, and subdue him. Painfully. Once I can focus my efforts. Right after the feeding begins, I think."

"If you're still capable of your fine tricks once it, whatever it is, no longer needs you."

The universes in his eyes flared to quasars. Her mind felt exposed, as if a shard of her skull tumbled away to reveal the throbbing meat beneath.

"I am no mere instrument to be disassembled when the job is done. I intend to join the world of man again. To feel and taste and walk in the sun, free and whole and full of life."

"Look at you," she said, her voice trembling. "You have no place among men."

The initial effect was as she'd hoped. The probing receded, derailed. What followed surprised her, however; an imperative demand which pierced her defenses and stabbed clean and quick into her thoughts. Her car was to be filled with fuel and ready for him to speed away once business at The Crymost was complete. He meant to run, to scurry away like the loathsome thing that he was.

"You will finish this with me," he said and stepped back from her. "You owe it."

"I will," she said, aware of his determination still burning like a brand in her brain. She would do as he asked, as automatically as she'd spoken his words into the *telly-phone*. Helpless, or nearly helpless.

But a crystal-clear opening remained in her thoughts, so narrow she was sure Roderick would not notice it should he enter her mind again. At its center, a name blazed, a quasar of its own.

micklogan, mick logan, *Mick Logan*.

CHAPTER SEVENTEEN

Mick sat on the bed next to Judy. Her phone was still in her hand. She had just finished speaking with Beth Ann. "Nancy has a sister on the peninsula in Egg Harbor who will take her in. The woman's disabled so we'll need to get Nancy up there somehow."

"You should go then, the three of you. First thing. I want you away from here and safe anyway."

She spoke as if she hadn't heard. "I'm helping you at The Crymost in the morning. Beth Ann says she'll stay in town and sit with Nancy while we do our vent pipe search."

"And there's no two ways about it, I suppose."

"Nope. And if I thought Beth Ann could make the drive to Egg Harbor in her condition, there'd be no two ways about me staying right up until the big boom. Believe it."

She kissed him, walked around to her side of the bed and climbed in.

He swallowed hard. His lips felt warm and rubbery. "I love you, Judy."

"I love you too, Mr. Logan. Try to sleep."

He turned out the lights and lay back, his hand cupped over hers under the blanket. He could tell her mind was racing, and he wondered what thoughts might follow her down into sleep.

Outside, The Crymost glow painted the sky.

PART SIX:

DARK
MIRACLES

CHAPTER ONE

At FIVE THIRTY AM, Nurse Debbie Schuster walked into room 323 to open the drapes. In her opinion it did little good to let in the light for the critical and comatose patients, but Hillside Hospital protocol said otherwise, and the view of Drury's east side wasn't a bad one. Her first thought as she stepped toward the window was how peaceful the room was at this hour. The incorrect quality of that peace struck her a moment later when she beheld the patient, the bank of monitors and the respirator equipment, all silent.

Her thoughts exploded, procedure pushing aside less immediate concerns such as why no alarms or alerts were triggered by the failing machines, or how a curl of strangely sweet smoke managed to rise out of the patient's pale mouth like a parting dream as she pressed her fingers into the carotid artery to check for a pulse she already knew was not there.

Then she rushed out to announce the patient in ICU unit 323, Axel Vandergalien, was dead.

CHAPTER TWO

Mick squinted against the eight o'clock sun as he and Judy got out of the car and walked up to the Kroener's house. Will pulled up, waved a greeting and followed them onto Harley's porch. A good day for something in town to go boom. But first, they needed to see what Harley was so worried about. All he said over the phone was, "We got something else in the wind. Get over here as soon as you can. Beth Ann and me put together some breakfast so don't worry about your stomachs, just bring your cell phones, check your messages if you haven't checked already."

He had checked his—one voicemail, but it was tangles of static. His readout was likewise garbled, just letters and numbers in random order. Gibberish.

Harley opened the door, his face grave. "Come on in."

The house was filled with food smells which, on any other day, would be delightful.

"I got part of something," Harley said and led them to the hutch in the dining room, "and I suspect it's only partial because of what we're up to. Like we're not invited."

"You lost me," Will said.

Mick took in the blinking light on the Kroener's old fashioned answering machine. "Who called you, Harley?"

"It's Chastity Borth doing the talking." Harley cued up the machine and pressed the playback button. "But I think the words belong to somebody else."

The machine clicked and whirred. Mick leaned close. Judy and Will leaned in next to him. The recorded voice was indeed Chastity, sounding as if she was speaking through a resonating metal pipe. Background noise rose and fell, drowning her out at times.

"Fellow Knoll citizens, this is Chastity . . . —orth . . . great remorse . . . find solace . . . community . . . meet us . . . won't you?"

The rest of the message was crackles of static.

Judy glared at the machine as it clicked off. "Meet us? She wants to set up another town meeting? After what happened yesterday?"

"This is the final move," Mick said. "Where Thekan feeds The Crymost. But when and where? Damn, I wish I could hear the whole message."

Judy cued up her cell phone, listened, and shook her head. "I have a message from Chastity, too, but it's the same as Harley's. Just bits and pieces."

"You're all too close to me," Mick said. "I seem to have a knack for scrambling Thekan's signals, remember?"

"Talking to Chastity isn't an option, I gather," Judy said.

Harley grunted. "I have a strong hunch she'll clam up if she sees us coming."

"My phone was dead this morning," Will said. "It's back at the bar, on the charger. I can get it and try it now."

"After breakfast," Harley said. "Mick and I can knock on some doors, see if somebody will tell us what's up, maybe let us listen to their voicemail, get the whole message."

"No. Let us talk to the neighbors," Judy said and waggled a finger between herself and Beth Ann. "You boys are forgetting about the machine at the village garage. If this call went to every phone in town, which it sounds like it did, the garage machine might be out of range of getting scrambled, or at least have something more complete. We might as well attack this from all sides."

Harley looked at her, his eyes sparkling. "You are a peach."

"That's why I keep her," Mick said and hugged her at the waist. She smiled, but there was a certain rigidity to it. "Let's eat," he said at last.

They filed into the kitchen where Beth Ann set out plates while Nancy Berns sat in a corner chair, studying the eastern window as if it were a dream.

CHAPTER THREE

At first Mick was worried about the village garage machine's ability to play anything back; he even said as much as they walked up to the desk, but Harley ran a thumb across the controls to wipe away the soot that covered everything: the desk, the window, the Swisher, like a blanket of shadow. It revealed a bleary message light, and he pressed the playback without hesitation. It immediately took off. When Chastity stopped talking he hit the stop button with a thoughtful frown.

"Tonight," Mick said at last, and felt the color drain from his face.

Harley rewound the message, played it again. "We were going to blow the double barrel today anyway."

"Which means we damn well better find that breather pipe fast. Or figure out how to make one, or we're screwed."

Harley nodded, almost curt, put up his hand and listened to Chastity Mellar Borth make her announcement once more. "She's struggling with it," he said. "Right . . . *here*."

" . . . we'll gather at . . . at *sunset*. Bring a special memento . . . " the message implored.

Mick considered it. "Maybe Thekan let her pick the time."

"Maybe," Harley said and tapped the controls where a digital counter displayed seconds. "But I've been stopping the message when she's done talking. From the looks of this, there's more to it."

They watched the counter tick down and listened to the rustle and clatter of a phone changing hands. "Come to The Crymost," Thekan's voice rose out of the machine so loud the plastic around the speaker made buzzing sounds. "At sunset, as she says."

"Sun sets around eight," Harley said gazing at the window.

"Gives us less than twelve hours. It suddenly doesn't seem like enough. Where are they when you need them?"

"Who?"

"The dead. At one time I had one riding my goddamned back, don't forget. Now they're all gone. Out of Knoll. Abandoned ship."

"Are you sure?" Harley said and pointed at the message machine again.

The counter flashed, but it showed no numerals now. It flashed L-I-N-R over and over again.

CHAPTER FOUR

Will pulled up and climbed out of his car just as they were leaving the garage.

"It's tonight," he shouted as he jogged around to meet them. "My phone is toast but I ran into Cheryl Abitz and she told me."

"Yeah, we've got it," Mick said. "Clock's ticking now."

His cell rang and he jumped a little. It was Judy.

"Connie Gassner tells me—"

"At sunset," he said. "Which means as soon as we find that breather, you're in the car and on your way north, understand?"

"I'll meet you at The Crymost."

"Yeah," he said and traded glances with Will and Harley.

He felt like a man at the edge of a tensing, volatile trap, unsure when the jaws might close, but certain they would. Soon.

Judy's car rode the uphill stretch of The Plank just as Mick, with Will right behind him, pulled over at the Pitch Road entrance. He got out and used a bolt cutter to nip the chain barring the entrance.

"Stronger up here today," Harley said after Mick was behind the wheel once again.

Mick wanted to agree. The Crymost was indeed exuding more than its usual palpable presence of sorrow. His attention, however, was pulled away by the choking gasp of his engine as an array of idiot lights winked to life across his dashboard.

Will's horn sounded, a single dying bleat. Judy rolled to a halt behind them, making them a stilled procession on silenced engines. Mick groaned. "I guess we hoof it from here."

He got out, his edge-of-a-trap feeling gaining some weight. Will strode toward him. "All three cars conked out at the same time?"

"My phone, too," Judy said as she slipped up next to Mick. "It's out."

Will grunted. "Like we're being warned off."

Harley nodded and glanced up the hill, toward The Crymost turnoff. "It can warn us all it likes. We got business we mean to get done."

"If it's a warning at all," Judy said. "Remember what Axel said last night? 'Its reactions are automatic, like an animal.' Maybe some of The Crymost's effects are involuntary. Pure reaction."

"And they spread like a glow," Mick said and let the possibility slide into his thoughts. "Or *with* a glow. Anyway, back to the matter at hand. One of us should be able to cover the ledge top easy enough. The rest of us need to comb through the greenery down below. What I wouldn't give for a metal detector right now."

"I'll cover the top," Judy said. "Girls up, boys down."

"We're looking for a heavy gauge metal pipe," Harley said as they walked toward the last gentle rise with its screen of shrubs. "Probably black—more probably rusted to hell—about eight inches in diameter, poking out of the ground. Somewhere."

"Needle in a haystack is what we're looking for," Will said and stamped his foot.

Mick patted his shoulder. "It's going to be a slow, steep climb down to the pond and we need to keep our eyes open the whole way, needle or not."

"Yes, eyes open please," Judy said and gave Mick a parting hug. "The Baylor Clinic saw enough of you yesterday."

He kissed her. "Thanks for helping with this."

She made no reply.

CHAPTER FIVE

Mick was drawn to a spot where the downward pitch of the land was grassy and more forgiving than the craggy face below The Crymost proper. He hiked down with the soaring view of the marshlands in front of him and Will and Harley on either side of him. A few times they needed to get a handhold on limestone fragments poking through the earth to successfully navigate, but their descent was steady. Near the bottom, they spread out.

"I'll check around the pond," Mick told them with uneasy thoughts of Peter Fyvie.

Limestone shelves ringed the pond, imperfect and yet precise, and he stepped up to the edge with a shiver. *A baptismal font*, he thought, *in a cathedral of tears*. To swim in the greenish water would be to weep from every pore and dissolve like a dream. And somewhere in its depths was Peter Fyvie's car, a mute hulk limned in silt, housing a single body stiff with bloat and rigor.

Again, the feeling his feet were perched on the edge of a tensing trap enfolded him. The Crymost's eyes were on them, of that he had no doubt. He found he was walking on the balls of his feet as he neared the place where the sheer limestone face of the drop-off terminated at the water's edge. No soft diggable earth here, only stone.

And debris.

Not every item tossed from above over the years was on target, he noted. Wooden dowels, gray with age, poked out like a ribcage from a coat of tangled greenery. He nudged it with his foot and the dowels, once finely turned and lacquered, reorganized to reveal a large hoop-like attachment. *Spinning wheel*; the term slipped by him with morose ease. He wondered what past-era grandmother spun up her thread on this ancient contraption, guiding the wool with carbuncled fingers while the huge vertical wheel whirled, throwing puffs of air like a saw blade. And he wondered which bereaved family member tossed the wheel over. Were they too blind with grief to notice when their offering smashed on the stones? Did they care? Because there are many wheels in heaven and earth, and each one turns in its own way.

He shook himself, skirted along the cliff face edge of the pond and picked his way across to the other side, searching and yet distracted. So distracted he did not notice the stifling quality come into the air. Not until he heard Will shout out, "What the hell—?" as a large shadow careened toward them from The Crymost ledge above.

More than once, Judy found the need to steer her attention back to the matter at hand. The people she'd seen here—ghosts, manifestations, whatever you called them—were trapped in her mind's eye. As if agitated by those thoughts, the air fluttered around her and filled with a creeping cold. Something was coming. Something bad.

She tried to call out—"Mi—"—and was cut short by a blow, full body, as if from a giant mitt. The air filled with images. People moved around her, or rather suggestions of people described by wisps of shadow. There were multitudes of them, overlapping, approaching the edge of The Crymost and dissolving there, each one unaware of the next. *Memories*, she thought. Memories and reaction. Incidental things riding on the back of what was coming.

She pushed her voice up and out as she stumbled to the drop-off amid shuffling, milling shadows.

"Mick!"

Mick's thought was *an old steamer trunk*, as the shadow dropped down The Crymost face like an inky teardrop. The trunk flickered in and out of existence as it fell.

"Look at it all," Harley declared.

Other objects were ejected over The Crymost ledge as well. Smaller, lighter for the most part, but it was to the trunk Mick fixed his attention. Its path toward the water was inevitable, a promise of something calamitous. A warning.

Will and Harley were ten feet apart, but equally close to the water's edge.

"Back off," Mick shouted to them. "Get away from the pool."

The trunk vanished at the water's surface, no splash, no sound. There was, however, an impact of a different kind.

The blow seemed to originate from within as if a large electrified club rapped the underside of Mick's skull. He sat down hard, a crag of limestone jabbing his tailbone. He saw Harley fall backward as if tossed by a mighty wind. Will dropped to the ground as well, his hands clamped to his head.

Defensive, Mick thought as he climbed to his feet. He staggered over to Will, who was on his side, knees drawn up.

"You dare not look at them," Will said through gritted teeth. His nails clawed across limestone. "They slip through still, but they can help you no more... Ah shit, ah *fuck*, I can barely move, and it feels like my head is going to explode."

Look at who? Mick wondered and glanced at the objects still falling from the ledge top: toys, jewelry, hats, and horns. Each one winked out of existence before reaching the pond. At last he bent over and clasped Will's hands. "Come on. We're going back up."

Harley stumbled over. He fetched a deep sigh, gathered Will up off the ground and held him like a broken doll. "I'll take him. You get yourself topside and check on Judy."

Mick glanced at the lip of the drop-off once more. He saw people there, translucent old-movie silhouettes stepping up by the dozen, leaning over with ceremony before casting trinkets out for the air and gravity to deliver to the pond. Another form, more substantial, stepped up to join them. It was Judy.

She waved. "Mick. Do you see them?" Her voice echoed down with the makings of a fevered dream.

"They're all around you."

"No." She pointed. "There."

He turned toward the place she indicated, only a few feet to his right.

Gray shapes moved near the north edge of the pond where the limestone rim touched the base of the drop-off. Three men, two of them crouching and packing loose earth into a common patch of ground and a third tamping the ground and stone down with his work boots. They flickered in and out with the same old-time movie presence. They did not speak but traded occasional morose glances. *They can help you no more*, Mick thought. *Like hell.*

"Harley. Over there," Mick shouted. "Is that them?"

"The one standing sure looks like Cy Vandergalien's dad in a younger day. *Francis*," he called out. "*Francis Vandergalien.*"

The standing man's head tipped just a little and he stopped his tamping. Then he winked out. The other two men disappeared a split second later. Mick's sense of alert remained, perched at some sort of apex.

"There," he said and strode toward the place where the men had been, and he hoped against hope the weed-covered object he spotted was what they were looking for. He pulled back old grass, kicked away decades worth of stone and dirt and gazed down at a stub of black pipe poking from the ground. "It's here. I don't know how they got it through the rock, but it's here."

"I'll be goddamned," Harley said, and then cast a contemptuous eye at the drop-off and the hail of objects. "We're good to go on the double barrel, then. Damned if we aren't."

"That's great," Will said, drooped in Harley's grip like a broken scarecrow. "I might not be able to see straight but the end is near. Got that, you Crymost mother fu—"

The rest of his words were drowned out by an earthy cracking and crumbling sound from the drop-off's rock face. Dust and melon-sized hunks of limestone streaked down as Mick rushed toward his friends.

Earth and rock rained down before he could reach them. Harley and Will became sepia silhouettes, and then they were swallowed by dust. Mick heard a single painful bark, unable to tell which of his friends it was, and then a door-slam blow to the back of his head made the world a ringing blur. He dropped to his hands and knees. Stones thumped the ground around him and pelted the pool with chuckling sounds. What seemed like hundreds of impacts died to a few, and then none.

"Guys?" he called out. The dust began to thin. "Harley? Will?"

"Here," Will poked his head from a nearby shrub. A coating of dust gave him the countenance of a powdered stage performer. "Harley threw me. I know he meant well but for Christ's sake, he *threw* me." Then, with a glance to his left. "Did you have to throw me?"

"Shit fire," Harley spoke up and made a tip-of-the-tongue sputtering noise. He got to his feet a few yards to Will's left. He was clutching his right elbow. A trickle of blood from his forehead described a harsh line on his dusty face. "I'd throw you again if I thought it would get us up top any quicker. We should get climbing before there's a round two."

"Lead the way," Mick said. "Will, how are the legs?"

"Pretty wobbly, still. It's this place. Gotta be. Damn, I hate feeling so helpless."

"Harley, can you take him?"

Harley shrugged. "Much as I'd like to, I think I'm on my own power. This arm. I suspect it's broken, Mick."

"Damn," Will said again.

Mick looked to The Crymost pond which was a calm, glassy oval of green. An eye, which sucked in sorrows instead of light and images. An eye regarding them with loathing.

Judy leaned over the ledge. "What just happened down there?"

"We got some more punches thrown our way. Some bad ones. But we found the breather pipe."

"Come back for me." Will stood upright but his knees wobbled as if made of loose sockets and ball bearings. "I'm just going to slow you down."

"I'll help you." Mick took a firm hold of Will's waist. "Slow and easy. Let's hope if The Crymost sees we're on the way out, it will hold back any more punches."

CHAPTER SIX

The climb was slow. Once, near the beginning, Mick lost his grip on Will and nearly sent him tumbling down the slope. Near the halfway mark, Harley sat down on a hump of rock, panting.

"Hold up," he said through gritted teeth as he hugged his damaged arm. "I got to sit a minute. This is the worst hurt since the cancer."

Mick and Will sat to wait it out. Judy, who regularly popped her head over the edge to check their progress, called down to him.

"Mick, I'm going to walk into town and get a working car up here. I'll park it on The Plank. I don't think any of you will be up for a hike back to Knoll once you get up here."

"You're right about that," he called back, his heart nearly bursting with gratitude.

Harley grunted. "Said it before and I'll say it again. She's a peach."

"Yeah," he said, not without a crack of worry in his voice.

CHAPTER SEVEN

Chastity noticed the intensity of the smell at about nine o'clock and tried to put it out of her mind, but by noon she was unable to keep from looking into it. The source was Roderick; of course, it was. Roderick had been in the guest room all day, sleeping she presumed, storing his energy like an old dry cell battery, releasing an odor of rot instead of ozone. She crept up the stairs and waited at his door.

The possibility that this was her last opportunity to end the dark magic presented itself, startling and abrupt. She pushed the door open, suddenly resigned to the idea if he was completely, *safely* in a deep sleep, she would make her move. But what might that move be? Slit his throat with a knife from the kitchen rack? Beat him with the bat she kept by the front door until his head was a senseless glob of shattered bone and bloody silver hair?

Two steps in, she stopped short. Roderick was stretched out on the bed, pale and naked, his eyes at a sleepy half-mast. His lips, a colorless gash, moved in twitches over jagged teeth. He was a wasting thing, his skin clinging close to the bone. *Vulnerable.*

She stepped up to the bed, her hands twisting against one another. One of the pillows was on the floor, ejected during his rest (*recharge, preparation*), and she crouched to pick it up. *So frail*, she thought as her gaze swept over his pale neck showing just a whisper of pulse, the hollows of his ribs, the flattened gray casing of his penis. She leaned close, the pillow in both hands as if it were a book she wanted to show him up close. She tensed her back muscles. Her jaw tightened until her teeth complained. Death. *It's coming all right, Judge Roderick. In fact, it's here—*

Pain shot up her arms in bolts. She stumbled backward and flung the pillow across the room as if it were the source. Agony awakened in a course of explosions down her spine. It nested between her legs where last night's aches were just beginning to abate.

Roderick's head rolled toward her, his heavy-lidded eyes burning with Crymost green as if his skull was stuffed with phosphorescence. On his lips, an almost pleasurable smile of admonishment. She was to deviate no more, that smile said. She was to make ready his departure and not play the precocious one.

Her pain amplified, invading her from skullcap to heel tips, and as if by a petulant hand she was flung toward the door. Blood coursed down her inner thighs and jetted from her nose. She caught herself on the doorframe with hands made of white hot agony.

"I understand," she said, the words hot and blood-tinged. "I'll do it. I'll do it all. Please stop."

The pain ebbed away. A sob rolled out of her. She collapsed in the hall, her hands clapped to her mouth, her thoughts roiling.

CHAPTER EIGHT

"You all look terrible," Judy said as she helped them into the car. "No clinic. I'm taking you into Drury, to the hospital."

While Judy drove with determinate ease, Mick evaluated his injuries. The heavy stain on his shoulder told him his stitches were torn open. His arm and his upper thigh housed the thump of deep bruises. His ankle also pounded, an extra injury he didn't remember getting.

"This is too much," Judy said at last. "We should all drive to Egg Harbor together, while we're able. Put Thekan and the rest of it behind us."

"I can't do that," Mick said, "not anymore."

She fixed her eyes on the road, her lips pressed together.

Harley sat forward. "Once we blow the double barrel, I'm all for high tailing it out of town, though. Let whatever happens take its course."

None of them spoke after that. Mick suspected each of them was evaluating how time was slipping away from them like a precious element down a deep, dark hole.

CHAPTER NINE

Mick was admitted first, even when he pointed out Harley's broken arm was more urgent.

"That might be so," a nurse in stretch polyester pants told him, "but you're the one who's bleeding. That bumps you up to first class."

She laughed. It jiggled her whole head and made her earrings—ridiculous Tweety Bird faces—waggle.

"I need to find a payphone," Harley said. "Let Beth Ann know where we're at."

"I feel bad about keeping her in the dark," Judy said from her waiting room chair. "You could use my cell but it has no signal, even this far away from . . . well, from *home*."

"Use mine," Mick said and tossed his phone over while the nurse held the door open for him. He gave her an earnest look. "How long is this going to take, anyway?"

"You need to be someplace special?" the nurse asked with a sudden glint of worry in her eye.

Or perhaps it was Déjà vu.

When he came out, feeling as if made of patchwork with a fresh, taut new bandage on his shoulder and elastic dressings on his arm, his ankle and his thigh, Judy got up to meet him. Will was in the chair next to her, his legs drawn up so his heels rested on the seat of the chair.

"I can't get more than two words out of him," she said in a whisper. "It's like Nancy, only different."

"He's been grabbed hard twice by The Crymost now. He's fighting to hang in there. You can see it on him. How long ago did Harley go in?"

"Ten minutes. Is it even possible anymore? This double barrel thing you want to do?"

He glanced at the wall clock. The hands crept toward two o'clock. "I'm for damn sure going to try. We all are. Right, Will?"

Will responded with a faltering "Yup. I'm still with you, Mick. I just don't . . . I can't always . . ."

"It's all right," Mick said and rested a hand on his shoulder. "Come on. Let's grab some coffee while we wait for Harley. It might be another hour."

Not one hour, but nearly two.

On the road at last, with Harley sporting a cast and sling like a loathsome trophy, Mick replayed Judy's earlier question—*is it even possible anymore?*—with real anxiety. Their injuries were going to slow them down, there was no doubt, and the angle of the sun seemed drastic and exaggerated for four o'clock.

Judy kept their speed at a respectable ten miles over the limit, the radio playing softly to cut the tension in the air.

"Holding it together, Will?" Mick asked and glimpsed in the rearview mirror.

He thought he saw a glimmer of green, twin pinpoints, in Will's eyes, but he couldn't be sure. If he did, it was gone as quickly as it came.

"Got my moments," Will said with a sideways glance. "It's in my head, you know. I can feel it in there, the way a stone feels in your shoe."

"You need me, Mick," Judy said. "You need as many hands in this as you can get."

"Beth Ann and Nancy need you," he said. "It's how Team Logan needs to do this, Jude. Girls up, boys down."

She pulled the car onto the highway without a word.

CHAPTER TEN

Knoll waited.

The Plank was devoid of traffic as if even travelers from Drury and points north and west, as well as Baylor and points south and east, diverted their usual routes. Some people puttered in their yards or walked their dogs, but with vacancy. Killing time. Waiting for the blush of twilight.

Will made a rusty, grinding laugh. "Cattle in a barnyard, grazing in the trough while the slaughterhouse truck rolls up at their backs." His eyes blazed green for the duration of a heartbeat. Mick saw it this time and it made him shudder. Then Will lowered his head in shame. "Shit, did you hear that? Maybe you should just tie me up and gag me."

"Take it easy. We'll get this done," Mick said. "Hopefully in short order. Right Harley?"

"Once we get the power to the double barrel, I'll want to test her out. If I don't find any bugs, it will be magic time. We can pull the trigger and be out of town in an hour. Short enough order for you?"

"There, you see?" He squeezed Judy's hand, which he'd been gripping since they drew near the town. "We'll be right behind you, more or less."

"Will you?" She shot him a glare laced with concern, a single name at its root: *Thekan.*

Beth Ann came out as they pulled up to the house and wrapped Harley in a powerful hug. They exchanged a few words and then Harley tapped the window on Will's side. "The ladies have some bags in need of loading, if you gents are so inclined."

Will went eagerly, leaving Mick and Judy alone. The air seemed full of words, none of which they were quite able to grasp. Finally, he said, "Just get them there. Get them safe. It's more help than you know."

"*You* be safe."

He didn't prepare for the kiss, didn't feel himself move in, but it was there, firm and forceful. They broke it mutually, with an intuition borne of years.

"Call me. When it's done," she said after him. "So I know you're on the way."

"When it's done," he said back and then went to the porch to help with the bags.

When the car pulled away, Judy and Beth Ann in the front, Nancy in the back, it was five pm.

CHAPTER ELEVEN

They made the short walk to the bar, Will in the lead swinging a propane-powered Coleman lantern to light up the double barrel room.

"Walkies," Harley said, handing one over to Mick. "Cell phones aren't cutting it down below. Maybe these will do us better."

On a first test they seemed to work just fine. Mick hoped their luck continued on that front. He put his walkie in his front pocket next to his cell and the velvet pouch. Chess pieces. He'd almost forgotten about them, but felt comforted to know they were there.

Will opened up and led them to the basement, rummaged in a back room across from the big walk-in cooler and wheeled the generator out for them.

"Never used it," he said.

It gleamed at them, a logical cluster of components in a cage of protective pipes, the tread of its hard rubber wheels barely dirty.

"Never even gassed her up?" Harley squatted next to it and gave it a once-over with his good hand.

"Never—oh damn, oh shit. I didn't think about gas for it."

"What do you think she runs on? Farts and good intentions? There's no oil in here, either."

"I didn't think about that stuff. Sorry, guys"

Mick wanted to take out his phone and check the time, but in a way, he didn't want to know. "Okay, you two get this thing down the tunnel and hook it up to the double barrel. I'll head over to Copeland's and get the gas and oil."

"Take my truck," Harley's voice followed him up the stairs. "Keys are in the visor."

Copeland's Gas-N-Go was dark except for a window sign flashing PIZZA in neon red and the pondering glow of the ATM just inside the door. The pumps were on, however, and Mick nearly groaned with relief. He rushed inside, called out for Roger and was met only by the brooding hum of the beer coolers. He grabbed a five-gallon gas can from a low shelf, thought about it briefly, then took a second one before going back outside.

Another car pulled up to the pumps, long and blackly sleek in the just-slanting sunlight. Chastity Borth's car. Mick was struck by a terrifying vision of Thekan grinning at him from the passenger side, eyes ablaze and dancing while jugs of windshield wash from Copeland's outdoor display lifted into the air like angry birds and slammed into him, pounding and bruising him. But as he drew closer, only Chastity got out. The car was otherwise empty.

He set his gas cans down and began to fill up. Nothing else stirred except for a lone shape dressed in something billowy and yellow. It rounded the Garden Street corner and cut across to join them. It was Connie Gassner, out for a walk in her zippered housecoat. She took a newspaper from the machine near Copeland's front door, then stood between their two vehicles, her slippers yellow shouts on the dull concrete.

"Coming to The Crymost meeting tonight?" Her eyes were burnt-out bulbs in a funhouse display.

"There'll be no meeting, if I have my way," Mick said.

No response from Chastity, other than a restrained yet startled jump. Mick saw it from the corner of his eye.

"I hope you're wrong," Connie said and swept at a tuft of gray hair lifted by the breeze. "Whatever helps guide this town out of its funk will be a blessing."

"I agree," he said, mostly to himself, "but things can't go on the way they are."

Connie blinked at him, a flicker of comprehension in her dead bulb eyes. "Take care of yourself, then, Mick. I'll hope things get better around here soon."

Then she cast a dismissive glance at Chastity and walked back toward Garden Street, her slippers scuffing an uneven rhythm in the quiet air.

"Me, too," he said. "Don't we all?"

Chastity looked at him hard and direct. Her lips parted and a word seemed trapped there, but then her pump kicked off. Tank full. She shook herself, seated the pump hose and drove away.

After the gas cans were filled he went back inside. He was sure Roger kept a generator of his own so his hope was all the necessary additives, including oil, would be on the premises. He went directly to the back storage room; what better place to keep a jenny and all the fixings?

Something nudged him, mentally, just as he passed through the door to the windowless back room. Nudged him too late.

Mick knew about the storage room door at Copeland's and how the inside was a blind side without a knob or latch, and you'd be sorry if you didn't use the doorstop to prop it open. More than a few townsfolk were caught by it to the good humor of all over the years. The idea struck him the moment the door slammed shut at his heels. He spun around knowing the exit would appear as nothing more than a flat sheet of steel but he lunged toward it anyway.

His foot caught on something as he plowed ahead. Cardboard. A stack of broken-down boxes piled layer upon layer until it was heavy and immovable. The next thing he knew he was falling, hands out, grease-scented air whistling in his ears.

He struck the floor hard, and he banged his temple against a metal toolbox. It filled his head with a brain-jolting sensation and his vision turned into smears of light and dark.

"Damn it," he said and rolled onto his back, fishing instinctively for the walkie.

It came out of his pocket in two pieces. Viable pieces; it was not broken, merely popped open at the seam. The batteries, however, tumbled out and rolled into the blur the world had become. Maybe in a minute he could collect everything up and make it work. He took out his phone. The screen was a senseless haze in the world, a blur. *Okay.* He rested his head back, drew in a gulp of air. *Let things settle. Give it time. Precious time.*

"Not going to happen," Will Adelmeyer said. He knew he said it and yet the words were not his. The need to take the heavy wrench off of the basement shelf wasn't his either, but there the wrench was, in his hand. *Hang on*, he thought, *The Crymost is driving.* "Might as well shut her down, Harley."

"Come again?" Harley Kroener asked him, hunkered over the generator now parked at the entrance to the tunnel.

Will shoved him, hard. Harley was a big man but he was off his guard and he stumbled against the wall. *Good*, a deeper part of Will commented, *stay over there. Keep away from me.* The force he put behind the wrench seemed to flow from somewhere else. When it crashed down on the generator, a shock of resistance assaulted him. Yet, he struck again, and a third time. Rapid, vicious blows.

"Here now," Harley barked.

The big man led in with his cast held forward as if to plow him out of the way. Will felt the wrench rise again, his arm a senseless marionette's limb, and when he brought it down this time it landed on Harley's cast, cracking it with a muffled crunch. Harley drew back, his face compressed with new pain, but his retreat was only a single step. He put his head down and rammed Will's gut with the top of his head. Will's wrench glanced off the back of the assailing skull and he stumbled backward, his insides feeling airless and on fire. He fell. Harley dropped over him, his face a working mixture of anger and remorse.

"Goddamn it, Will."

Will saw the fist coming and managed to raise his chin the slightest bit to receive it. The blow was numbing. His vision exploded into a plane of mingling stars. The wrench bounced out of his hand. *Good*, he thought, *make me stop. I want to stop*. Then Harley hit him again and made a sound like a sob. The room spun away. Seconds passed, or perhaps minutes. All he knew was his limbs felt his own again. He was sliding along the floor. The tightness of his shirt at the neck and armpits told him Harley was dragging him. Images began to leak through his cracked lids, iron-stained watercolors, but he knew the details well enough to realize what was happening before Harley let him go on a patch of frigid hardwood. The walk-in cooler. It was a good choice. It locked from the outside, and he mentally congratulated Harley on his quick wit.

"Jesus, Will," Harley said from the doorway. He flicked on the interior light when he said it. "I'm sorry about this."

The door slammed. Will felt it resonate through him with a note of finality, and then the outside locking mechanism slid home.

Good, Will thought again. His jaw hurt like hell. *Good*.

CHAPTER TWELVE

Mick was unsure how long it was before his arms and legs felt reliable again but at last he rose to his hands and knees. One of the walkie batteries was nearby, the other nowhere to be found. There were packs of double A batteries just outside; he could picture them on a peg behind Roger Copeland's cash register, for all the good it did him. He took out his phone again and this time his eyes registered. Five forty-five and no signal. Not in this little metal box. He got to his feet, shaky, and stepped up to the door, pounded on it, and groaned at the solid and nearly soundless *thunk* his fist made.

A gap between door and frame showed him a vertical pencil line of light near the floor. He knew full well the only way to climb from a dark pit was to find a hand hold in the overwhelming gloom. Sometimes the hand hold was your wife, but sometimes it needed to be your own wiles, and a little luck.

His gaze fell on a cluttered workbench-like shelf in the back of the room. He dove on it and felt almost giddy when he found an assortment of greasy but sturdy screwdrivers. He went back to the door with three of them clutched in his hand and was surprised when the tip of one fit into the door crack. He slid it upward, knowing the reach to the latch mechanism was a long and impossible one. When it bound up he pushed harder. His hand slipped and his knuckles crashed against the metal door, tearing skin. He sat down and cradled his aching hand, his breath sputtering.

Dull light near the ceiling above the workbench caught his eye. A duct protected by a grille housed a fan to vent the temperate air of the building. It appeared to be just wide enough for him to squeeze through. A handhold. Just as Hemingway said: luck in one of its many forms. Not always smooth or friendly, but you did with it what you could.

Mick stuffed his collection of screwdrivers into his back pocket and climbed onto the work bench, which drew out the pain in his thigh and ankle like lamentable taffy. He tore the fan grille loose. It surrendered with a ratcheting noise and he nearly fell off the bench for his efforts, but the first barrier had been bested.

The fan mechanism was next, mounted a few inches inside the opening by three bolts. The fan blade caught an errant outside breeze and twirled for him as he pondered it. He could see the outside through a second outdoor grille. The sun was pulling down shades of heavy gold. He glanced at his phone. Six fifteen. There was a wrench near his foot and he stooped to get it.

The work at hand made him think of a pleasant little bit of writing by Dumas, which in turn made him appreciate what it was like delving into a mad priest's tunnel to affect his escape. This led to Shakespeare waxing of hardhanded men never laboring in their minds until now. And the natural way such a comparison came to light reassured him his hands would never be as hard as some.

What followed this, in an odd and yet somehow appropriate way, was Robbie Vaughn proclaiming there were by-yourself kinds of people in the world. *Right, Mr. Logan?* And he had to agree that, yes indeed, there were.

At last the fan dropped over inside the vent housing. He tore it loose from its wiring and tossed it behind him. Then he hiked himself up into the vent hole and hammered at the outer grille until it dropped to the outside. He wiggled forward, glad no dead priest's body bag awaited him ala *Count of Monte Cristo*, only open air and sunlight.

An external water pipe served as a hand rail to help him ease his way to the ground and he sat against the building to catch his breath. Twin chimes from his phone startled him. Text message. An advertisement: *"Thank you for using Active Talk. Call us now or check online for new service specials just in time for summer . . ."* but he felt as if he'd struck oil. He had a signal once again. He thought about calling Will, then dismissed it. The tunnel blocked everything. Instead he got up and limped around to the front of the station, snatched a pair of batteries from the checkout stand and loaded up the walkie.

"Harley, you there?" he said into the mouthpiece. "I'm on my way now. Harley?"

He took up a can of plain 10W30 motor oil on the way out and tossed it in the truck. At last, a weak crackle from the walkie speaker. "Mick?"

"Jesus, Harley. Are you ready? I'm on my way."

"I'm in the tunnel." Harley's winded sound put his hackles up. "Our friend Will went a little bit ape shit on us. Smacked up the jenny pretty bad."

"Damn it." The lowering sun seemed to burn on the back of his neck. "Is it salvageable?"

"Should be. But the wheels are screwed up. I've been dragging her but its slow work, like dragging my ass through Hell. My wheels ain't so great either at the moment."

"I'll come as fast as I can."

"I'm just about to the end and I know what you're thinking, but there's no safe way to climb down through the mercantile anymore to meet me. You better use the tunnel."

"Agreed."

"I'll have the jenny hooked up by the time you get down here."

"Where's Will now?"

"Locked him up in his big cooler. He won't be a bother. Damn, it's already six thirty. I hope this works."

"Me too."

Mick's thoughts turned to Judy. He switched the walkie for the cell phone as he drove to The Chapel Bar.

CHAPTER THIRTEEN

Judy checked the dashboard clock for what seemed like the hundredth time. Fitful conversation with Beth Ann had died out around six pm, about the time the city of Grand Chute sprawled on either side of the highway.

"It's working okay, right?" Beth Ann asked and glanced with distrust at the cell phone on the seat.

"There's a signal. Has been since Oshkosh."

She glanced at her friend's fingers, which tapped at the cross around her neck, and she wondered if that particular telegraph system worked as well as saying prayers out loud.

Nancy's voice from the back seat startled them both. "I'm going straight to bed. Don't want to hear about how quiet the streets are out there."

Beth Ann turned around and her voice turned hard. "Judy. Stop the car."

"What? Why?"

"Stop it. Now."

She swerved into the breakdown lane and stopped with a lurch. As she cranked her head around, Beth Ann was already out of the car and tearing the back door open. Nancy sat forward, rigid, sweat dripping from her chin and the end of her nose, her face ashen. But what caught Judy's eye was the green light back there with her. It swirled away from Nancy's head in an expanding corona. Then it simply evaporated.

"It's gone," Beth Ann said with a magnanimous smile. "Oh great God, it's left her."

Judy climbed out and tore open the back door on the driver's side, barely aware of the whooshing traffic at her back.

"Driving away isn't the answer," Nancy said. Sweat-tangled hair clung to her face. "You put them on the gurneys, roll them away to get fixed. But it's just a stop-off, you know."

Beth Ann stroked her cheek with the back of her knuckles. "You be calm. You're going to get better fast, I think, now that we're away from Knoll. But we need to get back on the road."

"The pavement always ends. Bridge out." She let go with a pale imitation of an old Nancy Berns laugh. "But I'll keep still if that will help."

Beth Ann flicked her gaze at Judy. It was brief, like the glint of the cross hanging between her breasts, but it was also bold.

"Look at me," Judy told her friend. "You're better, too."

Beth Ann's left eye was clearer, as if someone had replaced the sanguine ball in her eye socket with a healthier, only slightly stained model.

"No headache," Beth Ann said. "None."

Judy's cell phone rang. She scrambled to the front and snatched it up. When the display showed her it was Mick she came close to shrieking with relief.

"Where are you? Is it done?"

"Not even close."

"Damn it, Mick."

"I think Harley is in bad shape. I'm going to him just now. And Will is out of commission the way it sounds."

"And you're going to try to finish this anyway, aren't you?"

"You already know my answer. I'm going into the tunnel soon and I know I'll lose this signal. But I need to know you're okay. I need to promise Harley that Beth Ann is safe too, so keep going. No matter what. I love you, Judy."

"Love you, too. I'll talk to you again soon, Mick Logan."

She barely got it out, her throat had turned to stone.

And then the signal broke.

She stood outside for a few minutes, checked something else on her phone and then went around to Beth Ann's side of the car. "How is she?"

"Better by the second, it seems."

"Okay, good. We're going into town."

What happens along the way is because of what you're all about.

Why didn't she listen to her instincts all along? Maybe because it still seemed a little like madness.

When Judy pulled into the car rental place, all was quiet. The young lady behind the desk put down her reading material—a battered novel by someone named Weaver titled *Wheel of the Year* that she didn't seem to be enjoying very much—and greeted her with a smile. A short time later an attendant pulled a late model Camry around to the front for her.

When she walked over to the Kroener's car to say goodbye, Beth Ann was already behind the wheel with the window rolled down. "I'll get us there," she said and reached out to clasp Judy's hand in a fierce grip. "I know it sounds silly, but angels go with you."

"Nothing silly about it," she said and reached in to give her friend a trembling hug. "I'll see you soon."

Nancy offered a cautious wave from the passenger seat. "Stay safe, Judy."

And it was done. Beth Ann pulled into a stretch of sun in a flash of chrome. *Like a cross glint. Angels go with you, too, my friends.*

Judy climbed into the rental and headed back to Knoll.

CHAPTER FOURTEEN

Time was a great crushing force now, squeezing the likelihood out of everything. Still, after he hurried through the bar and down the basement steps laden with a can of gas (only one because the second can was too awkward to handle and threatened to slow him down considerably), a container of oil and one of Will's flashlights, Mick was unable to keep from stopping outside the door to the walk-in cooler. "Will, you okay?"

There was a span of silence, and then, "Just great. If you can trust me. Hell, I don't trust me right now. I hope I didn't mess things up too bad."

"Harley thinks it will still work."

"I hope Harley is okay. I nailed him pretty good."

"He's holding his own. Look I've got to go. Stay calm. We'll come for you when this is done."

"I wish I could be more help. Damn, I hate it, Mick."

"See you soon."

He followed his jittering flashlight beam down the tunnel, unable to deny the new scratches in the floor where Harley had struggled with the battered generator. When he caught sight of a spot of fresh blood like a gleaming red coin, he stopped and put down the gas can to fire up the walkie.

"Harley, how is it coming?"

Static. A break of silence, then a wheeze. Finally: "Just got to the double barrel."

"Good. Sit it out until I get there."

"Like I'm some sort of goddamned old man?"

"Like I need you conscious and upright if you're going to help me finish."

No more words, just a conceding grunt and then the transmission went back to static.

When Mick walked in, Harley was kneeling next to the double barrel, hard at work. The Coleman lantern cast wild upshot shadows around him. A band of broken cast material circled his arm near the elbow and below it, his exposed arm was puffed and purple and his fingers wobbled like sausages. He acknowledged Mick with a type of resignation. "Take care of the fine wiring on this electrical cable. If you want. If I'm still the boss."

Mick's heart hurt. He would have smiled if things were different and there was no crust of nearly dried blood behind Harley's ear.

"Let me at it," he said, and reached down to open the toolbox sitting next to the generator. One of the jenny's wheels sat canted at a surreal forty-five-degree angle. Transporting the whole shooting match down here with only one good arm must have been a nightmare, and it made him look at his friend hard and long. "While I'm working, give me the lowdown on how we make this thing go boom."

"First thing we'll want to do is start up the jenny," Harley said and parked on the stack of rotting batteries. A trickle of fresh blood from behind his ear worked down his neck. "It's a cheap, donkey-backwards model, so you have to hold the choke down and then ease her back while you punch the starter. Starter's that button right there, cracked in two thanks to Will, The Crymost, and a Craftsman crescent.

239

It's loose but I think it will hold. As for this double barrel contraption, there's a starter switch for the pump on top. You'll see it when you stand up."

Mick finished the cable wiring and straightened up while Harley went on.

"We let the old girl run for a bit, get the juices flowing. Then we push the igniter lever forward when ready; it's that red lever on the side. After that, ten seconds to *boom*. Maybe twenty. My job, anyway. You've got to get moving."

"Where am I going?"

Harley tapped his watch. "It's coming up on seven thirty. Knoll is being Knoll about now. Early birds. You can damn sure bet a few folks are riding out to Pitch Road as we speak."

"Jesus, you're right. We can't do this." Mick threw up his hands. "Not if half the town is already up at The Crymost."

"It should take only one man to talk people into getting away from The Crymost, if it's the right man."

"Me? There's a few people I could convince, I guess. If they even show up. Roger. Maybe Corey Schelvan."

"The town respects you, Mick. Has for quite some time. And you've got something extra, something you brought with you from your days at that school, or maybe something born into you that landed you as a teacher in the first place. You can stand up front and have your say and it makes sense. It's natural. I've seen it time and time again, and if ever there was a time to use such a presence, it's now."

"I can try."

"It's either that or we give up right now. We hand the town over to Thekan and whatever else is coming down the pipe with a handshake and say happy trails."

Harley plugged the double barrel into the jenny's outlet, pressed the choke and then thumbed the damaged starter button. The jenny released a luxurious wet coughing sound and took off, filling the room with a moderate hum. Harley shuffled over to the double barrel, the light of success glimmering in his weary eyes, and switched on the pump. There was a metallic screech deep in the guts of the double barrel, aimed angrily at its creators, men who no longer lived. The fluttering, pumping sound that followed was unmistakable.

240

"I'll be damned," Harley said with quiet wonder and shut everything down. "We got ourselves a boom-maker. If it weren't for the jenny's exhaust I'd let her run. Once you give me an all-clear over the walkie, I'll get her going again. Aren't you headed the wrong way?"

Mick stood in the doorway leading to the jumbled ruin of stairs inside the mercantile cellar. "I'm going to find enough handholds to climb out this way. Luck comes in a lot of forms, and we don't have enough time for anything else."

Harley nodded and hunkered down by the double barrel. A drop of blood fell from behind his ear and stitched a mark down the front of his shirt. "Better get moving, then."

"Talk to you soon," Mick said. It didn't seem like enough.

CHAPTER FIFTEEN

Judy kept the speedometer spiked at 80, her thoughts racing as quickly as the scenery outside. She was being a silly bitch, going against the plan Mick and the others so carefully laid out. But weren't some of Mick's decisions driven by his emotions instead of the logic of on-paper schematics and the laws of combustion and detonation? Was her endeavor so different?

As she rolled at last into Knoll, she felt in the presence of a huge, dangerous and yet sleeping beast. She saw people walking at the other end of Garden Street as she pulled into her driveway. They wandered southeast with sullen slowness. Toward The Crymost.

She hurried into the house and ignored the chiding voice which propounded there were a hundred things she could take and there was no need to waste time going upstairs, but her mind was set. She bounded up the stairs and climbed into the attic, worried that what she wanted had been moved or—God forbid—thrown away in a flurry of spring cleaning. When she saw the torn and flattened carton marked CLASSROOM she let out a cry of defeat, but as she rushed over to it she saw the newer replacement box, unmarked but also unsealed, and greedily dug into it. What she wanted was right on top: chess pieces made of dull mineral. She scooped up a hasty handful, five pawns, and dashed down the stairs, an anxious whine building in the back of her throat.

She tossed the pawns on the car seat and started the engine. Or tried to. The engine cranked but would not turn over. She thought of the negligible caravan they'd abandoned earlier on Pitch Road—

(another effect like the phones. *Automatic*, Axel had said through bloodstained teeth. *Spontaneous, baby*, a floating young suicide had proclaimed)

—and got out again, giving the lengthening shadows a wild stare. Then she scooped the pawns off the car seat—one was lost; she now had only four—and sprinted down Garden Street.

By the time she reached The Plank her breath burned in her lungs and she cut back to a brisk walk. People dotted the sidewalks, some chatting as they walked while others sauntered quiet and introspective, all of them heading in a common direction, their shadows stretched out before them as if pointing the way to The Crymost. At the edge of town, a single car cruised downhill on The Plank—a traveler whose head swiveled every which way over the strange exodus of Knoll citizens. *Don't stop your car, Mister*, Judy thought as she hurried along, *the minute you shut off your engine it's game over. At least until my husband can blow the goddamned Crymost sky high.*

As the highway began its uphill grade, she poured on the determination, holding her one purpose out before her, and at last turned down Pitch Road. She weaved between the familiar abandoned cars there, her own included, and pushed a couple of people aside to squeeze through the shrubbery atop the last rise. A few townsfolk stood near The Crymost ledge, sullen, exchanging bits of conversation. She moved off to the grassy fringe and glanced once more at the pawns. She had dropped another somewhere during the walk, but three was still a good amount.

The broad view of the marshlands below The Crymost drop-off seemed to summon her, a goal nearly achieved. The sun shimmered at her back, a pending droplet of red-gold dipping toward the horizon. She shivered, certain the sleeping beast of this place was aware of her intent. It made her misstep and stumble and the pawns tumbled from her hands. The surrounding tall grass swallowed every last piece.

She moaned, squatted and ran her hands over the ground, and she managed to find two. She took them to The Crymost edge, her toes sticking over the drop-off. There were no ghostly figures this time, only neighbors in the light of late day, and the unmistakable presence of that which slept, but neared awakening.

"Help him, damn you," she said with an overall tremor. "You have to if I do this, because some of your reactions are automatic. Spontaneous, baby. So you protect the hell out of my husband."

She flung the pawns over. They made no ripple or splash in the pond. The only sound was the low utterances of Knoll people waiting in queue.

CHAPTER SIXTEEN

After she gassed up the car, Chastity Mellar Borth came close to driving hard and fast into the country, putting untold miles between her and Knoll, but in the end, uncertainty won out and sent her home. She didn't want to think about it now that she was at the house, because there was hope (*small*) and fear (*huge*) and the overwhelming worry about Roderick picking up on any of it, so she pressed her thoughts down like a tissue worked and worried to shapelessness in a funeral widow's hand.

He was awake. She heard him thumping about upstairs. Everything seeming very real now, and very close. A hard knot of part grief and part regret formed within her. It grew exponentially when she heard him cry out—a wail of revulsion and loss. If the intensity of the smell permeating the house was any indicator, she knew what the cry was about. His appearance had gotten worse. Her hand went to her pocket and tightened on her father's rosary, the strange gift that incited her request for all Knoll citizens to bring a special memento should they have one. Might it do some good? She could only hope it might be the basis of a little dark miracle of her own.

When she heard him coming down she went to the foot of the stairs to meet him. His odor preceded him and the clunk of his shoes was slow and uncertain. He was in the wool suit he'd worn to town, the cloak dragging from step to step behind him with a sodden weight. His derby hat was dipped low in an attempt to hide him from onlookers, but from this close the gaunt angles of his face were stark, gray, and stretched thin over jutting teeth, molded to eye sockets set so deep they were more like the empty pits present there during their lovemaking. But dry pits now. Bloodless, gray-black holes where gleaming irises rested far back inside.

"This isn't going well for you, is it Roderick?"

He stopped on the last step. His cordy throat worked around a deep swallow. "The reward is in the end. Always in the end. You need to trust more."

"Or less," she said and stepped away from him.

He pulled one of the dining room curtains aside with a withered claw. "Pull the car up close to the door. I may need help navigating the front steps."

"Maybe a bad fall is your end redemption."

His head snapped toward her with surprising fervor. His thin gray lips stretched into a sneer. "Careful. Endings are the subject of the day, after all."

Pain stirred in her joints, a warning bell chiming in the distance.

"I'll get my keys," she said at last.

CHAPTER SEVENTEEN

The stairway rubble was stacked almost to the gaping hole in the floor above, but it also proved to be a challenge, shifting and sliding apart every time Mick got a firm grip or a decent foothold, sending him back to the bottom again with the threat of rolling an ankle or wrenching his knees out of shape. At last he caught a firm beam, one he didn't notice at the start. It took his weight when he pulled himself up. Above it another handhold, broken but sturdy wood and a generous opening in the mishmash like a break in laden clouds. *One to the next*, he told himself as he gripped awkward protrusions and pushed off foot-friendly edges until he was in the gloomy belly of the mercantile's main floor.

Through the show window, he saw people walking along The Plank.

"Hey," he shouted and ran out to the shoulder of Highway L where Ken Wittkop and his wife walked. Ken carried a pair of aluminum tube frame lawn chairs. His wife, Nina, gripped a Bible with rigid fingers. "Don't go up there. Trust me, you need to go back into town. Go home, for God's sake."

"We're going to the meeting, I think," Ken said. "I've heard from the right people that it will help us get over our bad hump."

Mick shuffled backward to face them. It seemed to pull every muscle in his legs. "What if I told you The Crymost is what's causing the bad hump in the first place, and everybody on this road is walking right into something much worse than what we've already seen?"

Nina glared at him. "I'd say you're not as much a part of this town as I thought. The Crymost is a landmark. You don't speak out against something so sacred. Especially when you're in need. Come on, Ken."

She gave Mick a hard-shouldered pass and stepped up her pace, pulling her husband along by the elbow.

Mick looked around, his heart in his mouth, his teeth drawing blood from his lower lip. *Come on, Mr. Logan, get your lesson plan together.* He broke into a run.

Starting at the dump, Pitch Road was lined up with people like patrons waiting for an amusement ride. He glanced at faces as he pushed his way through and rushed onto The Crymost's limestone ledge. He knew them all, some well and some in passing. Children, some in pajamas, scampered around. He was unable to stop himself from picturing tiny beds in shaded rooms, their occupants wasted humps under the blankets. There was no desire to get out any longer. Mom was bundled up in her own bed, unresponsive to requests for food, or dad was under a blanket in the living room recliner, gazing toward heaven with cloudy eyes while the TV blathered and flashed and the flies buzzed around him in slow spirals. And outside something writhed unseen, glutted with delectable morsels, reaching for more.

A shape worked against the flow of the crowd, away from the ledge, and he recognized it with shock and a baffled type of chagrin.

"Judy?"

She hurried toward him, her face carefully set. He drew her into his arms, aware of relief bleeding through the other emotions warring in his head.

"I know, I know," she said and pushed back far enough to capture his gaze, "but I'm here alone. The other two are probably in Egg Harbor by now. I just had to do something to help you."

"Help me how?" His mind reeled. "You should get out of here. Now."

"The explosion?"

He flashed the walkie at her. "Harley's at the ready. My problem is getting everybody out of here, and fast." The sun sat on the western horizon behind them, a molten knob. It painted everything in hectic red. "It already feels like we're out of time—"

"Mick," she said and pointed.

A black car pushed through the shrub entrance of The Crymost path and drove onto the limestone flats, reflecting the sky in streaks like electric blood. Its engine died, and the crowd fell silent. Children flocked to their parents' sides. Did he hear a rumble from below, an anxious fuming from where the pool churned down there? Because it did churn, astir with wanting. He knew it without looking.

Chastity Mellar Borth got out from behind the wheel, head down, and hurried to the passenger side to open the door. Blatant servitude for the darkly draped passenger who climbed out in his low-set hat. Mick drew in a deep breath—his lungs seemed to have withered to nothing—and gave Judy a firm *stay there* gesture before he stepped away.

"There's another way to go about this," he said, projecting to the crowd with a power he thought he'd left at Lincoln Middle School. Heads jerked his way, a promising sign, and he climbed a ridge near the edge of the drop-off where he was visible to everyone. "Harley Kroener and I fix everything in this town, you all know that, and we mean to fix this, too. We have a plan we hope will push the darkness away from Knoll but it's dangerous, especially if you stay here. Will you trust me if I tell you to get off of The Crymost, and get off now?"

Thekan's voice rang out. "Yes. Who will you trust?" He stepped away from the car, his hands held out as if to clutch an unseen surface for balance. He seemed a wasted silhouette wrapped in a bagging suit, his hat brim and lowered head allowing only his jaw to catch the daylight, yet his voice was strong and atremble with fervor. "Hammer blows and crude workman's rivets are the answer if you are repairing a park bench, but some matters call for older voices and wiser ways." He stepped into the midst of the crowd and parted his hands. "Revered ways, you might say."

Mutters rippled through the masses, and at first Mick was convinced the sound was one of assent. But the response was a splintered one—there were those who offered knowing nods to

Thekan. The Jade family stood closest to him, their six-year-old son Tommy goggling at the man with a slack jaw brand of horror. Others stared at Mick with a dawning sense of interest, including Roger Copeland, who stood near the black car. The air stirred with a sense of awakening.

Another wave of vocalizations worked through the crowd, from only a few people this time as they looked at their hands—or more precisely at the objects in them, at the mementos they'd brought from home, just as Chastity had asked. Significant and curious. Glints of green light emanated from those items in the lowering daylight. Old Jim Schraufnagel stood close by and Mick was able to see a war medal in his hand. Green light flared across it, shrunk back, flared again in a cold imitation of a heartbeat.

"We sent as many as we could," Mick said under his breath. "It's all LINR."

Thekan stalked toward Mick. "There is no more time."

"You want revered?" Mick put all the force he could muster behind his words. "There are old voices, familiar well-loved voices, speaking out to you right now. Telling you what's right." He snatched Jim's hand and hoisted the glowing medal high for all to see. "Are you going to deny the gifts—no, more than gifts—the *warnings* your deceased loved ones sent back to you? *Can* you deny them?"

"You are not as wise as you think." Thekan stepped closer, his sunken eyes glinting like candles afloat in twin wells. "And you are no longer as safe as you believe. I have saved up a reserve of power just for you, Mick Logan. Just for *you*."

Mick once chaperoned an eighth-grade field trip to a science museum in Milwaukee. One of the displays offered the opportunity to feel the resonant vibrations brought about by various decibels of sound. A large silver dome offered a place for both hands, and the students talked him into experiencing the highest setting on the dial. The sensation was a whole-body, scintillating yet numbing assault.

A similar feeling gripped him when Thekan's eyes flashed at him. The world was swallowed, all sight and sound consumed. This time there was no laughter of students to help him focus once again. This time there was a disorienting sense of displacement, then a reverent hush, and the scent of carnations, and then the mumble of organ music all around.

His vision cleared. He stood in a funeral home peopled by small groups in various attitudes of discussion. An open casket sat at the far end of the room. Behind it, a minister in a white cassock busied himself in preparation for an upcoming service. The casket was Robbie Vaughn's—the handsome bronze and brass model was burned into his memory—and it was there he felt drawn. He stumbled up to the coffin, weak and anxious and peered inside. His breath caught in his lungs. The casket was full of brackish green water. Flecks of scum swirled near the satin covered lip. He was unable to see Robbie, but Robbie had to be in there, deep down, neglected for far too long.

He plunged his hands in; tainted water as cold as death. He leaned close until he was inhaling swampy vapors of decay. And he felt a whooshing sensation at his back as if a series of doors opened at once to let in the night air. The exposed, vulnerable feeling that followed unnerved him, but still he groped and delved into the water, hoping to find some part of Robbie: a shoe, a sleeve, a bloated and clammy hand, to grip it and pull him up, up . . .

The minister stepped up, his arms opened over the casket lid. "So this is the shuttered part that kept me out."

Mick looked up. The minister's cassock slid away in gray tatters. Not a minister at all but a judge. Thekan stood over him.

"Where is he?" Mick called out, his arms thrashing in the water and churning up greenish foam. "Do you have him? Where the hell is he?"

"Go after him, Mick Logan. Dive in. Perhaps you will find him if you go deep enough, down and down and down."

Down deep, in the dark. In the quiet, safe, airless dark. Where there was nothing. Where he was no one.

"*Mick!*"

Judy's voice exploded in his head. One of his hands struck an object, free-floating but hard, as if a pebble was suspended in the swill. He tried to draw it close and caught sight of it just before it was churned under again. A chess pawn, the mineral skin of it startlingly familiar. It was followed by a second one. New additions to the mix, he understood with amazing clarity, because his dear wife felt she needed to do something to help him.

Judy's exploding voice again. "Mick, he's doing something to you. Fight him!"

The funeral home wavered around him. Only Thekan remained solid, his stare intensifying. Mick plunged his hands deeper into the casket water with new determination. This time his fingers encountered a larger object. A flat thing almost as wide as his hand. He grasped it and pulled it out.

The funeral parlor blinked out of his view. He was at The Crymost again, with Judy clutched to his side and the people of Knoll looking on. In his hand was a foot-long slat of old lumber spiked on one end with two protruding nails. It made him think of a primitive war club designed to deliver a swat that resulted in snakebite damage. More than that, it made him think of Irma Casper the day he and Will visited her at the nursing home, the way she aimed her withered, forked fingers at her eyes and proclaimed "nails and a board" while she spent perhaps the last of her lucid moments recounting what she knew about the Honorable Judge Thekan.

He heard someone say, "What's happening to Mick?"

Another: "Yeah, what's going on up there?"

The lingering light told him what seemed to be an eternity had passed in only a few seconds. He felt dizzy, as if just stepping off a roller coaster. Like the funeral home, the wood in his hand faded away like a dream.

Judy shook him. "I thought I lost you."

"You ought to know better," he said back.

Thekan twirled to address the crowd, his eyes ablaze in the shadow crescent under his brim, his voice building like summer thunderheads. "It comes down to asking for guidance, people of Mellar's Knoll. The oldest of gestures and the oldest of practices—ask and wait, since nothing comes all at once."

Mick slipped out of Judy's arms and stepped forward on still-wobbly legs. "We don't want what you're waiting for, Thekan."

"One voice speaks for the whole town?" Thekan presented it with a wave of gnarled, beseeching hands. "Even after so many have come out for my counsel?"

"Your counsel will bring the town to its doom." Mick likewise addressed the town. "Listen to me. There's a cycle, some type of revisiting blight on this place, this Crymost, something hungry and awful and it means to sap the life out of us. And this monster is helping it. We need to leave now. And get as far away from Knoll as we can."

Shouts and cries from the crowd told him he'd done some good, and it would have relieved him if it weren't for the boiling and gurgling sounds from below the drop-off. The Crymost pond water churned full bore. The western sky was now a rusty smudge.

Thekan smiled, his lips splitting open in half a dozen places in dry, gray slits. "What comes will dine only on the living," he said and swept up close to Mick as if to dance, "but I think one more loss is in order. I at last have an *in* to your thoughts. So off you go, Mick Logan."

Another of those awareness-sucking waves washed over Mick. His crippled doors of defense flapped, broken shutters in a windstorm. Thekan's *in*. There was no funeral home this time. The Crymost and the goggling people of Knoll remained. His jaw locked. He was unable to turn his neck or use his arms. His feet however were forced into tiny backward steps, sending him toward The Crymost drop-off. *And down I'll go, like Robbie Vaughn, down to the Land of Nod.*

"No, Mick. Stop."

Judy lunged after him but Thekan caught her by the wrist, his teeth gritted, his eyes feral. "Broken," he said and flung her down.

Judy screamed and collapsed into the dirt. Mick watched with helpless rage as she rolled over and clutched her already puffing and purple wrist. Her eyes welled. In his head he let go a scream and it somehow pushed him closer to his doors of restraint, gaping doors thwarting nothing. He needed to call upon help, Crymost help, chess pawn help, and he hoped his suspicion on how to achieve it was correct.

Someone rushed toward him in the near dark, Bob Canham, calling, "Mick, come back here, man. You're gonna fall off."

Thekan whirled around and clapped his hands on the man's head to shake it as if delivering the most violent of healings. "Blind," Thekan shouted and cast the man aside.

Bob Canham sat up in the dirt howling. He groped at the air, his eyes turned to white clots.

Screams rose up. Another man rushed forward from the perimeter and Thekan gestured toward him, commanding "Fracture."

The man's thigh let out an audible snap. He went down with a bark of pain, his leg folded like a ruined wooden lawn chair.

Judy struggled to her feet, still clutching her ballooning wrist. Thekan stepped in front of her with an admonishing "Nuh-uh. No strength in your legs," and performed a gentle push to the air in front of her.

She sat down hard and cried out, "Mick Logan, come back here. Do you hear me?"

He pushed close to one of those gaping head-interior doors. Crazily he thought of Peter Fyvie offering advice while leaking onto his truck seats. Just trying to help. He'd received so much help. But in the end, it was all on him. *Some people were just by-yourself kinds of people.* Thekan raised his hands high. He wheezed, exhausted. "Who else wishes to challenge their fate?"

Judy struggled to stand once again but got no compliance from her legs. Her voice, however, was high and clear. "Run. All of you. Get away from here while you can."

A few people broke away from the crowd and began to hurry back to Pitch Road. Others, confused and uncertain, gaped at her, at Mick, and at the two men twisting in the dirt.

A laugh billowed out of Thekan in a dusty rasp. "Go on, then. Run. Your feet will not carry you fast enough any longer. Whether you're here, or crouched in your cellars, or cowering in your beds, it will find you. Why doubt my words, people of Mellar's Knoll? Why?"

"Because you lie," Chastity Mellar Borth's voice rang out. Light flushed over the crowd, and over the judge, as the headlamps on the black car came to life. She rushed toward Thekan, her face hard, her hands hooked into claws. "You're full of empty, dangerous promises and some hellish sort of trickery, and if what's in front of you doesn't serve you, you damage it or hurt it or outright kill it. What we shouldn't doubt is the reality of the dreadful thing coming over that ledge to get us. And you ought to know, you're serving it. We also shouldn't doubt what Mick Logan said." With a quick but graceful motion she snatched the derby from his head and flung it to the ground. "You are a monster."

The light blazed across his face, accentuated loose ribbons of rotted flesh on his cheeks, contrasted the deep wells of his eye sockets, flooded over the permanent grin of his jaw wrapped in a Papier-mâché rind of withered meat. The crowd shrieked and yelled. Mick felt the hold on him slip. He opened his right hand as if to receive a dark handshake and waited for The Crymost to react.

Thekan snarled at Chastity as if such insolence was unheard of.

251

"Do you realize those virile steps you took to confront me were your last?"

He slapped her with a forceful backhand. She sprawled in the dirt.

"This has got to stop," Roger Copeland's voice rose up as he fought his way to Chastity, his pocket watch still pulsing with ethereal green light in his grip. "Come on, we can take him down. Bill? Randy? For Christ's sake."

Indecisive murmurs rippled through the crowd. The murmurs changed to gasps as green light radiated over the edge of the drop-off. All motion seemed to stop except for a few people who cut out and loped back toward town.

Thekan took note of the runners and sneered at them. "Fodder."

"No different than you," Chastity cried out, pushing herself to a sitting up position at his feet. Her face creased and drooped as agonies settled in their old places like a burdensome disease. "In fact, you might be the most expendable of all. Look at you. How long before your face slides off your skull, Roderick? I give it ten minutes. How blind and foolish and ridiculous of you to throw yourself into this based on a promise. Because promises are empty things." She clawed the dirt. "Always."

"I should end you, cunt. But I like the idea of you suffering with immeasurable pain until the end of your days."

Mick became aware of two distinct sensations, each one stunning and empowering: his legs were under his command again (barely), and the length of coffin-water wood—its twin nails gleaming—was back in his hand, heavy, real, somehow *permanent*. Nails and a board, a little help for a by-yourself guy brought into being by—what? A true perfunctory response from The Crymost? Or a succoring outreach of focused energy from a few well-meaning souls? Whatever the source, he was willing to go with it. He shuffled forward.

"Come on," Roger Copeland shouted out again. He was near the front, his stricken gaze fixed on Thekan. "We can't let this thing push us around. Move your asses, people."

And some did move. People fanned out along the edge of the group, uncertain and threatening at the same time, reluctant sentinels awaiting either inspiration or divine order. Judy rose up and swayed like a woman on a tightrope as she waited for her bearings to return. Old Jim Schraufnagel broke away from the crowd, his father-in-law's medal glittering in his hand. *So many hurting*, his expression said, *so many in need of help*. He was close enough to ruffle Thekan's cloak on the way by, and it made Mick moan when Thekan's hand came up to grasp him.

"Ruptured," Thekan pronounced as his hand clamped on the back of Jim's neck.

What followed was a bright flash of green light centered on Old Jim's medal and a wounded yelp from Roderick Thekan. Jim staggered to the side, dumbfounded. Thekan glowered, rigid and stunned. Smoke rose out of his woolen clothes in thin curls. Mick managed another step forward, keeping his grip tight on the board.

Chastity's gaze flashed from Old Jim to Thekan. Her hand, shaking with pain and resolution, went to the pocket of her skirt. She pulled out what Mick thought at first was a string of tiny glowing pearls until he saw the crucifix dangling from the end. A rosary, each bead eerily alight. She reached up only a short way because one of Thekan's hands dangled just above her head. She looped the rosary over his wrist, then gripped the loose end tight with both hands forming a shackle. What appeared as a cluster of flashbulb pops leapt from the rosary, and Thekan let go a gritty howl, his face contorted with agonized betrayal and rage.

Mick tried to rush in and stumbled, his body not yet his to fully command. Blaring in his head, more words from his nursing home visit with Irma—*pure and powerful . . . tributes . . . we sent as many as we could*. And from Axel—*he's worried they'll get a whiff of the rot under his skin . . .*

"Use what you've brought," he shouted. "Your loved ones' tributes have an effect on this monstrosity. This *thing*. Bring them up here if you have them. Do it now."

"Damn straight," Roger Copeland shouted back and slung the fob chain of his pocket watch around Thekan's free arm at the elbow.

Thekan strained like a trapped beast balking heavy chains. "No. This is my time," he declared, his face crumpling with effort, shedding pieces of rot.

There was another flash, this one darker, accompanied by a sizzle and a reek of old decay. Chastity and Roger were flung away in opposing directions and sent rolling across the ground. Thekan shook his arms free of his ligatures and shimmied like a beast shedding water. Mick stood straight, drawing deep breaths, collecting his returning strength to make it count.

Judy lunged into the crowd. She encountered Sheila Wiedmeyer, who gripped a pair of old fashioned hat pins in her fist as if playing shortest-straw-loses, only these straws twinkled with green light. Judy snatched the pins so they jutted from her good hand like wiry daggers and then rushed toward Thekan.

Other people holding glimmering items pushed their way in, heedless of the banking Crymost glow which now illuminated the grounds. Mick felt his heart swell for them, for his Judy, and for the surge of power he felt in his own muscles as he lunged forward, sure at last, and brought up the board two-handed like a man preparing to hit a pop fly.

Judy was on Thekan in a second. *"No more!"* she shrieked.

She plunged the hat pins in a downward arc. They punched through the front of Thekan's shirt and sank in deep. Thekan glowered at them, the bulbous jeweled ends wobbling like antennae, and his mouth unhinged in a silent shriek. The seams of his suit opened and belched steam while scraps of old wool fell away in strips. His cloak flew into tatters. His hands swooped around as if to shred the air. His throat worked.

Mick leapt in. Thekan goggled at him, his face illuminated by the light from the drop-off, his lips quivering on the verge of forming a word.

"Go, you son of a bitch," Mick roared, "back to wherever the hell you came from!"

He brought the board around with a whistling swing. It struck flat and true against the bridge of Thekan's nose. Its nails punched into his brow with a grating crunch. Mick froze, suddenly mesmerized as Thekan convulsed, his mouth caught in a mournful scowl while dark oily fluids gushed down his face from behind the board he now wore like a strange, torturous mask. A constricted *guck, guck* sound came out from between his bony jaws. His hands flexed like insects in panicked dying throes. His skin drew in and darkened as if the last of the moisture evaporated from it. His shirt front fell away in shreds.

Mick reached out for Judy and she latched on, but neither of them was able to look away as the figure of Thekan began to totter back and forth the way a rusted pole yields to the wind. Thekan's stomach, now wasted and exposed, drew inward with a muffled crumpling sound and split open. Clumps of gray matter dropped out, dry and heavy, trailing comet tails of dust. Fully formed items followed, spilling from the hollow basket of ribcage in a dust-coated storm. Coins, a gavel, a brush and comb, a flask, markers of a life, trinkets reflecting tangible memory, spread out and wasted on the ground between his decaying shoes. With a strangulated wheeze Thekan dropped, the last of his brittle skin falling away from his bones on impact.

It was done. Almost done.

Judy pushed him away. "Mick." She indicated the massive, glowing bladder rolling over the lip of the drop-off like a storm heading inland.

"Yeah," he said and pulled the walkie from his pocket. To the crowd he leveled his best calm but authoritative voice. "Everyone, you need to leave here. Now. Get off The Crymost. Help those who need it."

Judy looked around, anxious. "Do you think the cars will start now?"

"It's worth a try," he said and began to walk with her in his arms. He never wanted to let her go again.

They were the first to approach Chastity who sat in the dirt, pale and stricken. She regarded her twisted and palsied limbs with remorse. Mick could nearly feel the pain radiating off her. "Ms. Mellar Borth, Let us help you. This area is going to blow sky high in about five minutes."

She tried to smile but could achieve only a sneer of agony. "There is no help for somebody who could do this to the town, to these people." She let her gaze drift toward The Crymost glow. "This pain is ten times worse than ever before. I can't walk. And if you touch me to help it will feel like you're ripping me apart. That's no way to live, and you're almost out of time. I'll wait here for you to finish it, if you don't mind, Mick Logan. It's what I want. And I'll pray you get it done before that green light can eat up what's left of me."

Judy squeezed his hand. Their eyes locked, the message in them mutual and grim. And then they ran.

"Harley," he said into the walkie as they caught up to the back of the departing crowd.

Harley's voice came soft, almost dreamy. "M-Mick?"

"You ready? We're just getting off The Crymost."

"Ready? We goan fishin'? . . . You sure it's okay with Cy . . . if we take off?"

He stopped and let the walkie dangle at his side. Green light washed across Judy's cheeks and forehead and it made her dread plain. "What's wrong?"

"Harley took a pretty good hit to the head down there. I guess it's worse than I thought. A lot worse. I'm going to have to go in and blow the double barrel."

"I'll come too."

"No. I've got to go in through the mercantile. The stairs are collapsed; it's a mess. You'll never make the climb with that arm."

"Mick!" Roger Copeland called from nearby. He was attending two other men who were guiding the blinded Bob Canham down Pitch Road together. He broke away and fought his way back through the crowd. "How long before The Crymost blows?"

"As soon as I can get down to the double barrel to do it. Listen, you and Judy work on getting everybody out of here. I'll give you as much time as I can. Then, you get her to the hospital."

"I will," Roger said.

Mick embraced his wife, regretful it needed to be a quick one. "Don't worry. I've got protection behind me. Two pawns worth, if I counted right. Thank you, Jude."

She hugged him back. Her breath was warm in his ear. "I'll never forgive myself if it's not enough."

He gave her a long, deep look—something too all-encompassing to be contained by words. Then he turned to Roger. "Thanks for everything. I mean it."

CHAPTER EIGHTEEN

The climb down to the mercantile cellar went quickly, as if on a subconscious level he stored away where all the easy handholds and footrests were. But a coldness, heavy and waiting, was on his back again. It was the reach of The Crymost, targeting his activity with idiot fascination and suspicion.

He called out for Harley when he reached the cellar floor and rushed into the double barrel room. Harley was slouched over the stack of old batteries, unresponsive, the walkie in his hand, the lantern hissing at his feet. Mick lowered him to a reasonable sitting-up position and then snatched up the lantern and hurried over to the jenny.

Harley's instructions came back to him in a measured cadence: hold the choke button and push the starter, activate the double barrel pump with a switch, the igniter is the red lever on the side. He went over it again and again, feeling unprepared and unsure.

The crack in the jenny's starter button seemed wider than before. He rested his thumb on it and brought his other hand around to work the choke, which was a spring-loaded pop-up. Above him, the pipe hole in the wall came alight with green radiance. It grew in intensity, rapid and rushing.

No time. No more time.

He pushed the choke down hard and gave the starter a preparatory nudge.

The starter button fell inside with a hollow rattle. So did the contact piece underneath it, leaving a deep hole like a surprised eye looking back at him.

"No. Goddamn it."

A living organ of light squeezed between the overhead pipes and reached into the room, slow, mesmerizing. He blinked away from it and squatted next to the generator, poked a finger into the now empty starter socket which sat like an open wound above the brand name Bishop. He probed it—the hole was of a much larger diameter than his finger—and found a contact plate inside which he estimated to be the size of an old fifty-cent piece.

"Okay. Come on now."

He pressed it down in the hopes of triggering the jenny's motor, but the plate tilted under his finger and pushed back with the resistance of spring steel.

"What the hell kind of half-wit engineers did you have, Bishop?"

He needed something larger in circumference and stronger than his finger. He glanced around. None of Harley's scattered tools seemed right. None of the debris on the floor was viable.

Predatory coldness radiated from the glowing mass as it nosed up to him. *So much simpler to stop now*, part of him reasoned, *so futile to fight. To live.* He appreciated how easily it infected Will's thoughts and scrambled Nancy Berns' sunny nature into mud.

He turned back to the generator and jammed his thumb into the empty socket out of sheer blind hope. No result, but he continued to force it in anyway. Perhaps with a little luck, a little of Judy's protection. *Come on luck, one more time. Come on two pawns.*

The idea unfurled in his head with an audible snap. He fumbled the velvet bag out of his pants pocket, at first certain the knight was what he needed. Or was it the king? One might not be long enough. The other might be too long and send the inner plate tilting with a *spring* while The Crymost enwrapped him and sucked his will away like a fly slurping sugar water. There was time to try one and only one.

The image of the chessboard aglow in March sunlight flared across his thoughts. For a pensive second, moves were contemplated by seated opponents and by a lingering shape in a nearby doorway. Then a young hand with bitten nails and the first white wisps of not-yet masculine hair took up a piece of carved mineral and placed it deftly, assuredly on the board, knocking the opposing king over with a polite thump. At last, small victory.

Mick took out the knight, inverted it and plugged it into the starter socket. Then he smashed his palm against it. Waves of green coldness swept over him like anxious breath.

Something inside the jenny clicked. He punched the choke nib, put his whole body into it, and felt his should stitches spread like wrangled shoelaces. The generator coughed and then caught. The roar of its motor was like a song.

He lunged at the double barrel, knowing he'd already stayed too long.

"I'm sorry, Jude," he said, his jaw tight, his throat tighter, as he flicked the pump switch.

The double barrel let go another of its waking screeches. A puttery, gyrating sound rose up from deep inside. The air ripened with fumes.

The Crymost glow pressed against him, images refracted on its surface: kaleidoscopic blooms of posters depicting old dead poets, of composition notebooks, student desks in neat rows, book reports with faulty grammar and poor comprehension, memories of a thousand conversations, a thousand more emotions and his own laughter, because laughing is what you do when you love your life. He saw it all, heard it all, and wondered vaguely where Judy belonged in the mix. Where Knoll fit in. Or Harley. He clamped down on the red lever as the glow enwrapped him with the tenderness of icy, loving hands.

And he realized the winds of the past are good air, but it's best to keep them at your back.

He flipped the switch.

"That," a young man's voice announced from inside his head, from the corners of the room and the very air around him, "is a checkmate, Mr. Logan."

The double barrel released a whirling sound, like a shaggy ball flying through the air. Ignition.

The glow tightened around him with a startled, strangling tension and then ejected him, pushing him out like an unwanted birth. It swirled back through the hole in the wall. He landed hard near Harley's feet. A distant sound bloomed under the hum of the jenny and the rusty labors of the double barrel pump. Explosion. It seemed to be a prolonged thud on the floor of the world. Everything jumped. The jumbled ruins in the next room collapsed, handholds gone. He closed his eyes and they stung with tears.

The landfill and The Crymost drop-off, he knew in ways he could never explain, erupted in a massive flash of blue flame and a cloud of blasted limestone. Chastity Mellar Borth teetered on the stony edge to face Knoll's beast eye to eye, invite it to a finality where greed and pain were as meaningless as dust while massive slabs of rock unhitched and descended with the ease of a fissured glacier. As the drop-off crashed down to a ruinous end, Chastity fell with it.

A vocalization traveled through the night air: a mortal whoop of betrayal as old as The Crymost stones themselves.

And there was another sound near Mick, a stirring snort from Harley. Mick reached out and rapped the bottom of his friend's shoe; it was all he possessed the energy for.

"Hey. Harley, we did it."

Harley's reply was almost mournful, at the tattered end of consciousness. "Aw damn."

Anything else Mick might have tried to say caught in his throat. The double barrel jumped and rattled. Its pump gave out with a loud clatter and its parts seized with a bang. There was nothing more to pump, and nothing more to ignite. Like a hero in an old tale, its purpose was fulfilled, and therefore its life was done.

Mick got to his feet, wobbly as a foal and the pains in his abused body began to check in from all quadrants. *Yet*, he smiled. "Sit tight. I'll get you some help."

The walk down the tunnel was almost dreamlike, and exhausting. When he got to the basement of the bar he found just enough energy to pull open the big cooler door, and then he collapsed, only half aware of Will reaching out to catch him.

"Jesus," Will said as he eased Mick down to the floor. "Is it done? Of course it is, because I feel—well, it's what I *don't* feel that counts. And I heard the boom."

"Hell of a face-off," Mick said and patted Will's shoulder with a grateful hand. "For all of us. Harley's still back there, by the double barrel. He's not good."

"I'll go. I'll drag him out with my teeth if I have to. I owe him big time after what I did. I owe you, too."

"Give me a minute and I'll help you."

"You stay right there," Will said.

Mick had to admit, it was good to have the old Will back. He nodded in concession. Many things would be back to the way they were, he supposed. He reached out, mentally, and hoped to nudge those two lucky pawns one more time. He was unable to detect them, however.

He lowered his head, listening to Will's diminishing footfalls and took the chance to rest. To rest at last.

EPILOGUE:
GOOD, LONG FUTURE DAYS

" THERE'S THE HOUSE HUNTERS," Harley said from the shady spot on his porch.

Mick and Judy walked up together and separated at the top step. Mick walked toward Harley's lawn chair perched under the sign reading THE KROENERS by the front door. Judy went to the far side where Beth Ann, in a shaft of midday sun by the porch railing, poured lemonade.

It seemed old and right, and it also felt strained. Judy and Beth Ann embraced overlong, the heavy wrapping on Judy's wrist keeping her arm at an awkward angle. Harley did not rise when he shook Mick's hand but the clap of their handshake was firm and deeper than ever before. Harley's arm, in a cast and a sling, added to the already infirm air about him.

"I know you're on your way to make that real estate offer, so we don't expect you to stay," Harley said. His eyes glimmered under his brow. There was a cane propped nearby, against a table where pill bottles stood behind a box of tissues like something shameful. "But we wanted to wish you luck."

"It sounds like a good offer," Beth Ann said and brought over two frosty glasses, one for each of them. "And if they accept it right off we can have another one of these tonight, with a shot of vodka mixed in to celebrate."

"Even me?" Harley's good-humored smile was as wide as ever, and yet thinner somehow.

"I'll measure yours with an eyedropper." Beth Ann laughed, an automatic response without real humor, like an echo. "And you shouldn't even have *that* much."

They all laughed some more, and then the women broke away

261

again. Once in their segregated groups (old and familiar as well-worn gloves) there was silence, except for the breeze through the leaves. Mick set his glass next to the pills and looked at the once towering man who now sat huddled like a crumpled ball of old paper. There seemed to be more gray in Harley's hair, and his eyelids drooped with the weight of exhaustion.

"It was gone," Harley said at last. "They can blame it on a goddamned botched-up test, but I know it was gone. I *felt* it was gone."

It. Never cancer (back to the way things were). Just *it.*

"I know." Mick pushed his hand against the bony nub of Harley's shoulder. The nudge was familiar, but that, too, felt thinner somehow. "I wish . . . ah, Jesus, I'm not sure what I wish."

"You did what was right. There's a hell of a lot of people in this town who owe you their lives, and they don't even know it. No denying it. And since we're talking about wishes, I'll tell you one of mine. I hope you and Judy get your offer accepted, and yet I don't. Just so you know where I stand."

"It's in Allycegate. Sixty miles. That's not far."

Harley cast him a look that said ten feet was too damn far when he was facing a dire prognosis, each day of his life paying out like thread from a nearly depleted spool. Then he slumped back in his chair. "This town needs somebody to rebuild it."

"I need some rebuilding time of my own, to be honest."

Harley nodded. "Yup, you do. Don't get me wrong. I want you to."

"You're still the boss."

Judy came over. "I thought Will was stopping by."

The voice from the porch steps made them all look around. "Oh, he is."

Will greeted each of them with a smile and a hug and thanked Beth Ann when she thrust a glass of lemonade into his hand. "I've got a lot to do today, but I couldn't miss wishing you guys luck."

"Business or pleasure?" Judy asked him.

"Business. Things have been slow, but Friday nights are fair, so I'm keeping the inventory up for now. I don't want to leave here if I can help it but, worst case, I got a line on a booze and sandwich place in Fond du Lac. It's been closed up for a while but I think it shows promise. It was called Trinity."

Beth Ann raised her eyebrows. Her fingers worked across the collar of her blouse, searching for a gold cross no longer hanging there. "Trinity?"

Will shrugged, sheepish. "Yeah. It . . . uh . . . used to be a church."

They laughed, rich and genuine this time.

"We need a toast," Harley said and struggled to his feet. Mick reached over to hand him the cane but Harley warned him off of it. "I'd do the honors, but I'm afraid the painkillers got me addled enough to start singing nursery rhymes instead."

"I can do it." Will stepped forward with his glass raised. "To Mick and Judy—actually to all of us. And to good, long future days."

As they clinked their glasses together a gust of wind rattled the shrubs and made the trees whisper and stir. They all looked out at the empty expanse of Backbank Street and beyond to where Knoll dozed in a state of wounded hibernation. Mick wondered which scars would fade in time, and which would remain. He glanced at everyone on the porch with a pang as they sipped their drinks.

"I heard from Nancy," Judy said and Mick was glad for the change of subject. "She's doing fine. She plans on spending the summer on the peninsula."

This was met with *ohs* and understanding nods.

"I hate to toast and run, but those cases of chicken wings aren't going to deliver themselves," Will said. "Goodbye, everybody."

He left them, handshakes and hugs all around before stepping into the sun.

"We need to go too," Mick said, "if we want to make the real estate office in time."

Harley settled back in his chair seeming shrunken and resigned. "Don't be strangers."

"Not a chance, my friend. In fact, we'll stop by late for those vodka lemonades whether we have any news or not."

"It's a date."

They were on the road with the windows down when Judy reached over to take his hand. "There's still time. We don't have to write that offer if you don't want to."

"I want to," he said. "Keep it all behind us. Where it belongs."

He dug in his pocket and produced the smooth mineral chess piece he kept there. The king. It flashed in the sun when he held it up for her to see. Then he tossed it out of the car window with a hitching sigh, committing it to the earth, the seasons, and to the vagaries of memory.

"Checkmate," he said, and gave the car more gas.

10/28/13-1/15/16

ACKNOWLEDGEMENTS

"Thank You" barely begins to express how deep my gratitude runs for those who offered advice, encouragement and expertise as I shaped *The Crymost* into a living, breathing novel. To Michael Knost and Kathy Ptacek, your interest, advice and encouragement—past and present— helped me in a hundred untold ways. To TM Wright, I have no doubt our conversations all those years ago guided me to this place. Rest in Peace, my friend. To Matthew Pea, Kathy Gerner, Heather Quickle and Lauren Walker, I value the professional and personal knowledge you shared with me far more than you can know. To Kari Eggert, your insight and assessments helped me to rectify and clarify that which was vague, your positivity allowed me to do it without hesitation. To Marc Ciccarone, I thank you with all my heart for believing in *The Crymost*. To editor extraordinaire Andrea Dawn, thank you for helping me take things apart and put them back together in a finer, more sensible manner. Your talent is rare and remarkable. And finally, to Julie Wild, my beautiful wife, unflinching first reader, my compass and my conscience, thank you for believing in me. I love you, always.

ABOUT THE AUTHOR

Dean H. Wild has spent his entire life in east central Wisconsin, living in various small towns near the city of Fond du Lac. He wrote his first short horror story at the tender age of seven and continued to write dark fiction while he pursued careers in the newspaper industry, real estate, and retail pharmacy. His short stories have seen publication in several magazines and anthologies. *The Crymost* is his first novel. He and his wife, Julie, currently reside in the village of Brownsville.

34476729R00165

Made in the USA
Middletown, DE
26 January 2019